MORE STREETS OF OUR TOWN

BY LARRY E. SARKIS

This book is dedicated to all my faithful readers. Thank you so much for making both
OUR TOWN ~ THE MYSTERY SERIES and
THE STREETS OF OUR TOWN a big success.
MORE STREETS OF OUR TOWN - the third book in the series is just as exciting and fun to read as the first two. Larry

Printing: Rick Rivera
J & R Graphics and Printing
RICKGRAPHICS@YAHOO.COM

Cover Design: Susi McCreary
Design and Print Production
SUSIMCCREARY@YAHOO.COM

Copyright 2011

Chapter 1

"John, let me know when we get to the award ceremony."
"I will, Larry."
As I relaxed into my seat in the back of the limo, I closed my eyes. Let's see, where was I? Oh yeah. I was at Mayor James Sanders' (we call him Mayor) house for a barbeque dinner when the barbeque grill blew up. It was rigged with a bomb to kill the Mayor. I jumped on him to save his life. In turn I took a lot of shrapnel in the back of my body. I took one large, long, sharp piece of steel near the center of my back.
That's why the story is opening with me lying in bed in the hospital.*
Oh, you're probably wondering who I am. I'm a onetime Real Estate Broker who accidently became the Commissioner of Police for the town of Pertsville. I'm Larry Towers. I was hired to eliminate crime in Our Town at any cost. I was given a free hand to do it. I established myself a team of experts to help me. The best our police force had to offer. I put the team together to protect me as well as to help me stamp out crime in Our Town. Let me tell you who they are. We have the Mayor who I've already mentioned. The Chief of Police, Pete Fortney an old time pro. Sergeant Lynda Stalls is my personal guard and fiancé. Lieutenant Thomas Harden, a good man to have around. Sergeant James Patrick O'Rily III, fourth generation police officer. Officer Robert Collins is big, mean and tough. This part of my team are all experts in either Karate or Judo. They're also marksmen with most weapons.
Also on my team I have two drivers for my limo. Officer John Watt is our youngest member who absorbs knowledge like a sponge. Yoto is an Officer and friend from my past. He taught the Special Forces how to kill. He's good....real good. My team and I are closer than any family. I have other people close to me that I'll explain as I go along.
Now let's see. I'm lying in my hospital bed and Doctor Samuel Kaplin is getting ready to examine me.
*Author's suggestion: this is a multi-book series. To know the characters and their exploits better you should also read "Our Town ~ The Mystery Series" and "The Streets of Our Town".

(We call him Doc. He is a surgeon who has worked with us more than once. We trust him so much that we put him in charge of opening a hospital for our police force. We also made him an honorary Police Captain.)

Doc asked, "Would everyone please take a walk so I can examine Larry?"

Everyone got up and moved toward and out the door of my room. Lynda was the last person left.

"Larry?"

"Doc, can Lynda stay?"

"Sure Larry. Everyone could have stayed, but they looked like they needed a change of scenery."

He was removing the dressing from my back as he was speaking.

"The wound looks good. You seem to heal quickly."

"I've been like that all my life."

"Keep it up, and you may go home tomorrow night rather than Thursday morning."

"If that be the case I'll be a real good boy. I hate being on my stomach 24 hours a day."

"Well, why don't we start a countdown? It's now Tuesday at 3:30 in the afternoon. If you're a good boy at 6:30 Wednesday evening you'll go home. That's 27 hours from now. How does that sound to you?"

"It definitely gives me a goal to work towards."

He finished changing my bandage. Which I thought was awful nice of him. He could have easily had one of the nurses do it. He put some light pressure on some of the other bandages on my body.

"Do any of these hurt?"

"Very little, by tomorrow I won't even know they are there."

"You're mental ability to shut out pain is amazing."

"Thank you, Doc. It took many, many years to perfect it. I'd like to change the subject."

"Go ahead."

"About our meeting at the new hospital site this Friday."

"I already figured the meeting was off."

"Wrong. The meeting is still on only the place has changed. You can meet Pete at the hospital site then you can both meet me at my penthouse." (The penthouse I live in is part of my pay plan. It's the whole top floor of the City Hall building. My office is in the same building on the second floor.)

"There are things I wanted to show you at the building site."

"Can't you show them to me on the plans?"

"Well, yes. I just thought it would be easier to picture my changes if you were at the building."

(We are remodeling a ten story office building we own into a police hospital. There is also a three story building in the rear across the parking lot. We are going to make it over into a convalescent home for our police force.)

"Doc, I already know the answer but I'll ask the question anyway. Can you keep a secret?"

"You know I can Larry."

"Due to the car accident I had a couple of years ago I have almost total recall; about 99.9 percent. So if you tell me what you want to do I'll be able to comprehend it."

"Wow! That's great! How many people know about this?"

"Just my team…and we don't talk about it."

"I won't either. So I'll see you Friday at four o'clock in your penthouse."

"Good. Are you about finished?"

"Why?"

"Without the sheet on me I'm getting cold."

"Lynda, help me cover our little boy before he freezes."

We chuckled.

"Lynda, when you're finished doing that go out to the boys. Inform them that I'm doing great. Then tell them to go home and get some rest. I'll see them at nine o'clock in the morning."

"It shall be done."

She walked out of the room.

"Are you slowing down a bit Doc?"

"Yes, Larry. Just like you I can follow orders. You said to slow down so I am. No more 18 hour days."

"Make sure you bring all the payroll figures for your nurses with you Friday. If you're using them to help you at the hospital we better start paying them."

"I'm using them both at my office and at the hospital."

"Seeing you're eliminating your office practice we'll start paying them."

"That sounds good to me."

"Well, Doc, if you're finished I'll get some rest."

"I'm finished. I'll see you tomorrow at 6."

"See you then."

As he left Lynda returned.

"Is everything all right with Doc?"

"Yes. Everything's fine. I'd like to get some rest."

"All right, I'm going outside for a little walk. Don't worry. I'll keep an eye on your room."

She left and I went to sleep.

I woke up when I heard the bonging that told visitors that it was eight o'clock and time to go home.

Lynda was lying in the bed next to me. When I opened my eyes she was looking at me.

"Like what you see?"

"Yes I do. I also love what I see."

"I love you too. I'm sorry I put you through this."

"There's nothing to be sorry about. I'm just glad you're going to be okay."

"So am I. It's funny."

"What's that?"

"I'm always preaching to the boys to be careful, and I'm the one that gets blown up."

"There's no way you could have known there was a bomb planted there."

"You're right. I'm glad I spotted it when I did. If I hadn't the Mayor and I would both be dead."

Yoto walked into the room.

"How're you feeling Larry?"

"As good as can be expected."

"I'm glad to hear that. Lynda, John will be here shortly with dinner."

"That sounds good Yoto."

"I thought I sent everyone home."

"I think being in the hospital has clouded your mind. Do you remember our job? Protect the Commissioner. Our lives for his.

Does that sound familiar?"

"Yes it does. Excuse me for asking."

"That's better. You know Lynda, every once in a while you have to put the boss in his place."

We all laughed.

" Why don't you go out and have dinner with the boys, Lynda? I'm going to get some more rest."

I slept right through until seven in the morning. I lay there thinking about what we'd tackle next. The door opened and Lynda walked in.

"Is that you Lynda?"

"Yes it is." She talked as she pushed her bed away from mine. "I just finished showering and getting dressed in the nurses' lounge."

"How are you holding up?"

"Just fine Larry."

"Good. Would you get on your cell phone and call Pete at home? I'd like to talk to him."

She got him on the line. She then laid her phone by my ear. "Pete."

"Yes Larry."

"Would you call everyone and tell them that there's no meeting until nine o'clock tomorrow morning? I want them to clean up everything they've been working on. This will give everyone time to catch up on their paperwork."

"I like the idea. I'll get right on it."

I nodded and Lynda closed up her phone and put it away.

"Would you like to give me a sponge bath, Lynda?"

"I'd love to."

The day went by uneventfully. At six o'clock Doc arrived. "How's my favorite patient?"

"Just fine Doc."

"I'll be the judge of that."

He looked me over and changed my bandage again. He had Lynda watch closely so she could do the job when he wasn't around.

"What do you think Doc? Can I go home?"

"The reason I was keeping you here in the first place was your inability to eat while lying on your stomach. So if you can lay on your side for me I'll release you."

I gently rolled up on my right side. I had a little pain but nothing I couldn't live with.

"Well? How do you feel?"
"Like going home, Doc."
"I need to order an ambulance from downstairs."
"Lynda, have the boys take care of that for Doc."
She said, "All right Larry," as she left the room.

Tom and John came into the room with Lynda. Lynda started to put my things together in a large brown plastic bag she had gotten out of her suitcase.

"The boys are getting you an ambulance. It'll be waiting for us when we get downstairs"

"Thanks Tom. Boy my clothes look a mess."

"I meant to ask you about that Larry."

"What's that Doc?"

"Your clothes, they seemed to slow down, in the case of your shirt, and stop, in the case of your shorts and underpants, the shrapnel. Why did they do that?"

"Doc, you know everything else. You may as well know this too. All the clothes worn by me and my team are bullet proof, even our underwear. Our ties are also special. They'll hold around 500 pounds of weight."

"Then that's why Jack (One of my original team, a driver. Yoto took his place. Jack's in convalescent care. He was wounded in book two, "The Streets of Our Town".), was shot twice but I only removed one bullet?"

"That's right. His jacket stopped the other bullet."

"Is there anything you haven't thought of, Larry?"

"I just try to cover all of our bases. I try to give us the edge. I feel the bad guys have had the edge long enough. Now, can we get out of here?"

"I have everything packed."

"Good, Lynda. John, give her a hand with the bag and suitcase."

They wheeled my bed out of the room and down the hall to the elevator. I was lying on my stomach enjoying the ride. I remembered last week when we were wheeling the Mayor out of here. Life sure takes a lot of strange twists. When we got off the elevator we went down a corridor and ended up at the rear of the hospital. My boys had the gurney off the ambulance waiting for me. They picked me up by using the sheet that was under me. Then they lowered me down on the gurney. John and Jim pushed the bed back inside the hospital while the boys put me into the ambulance. Some of my team jumped into the ambulance. The rest got into the limo. Yoto was in the driver's seat and Tom was riding shotgun.

As we pulled away from the hospital I asked, "Tom, did you have any trouble borrowing this ambulance?"

"I figured it wouldn't be a problem to borrow one of the units for an hour. But it turned into a national crisis. Paperwork, licenses, insurance, tests, and permits. No telling what I forgot."

"Then how did you get this unit?"

"Ask Snake." (That's Teddy 'Snake' Walker. He and Hans 'Cutter' Swanson, Sam 'Coop' Cooper, and Josh Walts were part of a group of 20 men I trained during the war. We did some secret missions together. These men are tops in their field. I taught them how to 'Walk Silent' and 'Walk Deadly'. These four men flew into Our Town to help me with some special problems we had.)

"Snake?"

"Yes, Larry."

"Wait a minute. Don't tell me."

"Larry we'll have it back before they miss it."

"The Commissioner of Police is riding around town in a stolen ambulance. Is that what you're saying?"

"Let me put it this way."

I almost couldn't hear him because of all the laughter inside the ambulance.

"I knew we needed a unit. The girl talking to Tom said she'd really love to help us. So I figured I'd grant her wish. I did understand her to say that she had six units. They keep four in service and use the other two in a rotation system. So I rotated one of the units for our use."

"Snake, will you ever change?"

"No, do I have to?"

"Not as far as I'm concerned."

"Good. Then I'll stay just the way I am."

I said, "As long as we borrowed this lovely unit I'm going to need some patch bandages for my back. Would you guys mind checking to see if they have any on board?"

As the boys were opening cabinets, Lynda asked, "Larry, should we be doing this?"

Snake said, "It's all right Lynda. The people I borrowed the ambulance from won't mind."

I said, "Thanks, Snake."

"Larry, this is kind of strange."

"What's that Josh?"

"You guys slide the end of the gurney over so Larry can see me." He was in the center of the truck.

"Got you in view, what is it?"

"You notice the small cabinet that's even with my face?"

"Yes. I can see it."

"It's the drug cabinet."

"What's wrong with that?"

"There's no lock on the cabinet."

"Maybe they're not using this unit right now so there's nothing of value kept in it."

Josh opened the cabinet and took out a bottle and blew dust off the top of it.

"That's strange."

"Here's the strange part Larry. The long cabinet below marked miscellaneous supplies is securely locked."

I said, "It would be nice to see what's inside, wouldn't it?"

Snake said, "I happen to have a key for that lock. Give me a little elbow room boys and I'll open it for you." (Snake is an expert at picking locks.)

It only took a few seconds and Snake had the compartment open. Josh slid the compartment door back.

I asked, "What's in there Josh?"

"Nothing but dirty uniforms, Larry."

"I have a problem with that Josh. Bring me a piece of clothing."

He walked over to me with a shirt in his hand.

"Let me smell it." He put it next to my nose. "Could someone here tell me why the uniform doesn't smell of being dirty? But it does have a slight smell of coffee."

Snake helped Josh pull everything out of the compartment.

"Nothing but uniforms, Larry."

"Hold on Josh."

I asked, "What did you find Snake?"

"A hollow bottom to the compartment, Larry."
"Are you sure it's not the bottom of the truck?"
"I'll let you know in a minute, Larry."

Snake took his penlight out of his shirt pocket and turned it on. He put it in his mouth and crawled in a little ways. His head, shoulders, and arms were in the compartment for a few seconds.

He pulled his head out and said, "Voila! One secret sliding compartment!"

"I can't see it that well Snake. Could you describe it to me?"

"The way they did this Larry is quite unique. The outside doors slide to the center. They stop short of meeting one another by about two inches. Two inches on the right and two inches on the left side. That gives you a hidden area of four inches. That keeps the keyhole completely out of sight. You'd never notice it unless you were looking for it. Once you unlock the sliding panel it slides completely over the other half of the panel. So by sliding both panels all the way to the right you have great access to the left side of the hidden compartment. The same is true if you slide the panels in the opposite direction."

"I see. Thanks, Snake. What did you find, Josh?"

"A very small amount of coffee grounds. I'm afraid they wouldn't even make a decent cup of coffee."

"Cute, Josh. Real cute. Do we all agree that in their spare time these boys run drugs?"

Everyone nodded their heads 'yes'.

"While you guys are getting me upstairs I want two of you to stay with this unit. Collect all the information you can about the truck so we can identify it later."

"Larry, would you like me to mark the outside bumper with the same material I used on the stolen trucks from Canada?"

"Snake, are the materials close by?"

"They're in the back of your pick up in the garage."

"It's a good idea. Do it. Now lock everything up and put everything away. We need to get me upstairs in a hurry so you can get this ambulance back before they miss it."

We did just that. Before I knew it everyone was back at my place.

"How'd it go Snake?"

"I put it back like it was and locked it up. Everything looked just the way it did when I took it."

"If that be the case then we need to get Pete here."

I heard the Mayor's voice from down the hall.

"He's in the kitchen, Larry. We stopped and picked up fried chicken for supper."

"Everyone to the kitchen for a plate of food, Lynda, bring me one please, with a lot of mashed potatoes and coleslaw. They're easier to swallow. Also make sure everyone is up to speed on what we discovered tonight."

Everyone left. This gave me a minute to collect my thoughts.

Everyone came back with a plate of food in hand. Tom, John, and Yoto helped me turn on my side so I could eat. As long as we were all together I figured it was as good a time as any to have a meeting.

Chapter 2

"Pete, I can tell by the look on your face that you found the ambulance situation hard to believe."

"I do, Larry."

"Well, either they're smuggling drugs or they're sloppy coffee makers."

John said, "Larry they don't make coffee in an ambulance."

"That's right John, that's why everyone is laughing."

When everyone quieted down I started.

"Pete, we need coverage of the ambulances 24 hours a day."

"All six of them?"

"I don't know. Aren't ambulance services licensed by the state?"

The Mayor answered, "Yes they are."

"Thanks Mayor for the information and volunteering."

"What did I volunteer for?"

"I need you to get together with whoever does the inspection of the units and do another one. It doesn't have to be a surprise inspection. They can let them know they are coming. Tom or Jim can go with the person as an assistant. You boys know what to look for don't you?"

They both said, "Yes."

"Pete, for now, follow all the units. After they finish the inspection we should know exactly which units we need to follow."

"Sounds good, Larry. I'll start lining up some men in the morning."

"If it was my operation I'd have two units set up. If it's larger than I think I'd need four units, one unit for each direction on the map. We also need to check out the company that owns the ambulance service."

"Larry."

"Yes Tom?"

"I'll do that, if Jim will do the inspections."

"Sounds all right to me Larry."

"Mayor, Jim's your man."

"Okay Larry."

"Tom… a complete rundown. If they have out of state owners have Sam and Wade help you." (That's Special Agent Samuel Erkins and

Assistant Special Agent Wade Brewer of the F.B.I. They help us on special out of state cases. I trust them so much that I made them part of my team.)

"I'll take care of it Larry."

"Robert, do some checking on their licenses, the areas they are restricted to, and the different hospitals they work for."

"Okay Larry."

"Yoto. You'll deliver Coop, Cutter, Josh, and Snake to the airport tomorrow. I think we need to give these boys a hand."

Everyone applauded.

"John, you'll be with me and Lynda tomorrow. Now if there's nothing else pressing tonight I'd like to eat and get some rest. Nine in the morning….here." (We have a meeting every morning at 9 A.M. in my office.)

Everyone took the hint. They picked up their plates and headed out of my room. Lynda fed me my dinner. She then washed me up for bed.

My night was sort of restful. Seeing that I only need 3 to 4 hours of sleep a night I did just fine. Lying there next to Lynda made me feel a lot better. Like the experts say, being home is much better medicine than being in a hospital.

It was nine o'clock and everyone was around my bed chatting. I sleep in a king size bed. I had the boys move me around so I was at the foot of the bed lying crosswise. With the double doors open to the sitting area, everyone was in front of me. The last people to arrive were Pete and the F.B.I.

"I'm glad to see everyone could make it this morning. Let's get right to it. We have a lot of things to cover. Let's handle this like a regular morning meeting."

"Then I go first."

"That's right Sam. What's new at the F.B.I.?"

"Quite a bit. Our major busts of the meth labs nationally netted us over 100 prisoners. On the trucks that the Canadians are stealing in Canada and bringing here we figured out who the crooked border guards are. There are two Canadians and two Americans. We have our two boys under surveillance and the Mounties are covering their two."

"Sounds good."

"It's progress Larry. But what we need to do is get the Canadians from here to return home for more trucks."

"You're figuring the border guards are just stupid pawns in this game?"

"Yes, Larry. The way we see it they're probably being paid X amount for each truck that passes through."

"I agree Sam. That's the same thing I was thinking. Jim, you've been keeping an eye on the operation here. How many trucks do they have on their lot?" (The problem we're talking about was brought to my attention by an elderly lady who lives in the condo complex that I lived in before becoming Police Commissioner. She told us about some Canadian people who bought a condo in her complex. Shortly after they moved in newer looking trucks started showing up. Upon checking out the situation we found that the trucks came from Canada. They were all stolen.)*

"As of yesterday Larry, they had twelve trucks."

"How many trucks do they usually have on the lot?"

"Eighteen to twenty."

"Sounds like they need more inventory."

"I agree, Wade. I also think the trucks may be on their way here."

"Are you figuring they already have the units they need?"

"Wade, it would only stand to reason that they would have a surplus of trucks. As everyone knows it's easier to steal trucks than to ship them. Seeing we know who the people here are, we need to continue our surveillance. I still feel they are smuggling more than trucks across the border. We know we need the people here to return to Canada so we can trail them to their accomplices."

Sam asked, "Larry, what do you suggest we do?"

"Sam, Pertsville is a large city (a million and a half people) and I don't feel these boys will slip away from us. I think we need to wait awhile. Hopefully they'll get homesick and make their move back to Canada."

"You may be right Larry. We'll wait."

"Do you have anything else, Sam?"

"I'll pass to Wade."

*Author suggests you read Book II of the Our Town Series "The Streets of Our Town" for the details of this case.

"We haven't finished processing the properties we took in the raid."

"How much time do you need?"

"Can we turn them over to you Saturday morning?"

"That sounds all right. Wade, coordinate it with Pete."

(When I took on the job as Police Commissioner any property in a drug related arrest would be forfeited to the Police Department. (Read Book I, "Our Town ~ The Mystery Series")

"I'll do that Larry. I pass to the Mayor."

"I have a few little things that we can cover now or they can wait." He looked at me with a look of concern on his face.

"Thanks for worrying about me. But working like this actually makes me feel better, so please continue Mayor."

"I have two things. One, I think everyone heard about the new camera systems that take pictures of people running red lights."

"Does it work?"

"Amazingly well Larry."

"Then why don't you get some?"

"They're very expensive."

Jim said, "Larry, maybe we need to give the town a loan."

"Cute Jim, real cute. Mayor, it's hard to believe that your budget is that close."

"We have the money Larry. But we have to hold onto it."

"Can I ask why?"

"You folks are the reason why."

"You're going to have to clarify that for me Mayor."

"It's like this Larry, the contract between the Police Department and the city comes due in about two months. We'll have to have money so we can negotiate a new contract with the Policemen's Association."

"I didn't realize we had a Policemen's Association."

John said, "You would if you got our paychecks."

"John, are you trying to tell me you pay monthly dues?"

"Is the Pope Catholic?"

"Let me think for a second….. I think I got it."

Tom said, "There's one good thing."

"What's that Tom?"

"With you flat on your side it can't be a big production."

15

Everyone laughed.

"How about a production that uses every person on the force?"

Tom came back with, "Wow! That's BIG!"

"Yes it is Tom. But before I go any further I'd like to know what happens to the dues you pay your association."

Tom continued, "I'm not fine tuned on it, Larry but I can give you an idea."

"Please do."

"The money goes into our local association for what is called working capital and a strike fund. Part of the funds goes to the state and part to the Federal Organizations."

"Thanks Tom. Mayor how much revenue will the camera tickets generate? Also how many cameras can you afford to buy?"

"If I had nothing else pressing . . . five cameras. Revenue is a minimum of ten tickets a day at one hundred dollars a ticket."

"Now people, let's look at this from a business point of view. Right now every officer on the Police Force is making more money with me as their leader. So here is what I have in mind. I want everyone to think about it as I say it. One, we'll renew our contract with little or no changes. Two, the city will buy us five cameras. Three, we will buy five cameras. Four, the city will install and maintain all of the cameras. Five, we will give a small percentage of the cameras revenue to the city for maintenance costs. Six, we'll dissolve the Policemen's Association and put their funds into our slush fund. Seven, we'll keep our Policemen's Association committee for grievances and contract negotiations. Eight, let me give you an idea of what these cameras will make for our slush fund. 10 cameras times 10 tickets times $100.00 a ticket. That's $10,000.00 a day, or over three and a half million dollars a year. Nine, everyone on the force gets another increase in pay. They no longer have to pay dues to the Association. Now give me some feedback on my proposal."

They all sort of looked at one another and mumbled for a few seconds.

"Can I get some help? Tom?"

"I'd love to help you Larry, but you don't need any."

"It's only a rough idea. There must be something I missed."

Pete said, "Larry, once again you put together a plan to help the men. You never think of Larry Towers. It's always 'What can I do for my troops?' The plan you just came up with is a sensational winner. I, for one will back it 100%. I'd like a show of hands of everyone who will back this plan."

Every hand in the room went up.

"Thanks Pete, I appreciate your kind words and everyone's support."

"Larry."

"Yes Mayor. Do you have something else?"

"I want you to know that I'll check the budget real closely. If we can afford another camera I'll buy it for you. I pass to Pete."

"We finally identified the two guys we shot at the pawn shop we closed up for dealing drugs. The three guys we arrested and one of the scumbags we killed were local garbage. But, the guy I killed personally hasn't got a rap sheet here. I have the file with me. Sam, would you run it through your F.B.I. computer for me?"

"I'd be happy to Pete."

Pete handed him the file.

"I'll let you know ASAP."

"Thanks Sam. Next, Larry you said we should start on the mobs." (That's what we call the gangs in Our Town. This scum isn't civilized enough to be called a gang.)

"Yes Pete, I'd like you to do a couple of things. Get some volunteers to check with the armed forces. They've closed down some of their facilities around town because of budget cutbacks. We'd like to lease a couple of these facilities for a dollar a year. In case of war we'll move out immediately."

Pete asked, "What do we need the facilities for?"

"I want to open a couple of new schools. 90 to 95 % of the kids who attend school today want to get a good education. But with the mobs around teachers lower their standards, so they can pass and get rid of their problems. But like sewer rats the problem doesn't go away it just multiplies."

Pete said, "So you're going to put all the rats on one ship, so to speak?"

"You got it Pete. Then they can sink, swim, or kill one another off. I don't care what they do. It'll be the kind of place you'd want to visit, but you wouldn't want to live there. It'll be a two way street.

They get in by their deeds and they get out by their deeds."

"What about teachers?"

"See if the armed forces can afford some help for us. Sam, check with the F.B.I. to see if they have any help for us."

Sam asked, "I take it you want big and mean?"

"Yes Sam, I do. Mayor, I'd like you to call your friend Warden Jackson at Flander State Prison. See if you can get him to work up a class on life in a prison. Ask him to use the boys who helped him before, plus anyone else he sees fit to recruit. I'd also like some women prisoners who are doing hard time. Promise them nothing but the opportunity to help clean up our town. They can arrange prison tours. Give them a free hand to select a program that they feel will help. I'd like to attempt to break these kids down, and then make good citizens out of them. I know I won't get all of them, but I'd be happy with 25%."

"I understand what you want Larry and it shall be done."

"Thanks Mayor. Pete, until we find out about the guy you killed I want you to be extra careful. If he's connected back east they will want revenge. That's usually the downfall of most bad guys. The reason they want revenge is because they don't know how to take defeat. They've been losers all their lives, now they've lost again. They think revenge will make it all better. Instead it usually costs them their lives. So like I said Pete, keep both eyes open and people around you."

"After seeing what happened to you and the Mayor, you don't have to tell me twice."

"Good. What else?"

"Do you remember we talked about the amount and variety of drugs we found in the pawn shop?"

"I do. I wanted to see if we could trace any of the drugs to their origin. Instead of doing that we're going to wait on Sam's report on your dead body. I have a feeling that body will tell us all we need to know."

"Sounds good, I pass to Tom."

"Larry, I'm also going to need Sam's help."

Sam replied, "Wait a minute! We finished the meth lab, we're working on the stolen trucks from Canada, we know about the pawn shop raid. Now how did you come up with a National problem in less than 24 hours?"

Everyone started to laugh.

I said, "I'm sorry Sam, didn't anyone bring you up to date?"

"No Larry, they didn't."

"Shame on you boys! Sam, we found another drug ring. It looks like their home operation is out of state. That's why Tom needs your help. Tom, explain the operation to Sam and Wade in detail later."

"I'll do that Larry."

Sam said, "You know I was only kidding Larry."

"Yes we did Sam, that's why we're all laughing."

"It's funny how you guys keep stumbling onto these things."

"The way I see it Sam, is like this; our town has ebbed its way deep into the grips of crime. Before they hired me the bad guys had declared their ownership of our town. It has taken time but we've slowly but surely taken our town back. Back to you Tom."

"I got a pretty good start on the information I needed this morning. The office with the information on the ambulance service opened at eight o'clock. I'd like to turn that information over to Sam and report on it thoroughly at our five o'clock meeting."

"Seeing we don't have a life or death matter pressing why don't we go back to one meeting a day? The morning one at nine o'clock. A show of hands if we all agree."

Everyone raised their hand so we continued.

"Tom, if you find out something Pete should know, call him direct."

"I will Larry. Now I pass to Jim."

"We're still watching the stolen trucks and people from Canada. Also the Mayor has arranged for me to do a surprise inspection with the State Inspector of Ambulance Services this afternoon at one. I'll give you my report in the morning. I pass to Robert."

"I checked on the license of the ambulance service and you'll never guess what I found!"

"What?"

"The same corporation runs one of our Airvac services."

"Thanks Robert, that helps clear up the picture. What kind of aircraft do they have?"

"Three helicopters and two light aircraft."

"Why is it that doesn't surprise me?"

Lynda added, "One W down and four to go."

"You're right Lynda. We know the 'What'. They are smuggling by means of ambulances of one kind or another. I think we also know 'Why'. That would be a great big profit. Mayor, also get Jim access to the aircraft."

"I've already made a note of it."

"Good, anything else, Robert?"

"I pass to John."

"As you notice, Larry is still here, which means I'm doing a great job of watching him."

"Cute John, real cute. I hate to say it, but if no one else has anything, I'm feeling a bit on the tired side."

"Larry."

"Yes, Coop?"

"I'll make it fast. Josh and I went to the night club again last night."

"The one you've been working on all week? What happened?"

He pulled a small plastic bag out of his coat pocket. He held it up so I could see it. "Pete has already tested it. According to him it's pretty good stuff."

"Who sold it to you?"

"The waiter we've been friendly with all week."

"Did he have it on him?"

"No, I waited at the table for him. Josh Walked Silent and Walked Deadly."

"What did you see Josh?"

"He went back to the Manager's office. I heard him talking to his boss. He explained how he could tell we were all right. Also, he was absolutely sure we weren't cops."

I said, "At least he got the last part right. Did you get a description of his boss?"

"Better than that Larry, I got the names of both of them."

"Give Pete and Sam the names. They'll check them out for us. Tom...."

"I know Larry find out everything I can about the restaurant."

"That's right. Who knows? We may soon be in the restaurant business."

Pete said, "Larry, if you keep this up we'll have to hire more cops."

"I know what you're saying Pete. But it'll all work out."

"I hope so."

"Believe me it will. If we get too many businesses we'll hire people to work in them and we'll just do the management. Now that brings up another problem."

"What's that Larry?"

"Well, Mayor, we now have two undercover men leaving town."

"I see what you mean."

"Larry?"

"Yes Coop?"

"Is this where Josh and I volunteer to stay and help 'win one for the old Gipper'?"

"That would be nice guys, but I can't ask you to stay any longer. You've been here almost a month. We'll work something out. Plus, I can't afford to pay you guys what you're worth."

"Josh and I talked it over last night. We know how important this is to you. We also know how much we love and respect you. And we never forget that none of your old team, that's all twenty of us, would be here if it wasn't for you. Both Josh and I have more money in the bank than we'll ever spend. So if you'll supply us with a place to stay and some spending money we'll stay until we put these boys on ice."

"Thank you for the nice words boys, and for your help. I think we can meet your terms for employment. Pete will work it out with payroll later."

Pete said, "Sounds good Larry. On that same thought we could make Coop and Josh some heavy hitters in town."

"You mean the idea I had last week?"

"Yes. The one about selling drugs that you never finished explaining to us. You had some dumb reason like getting blown up."

Everyone started to laugh.

"I was wondering how long it would take you guys to realize I was faking my injuries."

We all continued to laugh. When it quieted down I continued.

"That's what I like about this group. I say something and everyone remembers it. First, I have to admit, Pete that you are one step ahead of me. You're talking about what I was thinking a few days ago but

I hadn't put that thought and our boys together yet. But, it's a good idea. Coop, what do you and Josh think?"

"Can you explain it a little more, Larry?"

"Sure Josh. We'll set the two of you up in a nice house. Give you a couple of nice cars and give you drug buying money. We need to see how big your boys in the restaurant business are."

Josh said, "Sounds like fun. Count me in."

"Coop?"

"Me too, Larry. I wouldn't miss it."

"Who wants to handle the setup for the boys?"

"I'll take care of it Larry."

"Thanks Pete. Now does anyone else have anything?"

No one said a word.

"Good. A couple of things. Pete, you'll meet with Doc tomorrow at three o'clock at the hospital. When you finish you and Doc will meet with me here."

"Okay Larry."

"Yoto, you'll take Snake and Cutter to the airport this afternoon. You'll then return here,"

"It shall be done, Larry."

"Now, I'm awful tired. Snake and Cutter, thanks again for coming. We couldn't have done it without you. Have a safe trip home. Everyone else….let's get to work."

Snake and Cutter walked over to me and lightly we shook hands goodbye. They were good boys and I was going to miss them. After everyone left Lynda helped me get comfortable on my bed. She then kissed me and left the room. I shut down my mind and went to sleep.

While I was sleeping Yoto took the boys out to eat and then to the airport. Here's what Yoto said happened on their way to the airport.

"That was a good lunch Yoto."

"Yeah, I agree."

"Thanks guys. It was Larry's idea."

Snake said, "He's quite a friend."

"You can say that again."

"Okay Cutter. He's quite a friend."

We laughed.

"I'm going to miss you guys."

"We know Yoto and we feel the same way."

"When you guys stop being mushy I have a question."

"What is it Cutter?"

"We have over three hours before our plane leaves."

"Closer to four."

"All right Snake, four. Could we take a ride around the bad side of town? Maybe we could get some ideas to help Larry out."

"I don't see anything wrong with that," Yoto replied.

I drove the limo down to the south central part of town. We were driving on the main five lane street when a low rider pulled in front of us. I was going about thirty in the thirty five M.P.H. zone. The car in front of me seemed to stay the same distance in front of me. It was like he was following me from the front. There were four passengers in the car. I looked in my rear view mirror and saw another car with four people behind us. So I informed Snake and Cutter what was happening.

Cutter asked, "What could they possible do in broad daylight?"

"I don't know Cutter. To be safe I want Snake to reach between his legs and feel the lower part of the front of his seat."

"I feel a button."

"Push it in three times and a door will flip open. Take yourselves each a gun and a badge. You now work for the police force."

They did as I directed.

"We have to stop for the red light coming up. They could have gone through it but they didn't, so stay on your toes."

I pulled the limo up behind the low rider.

"I'm putting the limo in park in case they try something."

They did. As we sat there the low rider in front of us rolled backwards and our bumpers hit one another.

"One of two things boys, they want us out of our car so they can rob us and steal the limo. Or they want to claim an accident with whiplash. So heads up. Here comes the driver. Remember the four guys behind us."

By the time the driver made it to my door his other friends were getting out of the car. I looked in my rear view mirror again. The boys in the rear car were sitting and watching. The traffic signal changed and other traffic was driving around us giving us a wide berth.

"Boys, I'm going to play the dumb Chinaman."

"But you're not Chinese."

"We know that Cutter but they don't."

Snake said, "Be careful Yoto."

As I started to open the door I said to the boys, "I got the front."

As I got out of the car I thought these boys should be in school, or maybe working at a job. The place they shouldn't be is out in the streets picking on citizens. As I stood up and looked dumb the boy started in. As he spoke I walked in front of my open door.

"You know Chink, you're in a lot of trouble. And it's going to cost you a lot of money."

I spoke in my best broken English, "You hit me."

"That makes no difference. You see this?" He lifted the front of his shirt to expose a gun.

"You want to sell me a gun?"

"No. How dumb can one Chink be? I don't want to sell you a gun."

His other friends who got out of the car started laughing.

"Then you want to give me the gun?"

They started laughing again.

"No. I want you to have your passengers get out of the car. If they don't I'll draw my gun and kill you."

I motioned for my boys to get out of the limo. They got out on each side of the car.

As the boys in the front started to move, and the boys in the rear got out of their car, Cutter spoke in Swedish to me.

"Yoto." After that I had no idea what he said. I then spoke back to him in Chinese sounding jibberish.

Mister Big Shot with a gun in his belt asked, "What'd he say?"

"He wanted to know what was happening."

"What'd you tell him?"

"We have some children who think by outnumbering someone and by having a gun they can do whatever they wish."

"And that's right."

"It may be right somewhere little boy, but it's no longer the thing to do in Pertsville."

"You speak real brave for a man who's out numbered and unarmed."

"You're the one that's outnumbered. You had that problem the minute you got out of your car."

He started to move his right hand toward his gun.

"If you attempt to draw your gun," I spoke in a loud voice, "and if anyone else pulls out a weapon we will take it away from you and kill you with it."

"You talk awful big Chink."

"Oh. Did I forget to mention that we're Police Officers? Guys, show the children your badges. Now, for attempted extortion and threatening the lives of three Police Officers you're all under arrest. You can do it the easy way or the hard way."

I took one step toward the leader and he reached for his gun. I thought, 'How bold this garbage is'. In the middle of the day on a main street in town, they think they own this place. Death is the only thing that will convince them that they don't. I hit the boy with a side kick. My shoe hit his hand at the same time his hand reached his gun. He moaned as I heard his fingers snap. The kick not only broke his fingers, but also caused him to bend over a little. Before straightening himself up he pulled out his gun with his left hand. While he was doing that I hit him as hard as I could in the throat with a frontal kick. I destroyed everything inside his neck. He fell to the ground gasping his last breath. What a sick way to die. By the time he hit the ground his three friends were in front of me. I could also see Snake and Cutter out of the corner of my eye. They were standing between me and the four boys from the rear car.

"I said it before and I'll say it again. You're all under arrest! So you'll assume the position on the fender of the car closest to you." The three boys in front of me each brought out a switch blade knife.

"Need some help Yoto?"

"No Snake. You boys take care of the children in front of you. I'll handle the three in front of me."

One of the boys in front of me said, "We're going to carve you into little pieces for killing our friend."

"Two things, one; you animals don't have any friends. Two; this is your last chance to throw your knives away and give up."

"I know…you're going to kill us. What a laugh."

"Remember the rules. Once we start there is no surrender."

One of the other boys spoke, "You can't kill us if we give up and no longer have a knife."

"That's what you think. The day of the mob is over. You scumbags have three choices. One; go to prison. Two; leave town. Three; die. No more easy rides. No more bail. No more reform school. To be honest with you children I prefer your death, it costs the taxpayers a lot less money."

"But we have rights."

"Now you have me laughing. Now either fight or give up. I'm tired of talking to you."

"We're not going to prison. We've seen what will happen to us there. Let's get him boys!"

As they lunged at me I used a sweep kick to knock the knife out of the hand of the closest boy. I then spun him around and pushed him into his friend on his left. His friend managed to push the knife that was intended for me into the chest of his friend. As his friend sank to the ground, the third boy came at me. He lunged, and I slapped his wrist away. In doing so his body took a half twist away from me and exposing his side to me. I used a side kick with my right foot to smash his knee. I grabbed him by his hair while standing behind him. I pulled his head back and exposed the hand that contained the knife. He slowly raised the knife toward me. I grabbed his wrist and arm and drove the knife into his chest. I then turned to face the last scumbag. He was about a dozen paces from me. He was rolling his friend over so he could get his gun out from under him. He picked it up and started to raise it in my direction. When he had the gun pointed at me he cocked the hammer to fire. When he made that slight hesitation, I left the ground. I jumped up about six feet in the air flying toward him. Before he could readjust his aim with the pistol I hit him with a fatal flying head kick. I hit him and then the ground. I rolled and came back up on my feet. He dropped the gun as he fell to the ground. I looked over at Snake and Cutter.

"You guys need to do something with those children."

Cutter said, "Up against the car boys." They responded at a normal speed.

About that time two black and whites showed up. Each car had two cops in it. As they got out of the car I motioned them over to me. They recognized me and one of them asked, "What can we do?"

"Get the coroner's wagon over here. Those four boys resisted arrest." I keep calling them boys but they were between the ages of

18 and 24.

As the officer started to turn away I said, "Give me your cuffs." He handed them to me and left. "The rest of you will cuff the four prisoners leaning on the car." They walked over to the bad guys. They shook the boys down and cuffed them one by one. When they got to the third guy and started to cuff him he spun around and grabbed the rookie behind him. He spun the rookie around as a shield and pulled out the rookie's gun. He had his arm around the rookie's neck and his gun pointed in our direction.

"I'm not going to prison! I'm not going to be some monkey's whore! I'm getting out of here. If someone tries to stop me I'll kill this cop!"

Snake watched his eyes, and I drew his attention to me. As I spoke he pointed the gun at me.

"Don't anyone bother....."

A shot rang out. It came from Snake's gun. The boy hit the ground with a hole in his forehead.

I asked, "Does anyone else have a problem?"

The boy that hadn't been cuffed yet leaned over the fender of the car with both hands behind himself. The other cops cuffed and searched him. The rookie walked over to me, regaining his composure as he approached. He looked scared to death. Snake and Cutter had joined me.

The rookie came up to Snake and said, "Thank you for saving my life."

"You're welcome."

He then looked at me, "I think I made a big mistake, Sir."

"You did, and I want you to report what happened to you to your Sergeant."

"Yes, Sir, I will."

"Have him call me before giving you disciplinary action."

"Would you like my name and badge number Sir?"

"No. You're a member of this family. We're not going to discipline you we're only going to fix what's broken. I trust you to do as ordered."

"I will Sir. Thank you."

He walked away and I could tell he was still very shaken. I looked at Snake and quietly said, "Thanks from me too."

"That's what we're here for Yoto."

A third black and white pulled up. It was driven by a Sergeant. He walked over to me and asked what happened. I explained everything to him and left him in charge. I then took the boys to the airport. They still had a couple of hours before their planes left. I sat in the lounge with them and waited.

Chapter 3

Pete walked into my bedroom as I was awakening. "Larry, are you awake?"

"If I wasn't I would be now, what's happening Pete?"

"The war against the mobs has started."

"How so?"

"Yoto was taking Cutter and Snake to the airport….."

He explained everything that had happened to me and Lynda. "I don't know what we're going to do Pete. I can't leave those boys alone for a minute without them doing something to make me proud."

"You're right there. I don't know what we'd do without them."

"You know this couldn't have happened any better if we had planned it."

Lynda asked, "How's that Larry?"

"I consider this to be the strongest warning yet to the mobs, Lynda. I'd be willing to bet that a lot of members will be retiring from the mob business. What we need to do now is find out where they have their meetings. Where ever it is Pete, raid it. Arrest them for trespassing and whatever else fits the bill."

"You mean like drugs, stolen merchandise, and concealed weapons?"

"That's right, Lynda. Pete, talk to the Mayor. He gets status reports every week from the people we've helped to get rid of their graffiti problems."

"I'll do that. How're you feeling?"

"Pretty good. I can't wait to see Doc tonight so I can move around more. I think I'm healed enough to get out of bed."

Pete said, "Try to look at it this way; we're not in an emergency situation. So why don't you relax and get well healed so when you're needed physically you'll be ready?"

"That's good advice he's giving you Larry."

"All right Lynda. Between you and Pete I can't win."

Lynda asked, "Pete would you like something to eat or drink?"

"No Lynda. I have to get back to the office. My boss expects a report from me in the morning."

I asked, "Is there anything else new?"

"No Larry. I'll see you in the morning."

"See you then."

Lynda walked Pete out. She returned about five minutes later. She was wearing an apron. "You're hungry I hope."

"Starved is a better word."

After eating I slept some more. Around six o'clock Doc showed up.

"How's my favorite patient?"

"Feeling good, Doc. Real good."

"From what I can see you're looking great."

He changed my bandage and said, "You'll need to take it easy. I want you to get up and walk around, just a couple minutes at a time. Do this about a dozen times before I get here tomorrow. You may sleep on your side. You can also sit up in bed or on a chair as long as you have a lot of soft pillows supporting your back. Do you both understand my directions?"

"I do. Lynda?"

"No problem."

"Do you need any more pain pills?"

"I probably don't need any more since I haven't taken any yet."

"I forgot. You block out the pain."

"Yes I do. Now, where are you rushing off to?"

"The officer you assigned to my family teaches us karate every Tuesday and Thursday evening. I want to meet my wife and kids before our lesson for dinner."

"Then the whole family is learning?"

"Yes and I have to admit it's a lot of fun."

"That's great. While you're there stay completely focused. You'll be surprised at how much you can learn in a short time. Now get out of here."

"I'm gone. I'll see you tomorrow."

"See you then."

As Lynda walked Doc out Coop and Josh came in.

"What'd the Doc say?"

"Josh, it looks like I'm going to live."

Coop said, "Darn it! There goes my promotion."

"Cute Coop, real cute. Now if you're done joking around, Doc said I could sit up if I have a lot of soft pillows behind me."

"Then hold on a minute and we'll get some more pillows from the other bedrooms."

"All right Josh."

They returned with a half a dozen pillows and Lynda. They stacked the pillows up nicely, and then helped me to a sitting position.

"Oh, you have no idea how great this feels, the simple pleasure of looking someone straight in the eyes when you speak to them."

"I'm glad to hear that."

"Mayor, I didn't know you were here."

"I used my own key. And look at you! Sitting up like a big boy!"

Everyone laughed.

"My friends!"

"I know I'm your friend. I brought you two things. One; Judy for company and two; Chinese for dinner."

"That sounds good."

"I hope you didn't include us Mayor. Josh and I are going out for dinner."

I said, "I bet I know where."

"Yes, Larry. We're going to make another score tonight."

"What about the setup Mayor?"

"I talked to Pete before I came over. His report was; they'll be moved in before tomorrow afternoon."

"Good. You boys have a good time but be careful. Trust no one."

"All right Larry. We'll be late, so we'll see you at the morning meeting."

"Sounds good Coop. See you then."

They left and we had dinner. John had gone home early, and I wondered what had happened to Yoto. After we finished dinner the phone rang. It was Yoto.

"You had me worried."

"Thanks, Larry. It's nice to be cared for."

"Where are you?"

"Did you hear about what happened on our way to the airport?"

"Yes."

"Well, I had a bad feeling about the two cars that were towed in. I've been with our boys ripping them apart."

"Did you find anything?"

"A few thousand dollars under the rear seat of one of the cars."

"What else?"
"Nothing."
"Then what's bothering you?"
"Why did they want a limo? They couldn't sell it or get it across the border."
"Now you're making me nervous. I'll talk to Pete and the Mayor about it. Are you heading here?"
"Do you need me there?"
"Not really. Why?"
"I have a dinner date with Lyn-Yhi."
"Have a good time. I'll see you at the morning meeting."
"Thanks Larry. I'll see you then."
"Yoto!"
"Yes Larry. I'm still here."
"Tell our boys to take everything off the bottom of the cars including the gas tanks."
"I'll do it. Good bye."
"Good bye!"
I leaned back and relaxed for a minute.
"Are you okay Larry?"
"Yes Lynda, but someone else has a problem."
"What's up Larry?"
"I don't know Mayor. Yoto put out some food for thought."
"What do you mean?"
"Judy, I hate to do this to you."
"I know Larry. It's for my own safety. So let me take the dishes to the kitchen."
"I'll help you Judy."
"Thanks, Lynda."
They stacked up all the dishes and carried them to the kitchen.
"Mayor, Yoto asked a very simple question."
"The same one that's been bugging me all day?"
"I have to know your question before I'll tell you Yoto's."
"What did dumb, illiterate white trash want with a limo?"
"That's the question."
"I don't have an answer Larry."
"Someone is coming to town on a one way ticket."
"That's possible, or the boys wanted to ride around town in class."

"As strange as it may sound, that's also possible."

"What's Yoto been up to?"

"He's been with our boys at the storage garage tearing the cars apart. So far they've found nothing of importance."

"What should we do?"

"I'll talk about it at the morning meeting. That way everyone can worry with me. I hate to worry alone."

As we laughed, the Mayor agreed.

"You know it's almost eight o'clock? I better get out of here so you can get some rest."

The Mayor pushed the intercom on the wall and asked Judy and Lynda to join us. We said our 'Good Nights' and Lynda walked them to the door.

It was 9:45 P.M. Lynda had just finished giving me a lovely sponge bath when the phone rang.

"Hello." (Pause) "Yes Mayor, I'll tell him."

"What are you going to tell me?"

"The Mayor got a call from one of the council people. He said to watch Jack Parker on Channel Four News at ten o'clock."

Lynda opened the cabinet doors of our entertainment center and removed the remote control. She pushed the on button and the number four. She checked the sound and then lay down on the bed next to me. As she cuddled gently up next to me, I put my arm around her and squeezed her shoulder. She looked up at me and smiled.

"I love you."

"I love you too, Larry."

"You know how much I appreciate everything you're doing for me and I must say you're doing a great job. I don't know what I'd do without you."

"You get feeling a little better, and I'll show you what we can do together."

"Be careful! You're starting to excite this old man."

"That was the whole idea."

She moved her head up and we kissed. As my tongue wrapped around hers I squeezed her shoulder. When we broke from the kiss I said, "Enough of this! I'm only human."

Lynda's hand was in my lap. "I can tell." She said as she laughed.

"Cute, real cute. Now turn the volume up, the news is on."
We sat quietly listening.
"This is Jack Parker reporting our lead story of the day. There is some graphic material not for the weak at heart. It all started this afternoon when 8 mob members in two separate cars staged a false car accident. The boys had one car in front of the victim and one car behind him. All three cars were stopped at a traffic light. The car in front went into reverse and lightly hit the car behind him. When everyone got out of their cars the 8 boys attempted to rob the people and carjack their vehicle. The scum made only one mistake; they tried to steal a car with three plainclothes cops in it. When the fight was over there were 5 dead mob members and 3 arrested. I sit here and think of a different outcome. What if I was driving the car or one of my viewers? Instead of mob members laying dead in the street it would probably be one of us. What I'm trying to say is this; it's time we stopped the mobs in our town cold. If you know of people who belong to a mob I want you to call the police hotline. You don't have to tell them who you are. Just tell them about the mob members. It's time the mobs know that the police department is tired of their existence. They have 4 choices as I see it. They can go back to being a normal youth; they can go to jail; die; or leave town. The days of being in a mob have ended in Pertsville. What you've seen today is only the start. To the good citizens out there listening to me, remember this: in drive-by shootings last year 26 innocent people lost their lives, 20 of the cases are still unsolved. This tells me these animals are still out there to do it again. While the police are putting down the mobs in our town some innocent people may get hurt or killed. This is possible in any war. But if we all pull our resources together we may all get out of this safely. If someone does get hurt or killed at least we know they died so the rest of us can live in peace. So get to those phones, the police hot line works 24 hours a day. Let's keep cleaning up our town. The next time you talk to a cop, thank him for what he is doing. Now after our commercial break we'll return with the weather........."
"Turn it off, Lynda."
She pushed the off button on the remote control unit.
"What do you think, Larry?"
"I think Jack is either following orders or one very brave man. Get

me Pete...."

The phone rang. Lynda picked up the phone, "Hello? Mayor? He'll call you right back."

She disconnected the call and dialed Pete at home.

"Pete? Hold on Larry wants to talk to you."

She handed me the receiver.

"Pete?"

"Yes, Larry."

"Did you see Jack Parker's report?"

"Yes and I loved it."

"What about Jack Parker?"

"What about him?"

"You're a mob leader."

"All right."

"You just heard his report."

"I'd like to kill that big mouth S.O.B. to show the town that we're still in control."

"You made a good mob leader, Pete."

"Thanks for shaking my tree. I'm going to set up a little surprise for the mob that decides to hit him. First, I'll call Jack Parker at the station and tell him to stay there. Next, I'll call our boys and get things rolling and head over there myself."

"Good. You'll probably want to keep a surveillance team on him for a few days."

"I'll take care of it and talk to you in the morning."

"See you then."

I handed the receiver back to Lynda. She disconnected the line and dialed the Mayor back and handed me the receiver.

"Mayor?"

"Hi Larry. Did you like the report?"

"Yes. It was good. Whose idea was it?"

"Believe it or not, it was all Jack's idea with the permission of his boss."

"The man has guts."

"You don't think the mobs will retaliate against him do you?"

"Yes, I do, and so does Pete."

"That's why Lynda hung up on me?"

"Yes. I didn't want to lose any time getting Pete on the case."

"What's he going to do?"

"Protect and destroy. He'll report everything at the morning meeting."

"Then I'll let you get some rest and I'll see you in the morning."

"Good night Mayor."

"Good night Larry."

I gave the phone back to Lynda and she hung it up. She turned off the lights and we went to sleep.

Before I knew it I was sitting up in my desk chair in my living room waiting to start the meeting. Lynda had gone downstairs earlier to get my chair from my office. It's a tall backed, very soft leather, well cushioned chair. We added pillows to it to make me comfortable.

"Gentlemen, shall we get started?"

Everyone quieted down.

"Sam, get us started."

"I checked out everything for your boys and we hit the jackpot."

"Please go on."

Larry, we had to go through a lot of corporations before we hit the Lewed Corporation. It's owned by one of the larger families back East."

"Are you speaking about the restaurant or the pawn shop?"

"That's the jackpot, Larry. I'm talking about both."

"You're kidding! The mob owns both of the operations?"

"Yes and each operation is run by a nephew of the Don."

"Pete, you have a problem."

"That's right, Larry, he does. These boys will stop at nothing to get Pete."

Tom said, "Don't worry Pete we won't let them have you."

"Thanks, Tom. And just so everybody knows, I'm scared."

I said, "That's good Pete. That might be the edge you need to keep yourself alive."

John asked, "What do you mean, Larry?"

"John, if Pete wasn't afraid, he'd do something stupid and get himself killed. But the way he is now, he'll be extra careful of everything he does. Isn't that right Pete?"

"Yes Larry, you're right. The thing that bothers me is what are we going to do about it?"

"I don't know yet Pete, but you'll be the first to know the minute I figure it out."

Sam added, "Larry, I hate to interrupt but my boys in Washington gave us a big, green light on this operation. They want this family so bad they can taste it."

"I'm glad to hear that, Sam. I think we should stay calm and see what the Gods have in store for us."

"Can I at least put surveillance on the nephew running the restaurant?"

"Sam, you can tap all his lines, bug all his places, and read his mail."

"You sure gave in easily. Why?"

"Sam, these boys are trying to use real businesses to launder their money. As you can see, once scum always scum."

Wade asked, "Did I miss something, Larry?"

"No Wade. Everyone else got it."

"Got what?"

"Sam, why don't you explain it to him?"

"What Larry is trying to say is this….The boys were sent out here to set up clean businesses to launder some of the drug money from back east. Instead, the boys have decided to go into the drug business on the side."

"You know the family will kill their own, Larry."

"We know that, Wade. I'm just trying to figure out what story has gotten back east."

"Larry, I'll have our boys get the scuttlebutt from the streets."

"Let me know the minute you hear, Sam."

"I will Larry."

Pete said, "Wait a minute, Larry. Are you trying to say the boys back east won't send torpedoes out here to get me?"

"Until I hear from Sam, I won't know for sure. My gut feeling is this is a local problem? Use a local solution."

"You really think so Larry?"

"Yes, Tom. The last thing the nephew wants is his boss out here. The last thing they want to do is show their faces out here."

"I agree with you Larry."

"Thanks, Sam."

"Do you have any ideas, Larry?"

"Well Mayor, now that you asked."

"I smell another production."

"Just a small one Tom. I think the key to this situation is to know who is going to kill Pete. Does everyone agree? Hands!"

Everyone raised their hands.

John said, "We could always call and ask them who they hired."

Everyone laughed.

"That's not as funny as you may think, John."

"We're going to call them?"

"No. We're going to give them two professional killers."

"You don't mean....."

"Yes I do, Jim. They were good enough to kill me I think they can handle Pete."

Everyone laughed, making comments under their breath.

The Mayor said, "You're not serious are you Larry?"

"Dead serious, Mayor."

"I don't know about this."

"What's the matter, Coop?" I knew it had to be a joke so I went along with him.

"Two things. One, we only kill people with a rank of commissioner or higher. Two, you guys are ruining our bad reputation."

Everyone laughed.

"I'll try to save your tarnished reputation if you'll find it in your heart to kill this one lowly police chief for me."

As they were laughing they said, "Okay."

I said, "You thought it was going to be easy to get killed didn't you Pete?"

"Yes, Larry, I did."

"I hate taking you boys out of turn, but I need to know how things went last night."

"We made a good size buy. It made the owner so happy that he invited us to an after- hours party tonight."

"Good Coop. I don't have to tell you again to be careful. Always remember if it comes down to you or them I want YOU home safely."

"We'll remember Larry. We'll also give them a hint to what we're retiring from to become drug dealers."

Sam said, "I like the sound of that."

"So do I Sam. Now, do you want to continue?"

Sam continued, "Yes Larry. All's quiet in Canada. Pete, I have either two or three teachers for your new schools."

"Thanks, Sam. I'll make a note of it."

"Also Pete, we'll turn over the property from the meth lab bust tomorrow afternoon. Can we meet at the apartment house at five?"

"That sounds…."

"Pete."

"Yes Larry?"

"Instead of you meeting Sam and Wade tomorrow, have a couple of our people from the property committee meet with them. I don't want you exposed to the public any more than necessary. Do you understand?"

"Yes, Larry."

"Is that all right with you Sam?"

"Yes Larry, that's a good idea. Now I pass to Wade."

"I pass to the Mayor."

"I've been working with my people on our budget, and here's what I can do for the Police Force. A one percent increase in pay across the board. I can also afford to buy you a sixth traffic camera."

Everyone applauded.

"I don't know Mayor."

"That's more than I offered you yesterday, and you were going to take it."

"I know, but I got greedy overnight."

"I'm out of money!"

"Do you think I'd ask for more money out of your budget?"

"If not out of the budget, where will I get it?"

"Question?"

"Yes."

"If it's a person's first ticket or they haven't had one for two years they get an option, right?"

"Yes, they can pay the ticket and the points go against their license. Or they can pay $95.00 and take a one day defensive driving class."

"Who gets the $95.00?"

"Most of it goes to the teaching company we've contracted with that puts on the classes."

"The price of the ticket is usually higher than the class fee, right?"

"Yes."

"Here's what I propose we do Mayor. We will raise the price of the class to be the same as the ticket or $95.00, whichever is higher. You will take out your operating expenses and give us the rest of the money. Our volunteers will teach the classes and we can give the classes in one of our buildings. Can you break your present contract?"

"No, but the renewal comes up next month. They're bound to ask for more money. They've done that to us for the last two years."

"Think how good you'll feel when you tell them to take a hike."

"You're right. I will feel good. If I comply with your wishes do we have a contract?"

"As far as I'm concerned it's a done deal, hands from everyone who agrees."

All hands in the room went up.

"Then we have a contract?"

"Not quite, Mayor. I'm going to have to get over 1500 other people to agree to it. I'll have an answer for you next week. Who wants to play liaison between us and the men?"

"I can handle it."

"Me too, Larry."

"All right. Tom and John, you've got the job. Write up what you want to say and start with the Association Committee. Let them help you with the rest of the men. I don't see a problem with any of it, but I'd like our men to have a say in their lives. Make the voting easy. The only people to vote are the 'no votes', majority wins."

"We'll take care of it Larry."

"Thanks Tom. Mayor?"

"I pass to Pete."

"Where do I start? Let's see…I set up surveillance on the ambulance service. Jim will fill us in on the rest of that operation. I'm still checking on empty military buildings for your schools. I've got about a dozen volunteers for teachers. We're starting to line up raids on the mobs. I've gotten a lot of inside information from the Mayor, which he got from our good citizens."

I said, "I love it when the people of our town help us clean it up.

Continue, Pete."

"All right Larry. Coop and Josh will be in their house by four this afternoon. When you boys see your duds, cars, house, jewelry, and spending money you'll go nuts."

"Sounds good, Pete."

"I knew you'd like it Coop."

I asked, "Next, did everyone see Jack Parker on the T.V. news last night? Hands?"

A couple of hands didn't go up.

Pete resumed the conversation, "For the people who didn't see it, he was all for us. He asked his viewers to call us with leads about mobs in our town. It worked. Our phone lines have been going strong all night. And they're still calling this morning. Larry called me right after the broadcast. He figured Mr. Parker was now in a lot of danger. I called the T.V. station and thanked Mr. Parker for his broadcast. I then informed him to stay put until we get there to escort him home. He said it wasn't necessary, but I insisted. I had the closest black and white unit there in less than five minutes. They kept Mr. Parker in check until we got there. I sent a SWAT Team to his house to stake it out. I arrived first at the station. When my detectives finally arrived they had a bullet proof vest for Mr. Parker. Except for the two patrolmen everyone was in plainclothes. I told one of our female detectives that she had just fallen in love."

She asked, "With whom?"

"With Mr. Parker, of course. When the two of you walk out of the back door of this place you'll head through the parking lot to Mr. Parker's car. I want you two to hold on to one another and hug one another. Any trouble ….. you protect Mr. Parker."

"I will Chief."

"If you hold your revolver in the hand you're holding hands with no one will notice it."

"Thanks Chief. I'll do that."

I asked, "Are you ready Mr. Parker?"

"Yes, I've never worn a bullet proof vest before. It's kind of uncomfortable."

"If someone shoots at you it'll be the nicest piece of clothing you've ever worn."

"That's probably true Chief. I'm ready if everyone else is."

"Is this the usual time you leave?"
"Yes, I'm usually one of the last people to leave."
"Can we get out the front?"
"The night watchman can handle that for you."
I pointed to the detectives, "You four go out the front."
The night watchman said, "This way, gentlemen."

As we walked slowly to the rear door I said, "Remember you're responsible for anyone approaching you two. You have backup out there, but a close in target may be a risky shot, so it's up to you detective."

"I'll handle it Sir."

I figured enough time had passed for my boys to be out in the parking garage.

"All right, it's time. Be careful!"

As they started to open the door my detective said, "I will Sir."

"I meant that statement for both of you."

They walked out onto the parking garage. There couldn't have been more than a dozen cars in this part of the lot. As they got half way to Mr. Parker's car a young man around 19 to 21 years of age came walking up from behind a parked car. You could tell by the way he walked he was on a mission. He walked up in front of the couple.

"Aren't you that famous reporter, Parker?"

Mr. Parker answered, "Yes I am. Would you like my autograph?"

"I just wanted you to know that you said the wrong thing about the wrong people tonight. We run this town, and not you, or any police force is going to stop us. We're going to deal with you and everybody else who gets in our way the same."

"And how's that?"

He reached under his shirt and in his belt for his gun. He pulled it out and pointed it at them. While he was doing this he said, "We're going to kill you!"

Before he could fire a shot our detective pumped three slugs into his chest. He fell backward and fired into the air. As he fell to the concrete parking garage floor the car he'd walked out from behind started its engine and put on its lights. The people inside had to be hiding, because the car looked empty to all of us. The detective grabbed Mr. Parker's arm and pulled him into a state of retreat.

They were running toward the door of the building. The only thing between them and the door was a parked pick-up truck and a large concrete column holding up the parking garage. The car started rolling towards them. They ran past the truck and the car started to pick up speed. The detective knew they couldn't make the door. She pulled Mr. Parker by the shoulder over to and behind the concrete pillar. She pushed him against the pillar and turned the back of her body toward the oncoming car. The car had an arm out of every window, each one containing a gun, and they were firing them. Before the car got close to the pillar our four men in the parking garage seemed to pop out of everywhere. The nice part was they weren't looking around assessing a problem. They were filling the car full of lead. The car swerved into the parked pick-up. It hit the truck between the cab and the rear wheels right on the saddlebag gas tanks. In less than the blink of an eye the vehicles blew up. The noise was deafening to me inside the door. It must have been terrible for my people outside. There were only a couple of windows on my side of the building and they were blown out by the percussion of the blast. My boys that had done the firing all dove to the concrete floor which was a good move, otherwise they would have been knocked over. I ran out to Mr. Parker and my detective. The concrete pillar was large enough to protect them from the blast.

"Are you all right?"

"Yes Chief. We're fine."

"Mr. Parker, you said something about not needing our help?"

"I was hasty in saying that. Please forgive me. You had a great idea."

"To be honest with you it wasn't my idea."

"You're kidding!"

"No. The Commissioner called me after watching your report and said you needed help."

"Isn't he still laid up from the explosion?"

"Yes he is. Otherwise he would have been here himself."

"I'm glad to see you boys are in charge of our town."

"We don't want to be in charge of it; we just want to clean it up. With your help, and the help of all the good citizens out there we'll someday have our town in order."

"I believe you will, and I'll continue to help in every way possible.

I'll try to get some of my friends on the other T.V. stations to get on the bandwagon. Now, if you don't mind, I'm tired and shook up and I'd like to go home."

"I don't mind at all."

He turned to leave.

"Aren't you forgetting something?"

"What?"

"Your girlfriend!"

"Listen…she's cute and she's nice but I don't need a girlfriend. Wait a minute! I'm starting to see the big picture. More than one mob wants me dead."

"You're right on the money. Detective! There's a SWAT Team already in place at the house. Work it there the same way you did here."

They started to walk away.

"Detective!"

She stopped and turned around.

"You did a very outstanding job so far tonight, so keep up the good work and reload your weapon."

"Thank you Sir, I will."

I called the rest of my plainclothes men over to me.

"The patrolmen can handle this scene until their relief gets here. Everyone knows where Mr. Parker lives. I want two cars a block away East and two West, and wait for my orders. Get moving!"

They left the parking garage just before Mr. Parker. I walked over to my car, opened the trunk and pulled out a night vision scope. I got in the front seat and laid the scope beside me. I started the engine and headed to Mr. Parker's house. As I left I could hear the sirens of the fire trucks. As I pulled up to Mr. Parker's house I saw him and my detective encircled by eight young punks. They seemed to be jeering at Mr. Parker and my detective. I didn't see any weapons. I got on my radio to my men that I had posted around the area.

"I need two or three karate experts. Acknowledge!"

"One Sir."

"Two Sir."

Everything was silent for a few seconds.

"Will judo do Sir?"

"Yes. I'm going out to see what's happening. If I raise my hands in the air you boys will join me. If the boys in the circle show weapons and endanger our lives……..Combat Mode!"

I threw down the receiver and got out of the car.

I walked up on the crowd and spoke, "What's going on here?"

Looking at the boys they seemed to be between the ages of 16 to 25 years old.

"Unless you want to be beat to a pulp like your neighbor you better leave Mister."

"Why would you children want to do that to Mr. Parker?"

"Because, Mr. Bigmouth thinks he can stop us from running our town!"

"You boys don't look smart enough to properly run your mouth not yet run a town. My understanding is the day of the mob is over in Pertsville."

"Who says so?"

"I do, and the good people of Pertsville."

"And who are you Mister?"

"I'm Pertsville's Chief of Police Fortney."

I could hear undertones from the boys.

"Then I guess we'll have to beat on you too."

"Let me see, there's eight of you and three of us. Does that seem like a fair fight to you?"

"We don't care about fair. We only care about winning."

"That's how the low scum of this world would act."

"You're going to see how scummy we are."

"Do you know the rules?"

"What? There aren't any rules."

"Oh yes there are. They were put in place for you children. One; if you attempt to use a weapon it will be taken away from you and you will be killed with it. Two; there aren't any other rules. Lastly before we start I'd," I raised my hands in the air, "Like to bring in three people to take our places. Since you like the odds of eight against three, that's what it'll be. We'll sit on the porch and wait until the fight is over."

When I was through speaking my three boys were there to help out. I led Mr. Parker and my female detective over to Mr. Parker's porch, and we all sat down. I took my radio from my inside pocket and pushed the side button and said, "Move in, stay alert, and shoot to kill."

I guess some people would call it a fight, but I'd call it an exercise session for our boys. You could hear bones crack and break through the clear night air. End results; we didn't have to cuff the boys, they all had to go to the hospital, and that's the way it happened, Larry."

Jim asked, "Weren't you afraid they'd escape?"

"Jim, every one of them had at least one broken leg. Plus more different broken bones than we have time in this meeting to mention."

"I love it, Pete. Give the boys a 'well done' for me."

"I will Larry."

"What about Mr. Parker?"

"He's all right, Mayor. I left two men to spend the night with him. I'm going to keep him covered for another thirty six hours."

I said, "That should more than take care of the situation, anything else Pete?"

"That's about it Larry. I'll pass to Tom."

"Before you do, what about your meeting with Doc?"

"It's still on for this afternoon, and then back here to meet with you."

"Do me a favor."

"What's that?"

"Take someone with you."

"Tom, will you join me?"

"Sure Pete."

"Thanks. Now Tom, you have the floor."

"I'm waiting to hear from Sam on the out of state ownership of the ambulance business."

Sam replied, "And we're waiting for our people to get back to us."

"If that be the case, I pass to Jim. Maybe he's had better luck than me."

"The Mayor got me hooked up with the State Ambulance Inspectors. This particular ambulance service was set for an inspection in the next three months, so they didn't mind rescheduling a few things to do it yesterday. We spent the whole day and managed to inspect every transport they own. Six of twelve trucks are set up like the one we were in. The airplanes and helicopters all had plenty of space for extra cargo. I did find out one interesting thing. The helicopters seem to be built up more than necessary to do the job they are intended to do."

"I'll bet if you check the planes and the trucks closely you'll find the same thing."

"I bet we will Larry. I pass to Lynda."

"As you can see, Larry is doing much better. I hope to have him back to the office by the first of the week. You know what the Commissioner says, 'If you can't work, you can't eat.'"

"Cute, Lynda. Real cute!"

Everybody laughed.

"Now I pass to Robert."

"I found out that our ambulance boys have the run of the state. That's because of the extensive equipment they have."

"Pete, are you watching the ambulances?"

"Yes Larry. I have one man assigned to each ambulance."

"Jim's information should make it a little easier."

"Yes. Now I can use two man teams."

"Back to you Robert."

"I pass to Yoto."

"The man who has trouble finding the airport."

Everyone laughed.

"That's unfair, Larry. The boys only wanted to look around to see if they could make some suggestions to help you."

"To say the least, they opened a big can of worms."

"Are you mad at us boys?"

"On the contrary. I'm tickled pink. I was trying to figure out our next step when WHAMMO! My boys give it to me."

"It was by accident."

"I know, anything else new?"

"Yes. The boys that were going through the cars did as you asked. When they got under one of the cars they found a strange looking gas tank. By removing four simple wing nuts half of the gas tank came loose. There was a large, round opening on the top of the tank. The top screwed off."

"They didn't find any drugs, did they?"

"No Larry. That's what they thought they'd find."

"I don't know why Yoto, but I keep thinking of Police Officers."

"That's probably because they found three D.P.S. (Department of

Public Safety – State Police), uniforms and one night watchman uniform. They also found everything that goes with the uniforms down to the service revolver, belts and holsters."

I remarked, "Boys, Yoto thought there was something fishy yesterday. Why did these hoodlums want a white, standout limo to drive around in? So he completely searched the boys and their cars. What we now have is something that's going down in our town. And we have to figure out what, when, and where. If we do that the rest will fall into place."

The Mayor jumped in, "Larry, there's a ton of things happening every week. How are we going to find out what this stuff is for?"

"Well Mayor. We have quite a bit already. They need a limo, possibly a white one. Pete, check auto theft. We need to know if a limo is missing and everything about it."

"I'll take care of it."

"Next, they need three D.P.S. Officers for something. Jim, you and Robert take it."

"We'll check it out Larry."

"Thanks, Jim. Next, the night watchman uniform, if they got the right uniform it should really help us narrow this thing down. John and Yoto, that's your assignment."

They said together, "All right, Larry."

"Thanks guys. Pete, have the cars in the impound yard put back together and put a tracking device in them. When they're claimed follow them."

"It'll be done Larry."

Sam said, "Never a dull moment around this place."

"I have to agree with you, Sam, but I don't know if we can live with dull. Everyone in this room is a go-getter. But we could use a slow down. Talking about slow downs, if no one else has anything we should get to work. Does anyone have a problem with a short meeting at five tonight? If we can get everything wrapped up tonight I hope to give all of you and myself the weekend off."

The meeting was okay with everyone. They left and I rested and walked around the house.

Chapter 4

A little after four Pete and Doc showed up. Doc checked me out and re-bandaged my deep wound.

"I'm leaving everything uncovered except the deep wound in your back. You need to exercise more to get your strength back."

"I'll do it Doc. When can I go back to work?"

"Is that a trick question, Larry?"

"What do you mean, Doc?"

"You've been working since the minute you got your eyes open."

"I meant physically back to my office."

"I know. I was only kidding you."

"I know. What's your verdict?"

"Monday, two hours, then add an hour each day until the end of the week. By next Monday you should be at about an eighty-five to ninety percent."

"Will you check on me every day?"

"I'll try to. It seems all of a sudden I'm deluged with work."

"I don't understand your problem, but I guess I'll have to live with it."

"Now can I show you some changes I have in mind?"

He put some plans on my bed. He started out showing me some walls that had to be moved. He was so excited I didn't have the heart to stop him. He took a break when Lynda brought in a tray of glasses and a pitcher of orange juice.

"How much more do you have Doc?"

"Are you getting tired?"

"No. I was just wondering."

"You're bored!"

"No. Will you answer a question for me?"

"Sure."

"Are you showing me everything because I'm your boss, or because you'd like my insight?"

"Most of what I'm showing you are because you're my boss."

"We discussed this before. I had a feeling at that time you didn't believe me. So I'll say it again. This is your project. We are here to help you. When you're up to your fanny in alligators, you don't need the extra worry of what I'm going to think. What I know about building and running a hospital you can put on the head of a pin. I don't mind being a sounding board for you and your ideas. Other than that run with it, have a good time, enjoy yourself. This isn't a job…it's an adventure!"

"Are you sure? This is such a big project you're entrusting me with. Are you sure it's my project alone?"

"Doc, did Pete give you a check book?"

"Yes he did."

"How much money is in the account?"

"I don't know. Pete never told me."

"When you write a check who signs it?"

"Me."

"Who oversees the checks you write?"

"No one."

"Were you told you'd have to answer to anyone for anything including your check writing?"

"No. But I'm starting to get your idea. If there's a major problem I will hear from you or if I need help I can talk to you. Otherwise I'm Mr. Big at the hospital."

"I couldn't have said it better."

"Two things."

"What Doc?"

"How much money is in the checking account? And I want to show you a few more ideas."

"To answer your question about the money in the account, you can't count that high without making a mistake. Also, I'd love to see your ideas."

At five fifteen I walked Doc to the door. Everyone was already seated in the living room waiting for me.

"Like I said Larry, you never stopped working."

"You're right Doc. See you Monday evening."

"See you then."

I turned and walked into the living room. I sat in my chair and started the meeting.

"I notice everyone has a drink but me."

Lynda appeared in the living room with two brandies in her hands, "You do now." She walked over and handed me a brandy.

"That's better, a toast gentlemen to the fact that we're all still alive."

Everyone agreed and took a sip of their drink.

"Tom, were you with Pete? I didn't see you in the bedroom."

"Yes Larry, I was. When we arrived I crashed out here. I didn't want to add to the crowd in your bedroom."

"Good thinking. Let's move along. Sam, you're up."

"I'm still checking on the ambulance service for Tom. If they were clean it wouldn't take this long to check them out."

"Stay on it."

"We will. Pete, according to what we've heard, the family back east wants the nephew here to take care of the problem here, which is you."

I asked, "Any ideas Sam?"

"Yes Larry. The nephew has had plenty of time to hire someone local to kill Pete."

I said, "Pete, get on the phone. It's time all your boys get into the streets and find out who's been hired. NOW!!"

Pete went into the kitchen to use the phone.

"This is an order. I want you guys to work it out among yourselves. I want at least two of you with Pete 24 hours a day. If they're already hired they need to figure out Pete's schedule."

Pete walked back into the room. "It's done Larry. I should know something tonight."

"All right, for now keep your schedule erratic. We'll make it easy for your killers when we find out who they are."

"You think he hired more than one guy?"

"Yes Wade, I do. When they're no good you need more than one."

Sam added, "I'll agree with that statement Larry."

"Thanks Sam. What else do you have?"

"Jim, should I tell him or do you want to?"

"Go ahead Sam."

"Jim called me after the meeting this morning. He told me our Canadian boys are on the move. The minute his surveillance boys saw suitcases they called Jim and he called me. I've never seen such cheap people in my life. They have tickets on the red-eye special at midnight tonight."

"Stay low keyed and no one will know you're around."

"That's true Larry."

"What's next?"

"Wade and I will be on the plane with them. My friend Charles of the Mounties will meet us at the airport. He'll bring a surveillance team with him."

"How long will you be there?"

"We should be back Sunday evening."

"Then we'll see you at the Monday morning meeting."

"If everything goes according to our plan we'll be here."

"Anything else?"

"Yes. I picked up this report as I left my office." He handed it to Tom. "So far your ambulance corporation has taken us across five states and it stops with the Blanca Corporation."

"I've never heard of it."

"Well Larry, neither had we. As you look through the file you'll see what little we were able to get from Mexico and our border patrols. Blanca seems to be a legal end of a Mexican Cartel."

"Ouch! We stepped into it again."

Sam said, "You're right Jim. The trouble with this operation is we'll only get the people in the United States."

I asked, "Why is that Sam?"

"Larry, we don't get the cooperation we should out of Mexico. Their people are either working for the Cartels or they're afraid of them. In either case we have no idea who we can trust."

"Couldn't you send someone down there to eliminate the problem?"

"Yes Larry but if you eliminate one boss there are twenty people to take his place."

"Sounds like the problem I thought we'd have here. But we got lucky. When we eliminated a gang, we eliminated the whole gang."

"If we could make a dent in their distribution to the states it would help."

"We'll do our best to help you, Sam. Before you leave tonight ask your people to check on and get a list of all the properties the Blanca Corporation owns."

"I can do that and have it here for you Monday."

"That'll work. Tom, I want you and Jim to figure out how far the planes and choppers can travel round trip without stopping for fuel. Then get us a map that covers that area."

Jim asked, "You want us to use their base of operation as our starting hub? Then go out as far as we can in every direction then make a big circle on the map?"

"That's right Jim."

"And anything they own in that circle could be the drug distribution point."

"That's right Tom."

Sam said, "Larry, my people could do that for you. Plus it would save your boys some work."

"Sam, trust me on this one and do as I ask."

"You got it."

"Do you have anything else Sam?"

"I pass to Wade."

"I have everything set up for turning the buildings and personal property over to your people tomorrow. I pass to the Mayor."

"I pass to Pete."

"Everything is still in a holding pattern."

"While you were out of the room a few minutes ago I informed the boys that two of them would be with you 24 hours a day until your killers are taken care of."

"Thank you Larry. I like that. Hopefully we'll have them taken care of by Monday. Oh, I almost forget! Our two new drug dealers, Coop and Josh are all moved in."

"Josh, do you like your new place?"

"If we can keep it I may run away from home."

We all laughed.

"It's that good?"

Coop commented, "Larry, it's better than that."

"I'm happy you like it Coop. Don't forget. You boys need to show results."

"Didn't I tell you there'd be a catch Coop?"

"Yes you did, Josh, and I agreed with you. That's the way Larry is. There's no such thing as a free lunch."

"Yeah."

We all started laughing.

"All right you clowns. Knock it off! Did you move all your things from here Coop?"

"No Larry. We'll move them to the house before we go out

tonight."

"You both had better study your new house and put up a few booby traps. You can't be too careful."

"You don't think our new friends would do anything to harm us do you?"

We all laughed again.

"Just remember, with friends like that you won't be short on enemies."

"We agree, Larry. We will do the booby trapping, that's something we'd already decided on."

"That's good, Coop. Do you have anything else Pete?"

"I pass to Tom."

"I pass to Jim."

"Sam took care of things for me, I'll pass to Lynda."

"Larry should be back to work on a part time basis starting Monday morning."

Everyone applauded.

"Thank you gentlemen. Anything else Lynda?"

"I pass to Robert."

"I pass to John."

"Speaking for Tom and me we had a pretty full day. We laid out a ballot, and talked to the members of the policemen's association. They loved the idea. They are calculating their books to make sure how much money they have in their fund. The minute they receive the positive vote count they'll withdraw the funds from their account and turn it over to Pete."

"How do they know the count will be positive?"

"As one of them said to me, 'Only a fool would pass up an opportunity like this'. With their ratification first the rest of the men should follow suit. Only a fool would pass up an increase in pay plus a lifetime of benefits."

"I hope you are right John. That would make life a lot easier for the Mayor."

The Mayor commented, "It sure would Larry."

"That's all I have for now, I pass to Yoto."

"The cars we searched from the mob are put back together and ready to go, that's all for now. I pass to Coop."

"We're going out later tonight to the after-hours party we've been invited to. We'll tell you about it Monday."

I took over the meeting with my comments, "Well, it seems everyone has their weekend planned. So without further ado why don't you guys all hit the road? I'll see everyone downstairs in my office at 9 o'clock Monday morning."

Everyone left and Lynda and I had a relaxing evening together. In the morning Pete called.

"Larry."

"Yes Pete?"

"Our boys found out that three people have been hired to kill me."

"He's not taking any chances is he?"

"No."

"Do you know the hitters?"

"We know the two men and we have them under surveillance. I haven't gotten the name for the female yet."

"This young man is really trying to cover his bases isn't he?"

"You don't know the half of it."

"It's only Saturday morning. What'd I miss?"

"Coop called me just before I called you."

"How'd things go for them last night?"

"The nephew had gotten word from his man about the boys being retired. So he pressed them most of the night. He wanted to know what they were retired from. He finally got the boys alone long enough to find out. If they want any more drugs in this town they'd talk to him. So Coop told him what he wanted to hear. He was satisfied with their explanation."

"It sounds like we have the nephew where we want him."

"Yes, when we eliminate the people hired to kill me he'll have to call our boys out of retirement. This will cost him a lot of money and his life."

"You got that right Pete. But the first thing we have to do is keep you alive. Seeing I'm not out there, you and the boys will have to take care of things yourselves. If you need to get into your killers places Yoto can handle it. He's not as fast as Snake, but he'll get you in and out without being seen."

"That's good to know. I'd like to see if they have any plans for me."

"Work it out with the boys and tell me about it Monday."

"Okay Larry. I'll talk to you then."

I spent the weekend working out and resting, but Pete had a different time of it. This is how it went down:

"Tom, you're the last one to arrive."

"Sorry Pete, I did the best I could."

"No problem, just a statement. Larry asked that we handle this problem ourselves. In his condition, I agreed with him. I have the names and addresses of the two killers we know about so far. My men will call me with the data on the girl as soon as they get it."

Jim said, "I've been thinking about that Pete."

"And you came up with an idea?"

"No just a thought."

"Tell us about it Jim."

"What if he hired the girl over the phone? Now no one knows what she looks like. If she flies in she'll have to buy her equipment here. If she drives we're out of luck. But, I still think we should have our boys on the streets checking out all their weapon suppliers."

"Tom, call precinct one. Have them get the word out on the streets."(Precinct one has our largest communications center)

"Right away Pete."

He headed to the phone and made the call.

"Would anyone like something to eat or drink?"

They all wanted drinks so I made up a couple of pitchers of ice tea. We sat talking until the tea was ready. I brought the tea and glasses and put them down on the coffee table in my den. I poured everyone a glass and handed it to them. I then put coasters for their glasses around by each of them.

"These are nice. Do we get to take them home?"

"No John. You get to set your glass on it. I'm going to count them before you leave."

We all chuckled.

Tom asked, "Do you have any kind of a real plan in mind Pete?"

"What I've been thinking of Tom is this; as soon as one of my killers leaves his place, we drop by and check it out."

"Shouldn't we get somewhat closer to where they live?"

"Jim, right now we're about half way between their two places."

"You're kidding!"

"No, Robert. I'm not kidding. Remember me? I'm the Chief. I

don't kid. Larry, on the other hand is the Commissioner, he kids."

We laughed.

Robert said, "I see what you mean. Speaking of Larry how is he?"

"Robert, I have a feeling if he really felt needed, he'd be here. He knows we can handle it so he's resting."

"Yoto."

"Yes Chief."

"Larry said you can open doors, and get us in and out of places without being seen."

"I know I can open the doors, the rest is up to you. But I'll help all I can."

"Sounds good. I hate the fact that I'm being hunted."

Tom said, "Look at it this way Pete, if you weren't doing a good job you wouldn't be having this problem."

"I know you're right Tom. To tell you the truth, I wouldn't have it any other way. I've never had so much fun as I've had with Larry. When I first heard that he was made Police Commissioner I was a little put back. I could think of two, counting me, three other people far more qualified for the job."

"But that was the way the Commissioner's office used to be run."

"That's right Jim. Once I heard Larry's plan I knew I couldn't handle it. He was the only one who could."

Robert said, "Well he talked to us before he talked to you. I didn't want the job."

"Is that right Robert?"

"Yeah Pete, I stood up to leave and Larry told me to sit down and shut up. I've never been more glad that I listened to anyone in my life. What Larry has done for our town is nothing short of a miracle."

"I agree, and he's barely scratched the surface."

"That means we have plenty to do Pete."

The phone rings.

"That's right Jim, and I'll start by answering the phone."

As I picked up the receiver Yoto motioned everyone to their feet. It seemed he knew what the phone call was all about before I did. By the time I hung up the phone everybody was ready to leave. Larry had allowed Yoto to drive the limo. This made it easier for all of us to travel together. Yoto got behind the wheel, and the rest of us got in the back of the limo with the divider window down.

"Will you be able to find the place with only the address?"

"Yes Pete. See the monitor on the dash?"

I leaned forward to look over the front seat, "Yes I do."

"All I do is punch in the address and the computer directs me to the front staircase of the apartment building."

"I don't think there's anything this car doesn't have."

"I've never seen anything like it Pete."

I leaned back in my seat. "John, I want you and Tom to go to the manager's office and keep him busy. The rest of us will follow Yoto."

After parking the car we each went our separate ways. We followed Yoto to the apartment door. It didn't take him five seconds to open the door. We all went inside and we closed the door behind us.

Yoto stated, "Gentlemen, if you watch me and do as I do we won't have a problem."

Pete said, "Yoto, what if we just stand back and get an education?"

"That's a good idea. I'll explain as I go. First, could everyone squat down for me? That's good. I'll tell you when to rise. I'm now doing what you should do when entering a room. Place everything in the room in your mind. Now you should have a pretty good idea who you're dealing with. You may rise. Questions?"

Pete asked, "You're trying to tell us by looking at the room you can tell who we're dealing with?"

"Yes Pete, I'll show you. Everyone look around the room as best you can. Now let me explain. You have a low class wanna-be hunting you Pete."

"Would you explain further?"

"Sure Pete. The man is a local. He's lived here over six months. He's fairly neat and dresses the same. This is his first attempt at the big time. He's not highly educated and his only motivation for this job is money."

"Yoto?"

"I know Pete, how do I know these things? When we pulled up the sign said 'Leases Available'. A lease is generally six months to a year. If you look on the wall in the kitchen you see a calendar hanging there. Notice how many pages, each of which represent a month, are turned over. If a person moves, the first thing he does is rip off the useless pages of a calendar. But it's the last thing he does in the place he lives. He keeps his place fairly tidy. You'll generally find that people dress the way they keep house. His education is based on the fact that there is a comic book on the kitchen table and a small stack of comic books near the T.V. He's living in a lower middle class apartment which means he's not successful at what he does."

Pete said, "That's amazing Yoto. And you haven't even touched anything yet."

"That's the idea when you don't want someone to know you were visiting. I could also tell you he's left handed, wears glasses, doesn't smoke, and is a little overweight with bad eating habits. I'll explain the obvious. Left handed people set things down differently than right handed people. Remember only 12% of the populace are left handed. Also on the kitchen table there's a pouch of eyeglass cleaning papers. The vinyl seat on the chair at the kitchen table is indented in, he's overweight. The grease on the wall in back of the range top shows he eats a lot of fatty foods. Now we need to do our job and get out of here. Let's see if he follows the inexperienced pattern. Jim, you're the closest to the bedroom. Would you look under the bed and see if there's a rifle case there? Don't touch anything! Just look!"

He walked into the bedroom and squatted down.

"Yes there is and it's black in color."

"Now Jim, what would you normally do with a gun?"

"I'd slide it out from under the bed, set it on the bed and open it."

We all had walked into the room.

"Everyone look at the bedspread."

Yoto put his hand flat on the bedspread and pushed down. Then he raised his hand.

"You notice how my hand leaves an imprint on the bedspread?"

Jim stated, "The gun case would do the same."

"That's right Jim."

Yoto brushed the nap back up on the bedspread.

"You notice how the bedspread is on the bed. The lines in the bedspread line up evenly with the edge of the bed. The minute you slide the gun case out you move the bedspread."

Robert asked, "What do you suggest?"

"Robert, I suggest you raise the end of the bed a little, and Jim, you slide the gun case out the end of the bed."

They did as Yoto asked.

"Now, before you open it, or before you open anything, you examine it first. The case looks brand new."

Snap! Snap!

"Keep looking as you open the case."

Yoto got the case all the way open. The top went completely over to lay flat on the floor.

"This is quite an outfit Pete. You could be killed from over a mile away. As you can see there's regular ammo, armor piercing, and armor piercing incendiary, a scope, and silencer completes the package."

"That's heavy duty Yoto."

Yoto picked up the rifle and popped the bolt action open and fiddled around with it.

"It's no longer heavy duty Pete."

"What do you mean Yoto?"

"It may have been the best gun in the world for in assassin, but I have the firing pin."

Everyone laughed.

"As naive as he is, he probably won't even notice that it's gone."

"You really think so?"

"It's like this Robert, amateurs are just that. They look at a weapon for how beautiful it is and for what it's supposed to do. They have no real idea of how it all works. He couldn't tell you how many grains of powder each bullet contains to do each job."

Jim said, "Neither could I."

"I know, but you're not a professional assassin."

"I see what you mean Yoto."

"Now everyone walk gently." He said this as he closed the case. "Robert, lift the end of the bed again." Yoto slid the case back under the bed.

Yoto said, "Look around the room. Don't move anything. I'll take any door that has to be opened and the kitchen table."

Yoto got off the floor and went through the closest in about 10 seconds. He then moved to the kitchen. He examined the contents on the table and made some notes.

"Anyone see anything?"

Everyone shook their heads no.

Pete said, "I guess we didn't accomplish very much Yoto."

"We'll talk in the car. Let's get out of here."

When we got in the car Tom and John were waiting for us.

Pete asked, "How'd it go Tom?"

"We talked to the manager for awhile and since then we've been watching his office and he hasn't come out."

"That's good."

Tom came back with, "How'd it go on your end?"

"You'll have to ask Yoto. He's been giving us a lesson in espionage."

"Yoto?"

"Yes Tom. We've been having fun."

"What'd you find out?"

"If Pete will check and see where our man is right now, I'll know I'm right."

"What're your thoughts?"

"This guy isn't smart enough to do this job alone. We know he has a partner and he's probably working out a plan with him right now. I need to visit his partner's place A.S.A.P."

"Hold on a minute Yoto and I'll make the call."

It took me less than a minute to get Yoto the answer.

"You're right Yoto. The two scumbags are together."

"They won't do anything until tomorrow or whenever you're at an outside event. Do you have anything coming up?"

"Not that I can think of."

"Nothing at all?"

"Well, I'm doing a ground breaking at the Downtown Y tomorrow. They're building a new youth center."

"Downtown, hmmm, lots of tall buildings around, a nice place for an ambush."

"You've got to be kidding Yoto! They'd kill me in front of a lot of kids?"

"It's a job, nothing personal. They have to kill you and find a convenient place to do it."

"You sound just like Larry."

"When the student can sound like his teacher that indeed is quite a compliment. Thank you Pete."

"You're welcome. Now, what do we do?"

"I need to drop everyone off at your place Pete. Then I'll borrow Robert and continue on to where your killers are meeting. We'll park nearby waiting for your people on surveillance to call and tell us the two killers have left the area."

"Do you think they'll leave?"

"Yes. They have two things to do. One; before dark they want to check out their site by the Y. Have your surveillance boys find out all they can from their cars. They are not to leave their cars. We don't want to spook your killers. Two; after they finish up there they'll go to the apartment to check out the new rifle, they'll then go to dinner. While they are doing all that I'll check out the other apartment. When we finish doing that we'll return to your place Pete."

Jim asked, "How do you know he hasn't already seen the gun?"

"That's an easy one Jim. There was only one set of prints on the gun. That's why I only touched the wooden parts of the gun. Only touch places that won't show fingerprints."

Jim replied, "We do have a lot to learn."

"A smart person is one who wishes to learn. A dumb person is one who thinks he has nothing left to learn."

"I agree Yoto."

"Thanks Pete."

"Looks like you guys can have the evening off."

Tom said, "Sorry Pete, Larry's orders are; two of us with you at all times."

"But Yoto said....."

"It makes no difference what I said. No one is infallible. If I'm wrong, or if these guys are too dumb to do what's normal, you end up dead, and I have to live with that. So we follow orders."

"Excuse me for trying to give you some time off!"

"Pete, your life is what's important right now. Plus if we stay you have to buy us dinner."

"I see, Tom, now the real reason comes out."

We all had a little laugh.

Yoto and Robert dropped us off at my house and were on their way. By the time they parked I was calling them.

"Your boys are just pulling away from the curb."

"Thanks Pete. We're heading in. So let me know when they get somewhere."

"I'll call you the minute I hear."

Yoto and Robert were in the apartment looking around when I called them back.

"What took so long?"

"We were eating. Our boys called about ten minutes ago."

"Where are the shooters now?"

"In a restaurant eating dinner."

"Or establishing an alibi."

"What do you mean?"

"They had dinner here before they left. Check with your boys outside."

"Hold on, I'll get the radio in my other ear."

"Well, what did they say?"

"Nothing out of the ordinary."

"Find out what's ordinary."

"They're watching one of my neighbors walking his dog."

"Are you still wearing both your vests?"

"No, they're very uncomfortable."

"Well get them on and put Tom on the line."

"Yoto, what's up?"

"Tom, don't get Pete overly excited, but they are on their way to get him."

"Now!?!"

"Yes, Now! Check with the outside boys again and see what side of the street the man is walking his dog on."

"He's on Pete's side of the street almost in front of the house. Hold on a minute! They said a pizza delivery car is pulling up in front of the house."

"Those are your two hit men. You better get moving! Out!"

Tom started speaking as he was hanging up the phone, "Jim! John! Get out back and come around to the front. Our two shooters are on their way in! Shoot for the head! Pete, let's get your jacket on!"

"It's really tight with these two vests on."

"Let it be tight. You can use the extra protection." (Everyone on our team wears bullet proof clothing.)

I no sooner had my jacket on when the doorbell rang.

"If it's a man with a pizza box, he has a gun under it."

"All right Tom."

The man must have known me on sight. I no sooner opened the door when two shots rang out. He shot me through the screen door twice in the heart. The force of the bullets knocked me back into Tom. He helped break my fall to the floor. I could hear Jim and John outside shooting at my killers. All total I heard four shots. Tom was helping me up when Jim and John came in.

"Are you okay?"

"Yes, Jim. How'd it go outside?"

"They made two mistakes."

"Which was what John?"

"One, they didn't drop their guns. Two, they turned their guns on us. They were dead before they could get a shot off."

"Good work boys."

Jim asked, "How did Yoto know?"

"I don't know Jim. Get him on the phone and I'll ask him."

Chapter 5

Jim dialed the phone and when it started to ring he handed it to me.
"Hello?"
"Yoto?"
"Yes Pete, glad to hear your voice. Did everything go well?"
"I got shot twice in the heart."
"How are your shooters?"
"Dead!"
"Too bad. I wanted to talk to one of them."
"Where are you now?"
"Driving as fast as I can to the other apartment. I'll call you back in ten minutes."
"What did Yoto say?"
"For some reason he's rushing back to the other apartment Tom."
Jim said, "There's nothing of value there except the gun. Oh, did we mess up!"
"What do you mean, Jim?"
"The girl shooter flew into town. Does that help you Pete?"
"You can't be saying what I think you're saying."
"Yes I can." The phone rings. "Answer the phone and ask Yoto."
"Yoto."
"Yes Pete, the gun is gone."
"How'd you know what I was going to ask?"
"You're not idiots. Also tell the boys how I knew who the shooters were. They had eaten pizza in the other apartment before they left. There were pieces of crust in the waste basket and slices of pizza in the refrigerator."
"And that told you who my killers were?"
"Yes, because there wasn't a pizza box anywhere to be found."
"I see. If they were going to throw away the pizza boxes they would have also thrown out the rest of the trash."
"That's the way I saw it. We'll be back at your place in about fifteen minutes."
"See you then."
Tom said, "Boy is Larry going to be mad."
"I agree Tom. He's going to skin us alive."
"Tom, Jim, take it easy. Larry will understand."

John added, "That's what you think Pete. He gave us an easy assignment and we blew it big time."

Tom said, "I agree with you John."

"Okay boys. Please relax. I'll talk to Larry for you."

Tom replied, "That's not necessary, Pete. We'll talk for ourselves. You know what Larry always says, 'If you make a mistake admit to it. We'll fix it and move on.'"

"If that's the way everyone feels Tom."

"It is Pete."

Jim asked, "Pete how's your chest?"

"It's all right Jim. The bullets didn't even penetrate the first vest."

"The second vest probably saved you from some bad bruises."

"I think you're right about that John. I'm going to continue to wear both of them until this is over."

Jim stated, "That's a good idea Pete, but I suggest trying to be careful instead of counting on your vests for protection."

"What do you mean Jim?"

"The bullets she has in the rifle case. Your vests may stop the regular bullets but they'll only slow down the armor piercing shells."

"I understand what you're saying. Believe me I'll try to be more careful."

Yoto and Robert walked through the front door.

Robert said, "If you're going to be more careful I'd suggest keeping the front door locked."

"Robert, with all the commotion out front and all the cops in the area I didn't figure we'd have a problem."

Yoto added, "Can you recognize every officer on the force by his face?"

"No Yoto, that's really impossible."

"Then why can't our girl infiltrate what's happening outside and get to you?"

"You're right, Yoto. I'll be more careful. I hate to change the subject, but it's over 45 minutes since I talked to you."

"We got way laid."

"I hope she was cute."

"Not now John."

"Okay Pete."

"To answer your question, it was a guy and he wasn't my type."
Everyone laughed.

Tom said, "We have to keep it a little light Pete, or you'll die of a heart attack long before you ever get shot."

"I understand Tom. Now back to Yoto."

"When Robert and I went back to the first apartment I noticed a neighbor's door ajar."

"Was it next door?"

"Pete, it was across the hall and down one apartment. Anyone going up or down the hall had to pass this apartment. So we played a long shot and knocked on the door. The door opened a little more when we knocked on it. We were looking at a full length mirror on the coat closet door just to our right. I thought why would someone put a mirror there? I pushed the door a little more and used the mirror's reflection to see what was going on. The person inside the apartment was removing a camera that was on a tripod. After doing so he came to the door. 'If you're selling something gentlemen, I'm broke.' 'We're not selling anything.'" We showed him our badges. "May we come in?"

"Yes. What can I do for our city's finest?"

"How about answering some questions for us?"

"Shoot."

"Did you see or hear anyone entering or leaving the apartment next to yours?"

"Do I look like the kind of person who would spy on his neighbors?"

"We didn't ask if you were spying. Just if you heard or saw anything in the last half an hour."

"No, I didn't see anything."

"Why are you so nervous?"

"I'm not nervous."

I was standing in the approximate spot where the tripod had been. "Officer Collins, would you reopen the door about an inch?"

When he stepped away from the door I had a nice view of the whole hallway.

"By using the reflection in the mirror you have an excellent view."

"But I can't see if anyone comes out of the apartment across the hall."

"Who said anything about the apartment across the hall?"
"You did."
"No, we said the apartment next door."
"Then I misunderstood what you said."
"I still can't understand why you're so nervous."
"I'm not."
"Then quit biting your lips and putting your finger in your mouth and biting on it. Do you want me to continue?"
"No, I'm nervous."
"About what?"
"I'd rather not talk about it."
"All right, can we look around?"
"What if I say no?"
"We'll put you into protective custody and cuff you to a chair. Then we'll phone our office and get a search warrant."
"It seems I lose either way."
"Not really. It's a lot nicer when you give us permission to look around."
"All right, you can look around."

I asked Robert to stay with the gentlemen while I took a quick look around. The apartment was a run of the mill two bedroom apartment. One bedroom was set up as a dark room. In the other bedroom I found what I was looking for.

The young man we were talking to was either the greatest stud in the world or he had a great imagination. He had photos of girls in every sort of attire. So many different women it was spooky. The backgrounds were all different but the women were all doing the same thing....walking. I thought back. When we knocked on the open door we watched the camera and tripod being removed. It was now in the darkroom. The place the camera was set up gave a good photographer a view and a photo of everything that walked up or down the hall. The clincher was all the outfits the women wore with buttons. They were all buttoned backwards as if the photos were taken from a reflection in a mirror. So our young man is a Peeping Tom of sorts. I figured he was quite harmless if this is all he does. I walked back into the living room and started right in on the young man.

"Would you like to tell us about your photography work?"

"It's a hobby. Is there a law against it?"

"It depends on what kind of pictures you take, and whose permission you have to take them"

"They're all friends of mine."

"That's wishful thinking on your part. I know how you've taken the pictures and I don't care that you've taken them. If you come clean to us right now I don't think you'll have a problem."

"Are you sure?"

"Try us."

"As you can tell I'm very shy and reserved. I wouldn't know how to meet the beautiful women that hang around the apartment and pool area, so I take pictures of them and pretend they're my friends."

"Did you get a picture about a half hour ago?"

"Yes. She was so well built I shot a picture of her coming and going."

"Did she bring anything into the apartment?"

"No, but she was carrying what looked like an electric guitar when she left."

"Is the film still in the camera?"

"No."

"Can I ask where it is?"

"Hanging in the darkroom."

"Can we get it?"

"Yes. Follow me."

We went into the darkroom where he handed me the photos and the negatives.

"Thank you. You've helped us out. Would you mind if I make a suggestion to help change your life?"

"Please do."

"Go out and buy a small locking cabinet. Then lock up all the pictures you have around here of people who don't know you have them. Then take your camera down by the pool and take pictures of the building, flowers, trees, and anything else you like. Don't bother the girls. It may take a few visits, but before you know it the girls will bother you."

"You really think so?"

"I know so. Follow what I said and you'll be a very popular young man. Also, forget we were ever here."

"I will Sir and thank you."

"And that's the way it happened, Pete."

Tom said, "I can see it now, letters from the lovelorn answered by Yoto."

Everyone laughed.

"Thanks Tom. I'd probably make more money than I do here."

"Somehow Yoto, this job fits you better. Where are the photos?"

"We were driving by the station, Pete so we dropped off the negatives to have copies made. Here are the two prints we have."

Yoto handed the pictures to Jim. He looked at them and said, "Wow! She is a looker." He then handed the pictures to me.

"You can say that again Jim. She's beautiful!"

Everyone took a look and agreed.

Yoto calmly said, "A coral snake is also very beautiful but its bite can kill you in seconds. Just remember, Pete, you have a deranged mind working in a beautiful body."

"I will Yoto. Can you tell how good she is?"

Everyone laughed.

"That wasn't meant as a joke. I'm serious."

"And that's the way I took it Pete. I can make a few observations. On a scale of one to ten she's about a five."

"She looks more like a ten to me."

"John you're looking at her with the wrong part of your body."

"Sorry Pete."

"Yoto, what tells you she's a five?"

"Pete, if she was a ten like John said she would never have had her picture taken. When you're on a mission you have to watch and see everything that's going on. Her only thought was getting in, retrieving the rifle, and getting out."

"It sounds like she completed her mission."

"John, it doesn't do any good to complete your mission and lead the enemy back to your camp to kill your whole platoon."

"I see what you mean."

"Good. I know everyone else does also, a couple of other things. Her dress is too flashy. She wants to blend in, not stick out. Notice in the picture where she is walking."

Jim inserted, "She's in the middle of the hallway. The lights are in the middle of the hallway. Wouldn't it be smarter to walk as close to the wall as possible?"

"Yes it would, Jim. Like I said, she's not a ten."

I asked, "Anything else, Yoto?"

"Yes Pete. She's wearing contacts and two blond falls in her hair. This means her hair is lot shorter and thinner."

John asked, "Falls?"

"That's what we called them in my day John. They're false sections of hair that women use to make their own hair look fuller and prettier."

"How do you know she's wearing contacts?" Tom asked.

"If you look at the frontal photo Tom, pay particular attention to the top sides of her nose."

"They seem a little darker than the rest of her nose."

"She's trying to cover up the indented marks on the sides of her nose made by the nose pieces of her glasses. She's over compensated the makeup. She's also very athletic."

"Explain."

"All right, Pete. Look at her hands and fingers in both pictures. Notice her nails."

Tom said, "She doesn't have any to speak of."

"That's right, Tom, she breaks them off working out. Or, she's hyper and she chews them off. I believe she does both. Pete, I suggest you call the precinct and have them get that photo out on the streets as soon as possible. Tell them to forget the gun shops. They wouldn't have that kind of a firing pin. They wouldn't even have that kind of a gun."

"You really think she'll notice it missing?"

"It's hard to say Pete. The way the firing pin is recessed on that weapon…she may not notice it. Tell our men we're looking for someone who has seen her. If they find someone we'll take it from there."

"I understand Yoto and I'll get on it."

Tom interjected. "While you're doing that we'll work on dinner."

"Good idea Tom."

It was nine o'clock when the boys left. Tom and John stayed with me. The rest of the boys drove by the Y on their way home. It was ten in the morning when we were all together in my house once again.

"What did the area look like Jim?"

"It looked okay to me, but I'm sure Yoto can give you a different slant on things."

"Yoto?"

"Like I said before, it's a great place for an ambush. You'll be a sitting duck."

"That's reassuring. I'm glad I asked."

Everyone laughed, including me.

Jim stated, "Don't worry Pete. By two o'clock this afternoon we'll think of something. Won't we Yoto?"

"Yes Jim. I already have."

"You have a plan?"

"Yes Pete. I'm going to ruin Larry's weekend."

"You really feel that's necessary?"

"Pete, your life is worth more to us than Larry's wrath."

"All right, if that's the way you feel. Why don't you go down to the first bedroom, the one I have set up as my office. It has a speaker phone."

"Sounds good, I'll call everyone in after I bring Larry up to date."

"Want something to drink?"

"Yes Tom. When you come in bring me a glass of ice tea."

Yoto left and we walked into the kitchen. By the time we all had a drink Yoto was calling us.

"Is everyone in the room?"

"Yes, Larry, we're all here."

"I'm glad you're all right Pete. I understand the boys are having a bit of a problem keeping you alive."

"Larry, in defense of the boys….."

"Larry, this is Tom. We don't need any defense. We blew it."

"On the contrary, Tom. After going over everything with Yoto, I could only think of a few things I would have done differently. And remember, I have hind sight on my side. So I don't want you boys to feel bad. We'll all make mistakes from time to time. Just try to make them small ones and learn from them."

"What about the gun?"

"Is that you Jim?"

"Yes Larry."

"It's very simple, if you took possession of the gun she'd be out right now buying another one."

"I see, damned if we do and damned if we don't."

"Not really Jim. If she tries to buy a firing pin we may get her. If she doesn't her job is going to be a lot tougher."

"I see what you mean, Larry."

"Now, I can only suggest a couple of things. Pete, wear your two vests."

"I will Larry."

"Boys, Yoto and I put together a plan. He'll explain it to you on site. Follow his orders."

"We will Larry."

"Thanks, Pete."

"Larry, how're you feeling?"

"Great! Lynda and I are enjoying our time off."

"I'm happy to hear that. We'll see you in the morning."

"I'll see you then Pete, and be careful!"

"I will."

Click.

"Yoto, you have the floor."

"Thanks Pete. We need to stop by Larry's office and get a few high powered rifles with scopes, spotting scopes, and communication equipment out of our armory. (The armory is located behind a life size oil painting behind Larry's desk. It's a good size room filled with weapons and equipment. It also has a rear secret door out of Larry's office.) We also need six members of the SWAT Team with rifles with scopes. Larry wants her taken out as she is attempting to kill you. We're in combat mode."

"No prisoners?"

"That's right Tom. She's not here to scare Pete she's here to kill him. Turnabout is fair play. She deals in death so we're going to give her a personal dose."

I asked, "Will we be able to find her in time?"

"I think so Pete. You'll be standing with your back to the two o'clock sun. You'll be a good target for about five minutes. It'll take her 30 seconds to sight you in. Then with a clear shot she'll blow your head off. I forgot, the SWAT boys also need silencers and hand scopes. Have them meet us at noon behind the Y.M.C.A. Building."

"How are we going to search all the buildings before the ribbon cutting?" asked Jim.

"Larry and I analyzed it and we came up with this. She won't be in the Y.M.C.A. Building, which leaves three buildings to shoot from. The building straight in front of Pete will have too much sun for a direct shot. That leaves the buildings on each side of Pete. When we get there we can eliminate some of the windows because of the angle, once again a bad shot. Then by placing everyone around the area at strategic locations and with everyone having a grid to search we should be able to find her and eliminate her before she does any damage."

"I take it we don't tell the SWAT boys about her not having a firing pin?"

"Let me ask you a question back John. Do we know for sure she doesn't have a firing pin in her rifle?"

"Do you mean would I stand in front of her while she loads the gun, points it at me and fires?"

"Yes."

"Do I look stupid Yoto? Empty guns kill people."

"That's right. We have no assurance that she hasn't fixed the gun."

"If everything is done here I'll call SWAT and then we'll go out for an early lunch."

"Good idea Pete. Let's everyone get to the car."

Everyone was waiting in the limo when I got there.

It was 12:02 P.M. when we arrived behind the Y. The SWAT truck was waiting for us. We all got out of our vehicles and shook hands.

"Gentlemen, you've been briefed on the situation. The Commissioner asked me to put Officer Yoto in charge of this operation. Officer Yoto it's all yours."

"Thank you Chief. First thing is a direct order from the Commissioner. This is a combat patrol, no prisoners. If you get a positive I.D. on the target, and a clear shot, take it. If you hesitate we could have a dead Chief on our hands. Does anyone have a problem with that?"

No one moved or said a word.

"Good. I have a large diagram of the area. I'll lay it out on the hood of the limo. Our Chief told me everyone on the SWAT Team has a number. I'll tell you the assignment and the SWAT members will give me their number. When I'm finished with the six of you the Chiefs' personal team will overlap your areas."

After that was finished, I had one SWAT man on the roof of the Y and the rest of the team covered the top five floors with one man each. The men were arranged on the floors so they could see across the street in all directions.

"Remember, she's already in position to do this job. Our job is to find her before 2 o'clock. Number 3, we'll wait until you get on the roof. Give him a hand with the fire escape. Number 3, we don't want to spook her so keep out of sight. If you see something call for a confirmation then shoot. Last but not least gentlemen, you're all on your own frequency, so if I call for a radio check you'll answer 'OK' and your number. Nothing else! Is that understood?"

"What exactly will you say Sir?"

"Radio check. You'll say?"

"OK. 6."

"That's it! Don't forget it. Now get going and check in when you're in position."

As they were leaving they helped Number 3 onto the fire escape. When he was on the roof we headed into the building. What we didn't know was our shooter was on the roof of the Y Building watching us. When inside we stayed to the rear of the building.

Number 3 was the first to check in. It took about ten minutes more for the rest of the SWAT team to check in.

Little did we know by the time everyone had checked in Number 3 was knocked out and tied up. Our lady shooter was wearing his clothes and pretending to do his job.

Two of us stayed with the Chief and I sent everyone else out to look around. I told them to use their scopes to check everything out.

"This is Number 1."

"This is Yoto. Over."

"I see movement on the fifth floor of the building across the street."

"Hold on. Over."

"Number 5, can you see movement on the fifth floor of the building across the street?"

"Yes. It's a maid vacuuming an office."

"Thank you. Out."

"Number 1."
"Yes, Yoto. Over."
"A maid cleaning an office. Over."
"All right. 1 out."

We looked and we searched to no avail. I kept racking my brain. Maybe Larry and I were wrong. Maybe she's not here. Maybe the Chief is safe. That's wishful thinking and bunk. She's here, but where?

It was five to two when my team mates came inside.
"You boys look as disgusted as I feel."
"I know she's here."
"So do we Pete."
"I agree Tom."
I asked, "I wonder how the SWAT team is doing."
"The person on the roof seems ready."
"What do you mean John?"
"I was looking up and he was loading and then sighting in his rifle."
"Does anyone know why he'd do that?"
They all looked dumbfounded.
I picked up the radio and started with number One's frequency.
"Radio check."
"OK. 1."
I checked the frequency button between each call.
"Radio check."
"OK. 2."
"Radio check."
"Loud and clear."
"Radio check."
"OK. 4."
"Radio check."
"OK. 5."
"Radio check."
"OK. 6."
"Boys we now know where our shooter's hiding, on the roof and out in the open."
"I can't believe it."
"Believe it Pete. Also believe that I'll take care of it. For backup I

want Jim and Robert to take up positions outside. If I miss her you can get her. It's almost two o'clock Pete, I need you to have the Director give his speech slowly. Tom, you shadow Pete. Show Pete to her but not a clear shot. While she's watching Pete I'll get on the roof and take care of her. I need six minutes so get to it!"

   I took the elevator to the sixth floor. I got out and went to the furthest rear corner of the building away from the shooter. I climbed out a window and scaled the side of the building to the roof. I had two knives and a pistol with a silencer.

   She seemed vary narrowed in on Pete, which made me over confident. The sun was behind me. It threw a small shadow of me on her. As I raised my pistol to blow a small hole in the back of her head she leaned forward with her hands against the parapet and hit me in my gun hand and chest with a double footed mule kick. It caused me to fly backwards off my feet in one direction and my gun went flying in another direction. As I recovered and came to my feet she was only a couple of steps away with a knife in her hand. I raised my right foot and drew a knife out of my boot. She lunged and I blocked. I swung and she blocked. I thought, so far she's better than most men I know. It's such a shame when you have to kill skilled people. They could do so much good if they were on the right side of the law. I blocked her next downward slash. I then tried to lunge my knife into her breast area. She grabbed my wrist with the firmness of a man. We struggled. I had a hold of her wrist keeping her knife hand from me, and she did the same with my knife hand. I tripped her and we rolled on the roof. We kept rolling toward the rear of the building. We stopped rolling with me on top of her. Her knife had flown out of her hand so I let go of her empty knife hand to hit her in the face. As I drew back my arm she hunched up her body and at the same time she reached up with her empty hand and grabbed my hair and threw me over her body in a forward motion. I landed on my back and my knife went flying. I rolled over and saw that I was about three feet from the rear parapet wall of the building. I was barely on my feet when I saw her running toward me. She then left the ground and flew at me. She was about six feet in the air. She wanted to hit me with a flying head kick and knock me off the top of the building. If you know how to block a flying head kick it's easy to do. The secret is not to block the kick, but to redirect it. Using the heel of my right hand while shifting my body to the left I redirected her to my right. I couldn't see the look on her face because of the head gear she was wearing. All I could see for sure was her flying by me and past the rear edge of the building. I watched her all the way down to the concrete below. I don't think the fall hurt her, but the sudden impact with the concrete did her in. I picked the lock on the roof top door and headed into the building. I surprised the SWAT member on the sixth floor. I took his radio off his head and called in. John answered.

"John. Over."

"John. Yoto. Call an ambulance to the rear of the building. Then tell the Chief that it's all clear. Over."

"I'm on it Yoto. Out."

I handed the radio back to the officer.

"Number 3 is on the roof. He's unconscious and tied up. Go up and help him and I'll send the rest of your team up to give you a hand."

"Is that why you called an ambulance?"

"Yes. Also, I got the shooter and she won't need an ambulance. The morgue will take care of her."

I pointed him in the direction of the staircase up to the roof. I then headed downstairs. I stopped at our base radio and called the second floor. I explained to him to head to the roof. I then called the rest of the SWAT team and told them to head to the roof to help their downed man. After doing that I headed out back. The ambulance was just arriving. I had them shut down their siren and lights.

I told the ambulance attendants, "Wait here. They'll be down in a minute. Do you have a disposable blanket I could use to cover a body?"

They handed me one. I walked over to the shooter and covered her up. You talk about a bloody mess. The concrete was not at all kind to her. John walked up, "I called the morgue."

"Good move. How's the Chief?"

"He should be out front speech making right now."

A few minutes went by and then I heard that familiar voice.

"Officer Yoto."

"Yes Chief."

I walked over to where he was standing.

"I take it everything went smoothly?"

"Yes Sir, it did. All is safe and sound."

"That's great. I'm so relieved I'm buying dinner."

Jim asked, "Sounds good Chief. Where are we going?"

"No where Sergeant O'Riley, we're here."

"Here?"

"Yes, Officer Watt, hot dogs and hamburgers are on the menu inside."

"I think we can survive it Chief."

"I'm sure you can Lieutenant Harden. What about the SWAT team?"

"Chief, we'd really love to but we're due back at the station."

After the SWAT team left the rest of us headed inside. John stayed outside with the body and waited for the coroner. He was soon inside with us.

"Chief, you'll have the coroner's report tomorrow afternoon."

"Thanks Officer Watt."

I walked over to Yoto. "I heard how you scaled to the top of the building and fought my killer with your bare hands."

"I knew shots would scare the kids."

"You're right and thank you."

"You're welcome Chief."

"The boys were worried about how long it took you to subdue her."

"They had good reason to be. She was the toughest woman I've ever faced. If it wasn't for her mistake I don't know what the outcome might have been."

"Wow! I didn't know. It's a good thing you're smart as well as tough."

"We can thank Larry for that. He saved my life today without even being here."

"It amazes me at how much credit you give Larry."

"Remember when I told you he helped train twenty of the best military personnel in the world? That was men from all over the world."

"I see. I thought it was just our men he trained."

"No, and that's what makes him so great. He doesn't care what nationality you are, color, education, it doesn't matter. He plays straight from the heart to the heart. He gave us abilities we didn't even know existed, and he also gave us the Gods."

"I know. Someday he'll tell the rest of us about the Gods."

"When he feels the time is right, he'll do it."

"How should we play the rest of the day?"

"Chief, we should leave together and go to your house. We can work things out from there."

"Sounds good. We'll leave shortly. I have to do some more mingling."

"I'll tell the boys."

I spent the next half an hour shaking hands and thanking people for their support. It was a little after four when we arrived at my place.

Chapter 6

"You guys can have a seat or join me in the kitchen. I want to check my answering machine and get something to drink."

Everyone followed me into the kitchen. While the boys got out the tea and glasses I ran my machine. I had two messages. The first one was a robot selling something. I pushed the button that stopped that message and started the second message:

"Pete, this is the Mayor. I need to talk to you before tomorrow's meeting. Call me."

Tom inserted, "It doesn't sound urgent, but it does sound important."

"I was thinking the same thing Tom. Let's go into my office where I can put the call on the speaker phone."

We all retired to my office and I placed the call.

"Hello?"

"Mayor, this is Pete."

"Pete, glad you called."

"It sounded important."

"I needed your help and advice."

"I have the whole team with me except for Lynda and Larry. I can put you on the speaker phone if you think they can be of help."

"Good idea. Please do so."

I pushed the speaker button on the phone and hung up the receiver.

"Everyone say 'Hi' to the Mayor."

Together they said "Hi Mayor".

"Hi guys. I'm glad I got everyone at once. That saves me a lot of calls."

"Tell us the problem Mayor."

"It's one word Pete."

"What might that be?"

"Larry."

Everyone started talking together.

"Hold on boys! It's nothing serious."

"Then what is it?"

"It's his health, Tom. I'm worried about his health."

Jim asked, "Do you know something we don't know?"

"Jim, I think it's more like I see something that you don't see."

John asked, "Could you explain that for us?"

"Sure John. You guys stop me when I'm wrong. Larry gives everyone a job to do. Larry oversees all of them. Larry has the job of playing Commissioner and fulfilling all those duties. He then plans, directs, and is involved in the missions himself. He helps me run part of my office as well as yours Pete."

"You're right there Mayor."

"If we have a personal problem he's right there to help. Is everyone getting my point? He's going back to work tomorrow."

"Mayor, may I say something?"

"Yes, Yoto."

"He's not going back to work, he hasn't stopped working."

"That's my point. We have to figure out a way to get him away from work for about a week."

Pete asked, "Do you have any ideas Mayor?"

"Pete, I was thinking of putting him and two guards, Lynda and someone else, on a plane to somewhere for some bogus reason."

Robert asked, "Can we do the easy part first?"

"What's that Robert?"

"The person to go with him."

"Do you have someone in mind?"

"We need to send him all the protection we can."

"Who might that be Robert?"

As Robert opened his mouth to speak, everyone joined him, "Yoto!"

"What do you think, Yoto?"

"I'm humbled by the flattery and I accept the assignment."

"Like you said, Robert, that's the easy part. Now what about Larry?"

"Mayor, I have an idea."

"What is it Yoto?"

"First, we'll look better traveling as two couples. So I'd like your permission to bring my girlfriend along. I'll pay her way, Sir."

Pete said, "He's right Mayor. It will look better."

"I agree Pete. You can bring her along Yoto and we'll pay for it."

"Thank you Sir, now my idea. We just finished one of the largest meth busts in the world."

The Mayor said, "That's correct. Continue Yoto."

"I think either the Queen or the Prime Minister of England should give Larry some kind of an award."

The Mayor came back with, "I agree Yoto. That's a great idea!"

Pete said, "It seems everyone here also agrees Mayor."

The Mayor said, "That's good Pete. The only problem I see is Larry saying, 'Thank you, but no thank you'."

Pete said, "You're right Mayor. I understand Larry's good at turning down awards."

John came in with, "I agree Pete, but I know how we can get him."

"How's that John?"

We all expected some kind of a joke, instead we were all shocked.

"Larry loves his country and there isn't a thing he wouldn't do for it."

"I agree."

John continued, "Thanks Pete. Why don't we have the F.B.I. come up with something from the State Department that Larry can't refuse or turn down?"

"Great idea John."

"Thanks Mayor."

"Well boys I'll get things rolling here and let you know when I need your help."

"Just let us know Mayor and we'll be ready."

"Thanks Pete. I'll see everybody in the morning. Goodbye."

I said 'Goodbye' and hung up the phone.

I asked, "It's close to five. What should we do?"

Tom came back with, "That's simple Pete. Two of us will stay with you and the rest of us will go home. Do I have any volunteers?"

Yoto said, "I'll stay."

"Me, too Tom."

"Thanks Robert."

"What about Yoto?"

"You want me to thank a man who's getting a free trip to Europe?"

"Tom, you're not jealous are you?"

"No Pete. I'm envious as heck, but I'm not jealous."

We all laughed.

Robert came back with, "I think the best part was when he conned the Mayor into letting him take his girlfriend along."

"Yeah Robert, he was slick."

Yoto said, "Wait a minute guys."

Robert said, "We're only kidding you Yoto."

"That's the funny part guys. I was slick."

We all busted out laughing.

"Are you kidding Yoto?"

"No Pete, I thought I'd see how serious the Mayor was. He really loves Larry."

"That he does Yoto. I also feel the four of you will have a lot more fun together. That's why we're sending you away."

Yoto raised his glass as he said, "I agree Pete, a toast to Larry, Lynda and a fun trip."

We all clinked our glasses and took a drink.

After the boys left I called Larry and explained what had happened at the Y.

"Who was on the phone Larry?"

"It was Pete. He wanted to fill me in on what happened today, so I wouldn't worry all night."

"It was all good I hope?"

"Yes Lynda. It couldn't have been better. Is dinner ready?"

"Yes. You want to eat at the table?"

"Yes. I can handle it."

After dinner Lynda and I read in the living room. We had soft relaxing music on to help our bodies unwind. I wanted to be ready for work in the morning.

It was ten to nine when I walked into my reception area.

"Good morning Mrs. Thompkin."

"Good morning Sir. Glad to see you back at your office."

"I'm glad to be back. Continue to hold all my meetings for at least another two weeks."

"I'll take care of it Sir."

I said, "Thank you," and walked into my office.

"Lynda, would you get the tea and glasses for the group?"

"If you'll sit down behind your desk."

"I feel just fine."

"I'm not moving!"

"All right! I'm sitting!"

She grabbed Tom and John out in the reception area to give her a hand. The room was filling as they brought in the drinks. It was a little after nine o'clock, and I was sitting in my chair at the head of the conference table.

"Let's get started gentlemen. Has anyone heard from the F.B.I.?"

"Yes Larry. Sam called me last night and said they'd be at the meeting tomorrow."

"Thanks Mayor. Seeing they won't be here why don't you get us started?"

"I'll pass to Pete."

"I had a hellish weekend, and I'm glad it's over. We're still watching the ambulance company. Coop or Josh will call you later today. I didn't think it would be a good idea to have them here anymore."

"I agree."

"No word on a stolen limo yet. I'm still working on the military buildings. As far as I know Doc is still putting the hospital together. That about does it. I pass to Tom."

"Before you do, I'd like to have your assessment of the men and the weekend."

"I'll make it short and sweet. There isn't a thing worse than having to wake up each morning knowing this could be the last time you wake up. I tried not to show it, but I was a nervous wreck. The boys and I made a couple of mistakes, but overall I'd give us a 98 percent. I tried to get rid of the boys more than once. I figured I'd be safe in my house. I was wrong, and luckily the boys wouldn't leave. Larry, they had your orders to stay, and stay they did. I'm glad they did, and I'm glad it's over."

"It's only over if the nephew hires Coop and Josh."

Jim remarked, "I think he will."

"I hope you're right Jim. Now Tom, Pete passed to you."

"I pass to Jim."

"You know we were all tied up this weekend so none of us had a chance to check out our assignments. We'll all have reports for you in the morning."

"That sounds good Jim. Anyone else have anything?"

Lynda spoke, "Yes. Doc will be here tonight to look at Larry. We've had a good weekend. He'll be close to 100 per cent by the end of the week."

The Mayor said, "Thank you Lynda. We're glad to hear that."

"Now, if no one has anything else, you boys had better get to work. It seems you've taken the weekend off and now things are piling up."

Everyone was laughing as they left.

The Mayor stayed around and chewed the fat before he left. He asked if Lynda and I had our passports in order in case we had to go to Canada. We said we did but I told him you don't need a passport to go from the U.S.A. to Canada. He said he wasn't sure of that. After he left Lynda and I worked until noon. At that time we called it a day and went upstairs for lunch.

Around three o'clock the phone rang. We were sitting in the living room. Lynda had plugged in one of the extension phones near us so she reached over and picked up the receiver.

"Hello?"

"Lynda, this is Coop, can I speak to Larry?"

"Sure. Hold on."

She handed me the receiver. "It's Coop."

"Hi Coop. What's happening?"

"You called it and I think it's going to happen."

"Explain."

"The nephew just called to invite Josh and me to dinner."

"He took the bait."

"Pete told us what happened over the weekend. So that has to be why he's calling."

"Either that or he likes boys."

"As you would say, 'Cute Larry, real cute'."

We laughed.

"You know I was only kidding."

"I do."

"You know how to play your hand. Low keyed, you're out of the business. We need to get him and his suppliers."

"We understand Larry. You know Larry, with such a large demand for a good hit man maybe Josh and I should go into business for ourselves."

"Cute, real cute!"

"Gotcha back!"

We laughed.

"So you did. Just be careful!"

"We will! We'll also get all the information from our new partner before we do anything."

"I know you'll be out late so call me tomorrow and fill me in."

"Talk to you then. Bye."

"Bye."

I hung up the phone.

"Do we have the sucker on the line?"

"Yes Lynda we do. Tomorrow will tell us how the hook is set."

"I'd be willing to bet he swallows it hook, line, and sinker."

"I hope so. Why do you think so?"

"He's a youngster who thinks he knows everything. Instead he's extremely stupid."

"I've got to know why you think he's stupid."

"Anyone who is a blood relative of a family would not cross that family. But he thinks he's smarter than the Don."

"What do you suggest we do?"

"Personally, I'd tell the Don about his family and let him handle it."

"You know Lynda, that's one of the reasons I love you so much."

"What's that?"

"Your intelligence. Also your ability to listen and learn. Now you're even planning ahead."

"You like what I figured out?"

"Yes I do, it's the same plan I set up with Coop and Josh last week."

"Last week?!"

"Don't feel bad. All you need is a little more speed. Other than that I'm very proud of you. Now lean over here so I can give you a kiss."

We held each other and kissed for quite a while.

"I can see you're getting excited so I better go fix dinner."

"How can you tell I'm getting excited?"

"Because I am."

"I'll talk to Doc about that tonight."

"I wish you would. I'm getting tired of cold showers."

"Cute, Lynda, real cute."

We were laughing as she left the room.

While she was cooking dinner I was going over, and catching up on my paper work. I hate paper work. I'm very happy to have a receptionist/secretary to do most of it for me. Mrs. Thompkin has been doing her job for the city for over ten years. I allow her to run as much of the normal things of my office as she can. There are still things that need by personal attention. Mrs. Thompkin is not a member of my personal team. Between my speed reading and my 100 percent recall I was able to finish the paper work, take a nap, and have dinner before Doc arrived.

Lynda brought Doc into our bedroom.

"Good evening Larry."

"Good evening Doc. How are things going?"

"The most important thing is right here in front of me. I'll let you know in a minute how you're doing."

I was lying on my stomach and Doc was removing the bandages.

"What do you think?"

"It's amazing how well you've healed."

"It's the power of the Gods. They take care of me."

"You'll have to introduce them to me someday."

"Someday I'll do that Doc. What about my back?"

"Looks good. Is it giving you any problems Larry?"

"Not really Doc. Depending on how my body is turning, it gives me a little dull pain."

"That's expected. If that's your only problem you're almost as good as new."

"That's good to hear Doc. Thanks."

"Lynda, continue to change his bandage daily until Wednesday, after that let's leave the wound open."

"I'll take care of it Doc."

"Doc, I've been exercising a little and I was wondering…"

"What about sex?"

"Yes. How'd you know?"

"When a patient starts to feel good that's the first question he asks me."

"It looks like I'm normal and feeling good."

"In that case I want the two of you to take it slow and easy for the rest of this week."

"We will Doc."

"Good. Now that I'm done taking care of you, you can take a look at my progress with the hospital."

I sat up on the bed as he got his large portfolio. He took out drawings and notes with figures on them. As I looked at his work I commented on it.

"I love the way it's looking. You're playing down the outside and building up the inside."

"I feel if the place is neat, clean, and safe, that's all the outside needs."

"I agree. I like how you're adding more lights to the parking lot."

"I'm just about doubling what's there. What's there now is city code. But I feel when it comes to safety we throw out city code."

"I agree. I hate a dark parking lot."

"I brought you an outline of what's happening and what's going to happen. I was talking to some colleagues of mine, in general conversation, and I found two more doctors and their nursing staffs."

"So far I'm impressed. I knew you'd do a good job, and so far it's been excellent. Keep up the good work. Do you have an estimate of when you think you'll have the doors open?"

"Two to three months partially and four months completely. The rest home 60 to 90 days later."

"Sounds good. Really good. I'll read through your outline and if I have a problem with anything I'll call you."

"All right Larry. Depending on how you feel, I may see you at the end of the week."

"All right. We'll stay in touch."

"Oh, by the way, I put the hospital phone numbers on the papers for you. I'd try that number first. I seem to be spending more time there than at my practice."

"I'll do it Doc. I'm curious, how's your family doing?"

"Better than ever. You're my son's hero. If it wasn't for you he wouldn't have been ready for the bully. He said he couldn't believe how easy it was to redirect the bully's punches and make him land on his fanny. By the time the bully landed on his fanny the third time he started to cry. Now my son has a new friend who is learning how to get along with others."

"Sounds good, I'm glad everything worked out for you."

"Thanks to you."

"You're doing all the work. I'm just giving you the means. Now, get out of here and spend some time with your family."

"All right, I'm going but remember I've been thrown out of better places."

We were all laughing as Lynda walked out of the room with Doc. When Lynda returned to our room she was carrying two brandies.

"Do you mind if I take a shower before I bathe you?"

"No, go right ahead. I'll sit here and enjoy my brandy and think about what lies ahead for us."

By the time she finished I was really relaxed.

She walked out of the shower area wearing my favorite nightgown. It's simple in style, pink in color, with a little pink bow at the top between her breasts. Her long blonde hair cascaded on her shoulders. Her blue eyes sparkled and her body was lean and trim. She was 32 and in love with me. I'm almost old enough to be her father and I thank the Gods every day for giving her to me.

She stood there looking at me, "Is there a problem?"

I must have been staring at her. "No, why do you ask?"

"It's the way you're looking at me."

"And how am I looking at you?"

"With lust and desire, I hope."

"That, plus love and affection."

She picked up her brandy from the nightstand and said, "I'll drink to that."

I raised my glass in the air and clinked it to hers. Then I rose from the bed and walked towards the bathroom.

"What if I give myself a sponge bath and meet you in bed?"

"Sounds like a good plan to me. I'll fill our glasses while you're gone."

I seem to wash myself in record time. I slipped on some clean pajamas and headed back to bed. Lynda was sitting up sipping her brandy.

"It's kind of early Lynda. What would you like to do?"

"Why don't you slip out of your pajamas, I'll slip out of my gown and we'll both meet under the covers."

"I couldn't have said it better. I love to be with someone who loves me, and does things to make me happy."

I was talking as I was slipping off my pajamas. We slid together onto the middle of the bed. I shivered as her firm body made contact with mine. It seemed like an eternity since I held her last. The electricity of her soul seemed to mix with mine. I felt like a kid on his first date. As I put my arms around her she did the same to me. She had one hand on the back of my neck at the base of my head and the other hand on the left cheek of my rear end. As she touched me I must have given her a strange look.

"I don't know where else to touch you."

"Believe me, it's the right spot. I only see one problem."

"What's that?"

"You'll have to go slow and easy."

"I remember the first time we made love I said that to you."

"So you did. It just shows you how situations can turn around."

"I'll be gentle and I'll try not to hurt you. So don't be scared of this aggressive woman."

"Cute, real cute."

We slowly and gently held and touched one another. Her body was so warm and tender. We spent over two hours making love to one another. We slept side by side and woke up in one another's arms. To me that's one of the nicest things that can happen to a person.

"Good morning."

I said, "Good morning," then I kissed her.

She kissed me back and said, "I love you."

"I love you too, and thank you again for taking such good care of me."

"You're welcome. Are we going to work today or can we spend the day in bed?"

"Don't tempt me. But you know we have a lot to do."

"Larry, you're the biggest killjoy I know."

"Yes I am, now let's get ready for work."

We were in my office by five to nine. Pete and the Mayor walked in with us. The F.B.I. was the last to arrive at nine o'clock. As they started to sit down I opened the meeting.

"Good morning everyone, I'm glad to see we're all here. I think we better get started. Sam and Wade, welcome back. I'm glad you're here safely."

"Thank you Larry, we're glad to be back."

"In that case Sam, why don't you fill us in?"

"I'd be glad to. The trip was a great success. We followed our boys from here to their homes in Canada. We spent almost three days doing surveillance work. My friend Charles of the Mounties has all of their locations covered. We have photos of their friends, which the Mounties are still putting names to."

"I take it the bad boys are still there?"

"Yes, Larry, but now they have plenty of people watching them."

"When they do move, how're you going to handle it?"

"There will be a chopper available every night. Once they steal a truck and take it across the border the chopper will follow it and see where it goes. Hopefully when we're ready to move we'll have all the fish in one barrel."

"Is that it Sam?"

"Except we're glad to see you're doing better."

"Thank you I am, now shall we continue? Wade, do you have anything?"

"No Larry. I pass to the Mayor."

"I have the six traffic cameras ordered for you, and we've informed the company doing the driver's survival school that we wouldn't be renewing their contract."

"That sounds good, Mayor. If you could I'd like you to do something for me."

"Anything Larry."

"What's the ratio of cost of camera versus pole and installation?"

"About 20 percent pole and installation and 80 percent camera."

"Can we make the cameras portable?"

"You mean so we can move them from place to place with ease and speed?"

"That's what I have in mind."

"I'm sure our boys can put a pigtail on the camera and a female receptacle inside the box on the pole. What do you have in mind?"

"Two things. One; I want you to get together with Pete later and find out how many corners in town could use this particular camera. Then order that many posts and housings."

"No cameras?"

"Let's order four more cameras. That will give us ten floating units. Remember Mayor when we originally discussed this; you were buying five cameras and I was buying five? I like the way it is now better; you're paying for six and we're buying four."

"Let me make sure I understand what you are intending to do. You're going to put posts all around the city but only use ten cameras to service them."

"That's right Mayor. I also want signs posted to warn people about the cameras."

"Now you're going to warn them?"

"Mayor, the original purpose of these cameras is to deter the people from running red lights which causes accidents and deaths."

"I understand that."

"Well, a lot of towns don't. They use those cameras as a money maker. I know the cameras will pay for themselves and even show a large profit. What I really want them to do is to stop accidents and deaths."

"Sounds good, I'll handle it with Pete. Do you want us to report on our progress?"

"No, you two handle it."

"We will. Now I pass to Pete."

"Not a whole lot to report. I have the military working on giving us one of their buildings on the west side. They're also trying to get us a place on the east side. They said it may take a little while but they'll try to make it happen for us. The main reason being, is they love the idea. They also volunteered as many teachers as we could use."

"I love the sound of that. What else?"

"Coop and Josh got hired by the nephew to kill me."

"I'd be worried if I were you Pete. These boys are good. I remember when they killed me."

Everyone laughed.

"If they do that kind of a job on me I'll be happy."

"If all goes according to plan they won't have to try."

"Well, I'm hoping for the best."

"So are we Pete."

"Also the mobs in town are becoming very well known to us. You wouldn't believe the thousands of calls we've received, and are still getting from the announcements the T.V., radio, and newspaper reporters have made. The people in our town really want the streets cleaned up."

"I agree Pete. We've got good people in our town. I'm glad to see them taking advantage of the opportunity to help their town."

"Lastly still no limo missing in our town."

"There will be! I know it."

"No one's questioning that Larry. I'll keep watching. Now I'll pass to Tom."

"We're still keeping a close eye on the ambulance service, nothing great to report. We laid out a map like you suggested Larry. The planes and choppers can easily reach the border and return without refueling."

"That's what I thought, anything to make our job more difficult."

"It'll work out Larry. I'll pass to Jim."

"Seeing the Canadians have left town, there isn't very much happening here. I'll pass to Lynda."

"Doc looked at Larry last night and figures by Friday he should be close to 100 percent. I'll pass to Robert."

"Jim and I spent most of yesterday tracking down the three D.P.S. uniforms. It seems the badge numbers correspond to those of the special unit attached to guarding visiting dignitaries."

"We don't get an over abundance of those do we?"

"No Larry, but they also take care of the Mayor, Governor, and any other high ranking official. They're real good with motorcades."

"I get the idea, Robert. Yoto, what about the watchman uniform you're working on?"

"John and I have it narrowed down to three security companies. It would have been a lot easier if the uniform had a patch on it. That would have narrowed it down in a big hurry."

"Stay on top of it boys. Pete, check around the state for a missing limo."

"All right Larry."

"Robert and Jim, get a list of the assignments the special unit has coming up in the next 90 days."

"We'll take care of it Larry."

"Thanks Jim. Yoto, I want you and John to narrow our search down to one company. Do this by finding out the high level companies they guard. Then compare your list with Jim's and see what surfaces."

"It'll be done Larry."

"Good. Sam and Wade, on the Q.T. see if the President of the

United States is planning a trip to our fair city."

"It may take a little while Larry, but we'll get it handled."

"Thanks Sam. Anything else gentlemen?"

"Larry."

"Yes Tom?"

"John and I got the contract vote from the men. The Mayor will sign the new contract this afternoon."

"I take it a majority of the men liked my idea?"

"Not a majority Larry, all of them."

"I've always said we have a smart group of officers."

"We all agree with that Larry."

"Thanks Pete, anything else? Anybody? In that case, let's get to work."

It was around three in the afternoon when my private number rang.

"Hello?"

"Larry, this is Coop."

"What's happening Coop?"

"The nephew is really pushing hard for Pete's death."

"How'd you stall him?"

"We told him we had to wait a week or so for things to calm down. We didn't want to fail."

"What'd he say?"

"He agreed with us."

"Good. When you heading back east?"

"Tomorrow morning."

"Hope you have your story in order."

"I have something better than that."

"What is it?"

"I have a written contract with the nephew. Josh and I get his dead cousin's share of the drug business for killing Pete."

"You're kidding! How'd you get him to put it in writing?"

"Josh and I put the thought in his head and he came up with the idea all by himself."

"Ha! Ha! Ha! I knew he was dumb, but I didn't think he was totally stupid."

"He thinks he's the Godfather of the World. He knows everything and can do no wrong."

"All I can say is, you boys have done a great job."

"Thanks Larry. I'll call when I get back in town."

"I'll talk to you then."

Sam and Wade had explained to Coop on how to get in touch with the Godfather back east. He was to go into one of the Godfather's restaurants and leave word for him. A simple message, 'Godfather, I need to speak to you. I know of one of your businesses that is about to be destroyed'. He included his name, hotel, and room number. He would then go back to his room and wait to be contacted.

As the week continued everything seemed to move in slow motion. By Thursday's morning meeting, Yoto had narrowed the watchman uniform down to 2 uniform companies. Otherwise everything seemed to be at a standstill. The bright spot of the day came in the late afternoon when Coop called me. He reported on his trip back east.

"How'd it go Coop?"

"Scary, but fine Larry."

"Tell me about it."

"I left word for the Don Wednesday evening. I got a call at eight in the morning informing me that they would pick me up at ten."

"Were they on time?"

"Like a Swiss watch."

"Continue."

"They took me back to the restaurant I had visited the night before. They searched me thoroughly before allowing me past the front door."

"I bet they gave you a strange look when they found out you weren't packing."

"That they did. Then they escorted me to the rear of the restaurant. The Don was sitting in a large half moon shaped booth. He had just finished eating breakfast and was having his second cup of coffee. His boys stayed back and I moved in front of his table. I introduced myself and waited for him to speak."

"I bet he let you sweat."

"You know he did Larry. The way you did the first time I met you one on one. Just like you he wanted to see if I'd show him the respect he deserved."

"And you did?"

"You bet your bippy I did. Eventually he asked me what I wanted to see him about. I asked if we could speak privately. He said he trusted everyone there. I explained that I'd feel safer explaining the situation only to him. If he wished to relay the information later, that would be okay with me. He asked me to sit at the other end of the booth. I sat down and told him the whole rotten story."

"I hope you didn't leave anything out."

"No Larry, actually I added a few things."

"Good. Continue."

"He told me that he had his suspicions. But he was hoping he was wrong. I told him that I wouldn't have flown all this way if it wasn't for the fact that it was his nephew."

"I bet he liked that."

"Yes. He thanked me."

"Then what happened?"

"I started to implant our plan in his head."

"Did he bite?"

"Oh yes. I told him that my partner and I wouldn't get rid of his nephew for him because we knew better. We knew by doing this it would only show his weakness, his inability to handle his own family. That's the last thing we wanted to do. He told me that he believed me, but before he could take action against his late brother's last son, he'd need strong proof of what's going on in Pertsville. I showed him our contract with his nephew. I asked him if a large drug buy would do the trick. He agreed it would as long as he was there when it happened. I told him that I could arrange that for the same price. Then he bit again. He asked how much it would cost him. I told him two million dollars in cash or one million in cash and a favor if we ever needed one. He responded without blinking an eye. He told me that if all goes according to plan he'd give us two million dollars plus a favor. He shook my hand and put a piece of paper into it. He said that number will get me 24 hours a day. I thanked him and got up and left. His man was nice enough to drop me at the airport."

"Had you left your suitcase in their car?"

"Yes, and they searched it."

"They found nothing?"

"There was nothing to find."

"Good. When do you expect a drug shipment?"

"I don't know. It seems our nephew really wants Pete dead."

"You're going to have to convince him that business has to go on. Tell him you have a plan to get rid of Pete, but it's going to take a couple of weeks."

"Don't worry Larry. We'll get it handled."

"I never worry about your ability I just worry about you and Josh. So take care of yourselves."

"We will, and I'll call you when I have something else to report."

"Talk to you then."

At Friday's morning meeting I knew there was something wrong but I couldn't put my finger on it. It started out to be a short meeting. After I explained my conversation with Coop to the group I asked if there was anything else before we adjourned.

Sam spoke, "Larry I have a problem."

"What seems to be the problem?"

"I have a co-worker who hates awards and award ceremonies."

"I know the feeling."

"Well the problem is the President of the United States has requested this gentleman to receive an award."

"If this guy is a true American he'll do as his President has requested."

"I'm glad to hear you say that."

"I'm glad I helped you out."

Sam reached into his pocket and pulled out a letter and handed it to me. I opened it and read it. It was on Presidential stationary and signed by the President.

"Wait a minute!"

Everyone started to applaud.

Sam shook my hand and said, "Congratulations."

"You set me up."

"Yes I did and I think I did a pretty good job of it."

I said laughingly, "I have to agree. You sure did."

"What's the letter say Larry?"

"Tom, the President says Parliament wishes to present me with an award next week in London, England. It's for making the biggest meth bust in their history."

John said, "Some guys have all the luck."

"If that's what you call it John. We have a lot going on here. If it wasn't for the President I wouldn't go. Now I have a lot of planning to do."

"Larry."

"Yes Mayor?"

"We've known about this for a couple of days. So we took the liberty of arranging everything for you."

"How long will I be gone?"

"We talked about that among ourselves."

"I'm glad. What'd you come up with?" I could see a sad look on Lynda's face.

"First off, we couldn't send you anywhere without the proper protection, so we're sending Lynda, Yoto, and his girlfriend Lyn-Yhi with you."

Lynda was now smiling ear to ear.

"You still didn't tell me how long I'd be there."

"Until at least the end of the week."

"You want me to play it by ear?"

"That's what we figured, with the Brits, who knows what they'll have planned."

"All right Mayor. I'll do it your way. When do we leave?"

"Sunday. You'll get to New York about two hours before your overseas flight. You'll arrive in London Monday morning."

"All right, now that that's all settled when I'm gone I want everyone here to continue on with the morning meeting just like we were all here."

"I'll call you with the number of the hotel when we get there."

"Sounds good Larry. That way we can keep you posted on what's happening here."

"That's what I figured Pete. Now if there's nothing else some of us have a lot to do before Sunday."

As everyone left they seemed very happy for me.

Lynda and I had a lot to do before Sunday and we managed to get it all done.

Everyone saw us off at the airport. Lynda hadn't done that much traveling so she was thrilled to death about the trip. I don't mind saying that it made me happy to see her happy. Knowing we were flying first class the whole way made me feel even better for Lynda. I thought she'd been working so hard lately that a little pampering by the airlines would be good for her.

We were met in New York after we deplaned. The gentleman took us to the V.I.P. lounge to await our flight to Europe. With our F.B.I. clearances we went straight to our plane without stopping for checkpoints.

For some reason the Mayor had done the seating arrangement on the plane kind of funny. The first class section was about half full. Yet for some reason the Mayor had put Yoto and Lyn-Yhi in the two bulkhead seats on one side of the plane and Lynda and me in the two bulkhead seats on the other side of the plane. It actually made it rather nice. We were there together yet we were also very much alone. After a first class supper we were ready for some sleep.

I don't know how long I was sleeping when some low speaking voices awakened me.

"Sir, we'll do whatever you wish. Just don't hurt anyone."

As the stewardess walked by me she nudged me on my shoulder. She thought I was asleep so I pretended to be just that.

The man spoke, "Number four you stay here and watch first class."

"Umph."

Out of a small crack I made between my eyelids I could see our two hijackers and their guns. I have to admit that I've seen pictures of plastic guns before, but these were the first working models that I'd seen.

I quickly analyzed the situation. If Number One was heading to the cockpit with the stewardess and we have Number Four in front of us I wondered where Number Two and Three happened to be. First things first. We had to eliminate Number Four from our presence so we can formulate a plan to retake the plane. Little did I know that Number One had taken the cockpit and was talking to Heathrow Tower. He told them if they would refuel the plane he'd allow the women and children to leave the plane before he took off. He also said he'd have a few more demands once he was on the ground. To be honest about it I figured we'd retake the plane before most of the passengers knew it was high jacked.

I slowly reached my right hand across my body and removed my sleeve knife from my left sleeve. I then unhooked my seat belt so the hijacker could hear it. He then did what I knew he would do. As I was arising from my seat he was right on top of me. He put his left hand on top of my right shoulder to push me back into my seat. I smacked his right wrist with all the power I could muster causing the pistol in his hand to go flying. Boy, did he have a surprised look on his face. I kept raising my body and at the same time driving my sleeve knife into his solar plexus. After hitting his wrist with my left hand I used it to pull off his head set before he could notify anyone of his problem. As I held him close I could feel his life slipping away. I looked down at Lynda and she had her eyes wide open and a shocked look on her face. I turned my head toward Yoto's seat but never got my eyes that far. He was standing next to the guy I had my knife stuck in. He had the man's gun in his hand. I motioned for him to help me lower the body to the floor.

"Help me get his jacket off,' I whispered.

I put his jacket on. He was a big man and his jacket fit me nicely. I picked up his radio headset and his black baseball cap and put them on. I knew I'd have to cover the microphone every time someone would speak to me. I told Yoto to keep the gun.

The curtains on both sides of the aisle were closed between the first class cabin and the rest of the plane.

"Yoto. Recon."

I helped Lynda out of her seat. "Wake each person quietly. Tell them to stay extremely quiet. Get Lyn-Yhi to do her side of the plane." Lynda had to awaken Lyn-Yhi. Yoto had left his seat next to her so quietly that she slept right through it.

I stood at the front of our section like the hijacker. In case anyone came in they'd face either Yoto or me first.

It didn't take long for the girls and Yoto to rejoin me.

"Good work girls. Yoto, what's it look like?"

"Two people, a man to the rear on my side and a woman up front on your side."

"Can you get a clean shot at the man from between the curtains?"

"Not with this piece of plastic junk, but with my own gun….yes."

"That may be too noisy. We still have a hijacker in the cockpit. Talking about the cockpit and the crew where are the two stewardesses that were taking care of us? Yoto. Recon."

Yoto went up front near the cooking area and bathrooms. In a couple of minutes he walked back with the two girls. They looked scared and shaken. Other than that they were fine. I could see tape on their blouses around the wrist area. Yoto had cut the girls' bonds and pulled the piece of tape off each of their mouths. The girls were happy to be free.

After explaining the situation to the girls I asked them a direct question. "If we fire a shot back here will they hear it in the cockpit?"

Both the girls shook their head 'no' and one girl spoke. "With the engine noise and the soundproofing they will never hear a thing."

"Good. I love when a plan comes together. First thing we'll do is take out the two hijackers in the rear. Then we'll have to figure out how to get the one in the cockpit because we can win the battle out here and lose the war in there. He can kill everyone in the cockpit and destroy the plane before we can get through the door. Well first things first."

"Yoto you have the man on your side of the plane. I'll take the woman out when you fire."

"Isn't that dangerous for Yoto?"

"Yes it is Lyn-Yhi but that's why we get paid the big money."

"No one's paying you for doing this."

"Just an oversight my dear, now give Yoto a kiss and send him on his way." As she did that I kissed Lynda. I didn't want to take the time to explain to Lyn-Yhi that the danger was minimal. When Yoto fires his gun the sound will startle everyone including the female hijacker. Her next thought will be to the point of firing. When she turns that way with her gun I'll get her from behind. And that's just what I did. As she turned toward Yoto's position I walked silent and walked deadly. I came up behind her and with the palm of my right hand I smacked the back knuckles of her right hand causing her gun to go flying. In the same motion I continued my hand up to her face covering her mouth and nose with my hand. At the same time my left hand was driving my sleeve knife through her body from the rear. Yoto went to the rear of the cabin to check his kill. He pulled the dead man out of the aisle way and told the stewardess to cover him with a blanket. Yoto returned to me and took the woman off my hands. He turned her around and took her back to be with her dead partner. There was lot of low murmuring throughout this section of the cabin. I raised my hands and putting my palms down I slowly lowered my hands and the people quieted down. By this time Yoto and two stewardesses had returned to me.

"You girls need to inform everyone to stay in their seats and be quiet. There is still one hijacker we have to get. If he hears noise or feels something isn't right he'll blow up the plane. Do you two understand how important your mission is?"

"Yes Sir. We do."

"Good. We'll close the curtains on our way out."

"Don't worry Sir. We'll handle our end."

Yoto and I returned to the front of the first class cabin.

"How are things up here Lynda?"

"Just fine Sir."

I liked how she had quickly reverted to military mode.

"I now need a plan and I like how quiet everyone is."

"They know their lives depend on it."

"And they're right Lynda."

One of the stewardess' asked if she could speak.

"Yes ma'am. Please do."

"My understanding is we need to get our friend up front out of the cockpit before he kills someone."

"That's right. Or we need to get someone inside to kill him."

"I think I can get back inside but I don't think I could kill anyone."

"For right now just tell me your idea and leave the killing up to me."

"While you were gone I noticed a little girl with her parents four rows up."

"What about her?"

"She's asthmatic and she's using an inhaler."

"I noticed that."

"What if the captain was asthmatic and his inhaler was out here in the refrigerator?"

"If he had an attack someone would either have to come out and get the inhaler, or someone would have to take it into the cabin. Either way we get a shot at him. Good thinking Ma'am but how do we tell the Captain about this?"

"I can call the Captain on his head set and he can direct the call to whoever else has his head set on."

"How does he know you're calling?"

"A red light comes on."

"Will our hijacker be able to see it?"

"Only if he's in the pilot's or co-pilot's seat."

"Isn't there a small jump seat in the cockpit?"

"Yes there is. Do you think that's where he is?"

"No. If I was him I'd be in the navigator's chair. I'd be wearing his headset so I could be in constant communication with Heathrow Tower."

"If you're right he'll never see the light. We can talk to the pilot and co-pilot at the same time."

"That sounds great. Before we do that I'd like you to change clothes with Lynda."

"She'll never pass as me she has blonde hair."

"We'll have to give it a try. I don't have time to teach you how to kill."

The other stewardess said, "I'll be right back."

She went around the corner to the cooking area. We heard her open a cabinet and in a few seconds she returned.

"This should help out a lot." She had a dark wig in her hand. "I use it when I don't have time to get my hair done."

"I'm happy you do. Why don't you girls go and get changed?"

While they were changing Lyn-Yhi had gone to the family and borrowed the girl's extra inhaler.

When they had finished changing Lynda looked good enough to pass for the stewardess.

I said to the stewardess, "Now let's talk to the pilot."

We went to the intercom phone and the stewardess, in a few moments had the captain on the intercom phone. When he opened the line the stewardess told him not to say a word, just to listen to my instructions. She then turned him over to me. I had him patch in the co-pilot and I then explained that we had retaken the plane and what I needed them to do to help take out the last hijacker.

Two minutes later they started their act. I had put Number Four's headset back on.

"Number Four." (I could hear commotion in the background) "Get the head stewardess out of the bathroom. Untie her and have her get the Captain's asthma medicine. Hurry!"

"Umph."

My 'umph' must have worked because he disconnected. I think all the noise in the cockpit also helped to confuse him. While given enough time for everything to transpire I went over everything with Lynda.

"Bottom line once again, he's a cold blooded killer. He'll snuff you out like you were a bug. You take the tray in with the medicine, glass of water, and inhaler on it. Once you get close enough to him pour the tray onto him and fire. You better get him between the eyes. Remember your derringer has only one shot. If somehow the bullet doesn't do the job, you'll have my knife under the tray for backup."

"Don't worry Larry. Everything will be all right."

I kissed her and said, "Walk Silent and Walk Deadly." I knew she didn't know how to, but I wanted her to know the confidence I had in her. Someday I'll teach my whole new team how to Walk Silent and Walk Deadly.

Lynda went up and knocked on the door as I had told her to.

The communication officer opened the door from the jump seat. Lynda closed the door after she was in. She was standing in front of the hijacker, "I have your medicine Captain." She then spilled the tray onto the hijacker.

"What the hell are you doing?" said the hijacker as he started to stand up.

Lynda pulled back the hammer of the derringer and fired. Because of the hijacker's quick movements Lynda missed his eyes and caught him in the neck. The co-pilot was out of his seat and had a hold of the hijacker's right hand. It's the hand that held his pistol. The hijacker took his left hand and grabbed Lynda by the hair. While he was lifting her wig she was planting my knife in his chest. The co-pilot did as I had instructed him to do. He kept the hijacker from blowing out any of the windshields. Instead the gun fired three times into the communications center. The hijacker dropped the wig and grabbed Lynda's real hair as she pulled out my knife and buried it into his chest again. This time she hit his heart and before he got a good hair pull in, he was dead. As he slumped to the floor the co-pilot took his gun from his hand. Lynda pulled my knife out of his chest and wiped it off on his jacket. She stepped around the body and opened the cockpit door. I was standing in the doorway.

"I would never have done it without the co-pilot and your knife."

I said, "Thank you," to the co-pilot as he handed me the plastic gun.

"I only did what you told me to. We want to thank you and your people for getting us back our plane."

"Almost, but not quite."

"What do you mean?"

"An operation like this, there's usually a plain clothes observer. Hopefully this person will see or hear something to help save the others from having their plan foiled."

"So you think we still have one hijacker out there?"

"Yes Captain, I do."

"Any idea who it might be?"

"No idea. It could be a man or a woman."

Lynda said, "I think I have an idea for us."

"What's that Lynda?" I asked as she was kneeling down by the dead hijacker. As I watched she seemed to be smelling him.

"When I was trying to kill him I was pressed up against him."

"Don't worry, I'm not jealous."

"Cute Larry, real cute."

Everyone was laughing quietly.

"I'm sorry Lynda. Please continue."

"I smelled a woman's perfume on him. Here it is again."

I knelt down beside her and sure enough a sweet smell was emanating from his shirt.

"I would guess a woman about 5'4" to 5'5" by where the smell is."

Lynda said, "Sounds about right to me. Now how do we find her?"

"We don't. We let her show herself. Yoto give me a hand with this body."

Yoto asked, "What should we do with it?"

"Why don't we put this one and the other one in the bathroom where the girls were prisoners?"

"Good idea."

"Someone better radio Heathrow Tower and bring them up to date."

As we were moving the body out of the cockpit the communication officer was returning to his seat. We were barely clear of the door when he plugged in his headset. When he did all hell broke loose. There were crackling noises and sparks flying everywhere. Yoto and

I dropped the body and returned to the cockpit just as everything was quieting down.

I said, "What happened?"

The Communications Officer stated, "When I plugged in my headset everything shorted out."

"What exactly do you mean by everything?"

"I don't know I'm still checking."

As he was going through his check list I asked, "Captain, how are things your way?"

"I still have gauges, steering, power, and good vision. That's all I need to navigate this baby. Landing could be another problem, but we have a few hours before we have to worry about that."

The Navigation Officer said, "You can start worrying about that now."

The Captain asked, "Why is that?"

"We no longer have communications or navigation."

"Looks like I'll have to fly by the seat of my pants."

I asked, "Can you do that Captain?"

"It will be early morning when we arrive in London. If there is no heavy rain or fog and the traffic is clear I'll be able to bring her down."

"As you said before, we have a few hours to work it out. Right now we have one more hijacker to get rid of." I motioned Yoto out of the cockpit. "Captain."

"Yes Larry."

"Stay on your same heading at your same altitude."

"I already planned to."

"We'll be back soon to help you work things out."

"Thank you."

After storing the bodies and allowing our two stewardesses to smell the perfume I put my plan into action. We all hurried back to the main cabin. We now had all five of the stewardesses free and standing around the cabin. When they saw me I motioned for them to stay where they were. The rest of us walked to the back of the plane. I mentally felt that the girl had to be sitting on the opposite side of the plane as the rear hijacker. This is the section of the plane Lynda would take care of. I stood to the rear of the plane where I could see everything. I had Yoto coming up the aisle from the front and Lynda coming down from the rear. The two stewardesses were doing the same on the other side. They were telling the passengers that we were going to storm the cockpit and there may be some unexpected turbulence. We wanted them to tighten their seatbelts and where possible to move over so there was a vacant seat between them. Lynda was standing over the second row aisle seat when she gave me the prearranged signal with her left hand. Before she continued on to the next row she attempted to move the second person over a seat.

"Must I move? She's my sister."

"As long as you take responsibility for yourselves, it's okay with me. Let me double check with my supervisor."

Lynda straightened up, turned around and walked back toward me. As she did I walked towards her.

"What seems to be the problem? You signaled that you found the girl."

"I didn't find the girl. I found the girls."

"Girls?"

"Yes. Sisters, I told them that you would have to give them permission to stay seated together."

I reached down and raised my leg at the same time so I could pull my leg gun out of its holster. I handed it to Lynda.

"You're responsible for the second girl in. I'll take care of Number One. You go first."

Lynda stopped in front of the row and I stood even with the girls.

I spoke, "Ladies, all your friends are dead and you are under arrest for attempted hijacking."

The female in the aisle seat spoke to me, "Then I was right. You've already taken the cockpit and you've killed everyone."

"Yes we have."

"Then it's time I joined my husband and my sister." At that point she stopped talking and started chewing.

"What's she doing Larry?!"

"Cyanide capsule, I can smell it."

She shook her head up and down in a 'yes' fashion. That was the last movement she made. I looked over at her sister and I could tell she had done the same thing when Lynda was back talking to me. At least they got their last wish. They were holding hands as they left this world. Yoto and I moved the two sisters to the rear of the plane and put them in a rear bathroom with the other two hijackers we had killed.

Little did I know that while all this was happening, my friend from Scotland Yard, Dick "Winky" Hollender was the second person at Scotland Yard to hear of the hijacking. He hurried down to Heathrow to join the other people working on the case.

"What do you think Hollender? Any ideas for us?"

"The only thing I can say Sir, is that I sort of feel sorry for the people on the plane."

"We're glad to hear that. We're all praying for the passengers ourselves."

"It's not the passengers I was thinking of Sir. It's the hijackers."

"You feel bad for the hijackers? Why?"

"I have two friends on that plane Sir."

"So?"

"So, they hijacked the wrong plane."

"You think that much of your friends' abilities?"

"They're the same ones that put your drug bust together, Sir."

"I don't think your friends can take care of a plane full of hijackers."

"I have one hundred pounds that says when the plane lands it will be under our control and the hijackers will all be dead."

"I'll take that bet Hollender."

They shook hands and then went about their business.

It was close to four in the morning when the tower lost all contact with the plane. Winky was standing in the area when it happened. He could hear the tower operator trying over and over to make contact with the plane.

The Tower Operator said, "Their communications are out Sir."

"Nothing at all?"

"No Sir."

"Do you still have them on radar?"

"Yes Sir."

Winky moved closer so he could listen.

"We're going to have to assume that everything is out which means the pilot is flying by the seat of his pants."

"I know the pilot Sir. We were in the R.A.F. (Royal Air Force) together before I was grounded. If he has visibility and room he'll bring her down safely Sir."

"That's good to know. The only thing we need now is a way to communicate with them."

As he moved toward the tower supervisor Winky said, "Sir."

"Yes?"

"I'm Chief Inspector Dick Hollender of Scotland Yard. If you have a small jet and a signaling light I can be their eyes."

"You really think you can do this?"

"No problem Sir."

"You heard the man! Get him what he needs and get him in the air! We'll keep in touch with you."

"I'd also suggest you clear a large berth for that plane."

The control tower operator said," I'm already doing that Sir. I'm rerouting everything remotely close to their air space."

"Good."

As Winky was flying towards us we were trying to fix our communications system.

I said, "Gentlemen! This communications center looks really sick to me."

"I'm only the communications officer but I have to agree with you."

"I had no idea that three little bullets could do that much damage."

"Sir, it just depends on where they hit."

"Are you going to try to fix it?"

"I don't have the tools necessary to do anything."

"I have my Swiss Army knife if that will help."

"I have a packet of tools but I don't have the skill to fix this monstrosity."

"Yoto, grab the tools and let's see if we can get this thing open."

We couldn't. The screws were put on with power tools and we stripped some of them trying to unscrew them.

"It looks like you're right son. You can't fix it."

Yoto asked, "What now Larry?"

"Yoto, I think it's time we sit down, have a snack, and allow our minds to clear. Then we'll solve this problem."

We went back to our seats and relaxed. The stewardesses brought us some food and a bottle of champagne. Yoto and Lyn-Yhi moved to the seats across the aisle from us. I raised my glass, "A toast to the Gods and to all the help they gave us tonight."

"To the Gods," repeated everyone.

"Larry?"

"What Lyn-Yhi?"

"Are we in as much danger as I think we are?"

"I don't think the Gods will let us down."

"I've never been one to do a lot of praying."

"Don't worry. The Gods know if you are a good person or bad. In your case you haven't a thing to worry about."

"Thanks Larry. That makes me feel better."

Lynda asked, "Has anything new come to your mind Larry?"

"Yes Lynda it has. Yoto are you finished?"

"Yes Larry I am."

"I need you to go ask the Captain if he has a signaling light in his emergency equipment. If so, bring it here."

Yoto got up and left. When he returned he was carrying a heavy duty spotlight and a strange look on his face.

As he handed me the light I asked, "What's wrong?"

"The light with the forever battery isn't working."

"Is there anything else that can happen?"

"Yes there is."

"What's that Lynda?"

"I'm out of champagne."

"That I can fix." I refilled everyone's glasses. I then proceeded to check out the signal light.

"You're right Yoto. It's as dead as a doornail."

Yoto asked. "Any other ideas?"

"Give me a minute Yoto I'm still recovering from the dead flashlight."

Everyone laughed.

Yoto came back with, "You better recover in a hurry."

"Why's that Yoto?"

"Turn around and look out your window."

I looked out my window and saw a small jet pulling up parallel to us. Someone inside was flashing a signaling light at us.

"Let's head to the cockpit."

Everyone followed me to the cockpit. When I opened the door the communication officer was looking through everything in sight.

"Are you having fun?"

"I need to find something to signal the plane with."

"May I help?"

The Captain replied, "Did you get the light to work?"

"No Captain we didn't."

"Then what do you have in mind?"

"Your cockpit lights are on a separate circuit, correct?"

"Yes the copilot and I both have control of them."

I asked the copilot, "May I take your chair?"

The copilot got up and gave me his seat. He pointed to the control button as he moved aside.

The light from the small jet kept signaling in Morse Code. I used the cockpit light to signal them back.

"Yoto, it's Winky! Somehow I knew he'd come to our rescue."

"What's he have to say?"

"Before he'll tell us anything he wants to know how many hijackers and are they all dead."

"Winky hasn't changed. He has a bet with someone."

"I agree Yoto."

Winky and I conversed back and forth. He gave us our heading and followed us in. When the plane safely landed you could hear the clapping and cheers throughout the ship.

The crew and my party stayed on the plane. We soon had a flood of people everywhere. The stewardess had brought us another bottle of champagne and some rolls. We sat there eating and minding our own business as everyone scurried around us. It wasn't long until I heard that familiar voice.

Chapter 7

"Colonel Towers!"

I stood up and turned into the aisle way as Winky was coming upon me. I grabbed him and gave him a hug. "It's about time you got here!"

"It took time to land the other plane and then get back across the airport."

"No matter, we're glad to see you." At that point Yoto was standing beside me. They both saw each other and hugged.

"Yoto, you're looking good."

"So are you Winky."

We then introduced Winky to our fiancées.

"Winky, Yoto is curious."

"About what?"

"Ask him Yoto."

"How much money did you make off our ordeal?"

"One hundred pounds."

We all laughed.

"Winky, you'll never change."

"You're right Larry. I'm having too much fun the way I am."

It took about an hour and a half to get us off the plane. Winky had taken our luggage claim tickets from us when he had first started talking to us.

"Are you ready to go Larry?"

"We're past ready to go. Where are we heading?"

"There's a cart waiting for us when we get off the plane. It will take us out front where your luggage and limo are waiting for you. The driver will take you to your hotel. We have two suites next to one another for you. You're preregistered. All you have to do is give them your names and they will give you your keys. There's nothing important happening today, so relax and get some rest. I'll call for you at seven forty five P.M. for dinner. My treat."

"Sounds good seeing as we didn't sleep all night. What about customs?"

"It's been taken care of along with the reporters."

"I like how you run things in England."

"I knew you would. You always hated notoriety."

"We did the job and we know we did a great job so we don't need anyone else to tell us so."

"I agree. Now let's get you to your hotel."

We checked our luggage to see that it was all there and then got into the limo. We had a relaxing ride to the hotel. The driver pointed out a few landmarks on the way.

Our suite was simply beautiful. It had a small receiving area by the door as you entered. It contained a small marble top table against the wall with a live plant and a couple of silver coasters sitting on it. The chair was covered in velvet with a tufted back. I thought, 'if this is the foyer the rest of the rooms should be magnificent'. They were just that. The place made us feel at home. It was more European in style than our master suite at home. But other than that it was comparable.

No sooner had our bellboy left when there was a knock at the door. For the life of me I couldn't figure out what the bellboy had forgotten.

I opened the door, "Yes?" I was looking at Yoto and Lyn-Yhi.

"With a reception like that I think we'll go back to our own suite."

"I'm sorry Yoto. I thought you were the bellboy."

"I take it you couldn't get yours to leave either."

"You got that right. Either he thinks Americans are stupid or he was being overly nice. He showed us everything in the suite."

Yoto said, "The nice part was our boy made it a point to say how happy they are that we're staying here and if there's anything we need to just call."

"I'm glad to hear that. How's your suite?"

He did a three sixty turn around ours and said, "Furnished a little differently, other than that the same."

"Good. Do you like it Lyn-Yhi?"

"Larry if this is the way you travel, I'll go with you anywhere."

We all laughed.

"I'm glad you like it."

Lynda said, "So far it's much better than the plane ride."

"I agree with you Lynda. Now, I'm hungry. Would you like to eat together or separately?"

"Are you going to use room service?"

"Yes I am."

"I like the idea but we could have our luggage unpacked while we're waiting for our meal."

"Yes you could. So I'll take that as a 'no' Yoto."

"Not really Larry. Could we order the meal here and then go and unpack?"

"That's a good idea. We'll call you when it gets here. By the time the server puts it on the table you'll be here."

I had no sooner put the receiver in its cradle from ordering lunch when the phone made a funny sound.

"It won't bite you Larry. Pick it up."

"Cute Lynda. Real cute."

I reached down and picked up the receiver, "Hello?"

"Larry, this is Winky. I hope I didn't disturb you."

"No. We just ordered lunch."

"That's great. I forgot to tell you the dress for tonight."

"Please do. If we have it we'll wear it."

"Dinner jacket and bow tie."

"The girls are sure going to look funny dressed like that."

"I've always loved your sense of humor. The girls should wear evening dresses, high heels…that sort of thing."

"It shall be done, anything else?"

"Once again, you're the talk on everyone's lips."

"I'm glad the Gods put us there to help."

"You have no idea how many other people you made glad."

"Well, enough on that subject. We'll see you tonight."

"See you then."

I told Yoto and Lyn-Yhi about our dress code for the night before they left.

About 45 minutes later the food arrived. There's nothing better than good food and good friends. As they were leaving I told them we would pick them up for dinner. I closed the door and double locked it.

I said, "Believe it or not we're finally alone."

"Is this the part where you pick me up and carry me to the bed?"

"Yes it is."

"Oh goody!"

Lynda jumped up into my arms and we both started to laugh.

"I love you so much Lynda." I was talking as I carried her into the bedroom.

"I love you too."

I dumped her onto the bed. We had already removed the bedspread after we unpacked. The next thing I did was to jump in beside her. I was holding and kissing her like I hadn't seen her in months. She was doing the same to me. It was fun to once more playfully make love. It was over an hour later when we finally fell asleep in one another's arms.

My mind woke us up at 5 P.M. I nudged Lynda who was still naked and still holding me.

"Time to rise and shine Sleepyhead."

"Do we have to? Don't answer. I already know what you'll say."

I held her close and kissed her again. We had kissed for a couple of minutes when she said, "I can tell by the way you feel it's going to be 'hard' for you to get up."

"You're right but we're short on time."

"That's why quickies were invented."

"You don't mind?"

"Larry I love you too much to mind anything that you do to me out of love and I promise that no matter how short the time I will also have a good time."

We both had a good time and then got ready for the evening. At twenty to eight we were ready to leave so I called Yoto.

"Are you two ready?"

"Yes."

"Why don't you walk over? I'll open my door."

"We're on our way."

A couple of minutes later I heard the door open. Lyn-Yhi emerged out of the foyer and I could hear Yoto as he came into view.

"Look what we found out in the hallway." He had his hand on Winky's shoulder.

"He was probably trying to peak through your keyhole."

"You're probably right Yoto. To think there's never a house detective around when you need one."

We all laughed.

"You guys had better be careful. You're picking on the wrong guy tonight."

"Why is that Winky?"

"Remember Larry, I'm buying dinner."
We all slowed our laughter down.
Lynda said, "He's got a point there Larry."
"You're right Lynda. But I'd rather go hungry than stop."
Winky said, "He would too."

We were still laughing and carrying on when we got into the limo. The driver took us to a beautifully elegant restaurant. After one look at our table I knew it was a first class place. The table was set with a linen table cloth with napkins to match. The napkins were held together with gold napkin rings. But that didn't give the place away. What tipped me off was when I looked at the silverware and saw items I'd never seen before. My place setting alone looked like a service for eight. The nice part was by the end of the meal we had used every piece of silverware including the stem ware, two wine glasses, the champagne glass and the water goblet. It was 10:30 P.M., our meal was finished and we were having a brandy.

"Larry."
"Yes Winky."
"Are you folks up for a little fun?"
I looked around the table and saw no negative responses.
"It looks like we're game for anything you have in mind."
"I'd like to take you to one of our 'members only' casinos."
"Sounds like fun."
"I agree Lyn-Yhi."
Winky said, "Good. As soon as we finish our brandy we'll leave."
"Winky, don't you have to be in town for one or two days before you can gamble?"
"That's right Larry. Depending on whom you are and where you're from. So have no fear, tonight you're in with the in crowd."
We laughed as we finished our drinks.

The casino was done in class. It was nothing like the ones in the states. There were fresh flowers around the room, paintings on the walls, and statues around for the proper accents. The crystal chandeliers were out of this world. The people only added to the beauty of the place. Everyone was dressed in fancy clothes like ourselves. That's one thing I have to admit about our country; over the years we've lost a lot of our class and proper upbringing. That's why a lot of countries today look down their noses at us. Well, I'd better get off my soapbox and back to the evening.

We changed our money into chips and Winky took us on a tour of the casino.

"What would you like to play Larry?"

"I favor Blackjack."

"I hope twenty one favors you."

"You know we can always play the craps table. Do you boys remember.....?"

They both answered at the same time, "Yes we do!"

Winky said, "And that club in Monte Carlo still remembers us."

"You've been there since Winky?"

"Yes, and they asked how you were."

Yoto said, "I bet they did."

And I replied, "I agree Yoto. We're the last people they'd like to know about."

"Are we going to gamble?"

"Yes Winky. We are. Girls, what would you like to do?"

"Is it okay if we play the slot machines?"

"You girls do realize that they didn't get the name One Armed Bandits for being the best bet in the house."

Winky said, "Larry, they're not that bad here. They're set on a 50/50 split."

"You couldn't ask for more than that."

I handed Lynda a hundred pounds worth of chips and Yoto did the same for Lyn-Yhi. We both told the girls to have a good time.

Winky said, "Girls come close." They did as he spoke. "Try to get a machine near the high traffic areas. They're set to pay a higher percentage."

The girls thanked him and left.

"Shall we attack a table?"

"Lead on Winky."

Yoto and I sat at one table and Winky had to sit at another. Yoto and I were sipping on our brandy while we were playing our cards. The dealer was a real mechanic. If he worked like this in Las Vegas he'd take a one way trip to the desert. Some people think that the games in the casinos are rigged. They're wrong. With the odds of the games leaning towards the House, they don't have to cheat. The longer you play the better chance they have to win. I signaled Yoto what was going on and he watched more closely for the next few hands. We lost over 80 percent of the hands we played. We got up and headed towards the lounge area. We sat down on a nice comfortable couch and relaxed. We talked for about 5 minutes when Winky came walking our way. He had someone in tow. As he came upon us Yoto and I rose from the couch.

"Larry Towers and Yoto, may I present your host and manager, James Hawthorn?" We shook hands as we were introduced.

"Please call me Jim."

"Thank you Jim. You have a beautiful place here."

"But you don't enjoy losing."

"One thing I learned when I was young Jim, never play a game when someone else controls it."

"Winky, I think your friend is a sore loser."

"Jim!"

"That's all right Winky. I'm not here to insult your friend."

"Then you're serious, aren't you?"

"Let me ask you a couple of questions and I'll tell you how serious I am."

"That sounds fair."

"One, did you notice the Blackjack table we were playing on?"

"Yes I did."

"Two, do you use shills here?"

"No we don't."

"Three, Do you use mechanics to do your dealing?"

"The odds are in our favor. We don't have to."

"Then you have a small internal problem."

"Which is?"

"The blonde sitting in the seventh chair."

"I've seen her here a few times."

"He's feeding her large winning hands and everyone else more losers than winners. That's how he's keeping his daily figures up."

"I can't believe it. Are you sure?"

"Yoto?"

"I'm sure."

"I've noticed your camera system. It's a good one. If we could take a look at the tape of his table while we were there .I'll show you how he was doing it. As a matter of fact, in your position, with your knowledge I won't have to show you, you'll see it."

"Gentlemen, let's go for a walk. I'll take you on a tour of my establishment. I think you know where we'll end up."

I said, "Sounds like fun to me."

We took our walk around the casino and ended up in the main control room. There were two fellows watching a number of screens. Jim explained quietly to the older man what we needed. The old man then went about preparing it for us. While we were waiting Yoto and I were watching the surveillance cameras. I leaned over to Yoto and whispered in his ear, "Brunette in the blue dress on camera 8. Watch her."

He nodded his head.

I spoke quietly, "Jim, how much cash do you usually have on hand here?"

"That depends on who is going to be here."

"Could you explain?"

"Well, for example, we have a couple of sheiks that come to town a couple of times a year. They refuse to deal in checks. So we make it a point to have over two million pounds on hand."

"How much money do they bring to gamble with?"

"We allow them a million pounds a piece."

"So when they're here you have close to seven million dollars American here?"

"With today's conversion, close to that."

"Phew! That makes for one large payday."

"Only if they win Larry."

Winky interjected, "I don't think that's what Larry was referring to."

"You're right Winky."

"Hold on! You two are way over my head!"

"Larry."

"Yes Winky. I'll explain it to Jim. Please answer all my questions truthfully."

"I will Larry."

"Let's move over by the door so we don't bother your men working." As quietly as we were speaking they couldn't hear us, but I wanted to make sure. Actually I didn't trust the young man at the screens. There was something about him that didn't fit. "Jim, can you get me a picture of the young man working the screens? And grab his drink glass on our way out. Get both of the glasses so it doesn't look suspicious. Can you do that Jim?"

"Yes Larry. I don't know why but I will."

"The sheiks you were talking about will be here Thursday or Friday. Correct?"

"How did you know?"

"We'll get to that later. Do you also pay their expenses while they're here?"

"We supply them with some of their entertainment. Their entourage is too large for us to cover all their expenses."

"Let me narrow it down for you. Do you supply hookers for them?"

"We prefer to call them 'Ladies of the Night'."

"I don't care what you call them. Do you supply them?"

"Yes we do."

"How long will the sheiks be here?"

"They will be here Thursday night and Friday night."

"When they come in Thursday night do they bring their cash with them?"

"Yes they do. Their security is far better than mine."

"You take their money and give them a receipt for it?"

"Yes we do."

"That means you are responsible for it?"

"Yes we are."

"Do me a favor. Is your head of security working tonight?"

"Not usually. But he came in tonight after Dick called and said you would be here. He'd very much like to meet you."

"Where is he now?"

"He has a small office on the other side of the casino."

"We don't want to disturb anyone so I think it would be a great idea to send your young man over to get your head of security."

"I understand Larry."

He walked over to the young man and told him to nonchalantly walk over to the head of security office and ask him to join me here. If he's not in his office, find him and send him here. Then take your break that way you won't be seen walking back here together.

"I understand Sir. I'll take care of it."

He got up and left the room.

We walked back over to the screens. Jim quickly told Mr. Lenther who we were.

Jim said, "Mr. Lenther has been with me for fifteen years and I trust him."

I said, "What do you think of your partner?"

"To be honest Sir, he's a strange bird. I can't put my finger on it, but I don't trust him."

"We don't either. I want everyone to check cameras number 9 and 10. See the lady in the blue dress. Watch her for a minute and tell me what you see."

"She's good looking."

"Thanks Winky."

"She uses a lot of lipstick."

"That's right Mr. Lenther. She either has a lip problem or she's photographing the whole place with a lipstick tube camera."

"By George! I think you're correct."

"By George! I know I'm correct Jim. Now you need to call in an order of brandies for us and whatever else you need for Mr. Lenther and yourself. Mr. Lenther, could I have your drink glass?" He handed it to me. I carefully picked up the young man's glass from the counter and emptied the small amount of liquid in it into Mr. Lenther's glass. I pulled a clean hanky out of my back pocket and gently wrapped the glass in it. "Now all we need is a way to get this glass out of here without raising any suspicions."

"Sir, we could put it in my lunchbox. I get off shift in about an hour."

I said, "Great idea Mr. Lenther. Our limo is in the parking lot. Could you drop it off there?"

"Yes Sir. I'd be happy too."

Jim said, "I'll slip you a photo later. I'll get it from personnel."

"Thanks Jim."

Yoto said, "Larry!! Look!!"

As we looked back at the screen we saw our young fellow nod to our girl taking the pictures as he walked by her.

"I wasn't 100 percent sure until I saw that."

"Well Jim, you were the only one that wasn't. Now you better order our drinks."

As Jim was returning from the phone his head of security entered the room. "You sent for me Mr. Hawthorn?"

"Yes I did."

He then introduced him around the room. He seemed thrilled. He started to ask questions thinking he was asked here by his boss to meet us.

I spoke, "Mr. Gunther."

"Please call me Charles."

"All right Charles. We have a large problem to tell you about and only a short time to do it. So please hold all your questions until we're alone later."

I explained everything to him. I told him about the card mechanic and the major heist set for later in the week. He was a man in his forties, but he showed his astonishment like a youngster which to me was refreshing. By the time our young lad returned from his break we were getting the copy of the tape that had the card mechanic on it and were leaving. As we were leaving I heard the boy ask Mr. Lenther where his drink glass had gone to. He told him the boss had drinks brought in and the girl must have taken his glass thinking it was empty. He said it was all right, he'd order another one.

We returned to the casino floor and located the girls. I couldn't believe it…they were actually winning. We left them to their fun and retired to the lounge where our new friends were waiting for us.

Jim handed Winky the picture I had asked him for. Winky slid it into his inside jacket pocket.

"Did you have time to look at the tape?"

"Not all of it Larry, but enough to know that what you said was correct."

"How will you handle the situation?"

"I can't really answer that in front of Dick, he may be a friend, but he still works for Scotland Yard."

"Winky, can we go off the record?"

"You have my word Larry."

"Now will you answer the question for me?"

"We do the policing of the business ourselves. We never call for outside help. We will take the dealer out of town and break his arms, hands and fingers. Of course that's only after we beat on him for a while. We'll allow his girlfriend to watch. Seeing she bet with her hands and pulled her winnings in with her fingers, we'll break them. I know you probably think we're very barbaric in our actions but if we're to run a clean ship we have to be."

"Jim, I'll tell you a secret. In Las Vegas they'd give him a one way trip to the desert."

"You Americans are always trying to outdo us Brits."

We laughed.

"Now I'll tell you why I asked. The robbery of your place this weekend will be called the 'Ironic Robbery'."

Charles said, "I don't know about my boss, but I'd sure like to know why."

"Because if I'm seeing this whole operation correctly the crooks are using your money to finance their operation."

"Are you trying to tell me the dealer is also a part of this operation?"

"That's the way I see it Jim."

"I'm lost again."

Winky said, "Don't feel bad Jim, Larry does that to everyone when they first meet him."

Yoto added, "Winky's right Jim."

I said, "Thanks guys for explaining me."

Charles asked, "Could you give us some idea of what we're missing?"

"Sure Charles, if Jim will get us another brandy."

Jim caught the eye of the waitress and got up to meet her. He quietly gave her our order and then returned to the table.

"Did I miss anything?"

"Nope, I'm just about to start. In order to do this right I need to start at the beginning. The surveillance room."

Charles said, "Don't tell me there's something wrong in there."

At that point we all stopped talking while the cocktail waitress dropped off our drinks. When she left I started to continue when Winky interrupted me.

"Sorry Larry. I need to explain something to Jim and Charles. Larry isn't here to criticize any one. He's only here to point out what's wrong. When something is wrong you admit it then you can do what is necessary to correct it. I know it's a simple philosophy but it works."

"We'll be happy to follow it Dick."

"Thanks Jim. Now I give the floor back to Larry."

"Thank you Winky. Now the two people you have in the room. After examining the screens I would say that 70% of the casino action is on the screens to the right. Yet your experienced operator was watching the left side of the screens. I'm sure that if you talk to Mr. Lenther he'll give you a legitimate reason for the switch."

"He's not a suspect?"

"No Charles, he's not. Now think for a minute, gentlemen. The cameras on the right covered the area where the crooked dealer was dealing cards and strangely enough no one sees a thing. Why? Because they're working together. If they weren't our young lad would have turned in the dealer."

"So they are working together?"

"You're a hard man to convince Jim. So let me continue. A normal situation of theft with a dealer is done for one of two reasons. One, he's in love. I've watched them and if they're in love, I'm in love with that post over there."

"I believe you Larry. That post isn't your type."

Everyone laughed.

"Thanks Winky. Next time I want a date with a post I'll call you to pick it out for me."

Charles came back with. "After seeing some of the dates he's brought in here now I know where his real expertise falls."

"Thanks Charles. I'll get even with you for that."

We were still laughing.

Jim said, "Shouldn't we get back to the problem at hand?"

I answered him, "We will in a minute Jim."

I figured a little laughing and carrying on would only make this look like a normal conversation. So when the laughter finished I continued my explanation.

"Back to work gentlemen, if it's not love then its personal gain. But if you look at our perpetrators you'll see that's not the reason. He's wearing nothing fancy. The lady is wearing a dress she bought at a second hand store. I'm not sure of the rings on her hands, but I do know the string of pearls around her neck is a fake. Does anyone know who she's supposed to be?"

"Larry this is a members' only club, but as you've seen you had no trouble getting in with Dick."

"I noticed that. Your girl said 'Hi' to Winky and we just followed him in."

Charles spoke, "Which means if she watches outside for a group of four or more people she can just walk in with them."

I said, "That's the way I see it Charles. Then her dealer friend could supply her with the name of someone who had already left the club in case someone asked her who she was with. She'd give his name and say that he had to leave early, but told her to stay and have a good time. I'm sure if she told either one of you that story you'd believe it and tell her to enjoy herself."

"You're right Larry," said Jim.

"What gave her clothes away Larry?"

"Charles if you look at the side seams and the bottom hem you'll see where it's been sewn and not by a seamstress. If you're wealthy and lose weight you take your clothes to a professional seamstress or you buy new clothes. She did the job at home by hand."

"Her necklace?"

"Jim, when I was younger I learned that expensive pearls are strung with a knot between each pearl. Also the back catch has a safety chain. Hers has neither."

"Dick your friend is everything you billed him to be."

Jim said, "I agree with you Charles."

Winky added, "We all do Jim."

"Winky enough from you and your friends, I'm just doing the best I can."

"And we all think that's fantastic."

"Thank you Jim."

Charles asked, "Larry, what's our next step?"

"It's time we call in the professionals Charles."

Jim asked, "Dick and his people?"

"Yes Jim. This is no longer an internal situation. Its way above what your security can handle."

"I agree with you Larry. Dick, I need your help."

"And my help you'll get Jim. I'll get a hold of my boys in the morning and we'll figure out what we need to do or….."

Jim said, "Or what?"

"Or I'll ask Larry when they're going to strike."

Charles said, "He's good Dick but nobody's that good."

"I've got 50 pounds that says Larry can tell us Charles."

"I'll take that….."

I said, "Hold on Charles." Yoto and I were laughing as I was speaking. "Save your money Charles."

Charles had a shocked look on his face and Winky was complaining as he was laughing.

"Larry, you're no fun. I could use the money."

"Didn't I make you 100 pounds today?"

"Yes you did."

"Then that's enough for one day."

"Yes Sir, I'll let it be."

Charles said, "You can tell us when they'll do the robbery?"

"With the brain trust sitting here any one of you can."

"I'm lost again Larry."

"All right Jim. We'll walk through it together. You told me earlier that the sheiks would be here Thursday and Friday, right?"

"Right."

"When they come in they have better security than you do, right?"

"Right."

"That eliminates Thursday night. Now let's look at Friday evening. When the evening is over does the sheiks' security come in to get them and their money?"

"No, they wait outside. Our men walk them out the door to their security."

"When do you open the safe to pay them?"

"The safe is on a time lock. It opens every morning at 2 A.M. At that time we take out what's needed if anything. Usually we put the funds in from all the boxes from the tables."

"Then what happens?"

"After we put all the funds in the vault we lock the counter and bookkeeper in the safe. The time lock opens again at 8 A.M."

"Well you've listened to yourself Jim. Now what do you know?"

"They're going to hit us sometime Friday night."

"Think Jim. Rehash what you've told us."

"What do you mean Larry? That the safe is open at 2 A.M.?"

"Isn't that the only time they'll have the best access to your money?"

"Come to think about it that would be the best time for a robbery."

Charles asked, "Why not one of the other times when the safe is open?"

"It's like this Charles. With all the traffic, people, and cops on the street during the day, this time makes more sense. They can have a 20 minute to half an hour head start before anyone knows what's happening."

Charles said, "God I'm glad I came in to meet you Larry."

"So am I Charles. It's been a real pleasure."

"I'm also glad that Dick brought you here tonight."

"So am I Jim. I got to meet you and enjoy your hospitality."

"It blows my mind."

"What's that Jim?"

"How you can sit here so calmly after solving a crime and saving us millions of pounds."

"You're watching many years of training. I really don't get excited anymore. I get satisfaction. Charles I did want to ask you one thing."

"Anything Larry."

"Do you have enough information on the robbery?"

"Don't tell me there's more!?"

"Just a few things."

Jim said, "Would you tell us Larry?"

"Sure Jim, I thought you'd never ask."

We all laughed.

"Larry always likes to add a little humor to the situation."

"So I do Winky. So I do. A little fun is good for you."

"What else can you tell us Larry?"

"Jim I always work with the 5 W's. We already know 'When', Friday night at 2 A.M. 'Where', here. 'What', casino robbery. 'Why', for a large profit. So if everyone agrees with me the 'W' left is 'Who'. All right. 'Who'; we know three of the team, but we don't know the other two."

"I'm sleeping again!"

"I'm glad of one thing Jim you're man enough to keep admitting it."

Jim then asked, "How do you know there are two more people?"

"Let's pretend we're all mastermind crooks."

Yoto said, "This is the part I like."

Winky came back with, "Yoto, you have to have a mind before you can be a master of it."

I said, "Cute Winky, real cute."

We all laughed.

"If my guys are done funning we'll get down to business. Before I can answer your question Jim, I'll need to ask some. Remember, you're the mastermind. Why wouldn't you have ten people to help you?"

"Wouldn't that go down to shares Larry?"

"That's right Charles. No one in their right mind would do this job for a half a million pounds or less."

"But they would for a million quid."

"That's right Winky."

Jim added, "Around 5 million pounds gives you 5 people."

"Very good Jim. You're not sleeping anymore. Now you know where the first three are, where do we find the last two?"

"What about a driver for the get-away?"

"Good thinking Yoto. Let's put him aside for a minute and work on the other person."

Charles said, "I know this is crazy but I'd like a man inside my security team."

"What's crazy about it?"

"It can't be. Except for the new lad everyone has been with me for at least three years."

"Are you the crook Charles?"

"Are you kidding me Larry?"

"Just answer the question, yes or no."

"No I'm not."

"Thank you. I knew you weren't but it was my duty to check you out."

"I understand Larry and I'll work with Dick on checking everyone else out."

"Who knows I could be wrong."

"In that case no one will be the wiser, because they won't even know we checked them out."

"I agree Charles, now, our driver."

"He'll park out front."

"Would you park out there Jim, knowing the sheiks' security is waiting for you?"

"You're right Larry, I wouldn't. What about the alley?"

"I've noticed your exits. It's not easy to reach the alley from up here on the second floor. Plus the alley is too restricted. They could easily be bottled up there."

"Great. They can't go out the front and they can't go out the back. The only thing left for them to do is to sprout wings and fly out of here."

"That's a good calculation Jim. That's exactly what they'll do."

"Huh!?"

"Do you have a helicopter pad on the roof?"

"No. We rarely need one. We borrow the one next door."

"Is that building lower than yours?"

"Yes. Two stories lower."

"They couldn't have planned it better. They'll hook up a rope or steel line from your roof to the helio pad. Now all they have to do is take the elevator to the roof and slide down the line to the helio pad and off they go."

"Then they will sprout wings and fly!?"

"That's what you said Jim."

"Yes but I didn't mean it."

"Every bit of information helps when you're solving a crime."

Everyone laughed.

Jim said, "I have to admit it is funny."

"I'm glad to see you're more relaxed about it."

"Larry is there anything else you can tell us?"

"Well Charles, you're probably already aware of it, but I'll say it anyway. You're security person has to be scheduled to work Friday evening."

"Yes, I thought of that."

"Also think of this; it's easy for your people to switch shifts, so check everyone out. The person who has the most personal problems should be our person. Only time will tell."

"I'll keep an open mind Larry."

"Now I'd like to do some serious gambling on your craps table."

"Larry, I want you and Yoto to have a good time."

"Thank you Jim. We'll see you later."

We got up and left.

"Yoto, should we check on the girls?"

"Good idea Larry."

By the time we found them they were ready for a break. We took them to the ladies lounge so they could wash their hands and freshen up. For some reason coins make your hands very dirty.

Pretty soon they came out smiling and happy.

"You know Yoto we're blessed to have such wonderful women."

"Yes we are."

"Before we go any further I have a question."

"What is it Lyn-Yhi?"

"Is it customary in England for a lady to have three men's wallets in her handbag?"

"No. Why do you ask?"

"Because the lady in the lounge at the sink next to me had them in her handbag."

"Is she wearing a blue dress?"

"Yes Larry."

"Yoto! As fast as you can find Winky!"

As he turned to leave we saw Winky walking toward us. We hurried toward him. I quickly explained the situation.

"Winky. If it's our lady you'll have to become a purse snatcher. If not when she goes outside arrest her. After your boys leave with her give the wallets to Jim. He can quietly return them to their rightful owners."

Lyn-Yhi said, "Larry, there she goes now!"

"Different lady Winky."

"I know. I'll take her outside."

He left and we headed for the craps table. I used to throw a mean set of dice, and tonight was no exception. By the time Winky and Jim joined us I was about one thousand pounds ahead and so was Yoto.

"You keep this up and I'll be broke in no time."

"In that case, Jim, Yoto and I had better cash our chips in."

"You know I was only joking."

"I know Jim. But it's after one and about time we called it a night."

The play on the table had stopped momentarily between shooters. Jim motioned to his people to cash us in.

Jim said, "While they're doing that will you join me for a night cap?"

"We'd be happy to."

When we got to the lounge area we introduced the girls to Jim.

After ordering our drinks, Jim had the floor. "Larry, I want to thank you for turning Dick onto the pickpocket."

"I only relayed the message. Lyn-Yhi was the one who spotted the crime."

"It seems I owe you my thanks, Lyn-Yhi."

"You are welcome Sir. It seems being around these folks, crime fighting rubs off on you."

"Well keep up the good work."

"I will Sir."

It wasn't long before we had our money. We finished our drinks and were on our way. By the time we got to bed it was after two. I told Yoto that we would meet them in the hotel restaurant for brunch at eleven.

We spent Tuesday and Wednesday resting and sight-seeing. We had a limo at our disposal which made doing things a lot easier. It was nice to do things without a schedule or worrying about someone getting killed. It was great to just relax. That's what we did until 7:45 Thursday evening when Winky picked us up for a special dinner in my honor. The reason I was in London.

On the way to the limo Winky was being Winky, talking a lot about nothing. Right away it told me he was nervous.

"Relax Winky. I won't embarrass you."

"I know Larry. I'll be okay."

We arrived at a very nice restaurant where everyone, like us, was dressed in very fancy clothes. We were escorted to a private room away from the main dining room. Upon our entering the room five gentlemen got to their feet.

"Larry, before I introduce everyone to you, I have something to tell you."

"Is it the fact that there really isn't an award? That the people here are friends of yours trying to help you continue this charade?"

"When did you figure it out?"

"When the F.B.I. gave me the letter from the President's office."

"Was there something wrong with it?"

"Over the years I've gotten more than one letter from a President and none of them were like this one. Now why don't you introduce us to your friends then we'll sit down and I'll answer all of your questions."

After we were seated, Winky continued, "Then why did you come?"

"A lot of reasons. One, for so many people to love me so much that they'd go to all this trouble for my benefit is something you can't say no to. Second, everything there is under control. I work with too many competent people for it to be anything else. Third, Lynda and Lyn-Yhi both needed a vacation. I could continue but I think you get the point."

"Yes I did and I know of hundreds of people who are happy you made this trip."

"I know one person who wasn't happy to see us."

"That's impossible! Who could that be?"

"Your boss. He's a hundred pounds lighter!"

Everyone started to laugh.

Over the laughter Winky said, "You're right about that."

After a lovely dinner we retired to another lovely room to have our brandy. The furniture setting was more like a living room than a restaurant. It was very relaxing. The next couple of hours went well. Before we knew it Lynda and I were back in our hotel suite. We undressed, curled up in one another's arms and had a wonderful night together.

I woke up before Lynda and made a call to Winky. I asked him to join us for brunch.

We walked into the restaurant at eleven o'clock. Yoto, Lyn-Yhi and Winky were waiting for us. We said our 'good mornings' and took our seats. After we ordered brunch we all sat very quietly like something was going to happen.

Winky broke the ice. 'You know I can tell by looking at your eyes Larry, it's really eating at you, isn't it?"

"You know I'm on vacation."

"You've never had a vacation in your life!"

"I think I've missed something."

Lyn-Yhi said, "Me too."

I said, "Girls, it's nothing serious."

Winky said, "Don't tell me that you and Yoto haven't mentioned it to the girls."

"We didn't want to ruin their vacation."

Lynda came back with, "I wish somebody would bring us up to speed."

I said, "All right Lynda. There's going to be a multi-million pound robbery tonight at the casino. I'll fill in the details later. Now Winky, do your people want our help?"

"I convinced them that too many of our people may scare off the crooks."

"Yoto! We're in!"

"That's great Larry!"

Lyn-Yhi said, "I can't believe you people!"

"Not many people can Lyn-Yhi. We just hate injustice and fight it wherever we find it."

Winky said, "Well Larry, the way this is coming down is strange."

"What do you mean?"

"We don't have a pilot or a chopper. We only have a 'maybe' on an inside security man."

"You think we'll have egg on our face?"

"No Larry. Your instincts have saved my life more than once. I'd bet the farm on tonight."

"In that case, why don't we meet for supper? My treat."

"What time?"

"Nine o'clock?"

"I'll have everything in place by nine. I'll pick you up."

"Sounds good."

"I'll also pay for dinner."

"Wait a minute! I haven't paid for a thing since I've been here!!"

"And if you do I'll probably lose my job."

"What do you mean?"

"Scotland Yard said to give you the key to the city. The airlines owe you over two hundred lives. They said you are not to spend a dime while you are here. Jim at the casino wants to pay all of your expenses. The Mayor in the city of Pertsville wants to pay all of your expenses. Are you getting the picture of the kind of pressure I'm under!?"

We laughed.

"Yes Winky, and I'm sorry. We didn't expect anything from anyone. We were just doing our job."

"Everyone knows that Larry, that's why they want this to be a special vacation for you."

"Okay. We'll stop trying to spend our own money. Now are you happy?"

"Yes I am. Now I need to get out of here. I have a lot to get done before tonight."

"All right, we'll see you at nine. One last thing, check your chopper rentals for an eight-seater."

He said, "I will," as he walked away from our table.

"If what he says is true, Lyn-Yhi and I will spend the afternoon shopping. Let's see a diamond necklace and bracelet would be nice."

Lyn-Yhi said, "I like that idea Lynda."

"Girls, I don't think that's what Winky had in mind."

They both said, "Boo, on Larry," together.

We all laughed.

I signed the brunch check and we headed for our rooms to freshen up. Then I called for our limo. I picked up the phone and asked Yoto to join us. I hung up the phone and walked to our door and opened it. As I walked away from the door I could swear I could hear a female crying.

"Lynda!"

She arrived at my side in double time.

"What's wrong?"

"Listen and tell me what you hear."

All of a sudden we heard more sounds.

"It's a woman being beaten and her room is across the hall."

"I'm not even sure she's a woman."

Yoto appeared in our doorway with Lyn-Yhi on his arm.

"What do you two think?"

Yoto spoke, "We heard it as we got close to your door. The bedroom of the suite across the hall must be opposite your door."

I said, "I hate to delay our shopping trip but I think we ought to investigate what's happening across the way."

Yoto said, "I agree Larry."

I said, "Lyn-Yhi, go inside and call the desk and have them send some bobbies up here. We are going to talk to our neighbors."

As we walked down the hallway we could see two heavy set lads guarding the door. We were walking three abreast, which barely left air room between us and the walls in the hall. Yoto was on my left and Lynda was on my right furthest away from the men. I whispered to Yoto, "One." This told him the first person we come to is his. As we got even with the first guy Yoto stumbled into him. He said, "Excuse me." As he supposedly straightened himself up as well as the man he stumbled into, he hit the man. It was a short but forceful hit with the palm of his hand to the man's solar plexus. The man leaned forward gasping for air. Yoto then hit him between the eyes with a closed fist jab. The man fell to the floor like a ton of bricks. While this was going on the other man turned toward his friend and said, "What the hell's going on here?" The way he turned his body gave me a perfect angle for a frontal kick to the groin. The man doubled over, so I knee kicked him to the face. He returned to an upright position and hit the wall and slid to the floor in a heap. I held Lynda by her arm and looked over at Yoto. He'd stopped in his tracks the minute I did. I pointed to my eyes and Yoto knew that I wanted him to check out the suite. Lynda and I waited a few seconds and then entered the suite. Yoto was standing over a man who was slumped over the couch. We all turned toward and headed straight to the master bedroom. As Lynda reached for the door I stopped her. It had gotten quiet inside.

"Now you're a bad little girl and I'll have to spank you some more."

"You said you'd buy me a dolly and take me to a movie and then you'd take me home."

"So I lied little girl. You want a dolly to play with? I have one right here to play with."

"I won't touch you there and I don't care how much you beat me."

"You better do as the nice man says honey."

"He's not a nice man and I'm not your honey."

"You're right, I'm not nice and you'll learn to do as you're told."

I motioned to Lynda and Yoto, two fingers. They understood. I whispered to Lynda, "You get the woman."

She nodded.

Then I whispered to Yoto, "Open a window."

I slowly opened the bedroom door.

"Who's there?!" came a voice from inside.

I swung open the door, stepped into the doorway and spoke, "Your worst nightmare."

As I spoke I looked around the room. There were three people. A man to my left, an eight to ten year old girl in the middle of the room, and a woman to my right. They were all stark naked.

"That's what you think" came out of the man's mouth. He moved toward the dresser where his gun was laying. He picked it up with his right hand and pointed it in my direction. In doing so he moved his body around giving me a full view of his chest. I reached in my sleeve and pulled out and threw my sleeve knife all in one motion. I hit my target. The knife went deep into his right shoulder. The pain was too much for him. He dropped his gun and grabbed his shoulder. Blood was running all over the place as I approached him. I grabbed his hands and pulled them away from my knife. Next, I grabbed my knife with my left hand and twisted it. He fell to his knees crying out in pain. Meanwhile, Lynda and Yoto had taken care of their tasks.

"Get up on your feet!" I instructed him as I pulled up on my knife.

He was screaming with pain, so I helped him up. I grabbed what hair he had left on his head and lifted him to his feet.

"Aaagghhh! Stop! You're killing me!!"

I started to move him in the direction of the open window.

It's funny how scumbags can dish out pain but they can't take it themselves.

I heard noise come from outside the room. "Yoto!"

He left the room to stop the bobbies.

Lynda had her woman pressed up against the wall. The little girl had scooted herself up to the head of the bed. She had a pillow between her legs and was holding it against the front of her body.

When I had the man about three steps from the open window the woman yelled.

"Walt! I've opened the window! Jump out to the fire escape and get away!"

As he turned I pulled my knife out of his shoulder. He took two steps and dove out the window. As we all knew....there was no fire escape. We now had one dead, naked pervert down on the pavement.

I said, "You must have really hated him!"

"I was about her age when he kidnapped me. That was 16 years ago. I swore when the time came I would kill him for all the lives he's ruined. He was one of the biggest white-slave slavers in Europe."

"Let her go Lynda. I don't think she'll go anywhere."

"I won't."

"I bet you could fill Scotland Yard in on his whole operation couldn't you?"

"Not only could I, but I'd be happy too."

"I'm glad to hear that. Lynda, help the little girl get dressed. Ma'am you'd better put some clothes on as well. When you're dressed I want the three of you to join us in the sitting room."

I walked out of the bedroom and introduced myself to the bobbies. I explained that a crazy man had jumped out of his bedroom window. I then picked up the telephone and called Scotland Yard. When I got Winky on the phone I asked him to tell the officers to do as I tell them, and to speak to no one about what has happened here. I handed the bobbie the phone. After listening for a short time the bobbie handed me back the phone. I held the phone in my hand as I explained to the bobbies what I wanted them to do. As I was doing this, two more bobbie arrived.

"Cuff this guy and his two friends out in the hall. Put them in the extra bedroom and two of you stand guard over them until the Yard gets here. I want the other two of you to go down stairs. Make sure the body is covered completely. No photos by anyone. If you think someone has taken a picture confiscate the camera, if the person resists, arrest him."

They said, "Yes Sir," and left.

After they left I looked at Yoto. He was standing calmly waiting for his next order. Lyn-Yhi was standing next to him shaking her head.

I put the phone to my ear, "Sorry I kept you Winky."

"That's all right Larry. I hate to ask, but what have you gotten me into now?"

"I'd rather tell you in person. How's your timetable?"

"We're all set here. I can be there in half an hour."

"Sounds good. Bring some people with you that you can trust."

"How many?"

"Well, we have one dead, naked man in the street and three prisoners."

"How is it I knew you'd say something like that?"

"What can I say? I have trouble minding my own business."

"Larry, that's the biggest understatement I've ever heard!"

We started laughing.

"Could you hurry? The girls want to go shopping."

"All right, Larry," was his reply as he started laughing again.

I hung up the phone and looked at Lyn-Yhi. The bobbies, with Yoto's help were done with their work and tucked away in the spare bedroom with the prisoners.

I said, "What's the matter Lyn-Yhi? Too much excitement for you?"

"After everything you've done for me, saving my life and everything, I'm just so happy I can be a part of helping you save other people."

"I'm glad you feel that way. Like I said before Yoto, we have two women that would be impossible to replace." At that moment Lynda walked through the door with the woman and the child. The little girl's eyes were still red and puffy from crying.

"Yoto! Tell our friends we'll be in our suite and to stay put until the Yard relieves them."

I figured a change of scenery would be good for the little girl. As we walked into my suite the little girl asked if she could go home. I explained that we were police officers and that she was safe. I asked the little girl if she was hungry. Before she had a chance to answer our new woman friend answered for her.

"She ought to be. Part of the plan is no food, drink, or sleep until he breaks your spirit."

"The belt?"

"Torture makes the process go faster."

"Yeah, pain has a way of doing that."

I had Lynda call and order a bunch of different items. I figured whatever we didn't eat our guests would. They rushed the food up to us in record time. We were in the middle of eating when Winky knocked at the door. I opened the door and stepped out into the hallway. I quickly brought everyone up to date. Then I started giving orders.

"Whoops! I'm sorry Winky. I'm stepping on your toes."

"Not really Larry. I'm not in charge. My boss is."

"Sorry Sir."

"No problem. Continue what you're doing."

"The important part of this operation is that no one knows who died here today. Put him in the morgue as a 'John Doe', suicide victim. The three prisoners, keep them where no one can see or talk to them."

"Can I ask why all the secrecy Sir?"

"We have a person that spent the last 16 years with the dead scum bum, and she's biting at the bit to destroy his empire."

"I see Sir."

"I hope everyone does. Handled correctly we can put away a lot of scum and make this world just a little bit safer." I pointed to the two agents standing with us. "Now, I want you two downstairs. One of you can take care of the body, the other check on their room and what the hotel knows about it. You two take care of the prisoners in the suite across the hall. Winky, you and your boss can join me in my room. Whoever is taking care of checking out the hotel, when you've finished come back up here, I have another job for you." As the agents left I walked inside with Winky and his boss.

Winky introduced his boss to everyone. His boss's name was Simon Simons.

I was the last to shake hands with Simon. "I'm glad to meet you Simon."

"The pleasure's all mine Larry. When Dick first told me about you I thought he was on drugs. When he was done building you up I had but one thought, no one could possibly live up to that."

"Well……"

"Before you say anything I don't think he said enough. I'm proud to make your acquaintance. If ever you're in a situation like today don't hesitate to take charge."

"Thank you Sir. And thank you Winky. Now we better get to work. I'd like to get a nap before dinner tonight. Are you joining us at the club Simon?"

"Wouldn't miss it. Talking about that I have a surprise for you."

"What's that? I love surprises."

"You are in charge tonight."

"Wait a minute! That's too much."

"Are you being humble?"

"No, in order to run a battle successfully you need to know the strengths and the weaknesses of your forces and well as your enemies. I feel fairly comfortable with my enemy, but I don't know my own people."

"What about if Dick and I help you out?"

"What do you think Winky?"

"It'll be like old times Larry."

"Then I agree. Now we better get started."

Simon said, "Before we do I have one last question for you Larry."

"Please ask it, I'll answer it if I can."

"Why do you call Dick Winky?"

"That goes back to the war. It's only something that Winky can answer. It's not my place to do that."

"Now you really have my curiosity up."

"Larry."

"Yes Winky?"

"I feel close enough to Simon to tell him. Would you do it for me?"

"Sure. It's very simple. During the war we worked together, me, Winky, Yoto, and 18 other lads. We did special assignments together. Every one of the lads was a professional at different things. Winky and Yoto did almost the same thing. Winky was on the ground and Yoto covered the high places. Yoto can climb up a straight building wall."

"Then what was their specialty?"

"Your Dick Hollender has the ability to kill a man in the wink of an eye. So we called him Winky."

"God, I can't believe it!"

"It's true. But I wouldn't repeat it."

"I won't, honestly I won't."

"You see Simon, I didn't believe in taking prisoners, and I still don't today."

"So that's how Winky knew the hijackers would all be dead."

"That's right. We didn't feel the hijackers were selling church raffle tickets. They dealt in death and destruction so we returned to them what they gave to others."

"That you did Larry, and you cost me 100 pounds."

"So I did."

We all started to laugh.

After the laughter was over I had Lynda get the young girl out of our spare bedroom. I had left Lyn-Yhi in the bedroom to keep the girls company. Actually I sat Lyn-Yhi by the window to make sure no one left.

The little girl didn't have a lot to say. Between crying and mumbling we found out what had happened. She was bribed to go along with the nice couple in the limo. They had to stop at the hotel for some papers before going to the movies. When they got upstairs they took her into the bedroom. The man and woman got her out of her clothes. The man kept touching her in all the wrong places. She kept fighting him, so he started to beat her with his belt. Next thing she knew, we showed up. Now she wanted to go home. At that point our agents from downstairs had arrived back in my suite. I had Lynda return the little girl to the bedroom for a minute. I then asked our returning men for a report.

"I got the same story from the manager and the assistant manager."

"What was that?"

"You are not staying here."

"Could you make that a little clearer?"

"When Scotland Yard got the rooms for you the hotel was full. The hotel gave you suites that were being held for one of their larger clients. The client gets these suites because the four of them are very private. The trouble came when the client checked in. Both the managers were off the floor. There was a new person at the desk who is not aware of you being in two of the client's suites. So the clerk gave the client a key to his favorite suite and checked him in. That was only a few hours ago."

Yoto said, "Sounds like the Gods are at work again."

Winky added, "I agree."

I said, "So do I Winky. They do have a way of putting us in the right place at the right time."

Simon said, "I can't believe it! There are other people who believe in the Gods?"

Winky responded, "Not only do we believe in the Gods, Larry is the one who taught us about them. They've never let us down."

"Larry, can you explain them to me?"

"Someday soon Simon, I'll write a book about them."

"It would take that long to explain them?"

"Yes Simon, it would. Now it's time to get back to work. I'm sure we can rule out the hotel as an accessory after the fact. Is that all of your report?"

"Yes Sir."

"All right. Lynda, take the gentlemen into the bedroom and introduce them to the little girl. Then return out here with our other guest and Lyn-Yhi. Gentlemen, when the little girl feels safe and comfortable with you two, I'd like you to take her to the hospital and have her checked out. Then take her home."

"What about her parents?"

"She only has a mother. Explain to her what happened as vaguely as you can. No names, persons, or places."

"We understand Sir."

When our witness came out I introduced Sylvia to Winky and Simon. Simon took out a small tape recorder so he could record her statement.

"Before you start do you mind if I take Lynda, Yoto, and Lyn-Yhi shopping?"

"No Larry. Go right ahead."

"Thank you, we'll see you tonight. Lock up when you leave."

As we turned to go I heard, "Larry."

I turned, "Yes Simon?"

"I thought you'd want to hear this."

"I've heard the short version. That was sick enough. The powerful people involved here as well as other countries is too much for me to handle right now. If I had my way I'd set up a kill squad to eliminate these people. Reason being, is you'll never touch them using the normal channels of international law. So rather than being heart sickened by this case, I'd rather just avoid it."

"I understand and respect your position."

"At least we helped a little. There's a little girl in the next room who will go home tonight. That said we're out of here."

Chapter 8

We shopped and had a late lunch. I figured we'd have a late supper, about 10 o'clock. It was after six when we returned to our rooms. I asked Yoto to come by and get us at 9 P.M.
Lynda and I made love and then took a nap.
We were walking to the door, ready to leave when there was a knock. I opened the door and we were joined by Yoto and Lyn-Yhi.
We had a nice dinner and then headed to the casino. It was midnight when we arrived. The membership card that Jim had given me worked like a charm. As we walked upstairs to the casino I told everyone to keep their eyes open. The girls went to get change and Yoto and I went to the lounge area. The casino had changed since the first of the week. I had no idea of the kind of crowd this place commanded on a Friday night. There were people everywhere.
We sat down in the lounge and I said to Yoto, "This is going to be harder than I expected."
"I agree Larry. With the crowd he has here you'd think he was giving something away."
When the waitress appeared I ordered four brandies and gave her my membership card. After she left Yoto said, "Boy, are you thirsty!"
We chuckled.
When the girl returned she placed the drinks around the table. Then she handed me back my membership card. I thanked her and took a sip of my drink. Yoto did the same. By the time we returned our glasses to the table Winky came up and took a seat. He had no sooner gotten comfortable when Simon came up and joined us.
Simon's first comment was, "What's in the glass?"
"It's called brandy Simon."
"Alcohol and work do not mix."
"Simon, I'll have to argue that point with you."
Yoto and Winky started to laugh.
"Does that mean I don't bet any money on this?"
As we were laughing I said, "That's right."
"Could you enlighten me Larry?"
"Sure Simon. One ounce of alcohol works as a stimulant to the body. When you exceed an ounce it works as a depressant. I did a

research paper on the subject when I was in college."

"If that be the case I'll enjoy my brandy."

I said, "While everyone's doing that will someone fill me in on our situation?"

Winky nodded at Simon. "Larry, you have twenty men and women mingling in the crowd now, or they will be by 1:30 A.M."

"That sounds good. What about outside?"

"Snipers at every conceivable angle. We also have two men hidden on this roof and one with the chopper."

"Are they concealed well?"

"Larry, I couldn't find them in broad daylight."

"I like the sound of that. It's now time to look at the inside."

"Ask away Larry."

"I will Simon. Who knows what is coming down tonight?"

"Besides our people?"

"That's right."

"The manager, his head of security, and the old man watching the surveillance screens."

"That's it?"

"Yes Sir."

"What about the bad guys?"

"I didn't think of them."

"Would you do that now?"

Yoto and Winky were smiling. Simon said, "You two are really enjoying this aren't you?"

I said, "Tell him Winky."

"We've all been there. You're talking to the best. Don't try to outthink him. Just try to flow with him."

"I guess it would be easier that way."

"You noticed they didn't say to stop thinking? Just flow with my thinking."

"I understand Larry. You ask and I'll answer."

"Back to the bad guys."

"The sheiks got here about ten and guess who two of the hookers happen to be?"

"Did Winky identify them?"

"Yes I did Larry, the same two women who were here earlier in the week."

"Who else is here?"

"Our young lad at the surveillance screen and the blackjack dealer."

"What'd you find out about the security people who work here?"

"There are two lads who were hired almost three years ago. They're so far in debt that it's scary. They were hired within a month of one another and they've become good friends."

"Are they working tonight?"

"Believe it or not, they switched shifts with two other guys so they could be here tonight."

"Do they have any lady friends?"

"One of them goes with a lady who works in the counting room."

"Don't tell me! She switched shifts to be here tonight."

"Yes she did Larry."

"I was afraid of that."

"What Larry?"

"Simon, it's bigger than I thought."

"What do you mean?"

"Not only are they going to rob the club, but they are also going to rob the patrons."

"Why do you think so?"

"The number of players is getting too large. When we had 5 or 6 players it would be a snatch and run. Now with more players they need more money. They have a large enough chopper to take everything of value including hostages."

"Do we have enough people inside?"

"See if I have the count right Simon. Ten men, ten women, Jim the manager, Charles the head of security, you, Winky….."

"Winky and I are part of the ten men."

"All right. Then your twenty, the house's two and my four. That's 26. More than enough if deployed correctly."

"I'd better let my people know what's happening."

"In a minute Simon. Winky did you get the medicine for Mr. Lenther?"

"Yes Larry. He'll take it at 1:30 A.M. and in about five minutes he'll start throwing up. He'll then go home sick leaving the young lad to run the whole operation. It's a lot of surveillance screens to watch but I know the lad will be happy to do it."

"He will make things a bit sticky Larry."

"Not really Simon. A quarter to two the meanest, toughest, biggest, agent you have here will go into the surveillance room and work him over a bit. He'll then put a knife to his throat and have him tell his people that everything is okay."

"Keep in mind, once things start to go down, all the crooks will be wired. Is that also your thinking Larry?"

"Yes it is, Simon. I really have a strange feeling that we're missing something."

"If it's Charles and me, we're here."

I said, "Pull up a chair and join us. It's good to see you again."

"We're not interrupting are we?"

"Not at all Jim, I was just handing out assignments."

"Do we get one?"

"That's up to you. There will be shooting and people will get killed. Is your job worth that?"

"Larry, no one knows this, and I prefer it stays at this table. Not only am I the manager but I also own part of the club. So you can count me in."

"Charles?"

"This is what I was hired for, and I'm being paid far too much money for what I'm doing. So Larry, it's about time I earned my keep. Count me in."

"Just so you boys know I hadn't figured it any other way."

They both smiled at me.

"Now Jim, you need to write down the security combination for the surveillance room and give it to Simon. I'm sorry does everyone know everyone at the table?"

They all nodded their heads in the affirmative.

"Good, then I'll continue. Jim, have you talked to the sheiks tonight?"

"Not as much as I'd like to. For some reason we're overly busy."

"Here's what I need you to do. Our two girls that were here earlier in the week are now playing hookers with the sheik's party."

Jim said, "I recognized them."

"Good. You need to get the sheiks alone for a couple of minutes. Explain to them what is happening tonight. Tell them that the girls are both armed and extremely dangerous. They need to keep an eye on both of them. At fourteen minutes to two his men need to disarm the girls without anyone knowing it."

"I can handle that. I usually give them a gift at the end of the evening. I'll do it a little early."

"That'll work. Next, Charles. There's a young lady in your counting room."

"I know who she is Larry."

"Good. Your job is to make sure she's out of the picture at fourteen minutes to two."

"It'll be done on schedule."

"Thanks Charles. Jim, when you finish with the sheiks I want you to find Simon."

"All right Larry."

"Patience let me finish."

"Sorry."

Everyone started laughing.

Jim and Charles looked at me. "Don't worry about it Jim. It's a personal joke."

"All right Larry."

"You guys knock it off. Let's stay focused."

They started laughing again. Once the laughter died down I continued.

"Jim, did you bankroll the operation tonight?"

"Yes Larry, I did."

"That's good. What I need you to do is make sure seven of Simon's people have enough money to keep them at our friend's blackjack table until 2:00 A.M."

"You want them at all seven spots Larry?"

"Yes I do. We should have plenty of time to get that handled."

"We'll take care of it Larry."

"Thank you Jim."

Simon asked, "Larry, aren't you wasting seven people on one dealer?"

"Simon, aren't all of your people wearing bullet proof vests?"

"Yes they are."

"I'd rather have one of them shot than a civilian."

"I agree."

"Let's continue. Jim, I know you're armed. Are you Charles?"

"Yes I am Larry. And both of us also have vests on."

"Great. That makes me feel better. Charles, do you have a special place you take cheaters and trouble makers?"

"Yes we do."

"This part's a little trickier. If it sounds too difficult we'll do something else."

Jim said, "Larry…."

I put my hand up for silence. Everyone started laughing again.

Charles said, "You have to let us in the joke."

Winky spoke, "When Larry speaks everyone listens until he's done."

"And Jim keeps interrupting and that's what's so funny?"

Winky said, "Yes Charles. That along with the fact Simon had just gone through the same experience."

"I'm sorry Larry."

"You don't have to be sorry Jim. You didn't know. What you don't know you can't do. I'm very military minded and I run my men like an army."

"Then from now on you speak and we'll listen."

"Thanks Jim, back to what I was trying to say. I was thinking of two of Simon's boys without weapons or protection would get into a fight about quarter to two. Jim, you make sure you and our two security boys are in position to stop the drunks and take them to your security room. The minute you close the door Jim you'll draw your weapon and cover the two guards. At that time Simon's boys will take over. Do you think you can handle it?"

"I'll have to have the drop on the boys for two to five seconds, right?"

"That's correct."

"I can do it."

"After the guards are disarmed we'll have two of our women folk shadow them so they can return to the floor so everything looks normal. Simon, you'll take care of that please."

"I'll get it done Larry. I'll coordinate the whole thing with Jim and my boys."

"Good. That takes care of everything inside that we know about."

Simon stated, "If you keep saying that Larry I'm going to start worrying."

"Simon, as sure as I'm sitting here there will be an X Factor involved."

"X as in the Mysterious Mr. X?"

"That's right Jim. Everybody needs to keep their eyes open and their wits about them. I think it's time for you boys to get busy. I'm going to stay here with Winky and Yoto."

They started to rise out of their seats. As I spoke they sat back down. "Before you leave remember these words, no matter what I tell you to do; you do it without question or thought. If you don't it could cost all of us our lives."

They nodded their heads to show me they understood.

After they left I asked, "What do you think boys?"

Yoto said, "I agree with you Larry. There's too much going on. The boys here haven't the brains to plan this."

"I agree with Yoto Larry."

"So do I Winky, so do I."

We sat in silence for a few minutes enjoying our brandy.

Yoto asked, "What do you think the girls are doing Larry?"

"That's a good question Yoto. Why don't you ask them? They're right behind you."

We all stood up as the girls approached the table. As we all sat down Lynda asked, "What'd we miss?"

"Almost everything is handled."

"I don't like the word 'almost'. Is there a reason for it?"

"Yes Lynda. We've decided there's a 'Mr. X'."

Lyn-Yhi asked, "What about a 'Ms. X'?"

"From the mouth of babes."

Yoto said, "I agree Larry. Lyn-Yhi, I love you."

"I love you too, Yoto. What brought that on?"

I said, "It's what you said Lyn-Yhi."

"I'm sorry Larry, I don't understand."

"We've had no luck finding a 'Mr. X'. But for some reason we've neglected to look for a 'Ms. X'. Winky, get out on the floor and make sure everyone is looking for a 'Mr. X' as well as a 'Ms. X'."

Winky got up and left.

"Well Lynda, how's your money holding out?"

"It seems we're losing back what we won the other night."

"Don't worry about it. Just have a good time."

"We're doing that, aren't we Lyn-Yhi?"

"Yes Lynda. I've never had such a good time in my life."

"I agree," said Yoto.

"All right, I agree with the three of you. Now it's time you girls go back to mingling and playing the machines. Yoto and I will go back to crime fighting."

"All right Larry. We can tell when we're not wanted."

"That day will never come, not even in jest."

"I know Larry, but we're going to leave anyway."

As they walked away I said, "It looks like we're alone again Yoto."

"We're going to have to stop meeting like this. People are going to start talking."

"Cute, real cute."

We both laughed.

When our laughing subsided I said, "Yoto, why don't you take a stroll around the place to make sure everything is all right? I have a feeling we may have to Walk Silent and Walk Deadly. Check around the exits and elevator and let me know if anything has been moved."

"I'm on it. Be back in a few minutes."

I sat there and enjoyed my brandy waiting for people to return. It was 1:30 A.M. when Jim sat down with me.

"The sheiks were delighted with our efficiency. They said they'd have no problem taking care of their situation. I also suggested that by 2 A.M. they should be playing the tables furthest from the cashiers' area."

"Good thinking. That will keep the women out of the action, and the sheiks and their party out of the line of fire."

"That's how I saw it. The blackjack table is handled with our people."

Simon walked up and sat down. "I take it Jim filled you in?"

"Yes he did, anything else happening?"

"We're ready inside and out."

"Then all we have to do is wait, and not very long."

"I better get back on the floor."

"Good idea Jim."

"Me too, Larry."

"All right Simon I'll see both of you around the area of the cashiers' cage about five to two."

They both left. A couple of minutes later Yoto and Winky returned.

"How's it look, Yoto?"

"Nothing's changed."

"Good. Winky?"

"Everyone has their eyes open."

"That's all we can ask for."

"Is there anything else we can do Larry?"

"Yes there is. Winky you can keep me company while Yoto finds the girls and brings them here."

They agreed and Yoto left. Charles walked over and quietly took a seat.

"I just saw Mr. Lenther leave the club."

"Everything else okay?"

"Yes. Talk to you later. I have to get to the counting room."

"Did you see Simon's man go into the surveillance room?"

"Yes I did."

"Thanks. See you later."

He left and Yoto returned and Winky left.

"How'd you girls do Lynda?"

"We gave the club back a few more pounds."

"That's why they call it gambling."

"We know that Larry. We can win or lose. It's just more fun to win."

"I agree with you Lyn-Yhi. It's now almost a quarter to two. I think it would be a good time for us to mingle around the crowd, ending up at the cashiers' cage."

That's just what we did. I noticed that as we were mingling toward the cahiers' cage the sheiks' entourage was heading in the opposite direction. I could see the two pretend hookers snuggly locked away in the center of their group. Everything seemed to be going as planned.

As we got close to the cashiers' cage I could see Jim having a discussion with a woman. By the looks of their hand and arm gestures it was not a loving talk.

"Winky. Who's the lady with Jim?"

Winky moved into a position so he could see the person I was asking about.

"It's Jim's ex-wife."

"What would she be doing here at almost 2 in the morning?"

"The only thing I know for sure about her is she's a weird duck."

"In what ways?"

"After Jim married her she got into drugs, wild parties, and running around with the seedier side of life."

"Jim's money enabled her to do this?"

"Yes it did. He took it for a little over a year then she took him through a miserable divorce. He offered her a nice allowance."

"Probably a lot more than you would have given her?"

"You got that right. I told him to give her nothing. And after the court battle so did the judge. Well, to say it mildly, she was one bitter woman. She told him she'd get even with him if it was the last thing she did."

"Do you have any idea what you just told me?"

"My God! Ms. X!!"

"Bet you a weeks' pay."

"I wonder if Jim knows."

"He working with emotion right now not intelligence."

"Is there a way we can warn him Larry?"

"Take another look. It's a little late for that. She just took her mink stole off her shoulder and has it over her right arm, wrist, and gun."

"Now what Larry?"

"Winky, go to the cashiers' window and have her call Charles. He's in the counting room behind the cashiers' area. Tell him to cooperate and give her whatever she wants. We'll deal with them outside. You'd better hurry she's starting to move."

Winky got to the counter and got on the phone. He was talking as Jim looked my way. I motioned for him to go into the room. He understood and cooperated with his ex-wife. As they cleared the door Winky hung up the phone.

In a few moments Jim, Charles, and two ladies with guns came out of the room. The boys were carrying large money bags in each hand. As they came toward the door out of the cage, we were waiting for them. When the door shut behind them and locked I knew we had them, so I took over the situation.

As I spoke they stopped in their tracks. "Ladies, I'm Larry Towers with Scotland Yard. You're completely surrounded. I'd suggest you lay down your weapons."

"Copper! We have the guns and you don't! Unless you want a lot of dead bodies around here I'd suggest you do as I tell you."

"And what might that be?"

"I understand you've captured all my men."

"That's right."

"I want the two security guards bought here immediately."

"Is there a reason I'll do this?"

"I'll give you one right now."

She turned her body a little to her left and pointed her gun at Charles' chest and pulled the trigger. When the bullet hit him in the chest he spun around and hit the floor on his stomach.

"Would you like another reason?"

"No, you got my attention."

I nodded at Winky to get the two security guards.

"I hope you realize we have the building surrounded. Unless you're going to sprout wings and fly out of here there is no way to escape from here."

"You never know Sir. I may just do that."

At that point of our conversation Winky returned with the two security guards.

"Where are their guns?"

"I don't know. But I'm sure we can get them one."

"Then do it!"

"Winky, Yoto, give the men your guns."

I picked them because they still used an old style six shooter revolver. I figured if I'm going to give them fire power it would be the least I could give them.

They didn't pay any attention to the guns. They looked at them to make sure they were loaded. Then they pointed them at us.

"Boys, each of you grab a money bag and we'll head to the lift."

As they were grabbing the bags one of them asked. "What about the rest of the gang?"

"They didn't hold up their part of the plan, so let them live with their mistakes. Now let's get out of here."

We cleared a path for them so they could get to the elevator or lift as they call it. Jim's ex-wife kept her gun on him as they approached the lift. Then she covered us while her accomplices got themselves and the money bags they were carrying and the two bags that Jim had on the lift. She stepped onto the lift leaving Jim standing outside in front of the lift. "I told you I'd get even with you! You bastard! No one leaves me and gets away with it. I also told you I'd kill you and I always keep my word."

She had her gun pointed at Jim's chest. Next thing we heard was two blasts from the gun and two bullets hit Jim. He reeled backward and fell to the floor. She shot him as the doors to the lift closed. I looked at the top of the lift doors to see which direction they were taking. As we had thought, they were heading to the roof.

"Charles!!"

"I'm here and okay Larry!"

I took a few steps closer to Jim. He was already sitting up with the help of Yoto and Simon. They were the closest to him.

I asked, "How are you feeling Jim?"

"A little stunned and sore in the chest."

"Your head will clear and the bruises will go away. It's a good thing you boys were wearing bullet proof vests."

By that time Charles was standing near us. "I agree Larry."

"I thought you would Charles."

Jim said, "Simon, we want to thank you for making us wear these things."

"Yes, thank you Simon."

"You're both welcome."

"Now that we know for sure that they're on their way to the roof, I'll lay out our plan. Simon, have your people on the roof been notified the crooks are on their way?"

"Yes Larry. They were called the minute we saw the lift going up."

"Good. As much as I hate to say it, we need to climb some steps."

Lynda asked, "What about the elevator?"

"They'll put something in front of the doors to keep them open. The following people will go with me: Lynda, Yoto, Simon, and Winky. Everyone else will stay here and get everything back to normal. They should just about have their escape line connected. We better get moving."

Our boys on the roof had watched a man come to the roof a couple of hours earlier and hide a nylon rope line. After he left our boys switched the line. We replaced it with one that had a dead spot in the middle, which means they can roll so far on the line and then they stop and roll no more. That's where I wanted the four of them; stuck in mid air between the two buildings.

By the time we reached the exit door to the roof three of the crooks were on the line and the last one was getting prepared to slide off the parapet and join his friends.

Simon had hooked up his communications as we ascended the stairs. I had him inform his boys on the roof not to open fire without a direct order from us.

As Winky opened the door a hail of bullets hit around it. Winky quickly pulled the steel door shut.

"Winky! Make some noise and open and shut the door quickly and carefully."

He did and we heard one more shot.

"That's six shots. Let's move out."

As we walked out the crook slid off the parapet. We walked over to the parapet and carefully looked over it.

"Simon, tell all your boys to show themselves and their weapons."

"All right Larry."

I looked around as our men appeared everywhere. Their weapons were pointed at the four hanging on the line. We stood up so they could also see us. They started to reach for their guns with one hand while holding on with the other.

I said, "I'd look around before I reached for a gun." They saw the size of our force and quit reaching. "Now, while you folks are hanging around I'd like to see you drop your weapons. When that's finished, we'll throw you a rope and pull you in."

Without saying a word Jim's ex-wife drew her pistol and pointed it up to the line and pulled the trigger. The bullets tore the line apart. The four crooks and four money bags fell to the ground. From where I was standing it looked like an eight story fall.

Simon said, "I guess she didn't want to be taken alive."

"I think you're right Simon. After killing two people she figured she'd have to spend the rest of her life in prison."

"She didn't kill anyone Larry."

"Lynda, I know that, and you know that, but we neglected to tell her that."

Everyone broke out laughing.

"Simon, first thing I want your boys downstairs to do is bring the four bags of money back into the casino. We'll meet them there. Have everyone else take care of clean up. We have some gambling to do."

"Consider it done Larry."

Simon talked as we walked to the elevator. After we got off the elevator I broke the news to Jim.

Jim said, "She always said 'I'd give my life to be a star'. Looks like she kept her word she'll make front page tomorrow."

"She sure will. I'm glad to see you're over her."

"Larry, I wasn't until she tried to kill me."

"That does have a way of awakening your feelings."

We all laughed.

"Here comes your money Jim."

"Thanks Dick. I'd better get it back in the safe."

"That's a great idea. When you're done join us in the lounge area for a brandy."

"I will Larry. Wait a minute! I thought you guys said you were going to break my craps table tonight."

"We are. But the evening is young. So we're going to unwind for a little while. I want to give the place a little time to return to normal."

"Sounds good. Order me a brandy."

"You got it Jim."

We sat down in the lounge and I ordered a brandy for everyone and two extras. Charles had decided to stay with Jim, which I felt was a good move. When they arrived at our table Jim spoke as he sat down. "The whole way over here I was thinking of something stronger then brandy to settle my nerves."

Charles added, "I agree, maybe a double scotch."

"Gentlemen", I said, "Let me help you one more time. I know you've been through a horrendous night and you should feel on end and nervous, right?"

They both answered, "Yes."

"Here's what you have to ask yourself; do I want to be happy, or should I feel sad?"

They answered, "Happy."

"Right and why are you happy? Because you've outsmarted,

outwitted, and defeated your enemy without being hurt."

"That's right Larry."

"I know Charles. Now! That brings up the other side of the coin. Why you should be unhappy. Let us count the ways. One, ahh, ummm, can anyone give me a reason why we should be unhappy?"

No one said a word.

"Duh, looks like you don't need a depressant. So here's what I want each of you to do. When I tell you to I want you to take a deep breath and hold it until I tell you to let it out. Then let it out slooowly. Ready? Now, remember to hold it."

Not only did Jim and Charles take a deep breath but the whole gang joined in.

"All right, let it out sloooowly."

Our area sounded like the air being let out of a bunch of car tires. By the time everyone had finished we were all tied up in laughter.

As things quieted down I asked, "Do you feel better now?"

With a smile on their faces they said, "We sure do."

Everyone seemed to reach for their brandy glass at the same time.

I said, "A toast to my new friends; may the Gods protect them and care for them." I raised my glass a little higher and said, "To the Gods!"

They all repeated, "To the Gods!"

We relaxed for a while.

"Gentlemen, it's time we attacked Jim's craps table and see how the dice are doing."

Everyone agreed, although Jim pretended to be hesitant. We laughed and told him we'd go easy on him.

We all managed to win a few thousand pounds before we called it a night.

The rest of our trip was uneventful. We did a little sight-seeing, shopping, cocktail party and dinner and then the flight home.

I found all through my life the best part of any trip I take out of the country was when I arrived back in the good old U.S.A. Nothing is sweeter than being home.

Chapter 9

Everyone met us at the airport. It was 7:30 P.M. It was Sunday and I had asked the Mayor to let everyone relax, because tomorrow would be a long day. I asked him to send John to meet us. When we got off the plane everyone was there, even the F.B.I.

"Was there a miscommunication somewhere?"

John answered me, "Larry, you didn't order us not to be here. You only asked us not to show up."

"You're right John. Next time I'll speak more clearly so everyone will understand. Now, putting that aside, it's great to see everyone."

When we arrived back at my penthouse, the Mayor's wife Judy was there. She had put out a lovely spread on the dining room table. Everyone had something to eat as we filled them in on what had happened on our vacation. It was 10:30 P.M. when I finally threw the last person out. I knew I had to get Lynda to bed. If she didn't get some rest the jet lag would kill her. Even with rest it will have its effect on her.

"Good night Lynda and thank you for making my life so wonderful."

"Good night Larry. I love you."

"I love you too."

She kissed me and cuddled up in my arms. She was asleep in no time. I stayed awake for awhile going over everything that was happening before we left.

I woke up Monday morning feeling refreshed. I could tell by the way Lynda was moving around that she was still a bit sluggish and tired.

We walked into my office at five minutes to nine. Everyone was there waiting for us.

"Shall we take our seats gentlemen? I have a lot of catching up to do. I'd like to once again thank everyone for my vacation. The four of us had a wonderfully relaxing time."

Everyone broke out in laughter.

"Stop that! We did have a good time."

Yoto said, "Larry you can't kid a bunch of kidders."

"I guess you're right Yoto. But we did have a good time, didn't we?"

"Yes we did."

When the laughter subsided I continued. "Now if there is nothing pressing I'll start with the easy stuff and work my way up. That will give our minds a chance to get back into the groove of things. Tomorrow we'll go back to our regular meeting. Pete, how's the hospital coming?"

"Fine. Doc's right on schedule, or a little ahead of it. He'll be taking care of patients in less than ninety days."

"How're his volunteers coming along?"

"That's why he's so far ahead of schedule. He has more help than he knows what to do with."

"I hope our men aren't overdoing it."

"Our ranking officers are watching them carefully. Any minor problems are being reported immediately. That makes it easy to correct and keeps them from being major."

"I agree and a job well done Pete."

"Lynda, call over to the hospital today and have them put us on the volunteer list."

"I'll take care of it later Larry."

"Good. Pete, what about the other building we need for a school?"

"Thanks to the military we now have both an east and a west side location."

"Great."

"That's only the half of it Larry. The military are being so helpful that it's scary."

"What do you mean?"

"They asked if we could use a bunch of school and classroom equipment. By the time they are done with us we'll need little or nothing. They'll even set up barracks for us. If I didn't know better I'd think someone talked to them."

"What about it Sam? Did the F.B.I. have a hand in this?"

"Well Larry, it happened like this: I was talking to my boss and your old friend General Hatchaway. The way I understand it, the General spoke to his friend the President. The President is now very much aware of Larry Towers and what he is trying and succeeding at doing. The President was so impressed he told the General to support you any way he saw fit."

"Now do you feel better Pete?"

"Yes I do Larry. Sam thanks for your help."

"You're welcome Pete. I'm glad I could do it."

"I love it when you guys take on projects and get them done without my help. Keep up the good work."

John asked, "Now that we have the schools what are we going to do with them?"

"As I said before John, I have an outline in my mind. I'll need to talk to the school leaders to get their feedback."

When will you do that?"

"Pete when will you be open for business?"

"In less than thirty days."

"To answer your question John, in the next two weeks. I want to keep this project on the Q.T. I want to make the school officials have a large amount of the say of what will happen. I'd also like some of them to volunteer to help in some small way. Like getting set up, the kind of books needed; etc."

Jim asked, "Could you give us an idea of the kind of curriculum you have in mind for the students?"

"To be honest Jim, I have a feeling that most of the books needed will come from the grade school level. I'd be willing to bet that 30 % of them can read very little and 50 % are below the third grade level. The rest will be below the fifth grade level. Remember people, the smarter they get the easier they will be to handle."

"Won't that take a long time?"

"No John. Once we get their attention they'll learn very fast."

Pete said, "It's getting their attention that will be the hard part."

"I don't think so Pete. I'm hoping the Marines can handle that."

Sam interjected, "I think that can be arranged Larry."

"Thanks Sam. I'll leave it up to you and Pete. For now that closes that subject and we'll move on. Pete, how are the mobs doing?"

"After the job Mr. Parker did on his T.V. Program the other T.V. stations fell in line to help. When you were gone the radio stations and the newspapers also got on the bandwagon. If a child so much as sneezes the wrong way we know about it. If you remember I told you we had around 5,000 mob members around town. We now have a list of over 6,000."

"Sounds good. You want to make sure you know how many of those boys end up in our schools."

"I've already figured on cross-referencing them. I thought it would help our instructors to know who's who."

"What do you think Sam?"

"Larry, it's nice for them to know, but it's better for the instructors to treat everyone the same. If they show respect, they'll get respect. If they don't, they won't."

"I have a great deal of respect for the Marines. They were making men out of boys long before I was born. So we'll do it your way Sam."

"Pete and I will handle it Larry."

Pete added, "I'd like to say one thing Larry."

"What's that Pete?"

"The mobs are really lying low. Without them wearing their colors it's hard to tell them from normal kids."

"That's music to my ears Pete. It should get a lot better before it gets worse."

Jim asked, "Do you really think it'll get worse Larry?"

"Yes I do Jim. We'll eliminate 70 % of the mobs by educating them. The hard core boys won't give up without a fight."

Tom inserted, "We'll be ready for them Larry."

"You can bet your boots on that Tom. Now let's continue. Jim, the Canadian truck thieves, what are they doing?"

"They haven't made it back here yet. They're still in Canada."

"What about more inventory?"

"Truck thefts in Canada have gone up since the crooks have returned there. The Mounties and the F.B.I. managed to follow the bad guys when they stole one of the decoy trucks. With the homing device attached to it they had no trouble following it. The Mounties followed it to a large warehouse where they got the truck ready to cross the border. When it left the warehouse the Mounties followed it to their side of the border. The F.B.I. picked up the truck's signal on our side of the border. Sam told me that they followed the truck about ten miles from the border. Our boys on the ground following the truck stayed about a mile from its location. Our helicopter was able to fix its exact location. The F.B.I. flew some nondescript planes over the area and took some great surveillance photos. There's a house, a couple of small out buildings, and three very large barns. One barn is old and the other two are new. By the photos they are using the old barn to work on the trucks and the new barns for storage."

"Sam?"

"Yes Larry?"

"How do you want to handle this?"

"I'd like Pete and his men to work with four of our agents here to take down the local operation. The F.B.I. and the Mounties will round up the rest of the crooks."

"Great. You'll also take credit for the whole operation."

"I figured you'd want it that way so we will."

"Good. Next, has anyone lost a limo Pete?"

"Not yet Larry."

"Put an inquiry out around the state again. If that still gives you nothing check the states on our borders."

"I'll do it Larry."

"Robert, the D.P.S. uniforms?"

"Nothing more Larry."

"John, the guard uniform?"

"They guard a ton of places. I've had Jim and Robert helping me while Yoto was gone. It's hard to figure Larry."

"All right John, let's analyze it together."

"I was hoping you'd say that."

"I'm glad I was missed."

"Where do you want to start Larry?"

"Well John, how did you list the places that use these guards?"

"Kind of simply, I put them in the order of the businesses they protect."

"That's good John."

"It may be good, but there are still many possibilities out there Larry."

"All right John. Do you have the list with you?"

"Yes." He opened his file folder and handed me the list.

"Five pages front and back. I can see your dilemma John."

"Thanks Larry."

"I notice that you have a lot of places listed but only a few categories. So lets use the categories to limit our search. It helps to know what you're looking for."

"If we knew that we'd be done."

"Relax John I know what we're looking for."

Tom said, "I can't believe this. You've been in London for the last week and you know what we're looking for?"

"I sure do Tom. Let me continue. Categories; food stores, furniture stores, fast food restaurants, banks, one armored car company, night clubs, hospitals, parking lots, and movie theatres. Now does anyone here see any reason for these places to need three D.P.S. officers to give them an escort somewhere?"

No one said a word.

The Mayor said, "I don't know how we missed that Larry."

"I don't know either Mayor, I mentioned it before I left. But it's no longer missed."

"What's that leave us with Larry?"

"John, you have a dozen or so hotels and some special events to check out. Now that Yoto is back the four of you should handle this list and have a report for us in the morning."

"We'll get it done Larry."

"Thanks John. Sam and Wade, have you checked on the President to see if he's coming to visit us?"

"I haven't gotten a confirmed answer yet. I'll let you know the minute I do."

"I'd appreciate that. Pete, I noticed that you're still alive."

"Thanks Larry. It's nice to be noticed."

Everyone laughed a little.

"Cute, real cute, you know what I was leading up to. How are things going with Coop and Josh and the Don back east?"

"We're about a week away from killing me if that's your question."

"Partially, would you update me?"

"Sure Larry. I was only kidding."

"I know. What's the real scoop?"

"The whole thing took a bit of a twist on us around the end of the week."

"How interesting you should say that."

John said, "Larry's at it again."

Everyone started laughing.

"Just for that John, I'll let Pete finish."

"Wait a minute!"

"What Wade?"

"These guys may have seen you do this a lot but Sam and I haven't and would love to see you do it again."

The Mayor said, "Larry, there's nothing more flattering than a special request."

"You're right Mayor. You guys win. It's not that big of a deal anyway."

"Then would you tell us?"

"Sure Sam. When I was in London I tried to do the morning meeting in my mind at the same time you were doing it here."

Lynda inserted, "That's why you always looked a little preoccupied around four in the afternoon."

"Guilty as charged Lynda, so far everything you've said falls into my thinking."

"We believe you Larry, but what about the rest of the story?"

"Ye of little faith, Wade, if I figured it right, the boys supplying the drugs to the Don's nephew are the same bunch we've been checking out with the ambulance service. How'd I do Pete?"

"Right on the money, Larry."

"To continue, Coop has asked the nephew for a very large shipment of drugs and stated he'd like to meet the head of the drug operation. At that meeting the Don will show up. If the plan works right we'll get all the fish in one barrel. Now let me ask you Wade, how'd I do?"

"I don't know how you do it. But you're 100 percent correct."

Everyone started to laugh.

"So someone tell me where we are actually."

Tom answered, "Larry, Jim got tied up with Canada so I took over the case."

"Then fill me in Tom."

"What you said is true. We have the big meeting set up for Thursday evening at seven."

"What about Coop and Josh?"

"They're having so much fun we may never get them out of the lifestyle we made for them."

"I can believe it. They love putting on the ritz."

Yoto said, "Especially with someone else's money."

We all laughed.

"You're right Yoto. Now what else Tom?"

"They're meeting in the office at the restaurant. That's making bugging the place nearly impossible."

"I can see what you mean."

"We've been thinking about wiring Coop and Josh for sound."

"By the looks you're getting around the table, I can see no one likes your idea."

"No Larry they don't. If you noticed, I said 'thinking about it'."

"I'm glad that's all you've been doing. Wiring the boys is definitely OUT!"

Jim said, "Then you feel they'll search the boys?"

"Yes Jim. I do, if not the nephew, definitely the drug dealers. In their line of work they need to make sure new people are clean."

"That was our thinking Larry."

"Then Tom we need to look in a different direction."

"What do you have in mind Larry?"

"Let's look at the restaurant like any crime scene, Mayor."

"I know, Larry, get all the plans of the building from the city."

"Right Mayor, do you boys remember when we were in the restaurant that it had an eye in the sky?"

"Larry, I remember one in the bar area and two in the restaurant."

"You're right Yoto. Tom, find out who sold the cameras to them. They probably have a camera in the office as well. Sam! I need your people to go in and check out the units for the company. It'd be nice to use their own cameras to photograph them."

Sam said, "If my boys get the chance do you want them to bug the office?"

"No. If we can't use their own security cameras we'll forget it."

John asked, "How are we going to get evidence against them if we don't bug them?"

"I don't have an answer to that yet John. But we'll keep working on it. So far in my mind I have Thursday evening as the next big thing to happen. Is that right boys?"

"Larry, can I take over?"

"Sure Sam, if it'll answer my question."

"I can at least make Thursday evening a little clearer."

"That sounds great. Go for it."

"Wade and I have been working with Tom and Jim. We have

people all over the place watching these boys to see how they're getting the drugs into this country from Mexico. Your people here, Wade's people at the other Blanca Corporation locations, border patrols on both sides of the border. We know with the size of the shipment we asked for they'll have to go to their source for more product. We feel they'll move it Wednesday evening."

"How large a shipment are we talking?"

"I did a 'Larry'. I made the shipment so large that they have to make two trips to get it all."

"That's great. We'll have twice the chance of following them."

"That's the way I saw it."

"Sam, how are you going to track them without being seen?"

"I've set up radar triangular tracking. We know by the distance they can fly where to put the three units. One is in Mexico with a D.E.A. agent helping to man it. The other two are southeast and southwest of us. We'll identify them at take off and continue doing so until everyone is tracking them. The minute they land we'll have their pick up point, which should also give us their source."

"Larry, how does that work?"

"Lynda, seeing Sam is explaining it I'll allow him to explain how it works. This is a procedure we used a lot in combat to get our enemies' position for artillery fire. Tell her about it Sam."

"All right Larry. It's quite simple Lynda. When the plane lands each radar station shoots an azimuth reading through its' point of landing. This gives us three straight lines through the plane. We then take a reading where our three lines intersect the plane and 'BINGO' we know exactly where the airplane is sitting. Does that clear it up for you Lynda?"

"Yes, thank you Sam."

John, Jim, Robert, and Tom also said, "Thank you Sam."

I said, "Sounds like you have it under control Sam."

"I think so Larry. There are still a lot of things I wish I knew."

"If nothing else let's look at the bright side."

The Mayor said, "I knew there would be one Larry. What is it?"

"You know me Mayor I'm very optimistic and thankful for every little thing I get. The way I'm looking at this situation is if the deal went down right now we'd have plenty to be thankful for. One; the Don would kill his nephew and the F.B.I. would arrest him. Whether or not they got a conviction isn't important; they'd still take him out of commission for awhile. Two; we'd find the drug source and put our drug dealer out of business. Then we'd end up with ambulances, helicopters, and airplanes for our new hospital. If that's all that happens we've been very successful. Someone tell me if I'm wrong."

"You're right as usual Larry."

"Thanks Mayor."

The Mayor continued, "What are you going to do today Larry?"

"As everyone noticed as they entered my office I have piles of paperwork on my desk, Mayor."

"That will only keep you until lunch."

"All right Mayor, what do you have in mind? I hope it's safer than the trip you sent us on to London."

Everyone busted out laughing.

"You know I meant well."

"Yes I do. What about this afternoon?"

"I'm going by the hospital to see how it's coming. I thought you and Lynda might want to join me."

"Sounds good, I'll meet you at the limo at 1:30 P.M. If there's nothing else gentlemen, you'd better get to work."

Lynda and I went through all the messages and paperwork on my desk. We had lunch in and finished in time to meet the Mayor at my limo. Yoto had returned to drive for us.

As we were driving I said to the Mayor, "I know why you invited me."

"I told you the truth! Honestly!"

"Does a politician know the truth Mayor?"

Everyone was laughing including the Mayor.

"Larry, why do you think I asked you?"

"That's easy. You wanted to be driven around in a limo with your closest friends."

We laughed again.

"You got me there Larry. To be truthful I did miss you guys."

"We missed you too. Now that we're back the crooks are going to suffer. No more Mr. Nice Guy."

Everyone started to laugh again.

We pulled up and stopped at a red light.

"Yoto! Three o'clock!"

He turned his head in the three o'clock direction in time to see what I had seen.

"Got it Larry! I'll take a right and pull into the alley."

"Good. Lynda, call for back up. Three units; code two. Robbery in the drugstore on the corner. Four young white males plus us."

"Mayor, are you packing?"

"No Larry."

I reached down between my legs and found the button on the front bottom of the seat I was sitting on. I pushed the button three times and the door fell open. I reached inside and got the Mayor a hand gun. I checked the gun. It was loaded so I handed it to the Mayor.

"I'm going in the front and the Mayor is going with me. Yoto and Lynda, take the back."

We got out and moved swiftly.

As we separated I said, "Yoto, I'll give you twenty seconds. That should give you enough time to unlock the back door."

"Don't worry about us. We'll see you inside, if you're able to get that far without falling over from exhaustion. Isn't that what happens when you get old?"

We were walking as we were talking, "I'll get even with you for that." I was done talking to him because we were just about out of earshot.

"Mayor, when we get to the guy guarding the front door you need to be three steps behind me. I'm going to hit him once between the eyes and pass him back to you. You'll push him up against the wall and take the gun out of his belt. Put your gun to his throat and keep him quiet, if he makes noise shoot him with your gun. Got it?"

"Yes Larry."

We were rounding the corner, "Fall back!"

He fell back about three steps and we continued on not losing a step. As I approached the boy standing near the door I looked straight ahead like I was walking by. When I got even with him I threw a snap punch with my left hand and hit the kid right between the eyes. He had no idea what hit him. I recoiled my hand back then grabbed him with both hands and pushed him to the Mayor. "Use him for a shield. No one comes in or out this door!" I then proceeded into the store.

I entered the store by Walking Silent and Walking Deadly. No one noticed me in the store. I picked up a couple of items and held them in front of my body with my left arm. I could now feel the presence of Yoto and Lynda in the store. As I walked up by the cash register I could see the three guys that had entered the store. Two of them had pistols and one was holding the shot gun I had seen from the limo.

"Excuse me. Where do you keep the pickles?"

The boy turned my way upon hearing my voice. "Where did you come from?"

Now that I had their attention I had to keep it. The man with the shot gun was covering three employees and four customers. One of the other guys had a pistol at the head of what had to be the manager of the store, because he was opening the safe. The last guy had his pistol in his belt and was emptying the cash register.

"Now that I have your attention and you asked your question so nicely, I'll answer it for you. I came through the front door. Your look out is taking a nap. Oh, let me introduce myself. I'm Larry Towers the Commissioner of Police of Pertsville."

The guy holding the gun on the manager spoke, "Are we supposed to be scared or something?"

"I don't think there's enough brain matter between the three of you to be frightened."

"And what's that supposed to mean?"

"I'll make it simple for you. The three of you are stupid."

"That's not the way I see it cop. There's three of us and one of you. We have guns and hostages and you're unarmed aren't you?"

"I don't believe in packing a gun. Makes my suits look bad."

"Well I think you better move over there with the rest of the hostages before I shoot you where you stand."

At that point he took the barrel of his gun away from the manager's head.

"I have a better idea. If the three of you put down your guns and put your hands on the top of your heads, you'll walk out of here alive. Otherwise we'll carry you out of here."

They started to laugh, "You have balls cop! I'll say that for you. Without a gun you're going to kill the three of us."

"One of my guys will kill you and the Sergeant will kill you at the register. That leaves me to kill you with the shotgun. I'm going to count to two, I mean three (Yoto motioned to Lynda to shoot on two) at which time if your guns are not on the floor and your hands in the air, you'll all be dead."

They started to laugh once again.

"One!!"

The area went silent and no one moved a muscle. I waited a little longer than I had to but they did nothing. It was as if they were waiting to see how I was going to accomplish this. So I showed them.

"Two!!!"

As I said it I heard what sounded like one shot. The man with the shotgun turned his head toward his friends for a split second giving me enough time to pull out my sleeve knife with my right hand and in one motion I let it fly. It hit its target with no problem at all. I could hear the thud as it went deeply into his chest. He fell backwards to the floor firing his shotgun as he hit. I dropped my groceries to the floor and moved in on the men behind the counter. Yoto's target was humped over the manager at the safe. I pulled him off the manager and made sure the crook was dead. I have to admit the manager was really shaken. When I stood up and turned Yoto was checking the man Lynda killed who was in an upright position slumped over the cash register he was emptying.

Lynda was bending over my man to get my knife. As she put her hand on it the man I thought was dead grabbed her gun and was trying to take it from her.

"Yoto!"

He was closer than I and he had a gun. As I spoke his name I heard a shot ring out. Yoto had put a slug in the temple of the man's head.

As Lynda straightened up I said, "Now you can get my knife. While you're doing that I'll check on the Mayor."

When I walked outside I could hear struggling. The crook had the Mayor's hand containing his gun. The Mayor had the crook's hand which had a knife in it. At that point a black and white pulled up to the curb and two cops got out. I held my hand up and motioned them inside. They went inside.

"Mayor, if you wish, I'll kill him for you."

"No Larry, you gave me this job and I blew it! Now I'll correct my mistake."

At that point the Mayor took both of his hands and pushed them straight up into the air. Then he made like a windmill and brought both hands down. While the Mayor held the man's knife hand down he rose up and pointed his revolver to the man's chest and squeezed off three rounds. The perp stood still for a second or two then slid toward the ground. The Mayor let go of the man's arms and let him fall all the way to the sidewalk.

Two more black and whites arrived at the same time.

As I walked over to him I asked, "Are you all right Mayor?"

"Yes Larry."

"Good. Relax and I'll get things rolling."

One of the officers came over and said, "It's been called in Sir. There's a Sergeant on his way."

"Good. Get a blanket out of your car." As I was speaking another officer came up with a blanket. "You two get the area taped off and stand guard on the perimeter. You stay with the body until the area is secured then join the officers inside. And you, young man, go inside and give the other officers a hand. Also, send out my people."

"Yes Sir Commissioner, right away Sir."

The officer went inside and I got closer to the Mayor. "Are you really okay?"

"Yes Larry. I'm a bit shaken but okay."

"Was it the first time you killed someone?"

"Yes, and it was the hardest thing I ever had to do."

"Believe me, it doesn't get any easier."

"It doesn't seem to bother you or your men."

"You learn to lock it out of your mind. But it's still there. Ours is not an easy job. Remember when we first started? I said people will get killed and we'll have to do things we don't like? This is what I was talking about. As long as it's a life or death situation I want you alive and the crook dead."

"I know Larry. I hope I did well."

"I wasn't worried for a second." (Boy was that a lie!) "I knew you had the situation in hand. Just, next time, don't allow things to go that far."

"I won't. What happened inside?"

I was glad he changed the subject. "Everyone is safe and we have three dead crooks."

"Did they have a choice?"

"I asked them to surrender or die. They didn't surrender."

"I could tell that. I can't believe with everything we've accomplished that crime is still running rampant."

"Mayor, let me help your thinking. This town has been so low for so long you can't expect it to bounce back in a short time. We'll keep whittling away at it until it's a safe place to live. The nice part of destroying a criminal is he won't be back to hurt people again. Our main problem is, for the time being, they outnumber us. But, we're slowly but surely getting the upper hand. So fear not Mayor. We're winning the battles. Someday we'll win the war."

By the time I had finished Yoto and Lynda were standing with us.

"Is everything all right, Mayor?"

"Yes Lynda. Larry was just getting off his soap box."

"I'm sorry Mayor. I guess I got carried away."

"It's all right Larry. I enjoy hearing it from time to time."

Another black and white unit pulled up with the Sergeant in it.

"I'll fill him in Larry."

"Good idea Lynda. Yoto, while she's doing that bring the limo around. Mayor, let's take a quick check inside. I want to make sure everyone is all right."

"Sounds like a good idea."

Our boys had moved everyone to the home healthcare area. The people were all seated on everything from a wheelchair to a portable toilet. The officers were taking statements. Two of the women were still sobbing from the whole incident. Before I had a chance to get to them I was stopped cold in my tracks by a man I didn't know.

"Are you happy? You murdered three people today!"

"Make that four. We also killed one outside."

"Then you murdered four people today."

"You seem awful disturbed that four pieces of scum are off the streets."

"What disturbs me is you shot them down without giving them a chance."

"Were you asleep when I asked them to drop their weapons?"

"You didn't show them any reason to drop their weapons."

"Let me try to understand your reasoning. I walked into a situation where there were hostages and three crooks with guns. Am I correct?"

"So far, yes."

"Then, unarmed, I talked the crooks into pointing their guns away from you people and halfway towards me. Am I right so far?"

"I didn't notice that part."

"Then you also missed the part where I could see no way out of this situation except to eliminate the crooks. Do you remember me telling the crooks how they were going to die?"

"Yes."

"What I was actually doing was telling my people what to do. Remember how I messed up on the count to three and I said two? That's when my people knew what to do and when to do it."

"I thought you had planned this ahead of time."

"No Sir. I preferred that they dropped their weapons and surrendered. Any firing of a weapon can accidently hit the wrong person. That's why we only use extreme force when necessary. As I see the situation, you are all healthy and you'll be able to see your loved ones later on today."

The store manager had joined us and he inserted, "I personally want to thank you Commissioner for the chance you took for us. The man that had the gun to my head had already picked one of my employees and one of the customers that he was going to take into the back room and rape. I already told your officers that he just got out or escaped from jail. So if we didn't have your help this would have turned into a real blood bath."

The stranger asked, "Who was the customer he wanted to rape?"

"Your wife, Sir."

"Still think I was too rough on them?"

He was mumbling, "My wife? I can't believe it! Sorry Commissioner. You were right and I was wrong."

"Like I said before, I'm glad everyone is safe."

The manager shook my hand and said, "Thank you again Commissioner." With that said he went back over to console the sobbing women.

I asked the Mayor if he was ready to leave. He'd managed to get around the area to everyone. "Yes Commissioner. I'm ready."

As we turned to leave the Sergeant was approaching. "It's all yours Sergeant."

He saluted and said, "I'll take care of it Sir."

The Mayor and I walked out of the building and joined Yoto and Lynda in the limo.

As Yoto pulled away from the curb he asked, "The hospital?"

The Mayor answered, "Yes."

Chapter 10

The rest of the trip was quite uneventful. We arrived at the hospital a little before three. Doctor Kaplin was thrilled to see us.

"Larry. I'm glad to see you are home safely."

"Thank you Doc. Now, what's happening here? I've heard nothing but good reports."

"Let me show everyone around."

We spent half an hour looking at redesigned areas.

Doc said, "That's about it. What do you think?"

I said, "Well you're not as far along as I would have been."

Doc had a disappointed look on his face when he said, "I'm not?"

"No, you're much further."

We all laughed.

I said, "Doc, you're doing a superior job. Don't stop. Also make sure you have Lynda and me on your volunteer list."

Yoto added, "Also Yoto and Lyn-Yhi."

"I'll put the two of you down Yoto. Larry, Lynda called your names in this morning."

"Just making sure."

Doc said, "It was a great moral booster this morning. I don't think you know it but your men think the world of you. When the call came in this morning it spread through this place like wildfire."

"Glad I could help out. When do you think you can use us?"

"If I remember correctly, you push a mean paint roller."

"That's right."

"We're going to have a large paint party later on this month."

"Let us know and we'll be here. Keep doing what you're doing. I should have a surprise for you at the end of the week."

"I love surprises….."

"Don't try to con me. You want me to tell you what it is. I'll give you a hint. It'll save your budget over a million dollars."

"But I don't have a budget."

"Well, you'll be a million dollars ahead if you did."

"Whatever it is, we thank you."

"When we were driving in I noticed some work being done to the buildings and empty lots around here."

"The city came through and posted all the properties in the

neighborhood, including us. I did as the posting instructed. I called and after they found out who I was and which property I represented, they informed me I had nothing to worry about. They blanketed the whole neighborhood so no one could holler discrimination. I thanked them for helping clean up the neighborhood."

"It seems to be working. It looks like a bunch of properties are being cleaned up. Mayor?"

"Yes Larry?"

"Make a note to set up a small committee of volunteers to check on the non-respondent parties."

"We want to buy their properties?"

"Or trade them something we own for their property as long as we can negotiate our price. Right now they can't do anything with their properties. That makes them worth nothing. On second thought, have our real estate people look into this. I'd like to see all contracts before they submit them."

"I'll take care of it. You know I could get these properties condemned without any problem."

"We'll try it my way first, your way second."

"Okay."

As I kept looking around the building I had to mention it again. "I can't get over how you've utilized so much of the old building structure. You've had to save us a small fortune. How'd you come up with these ideas?"

"I don't know how you're going to take this but I had help."

"You were supposed to get help. That's why you have a checkbook."

"That wasn't an option."

"What do you mean?"

"I have two friends. One is an architect and the other is a builder. They've been spending most of their evenings and weekends with me."

"Is your wife jealous?"

"What?"

"Never mind Doc, it was my futile attempt at humor."

Everyone smiled.

"Back to your friends."

"A lot of times when they come over they bring their families."
"Are they becoming a part of our family?"
"Sort of Larry."
"Explain please."
"I could have asked them to give me a bid and do the job for us. But that's all they would have done."
"Which means what?"
"So far they've saved us over a million and a half dollars. And there's more to come. Whenever I have an idea they seem to make it a reality. Take the emergency room for example. The way this building is laid out, there is only one way to enter it. We decided that we couldn't have well patients and emergency room patients coming in the same door. So the entrance you came in will be for the emergency room. We'll have a smaller entrance at about the middle of the building for well patients and visitors. I had some rough sketches of what I wanted to do and what it would cost. Believe me Larry, it was scary!"
"So what did you do?"
"What I thought you would do."
"Which was?"
"If they'd take this job on like it was their own hospital I'd take care of them."
"That's it?"
"Yes, lifetime healthcare for them and their wives, including the rest home."
"You were right. I'd trade off future for present anytime."
Lynda said, "I'm sorry Larry. Would you explain that to me?"
"Sure Lynda. They are doing work for us now. We're giving them healthcare later. They could live to be 100 or they could die tomorrow. They've already saved us over a million and a half dollars. We're already so far ahead they'll never catch up, so it's really an unfair trade."
"I understand now."
"Doc."
"Yes Larry."
"What about their children?"
"They each have two about the same age as mine."
"You didn't include them in?"

"No Sir. I thought I'd leave that up to you."

"Tell them we thank them for all of their help. If they'll be here to help you through all this as well as help you in the future, they can include their children."

"Thank you Larry. That will make them feel good."

"You know me, they helped me first which makes it hard to say no."

Lynda said, "Larry, it's getting close to 5 o'clock."

Doc asked, "What does that mean?"

"Doc, that means we have to rush back to our office so we can be there in time to quit for the day."

Everyone started to laugh.

"I finally got a joke to work."

"Yes you did Larry, and I enjoyed it."

"I'm glad Doc. What are you doing for dinner?"

"Nothing, I was going to work right on through the night. I usually leave around nine."

"Doc, why don't you come with us for a bite to eat?"

"I'm not even going to think of a reason why I can't go. Let's get out of here."

He checked out and we left. We had dinner and great conversation for the next hour and a half. We then returned Doc to the hospital and we headed home.

Lynda and I left Yoto and the Mayor in the parking garage and headed upstairs.

"Do you mind if we stop at the office for a minute? I want to go through some of the reports a little more thoroughly than I did this morning."

"I'd rather go upstairs. I'm bushed."

"Go ahead. I'll join you in a few minutes."

"No. I'd better stay with you."

"Have it your way, but with your jet lag you wouldn't be very helpful anyway."

"That's what you think."

By that time we had reached the reception area door. I put my left hand lightly on the door knob and started to insert the key when I felt something strange on the knob. I held my keys fast in my hand as I brought my hand up to my face. I put my index finger to my lips so Lynda would know to be quiet. I turned the doorknob to find the door unlocked. Lynda proceeded to pull her gun out of her purse and then she sat her purse on the floor of the hallway. She followed me into the reception area. It was empty. I looked over at the door that led to my men's office and it looked secured. So I decided whoever was here had to be in my office. I motioned to Lynda that we were going into my office. I slowly turned the doorknob and found it locked.

I whispered to Lynda, "It's locked."

"I'll call for backup."

"No. We need to get in there before they stumble onto something they shouldn't see. We'll go in together. You with your right arm behind my back, me with my left arm over your shoulder. We'll look like young lovers. The only difference will be your gun in your right hand behind my back. If you have to shoot, shoot to kill."

She nodded the affirmative as she moved into position. I slowly put my key into the lock in the door. I could feel Lynda's nervousness as she held me. I could also feel my heart beating in my chest. There is one thing that everyone is afraid of and that's the unknown. Were we going to walk in and surprise more than one person? Were they armed? Would they open fire on us before we could get the drop on them? I turned the key as quietly as I could. For some reason I could hear every click of the tumblers as the key turned. I had my left hand on the doorknob so I started to turn it. Slowly, ever so slowly. I was so quiet I could hear myself breathing. When I had the doorknob fully turned to the right I started to open the door. As I pushed it slowly open the room became more and more visible. When I opened the door far enough Lynda and I stepped in. The light was on but I didn't see anyone. I heard sounds from behind the door, so I swung the door all the way open.

"Put your hands in the air!!!"

As I said that Lynda pointed her gun in that direction. We heard something crash and a woman scream to our right. We then heard a thud. We looked in the far corner of the room where I have a little group of furniture. We hurried to the area. There was a plastic bottle of furniture polish lying on its side on the table. And an elderly female maintenance person passed out on the couch. As I was picking up the furniture polish I heard laughing coming from behind us. I looked and saw Yoto standing inside the doorway.

"Larry, do you know how hard it is to get good help without you scaring them half to death?"

"If you say anything to anyone!.....oh, why not? It's funny to us. But when she regains her senses she'll be plenty mad."

Lynda was holding her helping her to awaken. "What happened?"

"You fainted," Lynda told her.

I asked, "Are you all right?"

She looked at me, "Commissioner, I'm a little shaken but I'll be just fine in a minute."

"Officer Yoto, get the lady a glass of water."

"Right away Commissioner."

The lady spoke again, "I'm sorry I'm here so early Commissioner."

"And I'm sorry we startled you so."

"I'll clean up this mess and come back later."

She tried to stand and fell back onto the couch. At that point Yoto came to her with a glass of water. "Here, this will help."

"Thank you."

She took a sip of the water and tried to relax. As I looked carefully at her face she seemed more stressed than the situation merited.

I was able to see her name badge so I asked, "Mrs." I used Mrs. because she was wearing a wedding ring, "Garcia you seem to have a larger problem than us busting in on you."

"It's nothing Commissioner."

"That 'nothing' seems to be really bugging you."

"I reported it to the police and I have an order of protection against him."

"Do you have someone stalking you?"

"I guess that's what it's called."

"It may help to talk about it. Would you like to do that?"

"I don't want to waste your valuable time."

"My time is your time. I work for you so please tell us what your problem is."

"All right Sir."

She seemed a little relieved just knowing that someone wanted to listen to her.

"Almost one year ago my husband died."

"How did he die?"
"He was drinking and he fell asleep in the bathtub and drowned."
"So it was an accident."
"I don't think so."
"Let me ask you this first. Was his death listed as an accident?"
"Yes."
"Now please tell us what you think happened."
"My husband enjoyed his beer. Every night after work he'd have a few beers, sometimes two, sometimes three, never more than four. If he had more than that he'd get sick to his stomach and throw up."
"Did you tell this to the police officers at the time of the accident?"
"Yes, but they didn't see anything out of the ordinary."
"What was your husband's first name?"
"Benis, we called him Bennie."
"Who do you think did the killing if it wasn't an accident?"
"The only person in the house at the time was his cousin Jose."
"Why would he want to kill Bennie?"
"Jose attempted to kiss me and touch my body the day before this happened. He told me he loved me and had loved me from the first time Bennie brought me home to meet the family."
"Did you tell your husband about what had happened?"
"Yes I did."
"What was his reaction?"
"He was mad and told me he would tell his cousin to leave our house that night when he got home from work."
"Where is Jose now?"
"I made sure the family got him out of my house before the funeral. I told them I wouldn't feel comfortable with another man in my house right now, so Jose moved back into his mother's house."
"Then he's been bothering you?"
"All the time for the last six months."
"Then why are you here so early?"
"He'll be waiting for me when I go home in the morning. He told me this on the telephone. He said that I shouldn't fight it any longer. We were meant to be together and tonight I'd be his."
"What time do you usually get home?"
"5 A.M."
"What about tonight?"

"I started three hours early so I could be home by 2 A.M."
"Has he ever said anything about killing your husband?"
"He made hints of it, but never said anything directly."
"Do you live in a house or an apartment?"
"A house."
"Would you cooperate with us if we could end your problems tonight?"
"Yes Sir."
"Sit here and enjoy your water. We'll be back in a few minutes."
I walked over to my desk and Lynda and Yoto followed me.
"What do you think people?"
Lynda said, "She has a real problem Larry."
Yoto said, "I agree with Lynda. What should we do Larry?"
"Lynda, find me Pete."
Yoto and I stood waiting as she called.
"Hold on Pete. Larry I got him on the first call. He just got home."
She moved out of the way and I took the phone from her hand.
"Good evening Pete."
"What did I fail to do, or what am I going to do?"
"You mean I can't just call to say 'hi'?"
Pete started laughing.
"All right, we have a problem."
"That's better. What can I do?"
"Line up the following."
"Hold on, I'm opening my pad. All right, shoot."
"I need everything available in an hour or two."
"All right."
"A complete surveillance team, they need to be able to get into a house and be out in half an hour."
"I'll get a couple extra boys."
"I need a file that was checked out and closed as accidental death. It was about a year ago and the name is Benis Garcia."
"I'll get it."
"While you're on your way to get it have someone blow up every photo in the file."
"What else?"
"Eight cops to cover the perimeter."
"Is that it?"

"Yup. See you when you get here. I'm in my office."
"See you in less than an hour."
He hung up.
"Looks like we're on the move again."
"Yes it does Yoto."
"Lynda, get Mrs. Garcia's address and a description of Jose. Then take her out into the reception area and make her comfortable. Have her get in touch with her supervisor and inform him that she is spending the rest of her shift with us."
"I'll take care of it Larry."
She left and I looked at Yoto. "Yoto, I think you better get on home and get some rest."
"I'm not really tired Larry."
"You know this will be an all nighter."
"I'll get some rest where I can."
"Sounds good. Why don't you go and relax until Pete gets here?"
"I'll do that." He walked over to the couch where Mrs. Garcia had been sitting and made himself comfortable. I sat back in my chair and waited for Lynda to return. It took her about half an hour to complete her task.

As she approached my desk I started my conversation, "Is she comfortable?"
"Yes, and she says she hasn't felt this relaxed since her husband died."
"I'm glad to hear that."
"She also said that you're everything she thought you to be."
"Boy that was a mouthful. What exactly does it mean?"
"She says a lot of her friends think you're a wonderful Commissioner and that you'd do anything to help our town. But you really surprised her with how quickly you jumped in to help her."
"A crime is a crime, none too big and none too small. We are equal opportunity crime fighters."
"If we were soliciting for business that would be a great motto for our T.V. ads."
"Cute Lynda, real cute."
"I knew you'd like it."

We were smiling as we talked. She was happy to be with me, but I could tell by her eyes that she was exhausted. I don't care who you are, jet lag will catch up to you.

"Lynda, we'll be at this all night. I'd like you to go upstairs and get some rest."

"I'm not that tired."

"One, you are that tired. Two, I'm going to need you fresh in the morning. Three, you can stay here until the time Pete finishes his presentation. Understood?"

"Yes Sir, understood."

She sat down opposite my desk and relaxed. I kept going over the problem in my mind. I believed Mrs. Garcia 100 per cent, but the truth doesn't always prevail in a court of law without adequate proof. We had to get the proof. I was hoping that someone had missed something in the investigation.

There was a knock at my door. I pushed the release button under my desk. The button allows the door to stay unlocked for 30 seconds. Pete walked in with a couple of large full envelopes in his hands. He headed straight for the conference table. I got up and Lynda followed. We also headed to the conference table. I looked over in the corner and saw Yoto also on his way.

We gathered around Pete as he poured the contents of the envelopes onto the table. He then took out a large, flat envelope from under his arm. He slid about an inch thick stack of large photographs out of it.

"That's everything we kept on the situation. We're lucky to have as much as we do. Usually when the case is called accidental death we only keep a small file of the case. They must have kept everything because of the wife's claim of murder."

"You're probably right Pete. Everyone grab something to read or look at. We're looking for something that doesn't fit. If no one minds, I'm going to read the reports first. Then I'll pass them on to whoever wishes to read them. I need everyone to start studying the photos. If you feel there is something wrong with one of them put it aside. Pete, before you get started go over to my desk and call your surveillance team. The information you need is sitting by the phone."

"What about a key?"

"Have them pick their way in. It'll save them time."

"They can handle that. Do you want them to cover every room?"

"Yes. They'll probably stay in the living room. But who knows about crazy people?"

"That's the problem. No one knows. Some people think they do, but they don't."

"You're right Pete. Sigmund Freud was right when he said, 'We don't know that much about the human mind, but this is still a well paying job.' Or something like that."

Everyone started laughing.

"I love your accuracy Larry."

"Thanks Pete. I knew you would. Now get going."

As he walked to my desk I started to read the reports.

"Yoto, I want you to get into your black SWAT outfit. I want you inside Mrs. Garcia's house. I want you to wire yourself so I can communicate with you. I want you to Walk Silent and Walk Deadly. I'm going to try to get her to work with us. I think she can easily get Jose to admit to the murder."

"You don't want me to move until he confesses?"

"You're there to protect and get a confession. Her safety comes first."

"I understand. Where will you be Larry?"

"I'll be out in the surveillance van. We'll keep you informed. Once he's inside he's yours. He could have her dead long before we could get in there."

"I understand Larry. She'll be safe."

"We'll be watching on the video screens outside to give you any help if you need it."

"Sounds like a good plan to me. When should I leave?"

"The same time Lynda does. Now back to work."

We spent the next half an hour going over everything. We boiled things down to three photographs. Two of them showed Bennie's body in the tub and one showed Jose talking to a detective. You could tell Jose didn't know he was being photographed.

"I asked, "Can anyone say why they picked these pictures?"

Yoto said, "I figured if there's something wrong it would have to be in one of them."

"I agree Yoto. Lynda, Pete?"

They both agreed with us.

"Lynda, will you get me my large magnifying glass from my

desk?"

"Sure Larry."

"If we can't see it with the naked eye maybe we can with a little help."

She handed me the glass. I slowly went over the photos. The tub, the floor, the body, nothing out of the ordinary. Then I started to look at the candid photo of Jose.

"BINGO!!!"

"You found something?"

"Did I ever Pete!"

"Yoto. Pull out the report that Jose gave the detective."

"Got it Larry."

"Did he not say that the bathroom door was locked from the inside so he kicked it in? Then he looked inside and saw his cousin under the water. He then ran to the telephone and called the fire department. He didn't enter the bathroom until they arrived?"

"That's the way I'm reading it."

"I want each one of you to take the glass and look at the cuffs on Jose's long sleeve shirt. Then tell me what you see."

They all came back with nothing.

Then Yoto said, "Wait a minute Larry. I do see a shade difference in the color at the very end of his cuffs."

"That's it Yoto."

"What's it? Larry, would you tell us?"

"Lynda, he's wearing a medium gray cotton/polyester mix work shirt. When exposed to water it darkens in color like in the photo."

Lynda said, "How'd he get it wet if he wasn't in the bathroom?"

"I don't think I have to explain that. He drugged Bennie's beer. He went into the bathroom after he fell asleep and gently submerged his head under the water until he was dead. He was very careful not to get himself wet, as you can see, not careful enough. He left the body under the water for a few minutes. Seeing no movement, he walked out of the room, locking the door behind him. He waited another five minutes before he kicked the door in. The rest is in the report."

Pete said, "You know Larry, at times I find the coldness of killers so hard to understand."

"I know what you're saying Pete. None of us understand it and to the end of time we never will. That's why I preach violence begets violence. If a person kills someone, and it's proven beyond a shadow of a doubt, that person should die. Instead they go to jail for life. Which means with good behavior he's out on the streets in less than ten years. Before you know it he's killed one or more people and he's heading back to prison. A person whose mind is three French fries short of a happy meal finds it very easy to kill over and over again. They have no respect for human life."

Lynda asked, "What about us Larry? We kill people."

"Yes we do Lynda. Does anyone of us get any joy or pleasure out of killing?"

No one responded to my rhetorical question. "I didn't think so. When we kill someone it's the last resort. There's nothing else we can do to rectify the situation. In most cases it's them or us. OOPS! I think I got on my soapbox again. I'll get off it so we can get back to work. Does everyone agree that we have a real live murderer in front of us?"

They all did.

"I know you understand Yoto that he's killed once."

"I know Larry. He won't hesitate in killing twice or maybe three times if he thinks she turned him in."

"Seeing the Gods helped us finish early, here's how I'd like the rest of the evening to go down. Pete, you're in charge. Get everything set up before you send Mrs. Garcia home. Tell her we have enough physical evidence to put Jose behind bars. Also tell her it would help our case if she could get him to confess to her how he killed her husband. Tell her we'll have people outside her house with listening devises to hear the confession. Rehearse her as best you can. With her not wearing a wire she should be at ease."

Lynda added, "Her not knowing the house is wired should really make her at ease."

"You're right Lynda. Also with Yoto letting himself in and staying out of sight, she'll act natural. I believe that will also help her get the job done as well as help keep her alive."

Pete said, "I better get going. As usual I have a lot to do."

I said, "Let's all of us feel sorry for Pete together."

"AAHHH," we all said together.

"Thanks a bunch guys."

We all laughed.

"I hate to ask what the rest of you will be doing while I'm working."

"That's easy Pete. Sleeping."

Lynda asked, "You changed the plan Larry?"

"Yes Lynda. We're going upstairs in a few minutes. Yoto, get your black outfit out of the office and come upstairs with us. You and I will leave from here at three o'clock. Which will put us at the house a half an hour to forty five minutes ahead of Jose."

Pete said, "Sounds like a good plan Larry."

"Thanks Pete. I'll see you in the surveillance truck later. Let's get going people."

We went upstairs to my penthouse. I gave Yoto one of the spare bedrooms.

"I'll wake you at two."

"Sounds good Larry."

As I walked to the master bedroom I knew that I hadn't heard the last of this from Lynda. When I walked in the room she was already in her nightgown.

I said, "You may look tired, but you're still the most beautiful woman I know."

"Thank you Larry. Hurry up and get ready for bed. It's almost ten o'clock."

I was in bed and asleep before ten o'clock.

Soon I was saying, "Yoto, it's two o'clock and time to get up."

"I'll be in the kitchen in less than five minutes."

I said, "All right," as I walked down the hallway to the kitchen. I had just finished toasting a couple of bagels when Yoto walked in.

"You better have one, you can use the carbohydrates."

"I agree Larry. Can I also have a glass of orange juice?"

"Take the glass by the bagel. I'll get myself another one."

While I was pouring myself a glass of juice Lynda came in. She was wearing a pink robe over her pink nightgown.

"I hope you boys aren't making a mess of my kitchen."

"I'm not doing a thing. It's all Yoto's fault."

We all started to laugh.

"You may as well blame me. Everyone else does."

"You poor boy," said Lynda.

We continued to laugh, the kidding around helps to take the edge off the stress of an operation. Yoto was going into the lion's den and then into the lion's mouth. I wanted him as loose as I could get him. I knew what we were doing would help.

After we finished eating I said, "Shall we hit the trail?"

"That's a good idea."

"I can be dressed in five minutes if you want the company."

"I'd love the company but there is no danger and I prefer to have you wide awake tomorrow."

"All right, I'll get some rest."

"That's my girl. I'll see you later in the morning."

Yoto and I walked to the elevator which we took down to the parking garage. We drove to the site in Yoto's car. He parked it around the corner and down the street from the surveillance van. I walked to the van and Yoto headed to the house. Within seconds Yoto had disappeared. I knocked lightly on the van's side sliding door. A sergeant opened it for me.

"Good morning Sergeant."

"Good morning Commissioner."

As I walked in I said, "Good morning Officer."

"Good morning Commissioner."

Pete said, "Good morning Commissioner."

"Good morning Chief, anything happening yet?"

"Officer Yoto contacted us as he entered the backyard of the house."

"Did you have good reception?"

"Yes, loud and clear. I told him the house was clear. He should be inside by now."

"He is Chief, if you turn back around and look at the screen."

"Thanks Sergeant."

We watched Yoto as he checked out the house. I love a well trained man. Yoto waved to each camera with an okay sign as he finished looking around. The house wasn't that large. As a matter of fact it was quite small. The reason Yoto walked around the house was he wanted to familiarize himself with the area. After doing that he settled down in the front bedroom. He sat on the floor at the foot of the bed. This gave him a good view of the front room and some of the front door. He picked the best position in the house to observe everything.

"He looks under control Commissioner."
"Not to worry Chief. He'll do his part. How's Mrs. Garcia doing?"
"Great. She's in great spirits."
"Do you think she'll do well?"
"Yes. I don't see a problem. She said she'd give her life to catch her husband's killer."
"I don't think it'll go that far Chief."
"Neither do I Commissioner."
"Gentlemen, nothing should happen for at least an hour. Your job is to watch the screens. The Chief and I will be napping. Wake us at the first sign of anything."
They both answered, "Yes Sir."
Pete and I rested fairly well.
I awoke when I heard the Officer saying, "Look Sergeant! You better awaken the Commissioner."
"That's a good idea Sergeant. But we're already awake."
As we were turning around in our chairs I asked, "What's on the screen?"
"A man that fits our suspect's description just appeared on one of the outside cameras."
We got up and looked at the screen. Sure enough, it was Jose looking for a safe place to hide.
I said, "Keep your eyes on him while I talk to the Chief."
We moved to the rear of the van.
"You have all your boys in a holding pattern don't you?"
"Yes Larry, I do. Is Yoto going to signal us when we are to move in?"
"When the area is safe and secure he'll tell us."
"What you're saying is he doesn't need any help."
"We both know that to be true."
"Is he in combat mode?"
"Only if necessary, with the evidence we have and Jose's confession on tape and premeditation, he should easily get the death penalty."
"I have to agree with you Larry. It'll be a pretty airtight case."
"Pete after the meeting in the morning, I want you to go to your office and get things in order and go home by noon."
"Is that an order?"

"Yes it is."
"Then I'll follow your instructions."
"Thank you."
"Now what?"
"If I have it figured right she should be getting home about now."
"Commissioner!"
"We're on our way Sergeant."
As we watched Mrs. Garcia walk up on the porch, we knew there was no turning back. As she stood in the dim porch light and inserted her key in the door lock we heard a voice from the shadows.
"Mary, don't be afraid. It's Jose."
She turned the key and opened the door.
"Don't run away! I have to see you."
"If you won't hurt me you can come in."
"I'd never hurt you Mary. I love you too much to do that."
"You know I find that hard to believe. I think all you want from me is sex."
"That's wrong. What makes you think like that?"
"What would you call a man that moves in on his dead cousin's wife when his body is barely cold?"
"Mary, it's been almost a year."
"Well you do have a point there."
"If I didn't love you would I still be here?"
"I don't know. Bennie loved me. He was a lot older than me but I know he loved me."
"Why would you say that?"
"There was nothing he wouldn't do for me."
"Would he kill for you?"
"No one ever loved me enough to do that for me."
"I would."
"I hope you don't mind if I don't believe you."
"Wait a minute. Why all of a sudden are you being so nice to me?"
"After talking to you on the phone I thought about what you said. I decided to see if you really cared for me. I've always cared for you. But with your reputation with the women I felt you just wanted me as one of your conquests. That's why I want proof of how much you love me."
I said out loud, "Don't push it Mrs. Garcia."

"You sure you didn't call the police again?"
"Believe me, I didn't call anyone."
"You don't mind if I prove it do you?"
"How are you going to do that?"
As he moved closely in front of her she stood still with her hands at her side. He grabbed her blouse with a hand on each breast area and yanked the blouse open.
"What are you doing!!??"
"I'm sorry. I wanted to see if you had a wire on you."
She pulled her blouse together and folded her arms on it to hold it closed.
"I think you've been watching too many movies. The police only want to come and help you if someone kills you. Otherwise they don't have time for you."
"That's sounds like how they work. I just had to be careful."
"Careful of what?"
"Telling you I killed Bennie, so I could have you all to myself."
"Nice try Jose, but it won't work."
"What do you mean?"
"The police said it was impossible for you to kill Bennie. They convinced me it was an accident because there was no struggle. So don't try to make me believe otherwise."
"What if I could prove it to you?"
"That's impossible. But the thought of you killing Bennie for me did excite me."
"I'm glad. Let me tell you how I did it. It started with me slipping him a roofie in his beer."
I said, "That's how he did it. He used a roofie. The medical term is flunitrazepamor or rohypnol, also known as the 'date rape drug'. Within 20 to 30 minutes it renders its victims unconscious."
Mrs. Garcia sat down on the couch and Jose sat next to her. By the time he finished telling her all the gruesome details of her husband's murder she broke down and started to cry. He grabbed her shoulders and pulled her up straight from her slumped over position.
"What's the matter? I thought you'd be happy that I killed him."
"How could you? I loved him!"
"Now you'll love me."
She spit in his face and said, "Not if you were the only man on this

earth." She stood up and yelled out for help. "Someone get this murderer out of here!!"

"Then you did talk to the police! They'll never take me alive! And that goes for you too."

He stood up and pulled a pistol out from under his shirt and started to point it in her direction. At that point Yoto came into the picture. He came out of the bedroom flying through the air. He went over the top of the couch and his left foot hit Jose's gun hand and his gun went flying. Mary and Jose were both startled to say the least. Yoto landed and rolled into the living room wall and raised himself to a standing position. Jose pulled a switchblade knife out of his pocket. It went 'click' and we could see the long, shiny blade.

Yoto spoke, "I'm a police officer. You drop your weapon and surrender and you will be arrested. If you fight you will die."

"The first thing I'm going to do is kill you. Then I'm going to kill that lying bitch over there."

Jose seemed to mentally snap. The look on his face could kill. He wanted nothing but death for everyone. No matter the cost that is what he wanted to accomplish. Jose kept moving his knife hand and arm back and forth. He then moved closer to Yoto and took a couple of fast swipes at him. One high towards his face and the other one a little lower, about chest high.

There's one thing you must remember when fighting someone with a knife…he wants to kill you. Even if that's not his exact thought. It's too easy for him to accidently kill you. Being a karate expert helps you. But even a karate expert will tell you that he'll probably get cut before he stops his attacker. That's why I always say, "No one wins a fight."

Yoto kept moving backwards as Jose kept in pursuit. Jose swung his knife from side to side. Every once in a while he would try to cut Yoto. Yoto moved down the hallway out of Mary's sight. Jose swung again cutting the front of Yoto's black outfit. On the return swing he missed his target. But Yoto didn't. He grabbed on to Jose's knife hand wrist and pulled him straight up in one motion towards himself. He then put his right hand on Jose's throat and shoved him against the door they were standing by. It flew open and they both stumbled inside. We could hear scuffling of feet and then a thud and a deafening scream.

"Get us up to the house."

As he was moving into the driver's seat the Officer said, "Yes Sir."

It took only seconds for our van to pull into Mrs. Garcia's driveway behind her car. As the Officer was driving I was still watching the screen. As the van stopped I was watching Yoto walk into view in the living room giving me the all clear sign. We left the van and walked up on the porch. Mrs. Garcia must have heard us because she opened the front door.

"Are you all right?"

"Yes Commissioner. A little upset, but it's a good upset. If you know what I mean."

"Yes I do, and may I say, you did a spectacular job. I'm very proud of you."

"Thank you Sir. Also thank you for giving me peace of mind, something I haven't had for the last year."

"You're more than welcome. I'm glad we were here to help out."

"Commissioner, may I meet the man in black?"

"Sure, but I don't have to introduce him. You met him earlier tonight."

As I was peaking Yoto took off his hood that covered his head and face except for holes for his eyes and mouth.

"Yoto, right?"

"Yes Mrs. Garcia. I'm Yoto."

She was now facing him, "Can I give you a hug?"

"I'd like that."

As they embraced, her emotions caught up with her and she started to cry again. So I left Yoto comforting her and walked back to the bathroom. Pete was bent over the body. I looked at the body and thought, 'I couldn't have planned it any better'. Jose was lying in the bathtub face up with his knife protruding from his chest. I remember what somebody once said, "The killer always returns to the scene of the crime." In this case he couldn't have been more right. Except for the water his body was in the exact same spot as his cousin's was. It's ironic how things happen. I turned around and walked out of the bathroom and back into the living room.

"Mrs. Garcia, Yoto and I will be leaving if you're okay."

"I'm fine Commissioner."

"Do you have somewhere you can go until about noon?"

"I guess that would be better. I could go to my sister's. She lives a couple of blocks from here."

"That sounds good."

"Can I ask what happened to Jose?"

"It seems an eye for an eye prevailed. He's dead."

"It was God's will."

"I agree with you. My boys will clean things up here and lock the house before they leave."

"Thank you Commissioner. I'll follow you out."

I walked back to the bathroom and told Pete I'd see him at the meeting. Then Yoto and I left.

When I walked into my bedroom it was 6:20 A.M. I undressed and crawled under the sheets. Lynda rolled over and slid her body next to mine. She didn't have her nightgown on. I know this because I didn't have my pajamas on. She put her arms around my neck and slid up on top of me. She gave me a very passionate kiss and of course I returned it.

"I can tell you didn't miss me."

"I also wasn't worried about you."

She was rubbing her beautiful body against mine as she spoke.

"There was nothing to worry about. I told you I'd be in the surveillance van."

"Don't tell me! You actually did as you told me you would?"

"Yes I did. I love you."

"I love you too."

She kissed me again and again. We made love and took a short nap before getting up to go to work.

Chapter 11

Everyone was on time for the meeting. As we all sat down at the conference table John had my first comment of the day for me.

"Larry, I understand you arrested a real dangerous desperado in this office last night. If it wasn't for your quick thinking and cunningness she would have polished you to death."

Everyone laughed.

"Cute John, real cute."

Jim also commented on the situation, "I'd love to have seen your face as you were scaring the maid half to death."

"If that's the last joke Jim, my face looked the same as it looks now, full of relief and satisfaction that the situation is over."

Tom said, "We get the hint."

"Thank you Tom. Somehow I thought you would."

The Mayor asked, "What did happen last night Larry?"

"As you can tell by looking at Pete and Yoto, it was an all nighter, Mayor. Yoto will fill everyone in on the details in their office later. Pete will fill the rest of you in on the elevator ride downstairs. I hope that makes everyone happy so we can move on. Sam, do you have anything?"

"Yes Larry. The President of the United States will be here Sunday."

"Is that confirmed?"

"Yes, it's been tentative for the last two weeks on a need to know basis."

"And we had no need to know."

"That's right. I'll get the rest of the information to you as soon as I get it."

"What kind of an event is it?"

"He's appearing at a fund raiser for a couple of Congressmen running for re-election."

"How long will he be here?"

"For something like this, usually two to three hours, could you hold all your questions until I know more? All I'm doing now is guessing."

"Sorry Sam. You did say you didn't have any details. We'll speak more on it tomorrow, anything else?"

"Not much. Let me go down my list. The schools are coming along fine. Canada is still on hold. Some of my boys are going into the restaurant this morning to realign the video cameras so we can use them for our surveillance. After they call me with the results I'll call you."

"Sounds good, anything else?"

"I pass to Wade."

"Seeing my partner hogged everything I'll pass to the Mayor."

We all laughed.

I interjected, "Sam's that kind of a guy Wade. You just have to learn to live with it."

"I know Larry. I'm trying."

When the laughter died down I nodded to the Mayor.

"Larry and I checked out the hospital yesterday. Doc gave us the grand tour. Even as rough as it looks you can still tell it's going to be great. The best part of the whole thing is that it's ours. Also, on the way to the hospital we ran into a little bit of trouble. Yoto stopped the limo at a light and Larry noticed something. What did you notice Larry?"

"The man with the shotgun pulled it out as they entered the store. From where we were sitting in the street I had a clear view of it. Now I'll shorten the story for the Mayor. We ended up having to kill all four of the robbers. The Mayor is no longer a virgin. He killed the outside guard himself."

The Mayor was looking down at the table as I spoke, "Mayor, It's nothing to be ashamed of .You didn't have a choice. It was your life or his. The only reason I told everyone about what you did is simple. You always wondered why I wouldn't allow you to go on a mission with us."

"Yes I did."

"Killing a person is not an easy thing to do for a sane person. Which means you could blow a whole operation by not killing somebody as you were instructed to do. So we end up dying because you're not christened under fire. After yesterday if you're needed for a mission I'll use you just like anyone else. This is an open order for everyone. The Mayor needs help with hand to hand combat. There's enough experience in this room to train an army. Work it out with the Mayor and train him. Anything else Mayor?"

"No Larry. I'll pass to Pete."

"Most of my stuff has been covered. But I still have a few things. We're minus four mob members after what you and the boys did yesterday Larry."

Everyone applauded.

"This is only the start. If I have it figured right there are about 1996 more mob members that we'll have to deal with."

Pete said, "That's right Larry. You did say there were about 2000 mob members we wouldn't be able to do anything with."

"And I haven't changed my mind Pete. The schools should save about 4000 of them. Two thirds of a saving is better than none."

"I agree Larry. Can I continue?"

"Yes Pete, go ahead."

"I have our real estate people checking out the properties around our hospital. I'll report their progress when they have some. I saved the best for last. I dropped by my office on my way here. I found this on my desk." He pulled out a piece of paper from his inside jacket pocket. Pete continued, "It's from one of our northern tourist towns. It says a limo has been missing for two days. More to follow."

"Great. Call them direct and get every piece of information you can about the car. Talk to the owner and the drivers. I want to know every little detail they can remember about the car."

Sam asked, "Larry do you really think they're going to try to assassinate the President in our town?"

"I need a little more reconnaissance Sam, before I can answer that question."

"I better alert the President."

"Sam, I wouldn't do that yet. Let me get a better handle on it."

Everyone started to laugh except Sam and Wade.

Wade said, "I thought we knew everything about this group and we were a part of it."

I stopped laughing long enough to say, "You are Wade."

Sam asked, "Then what's so funny?"

John asked, "Can I answer him Larry?"

"Go ahead."

"Whenever Larry wants more time to put something together it means we're in for a big production."

"A big production?"

I said, "Yes Wade, a big production. You guys could call the Secret Service and tell them about our suspicions. They'd stop the President from coming here."

Wade continued, "That's the idea, to keep him out of danger."

"All they'll do is pick another place and time."

"How could they do that?"

"They have inside help."

"I don't believe that."

Everyone started laughing again and Sam joined them.

"What's so funny?"

Sam said, "Wade, the look on your face when Larry finished telling us that we have a traitor in our midst."

"You believe him Sam?"

"Unequivocally Wade. He hasn't failed us yet. I'd love to hear how he's put it together."

"Wade and I will tell you. Won't we Wade?"

"Sure Larry, if you think I can."

"I'm sure you can Wade. Now Wade, when did you and Sam find out about the President's trip here?"

"This morning before we left our office."

"When did someone try to steal our limo?"

"Two, almost three weeks ago."

"We found D.P.S. uniforms, and a night watchman's uniform in the crook's car, which means what dealing with time?"

"It means they stole them before they tried to steal your limo."

"Just knowing those facts tells you what?"

"The crooks knew a month ago what we just found out."

"So either the crooks are clairvoyant or they have someone on the inside."

"That's only if the President is the target."

"We'll know that by the end of the day. Then we'll make our plans accordingly."

"Sounds good to me."

"Thanks Sam. What about you Wade?"

"I've always loved your productions. I'll wait to see what happens."

"Pete?"

"The minute I get the information on the limo you'll hear from me."

"Good, anything else?"

"I pass to Tom."

"I pass to Jim."

"I pass to Lynda."

"I pass to John."

"I pass to Yoto."

"As soon as you know where the President is staying let me know so I can cross check the night watchman' uniform."

Sam said, "I'll do that Yoto."

"Then I pass it back to Larry."

"Gentlemen, you all have your assignments. I suggest we all get to work."

The rest of the day went by smoothly. Everyone got the information they wanted and worked all day cross referencing it.

By the time I started Wednesday morning's meeting a lot of things had fallen into place. We all said our 'Good Mornings' and then we all started in.

"Sam? What's new?"

"If all you want is new, this will be a short meeting."

"That's right we have a lot to do."

"I got all the information I could about the President's visit. I already passed it on to everyone but you." He handed me a piece of paper. "Everything we know is on that paper."

"Looks good, are you going to be free this afternoon?"

"If you need me Larry just call."

"I will. Anything else?"

"I pass to Wade."

"Our man went into the restaurant yesterday and fixed their video cameras. If all goes well we'll have a front row seat for all the action."

"Sounds good Wade. Anything else?"

"Yes. We followed the ambulance plane last night. Our azimuth reading showed it landed about a mile from the border. We have the location but we haven't got the owner of the property yet. We should have that before noon. I'll call you when we have it. I pass to the Mayor."

"I pass to Pete."

"Before you start Pete I need to do something. Mayor?"

"What Larry?"

"Do you still have the clothes sizes for Coop and Josh?"

"Yes I do."

"We will borrow from everyone's wardrobe if necessary but I want Coop and Josh to have a complete outfit of our clothes down to their undershorts."

"You feel they may get shot?"

"Tom, all I know for sure is they'll be unarmed with a bunch of people who have no value for human life. They can't wear a bullet proof vest, so they'll wear our bullet proof clothes."

Sam said, "Great idea Larry."

"Thanks Sam. Now you can continue Pete."

"I'll handle the clothes today. I'll have a cleaning truck drop them off at their house. Will you tell the boys they are coming?"

"I've already taken care of it."

"All right, I have two things. The mobs are really scrambling. We've all but closed down their income through stolen cars. They have little to no drugs to sell. When they try a major crime they end up dead."

"Sounds like we have them on the run Pete, tell the boys to keep the pressure on them. Every time something bad happens to them they lose some old members and a lot of new members. Who wants to join a mob where the biggest thing you can look forward to is dying?"

"We'll keep the pressure on them Larry. The last thing I have is what I told you on the phone. The stolen limo was black on black, the same as the President's limos."

I said, "We all feel the President is a target for something."

Wade stated, "I thought it was an assassination."

"I don't think so Wade."

"He's doing it to me again Sam."

Sam inserted, "You bring it on yourself Wade, by assuming and not using the facts."

"You caught something that I missed?"

"Larry, can I walk him through this one?"

"Sure Sam. Go ahead."

"Do you remember that they stole a limo, D.P.S. uniforms, and a watchman's uniform?"

"Yes, that stuff will help them get to the President."

"If all they wanted to do is kill the President, don't you think that the inside man could do the job himself?"

"Well, yes he could."

"And if they're going to kill him here, a limo would not be a great escape vehicle."

"I agree with that. Wait a minute if they're not going to kill him, what are they going to do?"

"Did you forget kidnapping?"

"Impossible!"

"No very possible. That's why Larry and I spent so much time on the phone yesterday. Besides us, only one other person knows about this."

"Who?"

"General Hatchaway."

"That's all?"

"No. By now he should have told the President."

"Are you going to tell anyone else?"

"That's up to the President. If he likes Larry's plan, no one else will know."

"Excuse me!? You think the President will put his life in danger so we can catch some crooks?"

"Like I said, that's up to the President."

We were interrupted by the phone.

"Lynda, please answer the phone at my desk and take a message from General Hatchaway."

In a couple of minutes she returned with a smile on her face.

"What'd he have to say?"

"Larry, I'll quote the General, 'Tell Larry it's a go, and I'll be there myself'."

Sam said, "The General is good Larry. The message is understandable to us and no one else. You never know who is listening in on your phone line at the White House."

I said, "Lynda thanks for the message. Sam I agree with your statement about the phone lines. Now we need to go to work on the production. I'll let everyone know what I need from them later. Oh, one last thing. The plans you have bundled up next to you, Sam, are the hotel I hope."

"Yes Larry. I marked the possible paths in and out."

"Thanks. That'll be a big help. Anything else Pete?"

"I pass to Tom."

"I pass to Jim."

"Pass to Lynda."

"Pass to John."

"I pass to Yoto."

"And I give it back to Larry."

"Everyone knows what has to be done so let's get to it."

As they were leaving I was spreading out the plans for the hotel. After spending almost an hour on the phone with Sam, I knew what I needed.

"Lynda, call Pete and get him over here. Then look up the number of our old magician friend Nickolas J. Sorrono (Sorrono the Great) and see if he'd like to give us a hand again. If so, arrange a time this afternoon for him to meet us at the parking lot of the hotel."

She left for the phone. I continued looking at the plans. I knew what I wanted to do and I was hoping The Great Sorrono could do it for me.

"Larry."

I looked up and responded, "Yes Lynda?"

"Pete's on his way over. I was lucky, I got Sorrono at home. He was working on a new illusion."

"Will he meet us?"

"Two o'clock in the front parking area."

"Great. Now call Sam and have him meet us there. Also tell him everyone that will be there."

"I've already done that."

"Now who's the mind reader in the family?"

"Not really. Just following what you're always preaching."

"What's that?"

"Listen to what's happening and assess it and then act on it."

"You remembered that I asked Sam if he'd be available this afternoon."

"Yes and figuring that he was our liaison with the President he should be there when the plan is put into effect."

"Good girl! You're 100 percent correct. Now let's go upstairs and have some lunch before our meeting."

As we left our office I poked my head into the boy's office, "Yoto."

"Yes Larry."

"Meet me in the limo downstairs at 1:40 P.M."

"I'll be waiting for you."

With that said I closed the door and joined Lynda.

As we passed my receptionist I said, "Mrs. Thompkin, when the Chief gets here send him up to my penthouse."

"I'll take care of it Commissioner."

Lynda and I had just finished putting out a sandwich and some chips for the three of us when Pete arrived. Pete entered the kitchen area as Lynda was pouring the tea.

"I'm not interrupting am I?"

"Just to make sure you wouldn't we set a place for you."

"That sounds great. I'm hungry."

We sat down in the breakfast nook and started to eat.

"In the future if you need me make sure you call at lunch time."

"I take it you like the service?"

"Fantastic. It's not every day that you can walk in, sit down and start eating."

"Don't get too used to it. It won't become an everyday occurrence."

"I already had that feeling."

Lynda inserted, "I've never seen two guys who could say so much about nothing."

"We know that Lynda. But every once in a while it's fun to expound upon nothing for a few minutes."

Pete also responded, "I agree Larry. It helps to relax the mind. Now that we're relaxed you better tell me what you wanted before Lynda fires us both for wasting time."

We all laughed and Lynda blushed a little.

"I need you to contact your friend in Hollywood. We need the following: an actor who can pass for the President of the United States."

Pete said, "I don't believe it! Somehow you're going to switch the actor for the President?"

"That's right Pete, with the help of Sorrono the Great."

"In that case it may just work. He's good, really good."

"I'm not worried about our part. It's the actor that disturbs me."

"I'll do my best."

"I'll help your best a little Pete, $10,000.00 for a Sunday night appearance."

"It is funny how money always seems to help."

"The actor has to be the spitting image of the President, speech, mannerisms, and looks. There's one crook who knows him very well. That's the one we have to fool. That's also the one we have to catch. We have to bring him out of hiding. That's the reason for all of this. As we say in chess, 'we don't want the pawns, we want the king'."

"I agree. If you'll excuse me for a moment, I'll make a call."

"You can finish your lunch."

"I'll make the call first. It takes him two to three hours to get back to me, so the sooner I call the sooner he'll return it."

"I understand."

He got up and walked over to the kitchen phone, "It's really a shame Larry."

"What's that Lynda?"

"With all the productions you put on you'll never win an Academy Award."

Pete was laughing as he got near the table, "I agree with her."

"Cute guys, really cute."

We all laughed.

"We may never win any awards but somehow I feel the lives we save are worth far more."

"We agree Larry."

"Yes we do."

"I know you do. Did you leave your message Pete?"

"Yes I did. I hope he can get the job done for us."

"Did we get him in trouble the last time he helped us?"

"Seeing we paid him for all his equipment we blew up, as well as gave him a beautifully framed award of merit to hang on his wall, he was happy. Equipment and the makeup artist shouldn't be a problem. The actor is something different."

"Don't worry. The Gods will help us. We'll get it all handled. If your man finds us a good match Sam and Wade can convince him of his patriotic duty to his country and his President."

"I see what you mean. It would be hard for anyone to say no."

Lynda asked, "Are you boys going to talk your lunch hour away or are you going to eat?"

"Pete, the boss is on us again."

"Larry, if I didn't know better, I'd think there's something really bothering her."

"You want to talk about it Lynda?"

"Maybe it's nothing Larry."

"Why don't you tell us, and let us decide."

"All right, you've done a lot of things since you've taken over as Police Commissioner. And as crazy as some of them seem, they all worked out."

"Then what seems to be your problem?"

"The President of the United States?!"

"Could you explain?"

"He's the President! Hundreds of millions of people are going to be affected by what we do here. I'm sorry, but to me that's really scary Larry."

"And it should be. It's a big responsibility."

"But you seem to take it so lightly."

"There's enough pressure on us already. There's no reason to add anything extra."

"Then you're worried Larry?"

"Yes I am."

"Pete?"

"Down to my toes, Lynda."

"Now I feel better. I thought I was the only one worried."

"Lynda."

"Yes Larry?'

"Try not to show that you're worried."

"I won't Larry. I promise."

"Now let's finish our lunch."

As we left Pete in the elevator I told him, "I'll be waiting for your call."

Lynda and I returned to my office for about twenty minutes before heading downstairs to the limo. Yoto was waiting for us. I told him where we were going and we were off.

As we drove, I filled Yoto in on what was happening and what I hoped to accomplish at the hotel. I had the plans of the hotel with me for Sorrono to go over. As we pulled into the parking lot I could see Sorrono standing by his car. I could also see Sam a few spaces away waiting by his car. Yoto parked the limo. We got out and as a group, we approached Sorrono. Sam saw what was happening and also walked toward him.

"Mr. Sorrono!" I said as I shook his hand.

"Mr. Commissioner! I'm happy to see you again."

His English was still a little broken and he still had an accent, both of which I found to be very delightful.

"Let me introduce my friends. This is Special Agent Sam Erkins of the F.B.I."

They shook hands.

"My pleasure, Sir."

"I think you'll remember Sergeant Lynda Stalls."

"I couldn't forget anyone so beautiful."

They shook hands.

"Thank you Sir."

"And this is Officer Yoto."

"Officer."

They shook hands.

"It's a pleasure Mr. Sorrono."

Sam said, "If that's out of the way we can now get down to business."

"That's a good idea. Why don't we adjourn to my limo and allow Mr. Sorrono a minute to go over the plan and see the plans of the hotel? Mr. Sorrono, do you remember how top secret the last job you did for me was?"

"Yes, Mr. Commissioner."

"Well this one is a thousand times more important."

"The only man that important would be the President of these United States."

"You're right. That's who we're protecting."

"Tell me you make a joke. I was only funning."

"Agent Erkins tell Mr. Sorrono what we know so far. I'll tell him what we want to do if possible."

As Sam explained things I could see the look of total disbelief on the face of Mr. Sorrono.

"That's about it Commissioner."

"Thank you Agent Erkins. Do you have any questions Mr. Sorrono?"

"I still can't believe what I'm hearing. This is like stories you hear from the old country."

"The big difference is that our President has us to help him. Would you like to be a part of our team?"

"Oh yes! Please!"

I unrolled the plans of the hotel and showed Mr. Sorrono what I had in mind. I gave him three options and he ended up liking my favorite.

"Now I need to see and measure a few things to make sure we can make it work."

"I understand Mr. Sorrono. But I need you to know something."

"What? Pray tell."

"You'll have to build everything in your shop. You'll have to give me a time table of how long it'll take you to set it up Sunday evening."

"That will make it harder, but I can do it."

"I'm sorry I'm making it hard for you. The problem we have is we don't know if the bad guys have someone at the hotel working for them."

"I understand."

"Sam, there's one thing I need to know now from you, what's our cover for going through the hotel?"

Sam reached into his coat pocket and pulled out a bunch of name tags. "I have one for each of you. You're now city structural engineers. Make sure you return the badges to me before we leave."

"If we all work for the city we better all call each other by our first names."

"I'm Nick," said Mr. Sorrono.

"If everyone will look at their badge, you'll see that I put both your first and last names on it."

I rolled up a couple of sheets of plans with the one needed on top and gave it to Nick. I also rolled up some other sheets and gave one to Lynda and one to Yoto.

"Remember gentlemen, we're City Inspectors. We don't talk to or bother anyone but ourselves. When we get to the downstairs kitchen area we'll look at a couple of different areas as well as the one we're going to use. Sam, did you bring a tape measure?"

"Yes, I brought two."

"Give one to Nick."

He handed him a tape and a small clipboard with blank paper on it.

I said, "Looks like we're ready to move out."

We entered the hotel using the President's route.

I said quietly to Nick, "This is his way in. Did you see anything?"

"Just like the plan, nothing."

"Sam, let's hit the exit route."

We walked through the main ballroom to the right side and up onto the stage.

"This way Larry."

"Hold on Sam."

I stood where the podium would be and looked around. To the rear of the ballroom there were rooms on what looked like a mezzanine.

I pointed up at them, "What's in the rooms Sam?"

"I don't know. Nick, could you roll out the plans on the floor?"

"Yes Sam," as he kneeled down to do so.

Sam knelt down next to him and they looked at the plans together. We accidently had the right sheet with us.

"Here it is Larry. It looks like a projection booth as well as a reviewing booth."

"And it won't be in use Sunday evening?"

"That's correct Larry."

"If we are looking for a gun that is where it will be."

Lynda asked, "You did say gun and not a shooter?"

"That's right Lynda. All they need to do is fire a loud shot. That will scare everyone and cause mass confusion. The Secret Service will do as rehearsed. They'll cover the President and rush him out the escape route. In the confusion the bad guys will kidnap the President."

"The gun?"

"It'll work by remote control Lynda."

Nick said, "I can't believe it."

"I can Nick. So Sam, I want you to cover the podium with an extra bullet proof shield. We don't want an accident. My thoughts are they'll use a blank with extra powder for a louder shot. But I could be wrong so we're not taking any chances."

"I understand Larry. I'll take care of it."

"Also put surveillance cameras on the door to the projection room, and try to hide them. I want to know who the last agent is to check out that room."

"I'll take care of it Larry."

"Now that I've given Sam plenty to do we'll move out. Lead on Sam."

We walked back off the stage the way we entered it and out the rear door. We walked along a narrow corridor and down a flight of steps to another corridor with doors on our right. There were three doors on our right. At the end of the corridor there was a solid steel fire door that led out to the parking garage.

We walked in the first door and looked around. The kitchen crew was busy and didn't pay us any mind. As we looked around Nick played his roll to perfection. He looked up and down and all around. He made notes and measured the door opening. He did the same to the second door. After he finished we walked out into the corridor and headed to the last door. This door was wider than the rest. It was also the one I thought would work. Nick measured the outside and then the inside. He looked around and winked at me. I now knew that he agreed with me. This was the door we'd use.

"Yoto."

He moved closer to me.

"This is the door."

He shook his head in acknowledgment.

"I want two people down here Sunday evening to make sure the area is cleared around the inside of the door."

"Before the President arrives?"

"Yes. Two hours before. I want you in and out of here before the Secret Service checks the place out."

"It'll be done Larry."

I moved closer to Nick, "Take your time and get every measurement you could possibly need. This is our only chance to visit this area."

He did take his time. A half an hour later we were back in the limo.

"Nick, did you get everything you needed?"

"Yes Larry. The time is short. I need to build a mock up of the wall and the door so I can practice the substitution of the door."

"I have two experts at building mock ups if you'd like to borrow them."

"Can they work in my garage?"

"Yes they can and they'll work any hours you wish them to."

"Any?"

"On one project they worked 36 hours straight for me."

"Are they Police Officers?"

"Yes Sir, they are. I'll assign them to you as long as you need them."

"I'd love to have their help."

"Any idea what the materials may cost?"

"Three to four hundred dollars."

"They'll have cash with them to pay for it. Plus dinners and anything else you need. When would you like them?"

"How about after dinner tonight, my house about seven o'clock?"

He ripped the sheet of paper off his clip board and handed it to me. "This is my address and phone number."

"I'll give it to them and they'll be there."

"Can I take the plans with me?"

"Yes, and I don't have to mention it to you again about how top secret your mission is do I?"

"You don't Larry. Also, I'm glad I can help. Now I'd better get going. I want to have a material list done by the time my helpers arrive."

I shook his hand and thanked him as he got out of the limo. Everyone else also waved and said their thanks and goodbyes. At the same time he waved back.

"Sam you better get going as well. We'll see you in the morning."

"All right Larry. Everyone, see you in the morning."

Everyone waved goodbye as he left.

"Yoto, get us out of here."

"Lynda...."

"Get you Pete on the phone."

"Good girl."

She dialed the car phone, "Hi Pete, hold on for Larry."

I took the phone from her hand, "Pete?"

"Yes Larry."

"Two things. One, Sam just left and I gave him a job I want you to do. Call him in his car and tell him I want you to do the video work. I'll explain it to you later. Two, I need our mock builders to help Sorrono the Great. So give Officers Travis Weeks, and Betty Lou Counker the following orders: Meet with Sorrono tonight at his house at seven. Lynda will give you his address in a minute. They are to follow his orders to the letter. Before they leave your office explain to them what is happening and give them one thousand dollars."

"How long will they be assigned to him?"

"As long as it takes until the job is done."

"I'll take care of it. See you in the morning."

"See you then Pete. Here's Lynda." I handed the phone back to her.

While she was talking to Pete I sat back and relaxed. It was four o'clock when we returned to my office.

"Any important messages Mrs. Thompkin?"

"Nothing I couldn't handle Sir."

"Why don't you put the phones on voice mail and head home?"

"I like that idea Commissioner. I'll see you in the morning."

As I continued to walk into my office I said, "Good night Mrs. Thompkin."

"Good night Commissioner."

As we walked toward my desk I stopped and turned around causing Lynda to bump into me. I gave her a big hug and a sensual kiss.

When we finished our kiss she asked, "What brought that on?"

"I just felt I was neglecting you."

"You're not, but you can keep thinking you are."

So I kissed her again. I ran my hands up and down her back.

As we broke from the kiss she said, "If you keep this up I'll soon lose control of myself."

"You are such a sexy lady and I love you so."

"But it's time to get back to work."

"Yes it is. Forgive me for getting you all excited."

"I will not. You'll have to finish what you started tonight."

"I will. I promise. Now why don't you clean off the conference table while I do some work?"

When she finished she joined me at my desk. We worked on the paperwork until five. Before we left I had Lynda call Pete for me. I explained to him exactly what I wanted him to do at the hotel. He told me he would take care of it.

"What about Hollywood?"

"I got the ball rolling. Hopefully we'll know something tomorrow."

"All right, see you in the morning."

"See you then."

Lynda and I went upstairs and made a simple supper. We had a petite sirloin, a baked potato and some green beans. We had a pitcher of ice cold water on the table to drink. We relaxed and unwound as we ate. I tried to fill her in on everything I had in mind doing.

"I don't know how you keep it all in your mind, as well as the solution for everything else."

"It would be impossible if I didn't have everyone's support. I think the thoughts and they do the work."

"I'm sure if you keep thinking they'll keep doing."

"I agree with you."

We finished dinner, rinsed the dished and put them in the dishwasher.

As we were about to leave the kitchen the phone rang. Lynda picked it up and said, "Hello?"

"Hello Lynda this is Coop. Is your old man there?"

"Hold Coop, he's right beside me."

"Hi Coop."

"Hi Larry, I hope I'm interrupting something."

"Sorry, you're not. We were just leaving the kitchen."

"That's a good move. The bedroom would be much more comfortable."

"Coop, are you checking on my love life or do you have something important to say?"

"I just want to cover everything in general."

"We can do that. Shoot."

"The Don will be here in the morning. We'll be tied up all day

with him. That's why I'm calling you now."
"Has anything changed?"
"No. Everything is the same."
"Good. We'll see you tomorrow."
"Just one question before I go."
"What's that?"
"The clothes you sent us. Do we have to wear them?"
"Their almost as good a bullet proof vest and they work. So WEAR them!"
"You really think we'll need them?"
"You tell me. You're going to be in an office unarmed with a bunch of people with guns blazing and bullets flying everywhere. What do you think?"
"The clothes look great and we'll wear them."
"Good. Also, we'll be watching you through the video camera in the office."
"Are you coming in when the bullets start flying?"
"We'll play it by ear."
"Is there anyone you need to have alive?"
"Besides you and Josh everyone else is expendable."
"Good. That makes things a lot easier."
"You two be careful. I'll see you tomorrow."
"See you then."
We hung up the phone.
"Lynda I think it's time for a brandy and bed."
"Bed? At a little after seven?"
"Bad idea Lynda?"
"No, on the contrary Larry, it's the best idea you've had in a long time. Of course that's only my personal opinion."
"In this situation yours is the only one that counts."
"You get the brandies and I'll make sure the house is secured."
"All right Lynda. I'll see you in our room."
We met entering the hallway to the bedroom. I handed her a brandy as we walked.
"A whole night to ourselves, I can't believe it."
"Me either Lynda, let's relax and forget about everything and enjoy the night."
"Plus you have a promise to keep."

"It'll be my pleasure."

She took my drink from my hand and walked over to her night stand and put it down along with her own. As she sat her drink down the phone rang.

"Now who could that be?"

"If you pick up the receiver Lynda, you'll probably find out."

"Hello?"

"Hi Lynda, is Larry there?"

"Hold on Sam."

I walked over to Lynda and took the phone from her, "Good evening Sam. What can I do for you?"

"Have you heard from Coop or Josh?"

"Yes I did."

"Any changes in our plans?"

"Only one."

"What's that?"

"The Don will be with them all day tomorrow so we can't talk to them."

"That's it?"

"That's it. I'll see you in the morning."

"See you then."

I hung up the phone and took Lynda in my arms. She was still standing next to me. I kissed her like we were on our first date. After kissing her a few times I moved my lips down her chin and kissed her neck. I moved up her neck and nibbled on her left earlobe. Next I kissed my way around her neck to her right earlobe. By this time she was excited enough to be panting a little. I was getting excited myself. She was running her fingers through my hair, up and down my back and around to the front of my body. As I was kissing her she was unbuttoning my shirt. So being the gentleman that I am I unbuttoned her blouse. As I allowed my shirt to fall to the floor she did the same with her blouse. I reached between us to unhook her bra when the phone rang.

"I'll get it Lynda."

"Good thing, I'm not in any condition to."

"Hello?"

"Hello Larry, this is Pete. How are you doing?"

"I'm working out. What's up?'

"I was wondering if you…."

I interrupted him, "Talked to Coop?"

"Yes, that's right. Have you?"

"I did. Everything is a go with no changes. We can't talk to him tomorrow because the Don will be with him all day. Now I need you to do something for me."

"What's that?"

"Call everyone except Sam and tell them what I just told you."

"I'll do it. It there's nothing else I'll see you in the morning."

"There isn't. I'll talk to you then."

I hung up the phone and returned to Lynda. She was standing right where I left her. She had her eyes half closed and her hands to her side. I put my arms around her and kissed her beautiful red lips. She responded to the kiss and put her arms around me. I held her close and kissed her a few more times. I then slipped my right hand between us and unhooked her bra. We were now both naked from the waist up. I held her close to me squashing her chest against mine. That is such a wonderful feeling. We kissed some more. I worked my head down and kissed her breast which added to her excitement. I unhooked and zipped down her pants. She was doing the same thing to me. Our pants fell to the floor and we stepped out of them. I pulled her close to me again. The only thing between us was our underpants. At this point we walked over and crawled onto our bed. As we rolled into one another's arms the phone rang. I rolled away from Lynda and answered it.

"Hello?"

"Hello, is Terry there?"

"You have the wrong number."

"I'm sorry."

I hung up the phone and rolled back over to Lynda.

"Why don't we get an unlisted number?"

"We have one Lynda."

We stared at one another for a few seconds before we broke out in laughter.

"I can't believe it. We don't get that many calls in a week."

"I know Larry. I bet it's a deep dark plot to get us."

"I bet you're right. It's the conspiracy of the century."

We started laughing again.

"That's what I like about you Lynda, you're not only my lover but you're a fun person to be with. Now where were we?"

She put her arms around my neck and prepared to answer when the phone rang.

"You were answering the phone again."

We were laughing as I rolled over to get the phone.

"Hello?"

"Hello Larry. The Mayor here."

"Didn't Pete call you?"

"Yes, that's how I knew you were home."

I laughed and said, "What can I do for you Mayor?"

"Did I say something funny?"

"No. It's just a joke between Lynda and me. Now what do you need?"

"Remember I mentioned to you that Judy's birthday is Saturday?"

"Yes I do."

"We want to go out to a movie and dinner. We'd like our best friends to go with us."

"Now I got it. You called your best friends and they can't make it so now you're asking Lynda and me to go."

He laughed and said, "You saw right through me."

"We'd be glad to join you. But didn't you want to have a barbeque Saturday?"

"We're still going to do that Saturday afternoon, but I thought we'd go out Friday night."

"Great. Why don't we fine tune the plans in the morning?"

"All right. I'll talk to you then."

I hung up the phone and rolled back over to Lynda. As I looked into her eyes we both started laughing again.

"I just figured something out Larry."

"What's that?"

"Our telephone could easily be marketed as a birth control device."

We laughed.

"You are definitely correct."

I kissed, held, and made love to her for the next two hours. We woke up in the morning still holding one another.

"I do love you Little Girl."

"And I love you."

"We better get going. We don't want to be late."
We kissed, rolled out of bed and headed for the showers.
It was five to nine when we arrived downstairs.
"Good morning Mrs. Thompkin."
"Good morning Commissioner and good morning Ms. Stalls."
"Good morning Mrs. Thompkin."
"Mrs. Thompkin you can start scheduling things for me on Monday."
"I'll take care of it Commissioner."
With that said we walked into my office. Everyone was sitting around the conference table drinking ice tea and talking to one another.
I stood in front of my chair and said. "Good morning gentlemen."
They replied together with 'Good morning'.
"Before we get started I have a question. Does anyone have anything new and important to talk about?"
The Mayor raised his hand.
"Yes Mayor?"
"Saturday is my wife's birthday. Judy and I would like everyone here, with or without a date to join us for a barbeque at my home at 1:30 in the afternoon. Would you please R.S.V.P. by tomorrow? That's all Larry."
"Anyone else?"
No one said a word so I continued, "I think we should spend our day making sure tonight is a success and that nothing happens to Coop and Josh."
"Larry."
"Yes Jim?"
"Would you mind going over everything we know about tonight?"
"I can but I'd like everyone to jump into the conversation. To start with Coop should be picking up the Don from the airport this morning. The Don will spend the day with Coop and Josh. They'll handle that situation themselves. Pete, did you supply Coop with a closed in van to transport the Don?"
"I took care of it. We had a real plush one at the motor pool. It should impress the Don."
"Good. That takes care of the day. Next we have the night. It's going to be a little trickier. Sam, where do you have your

surveillance units set up?"

"They rented an apartment across the street from the restaurant. They have a pretty good view of the front of the building and its parking lot. They have orders not to tune in the video until we give them the word tonight."

"I like that. Do you have anyone on the inside?"

"Wade and I will be there for dinner at seven."

"Alone?"

"No, we have reservations for four. We're taking two female agents with us. We ordered a birthday cake to make it seem normal."

"That's a nice touch. It's a shame I didn't think of it."

"What time will you be there Larry?"

"I'll get there about 6:20 so we'll be in time for their early bird specials."

"That's almost as good as my cake idea."

Everyone laughed.

"Who's going with you?"

"Yoto, Lyn-Yhi, and Lynda."

Tom asked, "Larry, how is Lyn-Yhi taking all her exposure to crime?"

"Tom, she seems to be handling it just fine. But Yoto could give us a better answer to that question."

"What you just stated is true Larry. She had never given much thought to crime fighting until the night we saved her from the team of rapists. Since then she's been obsessed with learning martial arts, how to handle weapons, as well as handling herself. It hasn't been very long but I'd put her up against any rookie coming out of the academy."

Pete asked, "Is there a reason you've worked so hard with her?"

"Yes Pete. I fell in love with her and her with me. In order for a relationship to work you must both have something in common. Now we do."

Once again I picked up the conversation, "Now that we have the answer can I ask you why you asked the question Tom?"

"I think Pete caught it. That's why he piggy backed on what I asked."

"Sorry guys, I missed it."

"You have to be a cop for a long time to get it. It's a simple overlooked word...liability."

"Liability?"

"Yes Larry. If there's trouble and Lyn-Yhi shoots someone she can be arrested and sued."

"I agree."

"But if she works for us she won't have a problem."

"I see your point. Do you and Pete have a solution to our problem?"

"Pete?"

"No, go ahead Tom. You were the first one to see the problem."

"I propose we put Lyn-Yhi on the payroll as part of the Commissioner's personal team."

"Full or part time?"

"That's up to Yoto, Larry."

"Yoto?"

"I'm flattered gentlemen. I'd like to see her sworn in and to see her carry a shield. But I'd rather leave her as an undercover agent that we can use whenever we need her, if that's all right with everyone."

I asked for a show of hands and everyone agreed.

Pete stated, "Have her stop by and see me on her lunch hour today Yoto. I'll take care of her at that time."

"I'll have her do that Pete."

I said, "Now if everyone's happy we'll continue."

They all smiled and we moved on.

"Sam, how many people are you committing to this?"

"Locally Larry?"

"Yes."

"The four of us in the restaurant and the four guys in the surveillance room."

"Pete, you're covering everything else?"

"Yes Larry."

"Sam how are you covering the drop point this side of the border?"

"It's being over covered."

"Explain."

"We'll be there, along with the local police, border patrol, D.P.S., and A.T.F. (Alcohol, Tobacco and Firearms)."

John came in with, "I think the only people you're missing is the

Coast Guard."

Everyone laughed.

"Thanks for your observation John, but I can tell that Sam already knows that."

"That's why I said the location was over covered."

"We have to agree with you Sam. How many agents are yours?"

"Two and that's two more than we need."

"Does everyone realize that this is your bust?"

"They do and everything we seize comes up here to be stored."

"Your two boys will make sure of that?"

"They will, or they'll be looking for new employment tomorrow."

Wade said, "You know Larry, that's quite a large ranch you'll be getting. What will you do with it?"

"I have some ideas, but I'm sure everyone else does too."

"Not me Larry, I'm a city boy."

Everyone laughed.

"Thanks John. I'll remember that. For everyone else we'll cover the matter soon enough. Sam, the Blanca Corporation?"

"We've had to go through a lot of mazes and hoops to get the end results."

"Which are?"

"Locations in three adjoining states."

"Are you going to hit them all?"

"Yes Larry. This branch of the operation has given us probable cause for Federal warrants for all of their locations. We're going to hit them hard and fast. Then we'll take their places apart and go through them with a fine tooth comb. We even have I.R.S. coming in for a visit tomorrow. I don't think they're going to be happy campers."

We all agreed with Sam.

"What if you don't find anything on their other locations?"

"We have complete surveillance of the operation here. So regardless of the outcome of the rest of the operation, this part is history."

"Sounds great Sam. The F.B.I. is on the ball."

"Larry, the way you lay out a plan, our job is easy."

"I'm glad I could help out Wade. Can anyone tell me about the Don?"

"He took off this morning and should be here around 11:30 A.M."

"Thanks Wade. To reiterate what I told you last night: Coop will pick up the Don and two of his lieutenants at the airport. He'll bring them to his place for the day. Then he'll allow the Don to use one of his vehicles. Coop and Josh will drive to the seven o'clock meeting together. The Don and his people will follow later. Coop asked for twenty minutes to set everything up in the office. We can only guess what will happen after 7:20 P.M."

Jim asked, "What about Coop and Josh?"

"The only thing I can tell you is that they'll be unarmed, the only two people in the room that will be unarmed."

John asked, "Why did they accept those terms?"

"They had no choice, John. They're the new boys on the block. The drug suppliers didn't want to expose themselves to someone new. The only way they'd meet was if they felt real safe. Knowing they have the upper hand was what they needed. Also, I'm sure their boys will be at the door."

Tom asked, "Do you think they'll have two boys at the door?"

"If I was running the meeting I'd have a man on each side of the door, one standing outside and the other one sitting next to the door on the inside."

The Mayor came in with, "That would be a smart way to do it."

"Yes Mayor it would. So when we get there we'll find out how smart our adversary is or isn't."

"It sounds like fun Larry. I wish I could be there."

"Mayor, there'll be plenty of places for you to be later. Don't rush it, there's plenty of corruption in our town to go around. Before we finish cleaning it up we'll all have had more than our stomachs full."

"Good. I understand Larry."

"Now back to our problem at hand. Sam and Wade, I don't want anyone to enter the office before I do. Do you boys understand?"

They both said, "Yes Sir!"

"Jim and Tom, I want you two in the F.B.I.'s surveillance room. Lynda will be wearing her hair to one side. It will conceal her ear phone receiver. Jim, you'll feed her everything that happens outside the office. Tom, you'll supply a blow by blow of what's happening inside the office. Tom, you'll continue your dialogue until you personally see my face on the monitor in the office. Do you understand gentlemen?"

They answered together, "Yes Sir!"

"John, you'll drive the limo. You'll drop us off at the door. Then you'll park to the rear of the parking lot. Understand?"

"Yes Sir!"

"Robert, you'll be with Pete in his car outside the restaurant. The two of you will coordinate all the outside units. Understood gentlemen?"

Together they said, "Yes Sir!"

I love it when my men answer me like a well oiled military machine.

"Gentlemen you make me proud to be associated with you."

I stood up and picked up my glass of water and said, "A toast to a successful mission tonight. May the Gods be with us and may we all return safely! To the mission!"

They all stood up, held up their glassed and repeated, "To the mission!"

After we sat back down I continued, "Spend most of your day preparing for tonight. Tom, you and Jim need to work on a good sound system for Lynda."

Tom said, "There's a good unit in your armory, Larry."

"That's good. Just make sure it's in good working condition. I don't want to sit there blind."

"It'll be done Larry."

"Sam, I forgot to ask, when are you hitting the in city, out of city, and the out of state operations?"

"They will move only on a direct voice command from either Wade or me."

"Great. So nothing will happen until we're secure."

"That's right. The safety of Coop and Josh are first in our thoughts."

"Thanks guys, I'll tell them that when I see them tonight. Before closing, have I missed anything?"

Sam asked, "One small question Larry."

"The answer is the same as before. This is an F.B.I. action. We're just here for back up. You take all the credit for it."

"I understand Larry. How'd you know that was my question?"

"It was the only one you hadn't asked."

"You got me there."

The Mayor spoke, "You know Larry you would think the drug dealers would get the hint that this is no place to do business. Instead, they just keep coming."

"Mayor in a normal business operation that might be the case, but drugs aren't normal and believe it or not, we're partially to blame."

John jumped in, "Hold on Larry, how are we to blame."

"That's easy John. We destroyed the local gangs. This makes the buying of drugs on the street very scarce. This is where the old rule of supply and demand steps in. Large supply and small demand gives you a small profit. But a small supply and a large demand gives you astronomical profits. Which are hard for anyone to pass up."

"I understand Larry."

"Good John. I hope everyone else does also. I said it at the start that it would take three to five years to clean up our town, and I'm not changing my mind. The crooks are still ahead of us. But we keep chipping away at them. Soon we'll be ahead of them. They won't be bold anymore because we will instill fear into them. Gentlemen, that day is in our future. We've been lucky so far. The people we've dealt with have ended up dead. The good part of dead is the crooks won't be back on the streets in 6 months to 7 years to start trouble all over again. Also they won't be able to run their gangs from inside prison. Eliminating the gangs this way gets us to our goal a little faster. Is everyone with me on this?"

They all nodded their heads and said, "Yes".

"Does anyone have a question or comment before we leave?"

The Mayor asked, "Will you call me when it's over Larry?"

"Sure Mayor, I'll do that, anyone else? Then I guess we're all set."

Everyone started to get up out of their seats except me. Pete was the first one to settle back into his seat. Sam and Wade followed suit.

As John was sitting back down he said, "It looks like we missed something boys."

Everything went quiet as they sat back down.

Sam spoke first, "What is it Larry?"

Jim joined in, "Yeah Larry, what could it be? We have tonight wrapped up in a package with a ribbon on it."

"Just a little point gentlemen, Pete, our boys are supplying the money correct?"

"Yes Larry."

"The Blanca Corporation is supplying the drugs, right?"

"Right."

"Where, when, and how are they doing that?"

"I don't know. Sam hasn't told me yet."

"Sam!?"

"Larry, they flew the merchandise in. We know where it is, but that's all we know."

"Heavy surveillance?"

"Yes."

"Then you'll know the minute it moves?"

"Yes."

"Where do you think they'll take it?"

"I was thinking the restaurant."

"Seven o'clock in the evening, patrons everywhere, help everywhere else, is the restaurant really a good idea?"

"No Larry, it isn't. We just can't think of another place for them to make the drop."

"You can see why you have to rule out the restaurant."

"Yes I do Larry. But what's that leave us?"

"Your boys on surveillance with the dope will call the restaurant surveillance team the minute the dope leaves their location."

"Then they follow the dope."

"Nope, as far as I'm concerned they can take the rest of the evening off, or they can coordinate themselves with Pete."

"If we don't follow them how will we know where the drop point is?"

"Have they talked about the drop point over the phone?"

"No."

"My guess is it's a building within three miles of the restaurant. It's a place they've used before and the nephew will have some of his people there. They'll be waiting for the shipment to check it and help unload it."

"Then we need to find a building owned by the nephew."

"Keep in mind it could be in the dead nephew's name."

"We'll check both of them."

"Now you're cooking with gas Sam."
"I hope so Larry, I almost blew it."
"Nah, I wouldn't let that happen to you. You're too nice of a guy."
"Thanks Larry."
"Now gentlemen I think it's time to get to work."
Most of my men left my office conversing among themselves.
Jim and Tom went into the armory behind the large painting behind my desk. Lynda stayed seated at the conference table with the Mayor and me.
"What do you think Mayor?"
"Personally Larry it seems a little shaky."
"I agree. But with the scum we're working with we can't get perfection."
"I really feel for Coop and Josh being in that den of thieves unarmed."
"I'm glad you're worried. That tells me everyone is worried. That means they'll do their job as precise as they can."
"Larry, I've known you long enough to know when you're worried. This isn't one of those times. Why?"
"Everyone thinks the boys are unarmed."
"Won't they be?"
"I'll tell you the only thing I know for sure."
"What's that?"
"They will not be wearing a visible gun."
"Then they're going to hide a gun on their person?"
"No guns."
"I don't understand Larry. If you don't have a gun you're unarmed."
"Mayor, you're starting to confuse me. I'll explain everything to you tonight."
"That sounds like a plan. I better get to my office."
As the Mayor left Tom and Jim came walking up.
"Larry, how would you like to wear a cufflink shirt tonight?"
"I could do that."
"Then you'll not only be hooked up for sound but you'll also be able to communicate with us."
"What do you have?"
He showed me a small jewelry box. He opened it and displayed a

lovely set of black cufflinks.

Lynda said, "They really look nice."

Tom said, "Not only that Lynda, they're also a radio. The left one sends and the right one receives. To activate them you twist them clockwise."

He took one out of the case and handed it to me. It was square in design. The top black body looked like wire mesh. The stem coming down was silver. They were plain but chic. I twisted the top of the cufflink to see how easily it operated. I then handed it back to Tom. He returned it to its box.

As he handed them to me I said, "Thank you, I'll enjoy wearing them tonight. Do you have something for Lynda?"

Jim handed her what looked like a small hearing aid.

"You can wear it in either ear. It only receives. You'll want to turn it on and adjust the volume before you leave the limo."

"Does this tiny little dial do the trick?"

"Yes Lynda, and don't sell it short. It's a sensitive and powerful little unit."

"I'll be careful Jim."

"Tom, do we have enough range with these units?"

"More than enough Larry."

"How about the batteries?"

"They're all brand new."

"A job well done boys, thank you."

As they said 'You're welcome' Jim handed Lynda a small black cloth bag with black pull strings.

"What's this for Jim?"

"It'll keep your hearing device clean and safe."

Lynda opened the bag and put the device in it. She pulled the drawstrings closed and slipped the bag into her inside jacket pocket.

"You boys better get going. It'll be time to move out before you know it."

Tom said, "We're going Larry."

They did and Lynda and I were alone. We spent the next forty five minutes doing paperwork. At a quarter to twelve John came in to get us and we left for lunch. We were back in my office by one. Lynda and I continued to do our paperwork. Paperwork is the part of this job I hate. At five to three my phone rang. Lynda picked it up,

"Hello."

"Hello Lynda. Can I speak to Larry?"

"Hold on Sam, I'll give him the phone."

"Yes Sam. What's happening?"

"We found the building."

"Are you sure?"

"Yes. Some of my boys physically checked it out before I called."

"Who owns it?"

"You were right. It was the dead nephew."

"What took you so long?"

"Sorry. They had six properties to check out. The sixth property fit our bill. It's the only one that was large enough to drive a truck into for unloading."

"Is it close to the restaurant?"

"Within a mile."

"Good work. Try to be careful with the building."

"I was wondering about that. I know your policy. Whatever the police force takes in a drug raid they keep. Did this building slip through the cracks?"

"I don't know. But I will check on it. Which makes me curious, was it listed in his name?"

"Not really. He used one of his corporations from back east."

"And you just happen to know all the back east corporations he owned?"

"Remember when I told you how excited Washington was about getting the Don?"

"Yes I do."

"After talking to them they sent me all the files on both the nephews and the Don."

"I'd love to know about everything they own here A.S.A.P."

"I'll have someone fax you the information before five."

"Don't fax it to me. Send it over to Pete with a cover sheet explaining what it is and that I'd like some of our boys at all the places tonight so we can impound everything on the list."

"I'll take care of it for you Larry."

"Thanks Sam, anything else?"

"What if we need to talk when we're in the restaurant?"

"Seeing you'll be there last try to sit within eyesight of our table. If you need to talk to me stand up, take a drink, and then head to the bathroom. I'll do the same if I need to talk to you."

"Sounds good, see you later."

"See you then." I hung up the phone. "Lynda what do you say to quitting early and heading upstairs?"

"The best idea you've had all day Larry."

We put everything away and headed out the door and up to my penthouse.

We rested, checked our weapons, and then got ready for dinner.

John was waiting in the limo with Yoto and Lyn-Yhi when we got to the parking garage.

The rear door was open so we got in.

"Good evening everyone. I hope you haven't been waiting long."

Yoto spoke, "We've only been here a minute or two."

"That's good. Shall we be on our way?"

John started the engine and headed toward the restaurant. As he drove I brought everyone up to speed on what was about to take place. They listened attentively. When I finished I changed the subject.

"Lyn-Yhi you look very nice tonight."

"Thank you Larry."

"Lynda and I would like to congratulate you on your new job. I hope it makes you happy."

"Oh Larry it does. It was such a shock when Yoto told me. And I have to admit that I had watering eyes when Pete swore me in."

Lynda said, "Everybody feels that way. You have so much pride you think you'll burst."

"That's how I felt. I want to thank you Larry."

"It wasn't my doing. Other members of the team brought it up and we discussed it and voted on it. Just so you know how the team feels about you the vote was unanimous."

"I hope I can live up to your expectations."

"That shouldn't be hard for you to do. We don't have any expectations for you to live up to."

"Then why did you make me a police woman?"

"Somehow you keep getting in the middle of our cases. So we figured as long as you're risking your neck you may as well get paid for it."

"Does this mean I don't quit my day job?"
"That's right. We'll only use you from time to time."
"I can live with that."
"Good. Once again, welcome aboard."
"Thank you and please thank the rest of the team for me."
"I will. Are you still training hard with Yoto?"
"Yes I am."
"How's she doing Yoto?"
"I'll put her up against any two hundred pound guy."
"That's good to know. Lyn-Yhi, do you have your gun in your purse?"
"Yes Larry."
"Has Yoto explained to you how hard it is to kill someone?"
"He said the first time is really tough."
"It is. Try to remember this; the people we are dealing with will not hesitate in killing you. So it's very simple, if you want to die or if you want to live, it's up to you. When we're in combat mode we don't take prisoners. If you're given a target it's your job to kill him. Everyone else has their own target to worry about. So no one has time to worry about you. Do you understand?"
"Yes Larry. I'll hold up my end."
"Good girl."
"Lynda?"
"Yes Lyn-Yhi?"
"Have you killed anyone?"
"Yes."
"How was your first time?"
"Larry and I were kidnapped and it was a life or death situation. There were four people who had to be killed. Larry took out one with his sleeve knife, Yoto got two with his pistol, which left me with mine. I had a one shot derringer. He was drawing his gun while I was drawing, cocking, and firing mine. I got him right in the eye. It happened so fast that I didn't have time to think about it.*
With the people we're working with tonight, if you have to kill someone you'll do it by reflex because they won't give you time to think about it. So don't worry yourself. Just enjoy the evening."
"I will. Thank you for the advice. I feel a lot better now."
*Author suggests reading Book I "Our Town ~ The Mystery Series"

John said, "I'm glad to hear that because we just arrived at the restaurant."

Lynda and I checked our radios with Jim before we left the limo. I twisted my left cufflink. "Jim, are you there?" I twisted my right cufflink and listened.

"Yes Larry, I'm reading you loud and clear."

"Lynda, can you hear him?"

"Yes Larry, loud and clear."

"Jim, tell Tom we're going in now."

"All right, talk to you later, out."

The four of us got out of the limo and John pulled away to take up his position in the rear of the parking lot.

After entering the restaurant and being led to our table I could see the back of Josh's head entering the hallway that led to the manager's office. I thought 'they're here early. Their plan must have changed.' The floor plan of the hallway was kind of normal for a nice restaurant. First door on the left was the men's room. Second door on the left was the ladies room. A few feet further down the hallway on the right was a large manager's office.

After we were seated Lynda spoke softly to us, "Josh and Coop just entered the office. They're being frisked."

We discussed earlier that we'd try to ask questions or make comments so it wouldn't look like Lynda was doing all the talking.

I asked her, "How many people are in the office?"

Lynda answered, "Tom said 'our boys, the nephew, and three men he doesn't know'."

Yoto asked, "Did he give you locations?"

"Yes. Two of the people he doesn't know are standing by the door. Everyone else is seated around the desk."

"Yoto."

"Yes Larry?"

"Have you been looking around the room?"

"Yes Larry."

"What do you see?"

"Eight people that don't belong."

"Three different tables?"

"Yes."

"Four, two and two?"

232

"Yes."

"I think I have to go to the bathroom. Before I leave, what's going on in the office Lynda?"

"They're joking and getting to know one another with small talk, nothing important."

"Good. We'll be back in a minute."

Sam and Wade's party had just arrived. It was a good thing they were early. I got up and made sure Sam saw me take a sip of water. Then we left the table and headed to the men's room. When we walked down the hallway we noticed one guard standing outside the office door. After entering the men's room Yoto and I went to the bathroom while waiting for Sam. Sam came in and went to the bathroom while we washed our hands. Yoto had already checked the stalls to make sure the room was secure.

"What seems to be the problem Larry?"

"Nothing, we just noticed how nervous you looked and figured you had to go the bathroom."

We all laughed.

"Thanks, I did."

When we finished laughing I got to the point, "Inside the office right now we have the nephew, Coop, Josh, and three strangers. You did notice the guy outside the office door as you came down the hallway, didn't you?"

"Yes I saw him."

"How about the eight guys in the restaurant?"

"What eight guys?"

"You have four guys sitting together, two tables to your left, and two guys at the table to your right, also the table behind them with two guys."

"Are you sure?"

"I'm betting our lives on it."

"What do you want me to do?"

"The table of four belongs to our local drug dealers. I want your ladies to silently keep them there when the other two tables get up to join the Don when he comes through the dining room area."

"It shall be done."

"Can you trust them to get the job done?"

"I don't know. Their files say they can handle it, but I've never worked with them before."

"All right, small change in the plan, have your female agents get the drop on the boys. Then Lynda and Lyn-Yhi will back them up. I know Lynda can handle the situation by herself. So ask your people to follow her lead."

"I'll take care of it Larry."

"Good. You and Wade will follow Yoto and me to the office."

"We understand that part."

"Do you want me to give you a high sign when the Don is heading into the restaurant?"

"Yeah, that way the girls can get ready to make their move."

"All right, I'll do it. Now before we leave I'll call Tom to see if there's anything new." I called on my cufflinks and I found out that they were in the middle of negotiations in the office. "Yoto and I will leave first."

We walked back to the table. We sat down and I explained our plans to the girls.

When I finished Lyn-Yhi asked quietly, "How do you know they're out of town bad guys?"

Lynda said, "I was also wondering that."

I answered them both at the same time, "You know observation is a big part of police work. Team that with years of knowledge of knowing what to look for and you answer your question. Take the four men at the table together. Yoto, tell the girls a little bit about them."

"The four of them have an age, dress, and looks that don't fit together. They're all preoccupied. So far they've ordered and re-ordered cocktails. They keep their eyes on the hallway leading to the office."

Lyn-Yhi asked, "Are you sure they're preoccupied?"

"A few minutes ago Larry and I walked into this room with two very beautiful ladies. One of the men glanced our way for a second and then back to the hallway."

"What about the other people Larry?"

"Some of the same reasons Lynda. The biggest give away is their dress. No one in the west dresses like that. They have to be the Don's people. Any other questions?"

Lynda said, "It'll have to wait Larry, the Don's on his way in."

"He's a little early. You girls know your assignment, don't let me down."

As I was giving Sam the high sign the Don and two of his men walked through the restaurant. He stopped at one of the tables of two men. Then the Don and the two men with him continued toward the office. The two F.B.I. ladies got up out their seats and moved toward the table of four. I nodded at Lynda and she and Lyn-Yhi also headed toward the table of four. At that same moment the Don's four seated men got up and followed him toward the hallway. At that time the table of four men started to stir. At that point the agents moved closer to their table and leaned over them. One of the agents leaned forward and put her small handgun in front of one of the men's shoulder. "F.B.I. gentlemen, please keep your hands on the table in front of you. We don't want a scene, but we will kill you if necessary." The other lady poked her hand gun into the back of the closest man to her. Before the four of them could regain their composure Lynda and Lyn-Yhi were each in place covering the other two men.

One of the seated men, realizing their position said, "Do as they say. They got the drop on us."

Lynda said, "You have more intelligence than I gave you credit for."

"It's very simple, you can hold us here but you can't arrest us for having dinner."

"You may be right but for now just make yourselves comfortable. This may take a while."

Knowing the girls had their situation well in hand I was on my cufflinks talking to Tom, "What's happening Tom?"

"Everything's the same Larry. Wait a minute! There's a knock at the door."

"That will be the Don."

"The guard is opening the door slowly. Now someone is pushing the door open knocking the first guard into the second one. Everyone around the desk is rising up and drawing their guns. Too late the boys coming through the door have them cold. Everyone has their hands in the air. One of the Don's men is gently pushing everyone down into their seats. The drug supplier is the only one talking. Or should I say babbling? Because no one is paying the least bit of attention to him."

I said, "Everyone is seated except the nephew?"

"You're right Larry, and someone else is coming through the door."

"Is he a big man wearing a white carnation in his lapel?"

"Yes, that's him."

"That's the Don. Keep talking."

"He's walking over to the nephew. He's asking him why he betrayed the family. He had a simple operation. No hassles, all he had to do was launder money. But no, that wasn't good enough for him. He had to sell drugs. That's something the Family may have been able to tolerate. But your deed got your cousin killed."

The nephew said, "The Chief of Police killed him and I'm going to get even with him. He killed one of ours and he deserves to die."

The Don said, "I agree with you. Your cousin's murderer should die and will die."

"The Don is taking the flower out of his lapel Larry, and putting it into the nephew's lapel. This is starting to look like a Hollywood movie."

"Just keep to the facts Tom."

"All right, the Don has put his open hands on each side of his nephew's face and he's now kissing him on the lips. I didn't notice this before but one of the Don's men is standing behind the Don."

"He's protecting his back."

"The Don has taken his hands off the nephew's face. He's now turning around and the man behind him is handing him a handgun with a silencer on it. He has just turned back around to face his nephew. My God! The nephew also has a gun. They're firing at one another and they're both hit. Coop and Josh are scrambling to the furthest corner from the action. Everybody is now firing at everybody else. All of a sudden I can't see too much. There's a lot of smoke. Like someone detonated a smoke grenade."

"That would be Josh or Coop."

"But they were thoroughly searched when they entered the office."

"They used exploding 'smoke buttons' off their suits. What's happening now?"

"I don't know. There's still too much smoke."

"Let me know when everything is quiet."

There were two reasons why I didn't want to rush into the office. One, with all the smoke, one of us could easily get killed. Two, Coop or Josh could get killed. Did I mention that I gave Coop and Josh the orders of 'see that no one except them walks out of the office'? If they had prepared themselves correctly, they would each have a small throwing knife inside their belt. The belt buckle is the knife handle and the blade slides out from between the leather part of the belt. The other side of the belt has a small black metal tip. When twisted around clockwise and pulled on it produces a choke cord. With these weapons they would be able to kill someone and then use their gun to kill whoever is left standing.

"How're things looking Tom?"

"Nothing Larry."

"Like in you don't see anything?"

"Also I don't hear anything."

"Keep your eyes on the screen. We're going in. Can you see the office door?"

"Yes I've got a good view of it."

"When it swings open I want a report from you before we enter the office."

"It shall be done."

I got up and motioned Sam and Wade to the hallway. They joined Yoto and me and we walked as far as the men's room.

"Wade, I want you to go back into the restaurant and explain to the patrons and employees, quietly that there is smoke at the other side of the building. Tell them to pick up their belongings and leave the restaurant. Then call your boys in from the stakeout across the street."

"All right Larry."

He turned and left. I motioned Yoto to the office door. He kicked it open and stood there with his gun in hand.

I listened to my radio as Tom said, "I could see the door open but nothing else is happening."

I started to open my mouth when I heard a familiar voice. It was Coop, "There's nothing in here worth getting your clothes all smoky smelling over. We're coming out."

A few seconds later Coop and Josh came strolling out the door. They had small paper type filter masks over their mouths.

"What's it look like inside?"

"A bunch of crazy people. They shot and killed one another. I've never seen anything like it."

"When your eyes get adjusted a little better you'll see that it's okay to talk to us."

Coop looked around and said, "Oh, it's you Sam. I'm sorry. I didn't get a good look at you coming out."

"I'll forgive you Coop. What really happened?"

"The Don killed his nephew who in turn killed the Don."

I said, "A Family that kills together dies together."

Sam replied, "That's a nice way to put it Larry."

"I thought you'd like it Sam. You have my permission to use it in print if you wish."

"Thanks Larry. I'll think about that. What else happened Coop?"

"There were bullets flying everywhere. I sent Josh to the door. He crawled over to the Don and his nephew and picked up the gun that had the silencer on it. He grabbed the nephew's gun and threw it to me. At that time he headed to the door and I ripped two smoke buttons off your suit and threw them in the direction of the shooters. I put my mask on and cut down two of the Don's men. They were the only ones left standing. They fired back and I got hit twice."

"You're not bleeding?"

Josh said, "Neither am I Sam, and I got shot three times."

"How'd you boys manage that?"

"Larry lent us his suits."

"That explains it. Bullet proof clothing."

Yoto said, "Don't leave home without it."

I said, "I think Coop and Josh would agree with that statement Yoto."

Coop said, "You're right about that Larry."

Sam asked, "Are you sure of the situation in the office?"

Josh answered, "Yes Sam. I checked everybody in the room. They're all dead."

"Good. How many did you get Josh?"

"One Sam."

I said, "Job well done boys. Sam, all is secure here. You need to get on the phone and get the rest of this ballgame moving. While you're doing that I'll get Pete to work on his raids."

"Check your watch Larry. It's now 7:40 P.M. At 7:55 P.M. have your people go."

"Consider it done Sam."

With that said he left. I called Tom on my cufflinks and caught him just as he was leaving the surveillance room. I gave him the plan to relate to Pete.

"When you finish that Tom, come over and join us for a drink."

"We'll be there shortly."

While I was talking I was facing the open end of the hall. To my delight Sam had sent one of his female agents to me.

"Agent Erkins thought you could use my help Commissioner."

"He was right. I need you to keep this room secure. No one in and no one out."

"Understood Sir. It shall be done."

"Gentlemen, follow me."

We walked back into the restaurant. The four men the girls were guarding had their right arms under the table. It looked like the girls had handcuffed each one of them to a leg of the table.

"Good work Ladies. Sergeant Stalls and Officer Lyn-Yhi will join us in the bar. That's only if you feel comfortable watching the prisoners by yourself Ma'am."

"They're secure Commissioner. I can handle it. Also, backup is on the way."

"Sounds good, shall we go ladies?"

When we walked into the bar Sam and Wade were still busy on their cell phones.

"Seeing we now own the restaurant, the drinks are on me."

Everyone laughed.

"Who wants to play bartender?"

No one said a word.

"What? No volunteers? Not only do I have to buy the drinks, you also want me to serve the drinks."

Everyone applauded.

"All right, you win."

I walked around the end of the bar and walked up to where everyone was seated. I picked up a brandy snifter and a bottle of good brandy. I filled the snifter half way, "Now that I've taken care of me what would the rest of you like?"

Sam and Wade were off the phone by the time I needed their orders. Everyone was sitting quietly waiting. No one had touched their drinks. It reminded me of the old days. When we successfully finished a mission we'd have a toast. We'd salute our fallen comrades and give thanks for being alive.

"Who'd like to give the toast?"

Yoto spoke, "It was Sam's mission."

"Thanks Yoto, but Coop and Josh made the mission a success. Would one of you boys do the honors?"

Coop said, "That's a good idea Sam. Josh, you have the floor."

Josh picked up his glass, "To all our fallen comrades of our past and to the Gods who protected us this night."

We all said, "To the Gods!"

We all took a drink and set our glasses down.

"Sam, Pete will be rolling in here in less than five minutes, how about your boys?"

"Everything's set. They'll report into our cell phones when each area is secure."

"Then all we have to do Sam, is wait."

"Larry, while we're waiting can I ask you a question?"

"Go for it Josh. You have the floor."

"Coop and I were wondering what we're supposed to do with two million dollars in cash?"

Lynda answered, "You could throw a big party for all your drug friends."

"That's a good idea Lynda. But after tonight all our drug friends are dead."

We were all laughing.

"You guys are cute, real cute. One of you can drop the money by my office in the morning."

"Larry, Coop will do that. Won't you Coop?"

"Yes Josh, I'll do it. Now, can I get another drink? The service in this place really stinks."

I came back with, "You're right Coop, good help is hard to find, hopefully the price of the drinks make up for the service."

We laughed.

As I was giving him and Josh another drink Tom, Jim, and John walked in. John spoke first, "Did I hear something about free drinks?"

I said, "Yes you did John. Seeing that you're our designated driver you may have any soft drink you want on the house!"

Everyone started to laugh.

"You sure can ruin a good evening Larry."

"I know John. I'm a killjoy."

"That's all right Larry. Give me a coke and I'll forgive you."

"Thanks John. Sam, I think your boys have arrived."

Sam swung around on his bar stool and said, "You're right. We'll be back in a few minutes." With that said, he left and Wade followed.

I said to Coop and Josh, "You don't know how relieved I am that you boys came out of this in one piece."

"Thank you Larry. We're sorry we worried you. Also, once again, thanks for lending us your suits. I never thought they'd work so well."

"Coop, I'm glad they worked for you. That's our edge against the bad guys. Every little edge helps."

Tom and Jim ordered a drink.

"Why don't you boys pull a couple of tables together while I make your drinks? That'll make it a lot easier for us to converse."

Everyone seemed to react to my suggestion. They got down off their bar stools and started to move chairs and tables around. In about a minute we had a nice area to sit in. I put the boys' drinks on the bar. I motioned to them with my right arm while pointing to their drinks with my left. They came up and got their drinks as I picked up my brandy snifter and a half full bottle of brandy. I walked around the end of the bar and headed for my seat at the table. I no sooner got seated and was refilling my brandy snifter when Sam and Wade returned.

"How goes everything gentlemen?"

"Fine Larry. It couldn't be better. My boys will wrap everything up here. I hope you don't mind but some of your boys arrived and I brought them up to date. They said they'd help my boys, but their primary mission was to secure the restaurant and everything in it. I'll tell you how efficient Pete is. As we speak, a locksmith is outside changing all the locks on all the doors."

We laughed.

I said, "We have a great team Sam. There's no doubt about it....."

A cell phone started ringing. Everyone reached for their phone. Wade was the lucky one. "Hello?"

We all enjoyed our drinks in silence so he could hear his conversation.

"This is Wade. You're kidding! I don't believe it! I want one of you there personally until I get there in the morning. That's an order! I don't want anything moved until our boys arrive. We'll be coming by chopper and we'll be there in the morning. See you then."

Wade disconnected the call. "Larry, that was our team down by the border. Do you have any idea of what happened?"

"Not this time Wade. You better fill us in."

"The bad guys must have had motion sensors set up because our boys couldn't get within one hundred feet of the house. At that point automatic weapons opened fire on them. We got a D.P.S. officer and Sherriff's deputy wounded."

"Their condition?"

"Flesh wounds, nothing serious."

"Our boys returned fire?"

"Yes. You remember we said there was a small army there? Well there was. When they opened fire it was like all hell broke loose in Georgia. The next thing our boys saw from the building was a white cloth on the end of a rifle. They held their fire and yelled at the crooks to come out of the building. At that time it happened."

"What?"

"The building blew up and collapsed to the ground."

Coop pointed out, "That's two different statements Wade."

"What do you mean Coop?"

Coop answered, "It's very simple. The building either blew up or it collapsed to the ground. It couldn't do both."

"Why not?"

"If you blow something up what do you have left?"

"A bunch of little pieces of something."

"Correct, and little pieces don't collapse."

"I see what you mean Coop. But that's what my man said."

"Something stinks in Denmark Larry."

"I agree Coop. Why don't you take a chopper ride with us in the morning? Maybe your explosive expertise can help us."

"I'd love to join you. I have to bring the money back to you anyway."

I asked Wade, "What time are you thinking about leaving?"

"How does eight o'clock sound?"

"I'd prefer seven o'clock. We have a big day tomorrow. You do remember that we're hosting the President on Sunday?"

"Yes I do and seven o'clock is fine."

Within the next half hour all our units had checked in. Everything went as planned. All the raids were successful. Once again the Gods were watching over us. Not only did we get a restaurant, including the building and the land, we also got a couple of homes and a few other pieces of property. The thing I liked the most was the ambulance service we took over. Seeing our new hospital had no ambulance service yesterday, today it has the best service in town. I love when things come together.

When I talked to Pete on the phone I told him about tomorrow. He suggested I get something to eat and call it a night. He said he'd wrap things up. I told him I liked his idea and that I'd see him tomorrow. I also told him we'd have our morning meeting whenever I returned. He said that he'd notify everyone who wasn't with me.

It was around ten thirty P.M. when Lynda and I got home.

Chapter 12

In the morning I asked Lynda to keep an eye on the office until I returned. She said she would.

It was a nice, clear, warm morning. We had a nice flight south. Inside the chopper we had a pilot, co-pilot, forensic man, Sam, Wade, Coop, and me. The flight down was quiet and uneventful. The nice thing about riding in a chopper is that you can land almost anywhere. As we approached the building Coop spoke first. We all had headsets on so we had no trouble hearing him.

"It's as I thought Larry."

We were approaching from the northeast.

"Are you sure?"

"Could we swing the chopper around and approach from the south?"

"Pilot? Will you do that?"

"Yes Sir. Do you want me to maintain the same altitude?"

Coop answered him, "Could you take us up about another thousand feet?"

"Can do!"

The pilot did as he was instructed. As we once again approached the cabin Coop said, "I got it Larry. I'll explain it on the ground."

"Pilot, take us down."

"Yes Sir."

We landed and disembarked the craft before the propellers stopped turning. We moved as a group toward the cabin. We stopped for a minute while Sam and Wade went to talk to their men.

As we were waiting Coop and I were surveying the people Sam and Wade were talking to.

"What do you think Coop?"

"About what?"

"The whole situation."

"Josh and I taught you enough about explosives to where I don't have to explain the building to you."

"You're right. I caught it on our first approach."

"So did I."

"Then why the second approach?"

"What you always taught us Larry, if it looks too easy they won't need us."

We laughed.

"You're right there Coop. What else did you see?"

"For all the drugs that come in and out of here there isn't enough use around here."

"I agree. The road, the parking, the general use of the area tells me something isn't normal."

"I agree with you Larry. I can't wait to hear what the F.B.I. expert has found."

"Don't be too hard on him Coop. He may not have our expertise, but we're all on the same side."

"I know Larry. But sometimes I get tired of teaching."

"That's the only way they'll ever learn."

"Well here they come, Larry, so get ready."

We both laughed.

While Sam and Wade had been talking to their men, the forensic man had been looking over the situation at the cabin. He poked a bit, and smelled a bit, then shook his head and walked over to us. At the same time, Sam and Wade returned.

"What'd you find out Sam?"

Before he could open his mouth, the forensic man spoke, (I hate people who speak out of turn) "I don't know what he found out, but it looks like you people have wasted my morning."

Sam asked, "You didn't find anything?"

"Just what you reported, a building blown up, under the building we're going to find three bodies. I think you could have done this job without me."

I stepped in, "May I ask you a question?"

"Sure Commissioner. What is it?"

"Could you tell us how the drugs were being smuggled into the United States?"

"The border crossing isn't that far away. The drugs were smuggled across the border and brought here for distribution."

While he was speaking, the border patrol from both sides of the border had walked over.

"Did you gentlemen hear?"

"Yes we did Commissioner, and I don't see how it could possibly have been accomplished."

"That also goes for the Mexican side of the border Senor."

"Would the gentleman from Mexico tell me why this isn't possible?"

"That is easy Senor Commissioner. My friends on your side of the border work pretty close with us. They told us of the latest shipment coming through. I put extra men and dogs on patrol and at the crossing."

"Sounds like what I would have done."

"Commissioner, I did the same thing on our side of the border. We found nothing."

The forensic man said, "Maybe I was a bit hasty in my thinking Commissioner."

"I know you were. The next time you go out on a forensic job, make sure you take your time in studying the situation. Also make sure you know all the questions that need answering. Lastly, leave your problems from home there! Don't bring them on the job with you! Do you understand all that??!!"

"Yes I do Commissioner and I'm sorry. Is there anything else I missed?"

"Do you know why the people blew themselves up?"

Everyone looked surprised and he said, "No."

"Seeing this was a major operation, do you know why very few people visit here?"

"No."

"Do you know how the building was blown up?"

"Probably C-4."

Coop answered, "Wrong."

"Are you sure? No one uses dynamite anymore."

"Coop, explain for everyone."

"The first thing you have to remember is C-4 Plastique is something you have no control over. It's used to blow up and destroy things. Dynamite on the other hand is something we have some control of, because when it blows it does so in a downward manner. If you look over at the building you'll see that it wasn't an explosion. It was an implosion."

"You mean like they do to the big hotels?"

"Yes Sam."

"Why would they do that to a small cabin?"

"I would say they are trying to hide something."

I said, "And I agree with Coop."

Sam asked, "Are you sure of this?"

Coop answered, "As sure as I'm standing here."

I said, "Let me step in. Coop is on my team. When it comes to explosives, he's one of the best in the world. You could probably ask him how many sticks of dynamite they used and he could tell you."

"I could Larry, but that's kind of worthless information."

"Now gentlemen, our next task is to roll up our sleeves and remove that cabin from its site and see what's under it."

With the help of our chopper, cars, and four wheel drives, we had cleared away all the debris and the three bodies by 11 A.M. We were now looking at a wooden floor with a brick wall foundation.

Sam's forensic man spoke, "Commissioner I'm missing something? Or have we gone through everything and still found nothing?"

"On the contrary, we found what we were looking for."

The forensic man started to laugh and everyone joined in.

Someone said, "We found the floor!" and they kept laughing.

I allowed them to laugh. I looked at Coop who had a disgusted look on his face, "Let them relax a little." We waited until everyone quieted down.

"If you're all finished, I'll answer your question gentlemen. If everyone will direct their attention to the floor, and please notice something funny on the floor."

"The large throw rug?"

"Thank you Wade, it is the throw rug. The whole building was blown up and the throw rug is still in place. I wonder why. Coop, would you show everyone why the rug wouldn't move?"

"Yes Commissioner."

He walked on the wooden floor and over to the rug. By taking a closer look he noticed the fringe on one side of the carpet was longer than the other. He felt around the longer fringed side and found a handle with a key hole in it. He reached in his back pocket and pulled out a small leather case. It had a zipper around three quarters of it. He unzipped it, took out a pick, and picked open the lock. He then opened the trap door. When he lifted the door the rug went up with it. I asked one of the officers to throw Coop a flashlight.

"Coop, go down and see what's there."

He disappeared down some steps into the basement of the cabin.

Everyone was mumbling among themselves. They couldn't believe their eyes. This small cabin had a basement. Homes in this area don't even have basements.

Coop walked up out of the basement carrying something under his arm. He walked over and handed it to me.

"There's a bunch of these down there. I think I know what it is, but it's awfully large."

"Are the walls all dirt?"

"Yes and so is the floor."

"Was there any fresh dirt by the south wall?"

"Yes there was."

"I think if you sift through the dirt you'll find two things. One, the detonator, and two, the way they smuggled the finished drugs to this location."

"I'll be back in a minute."

Coop went back down into the basement and Wade followed him. We waited and in less than five minutes they appeared from the basement.

"You were right Larry. I have the detonator."

"Thanks Coop."

"Larry, we also found some sort of cylinder in the south wall. I have an idea what it is, but I'm not sure."

I held up the container from under my arm. "Does everyone recognize this container? If not, think about when you go to the drive through window of your bank. You put your deposit in a smaller container exactly like this."

I could see on their faces that it finally registered with everyone.

One of our border patrol men spoke, "The bank is such a short distance from the car to the teller. With these units there is a weight factor where you can only put three rolls of coins inside at a time. And what you're trying to say is they used this method to send a small amount of drugs miles underground. I don't think so."

"May I explain what you seem to be short of knowledge on?"

"Please do, but I don't think you'll convince me or anyone else standing around here."

Coop said, "Yea of little faith."

"Relax Coop and I'll explain it to them. The system we're talking about is called a pneumatic tube. It's been around and widely used since the 19th century. Some people think it's obsolete, but it's far from that. Its use has been increasing every year since the early 1980's. The system is powered by air pressure. By the looks of the cylinder container I'm holding I'd say that the tube downstairs is about 12 inches in diameter."

"That's about right Larry."

"Thanks Coop. The container in my hand will hold about thirty to forty pounds of drugs. It will travel through the tube at about 25 M.P.H. Does that seem cost effective to everyone?"

The same man spoke, "I said I was hard to convince. This cabin is almost a mile and a half from the border. That's a long way to push something through a tube."

"Not really. The New York Post Office System had a 27 mile pneumatic mail system from 1897 to 1953. The system comprised of tubes eight inches in diameter and located from four to twelve feet underground. The two foot long cylinders carried 21 pounds of letters through the tube at 30 M.P.H. This was done solely by air pressure. Now, who has a problem with this system?"

The man spoke again, "You've convinced me Commissioner. Now what do we do?"

"I'd suggest two good metal detectors."

"Two?"

"Yes Sam, two. One will start from here and the other will start close to and on our side of the border. Hopefully the man at the border will find the buried tube before the man here has to walk the whole mile and a half."

One of the Mexican border patrolmen asked, "Commissioner, are you saying we can follow the tube backwards and find the drug smugglers on our side of the border?"

"Yes and no."

The same border patrolman asked, "What do you mean 'yes and no'?"

"If it's a direct hook up you have them. But if they use a couple of relay stations with rocketeers redirecting the cylinders your big shots could be anywhere."

"Any suggestions, Commissioner?"

"Yes Wade. See that the raiding party has a couple of these cylinders with them. After the raiding party takes down the first relay station, have them hide a homing device inside a cylinder. Before you send it out of the first relay station send out four cars about a mile in each direction, then send the cylinder. Keep doing this until you find their head quarters. I have a feeling you won't find anything at the relay station. Their headquarters is in a basement probably with a business front. What this means is that the cylinder will arrive with no one there to see it. This should allow your boys to hit them before they have time to dispose of anything."

The head of the Mexican border patrol said, "I'll only use my most trusted men."

Sam said, "You can borrow some of mine if you wish."

"We always work closely with your border patrol."

I said, "I'm sure they'll be happy to help you again."

Our border patrol man from the U.S. side said, "You're right Commissioner. It'll be our pleasure."

"Good. Now that it's taken care of, where is our forensic expert?"

"I'm here Commissioner."

He had worked his way to the rear of the people standing around me.

"Aren't you glad we didn't listen to you?"

"Yes Sir, I am."

"Everyone take a lesson from this. If you can't come to work and give 100 percent…stay home! If we had listened to the first assessment of this area we'd be home by now and the drug suppliers would get away scot free. Enough said on the subject. To all you gentlemen on the border patrol…Good Luck!"

They said, "Thank you Commissioner."

"Oh, I almost forgot! Coop, tell us why the three boys inside the cabin blew themselves up."

"Whoever set the charges believed in the statement 'Dead Men Tell No Tales'." Coop then pulled the detonator out of his pocket. He held it up and showed it to everyone. "As you can see it reads three minutes and thirty seconds. I'm sure the boys inside were told they had five minutes after they activated the detonator to get out of the cabin. The important thing that one of the men had to do was to quickly get downstairs, cover up the tube with dirt, and set the detonator. Knowing he only had five minutes he needed to swiftly get upstairs and lock the secret door. Then they could surrender or do whatever they wished. They thought they had five minutes but the detonator was rigged to go off in one minutes and thirty seconds."

Wade asked, "Is that why they started to surrender and the whole building blew up?"

"Yes Wade. That's why." I thanked Coop for his wrap up explanation. "Now if no one else needs us, we're out of here."

We said our 'good byes' and headed for our chopper.

Chapter 13

It was almost one o'clock when we arrived back at my office. Lunch was waiting for us. I had called ahead and had Lynda go out and pick up lunch for us. I also asked her to call everyone for a two o'clock meeting.

Everyone arrived at two. As we sat down at the conference table and got comfortable I said to the Mayor, "We're all back in one piece."

"I'm thankful for that."

"Did Lynda fill you in while I was gone?"

"Yes she did. Except for Coop and Josh, you guys had kind of an easy time of it."

"Yes we did. But we left a lot of work to be done at the border. If the border patrols from both sides of the border work together they should put a lot of people in jail."

"I'm happy for you Larry."

"Thanks Mayor. What we've done is great, but it's still only the start of cleaning up our town. We still have a long way to go."

"We'll just keep hacking away until we get there."

"Yes we will Mayor."

Everyone was listening to our conversation.

"As long as I have your attention, we may as well start."

I pointed to Sam.

"As everyone knows, we've been tied up with this drug bust. It was nothing less than a complete success."

Jim interjected, "We knew it would be Sam, you were running it."

"Did you see me on T.V. Jim?"

"No, the Mayor told me."

"How was I Mayor?"

The Mayor slid over the video tape he had in front of himself to Sam. "I taped it for you so you can critique yourself."

Sam stopped the tape and said, "Thanks Mayor. I'll enjoy it."

"Is that it Sam?"

"No Larry. I found out the President wishes to meet you before his speech Sunday evening."

"I'm honored. Give me the particulars as you know them."

"I will. Now I pass to Wade."

"I'll turn it over to the Mayor."

"Just a few things, I've started to talk to the school officials around town."

"You're covering all the schools in our town, aren't you?"

"Yes Larry. Every school seems to have some kind of a problem. Big or small I think they should be addressed."

"I agree Mayor. Children are in school to absorb knowledge, not violence. There will always be small problems. That's why they have discipline in schools. Once the dopers, killers, and gang members are removed, the officials at the schools will be able to handle their own problems. That's how it was when I attended school and that's how it will be again. Without an education a human being becomes a burden on society instead of an active member of the community. Whoops! Once again I'm on my soap box. Sorry everyone. I'm telling you things you already know. I wish someone would stop me when I do that."

Jim said, "Larry, we enjoy listening to you."

"Thanks Jim. Now we need to get back to the Mayor."

"I'll let you know in about a week when and where we're going to meet with the school officials. It depends on how many people we have showing up."

"Sounds good, what else do you have?"

"The hospital is coming along great. I told Doc you'd be by today with his surprise. I hope I didn't speak out of turn."

"No you didn't. I was thinking about taking a few of the ambulances over to show him today."

"Sounds like a great idea. Can I drive one?"

"Sure Mayor and John will drive one. Who wants to drive the third one?"

Jim volunteered, "I haven't been there for quite a while. I'd like to see the progress that's being made."

"You're in Jim. We'll leave after the meeting. Yoto will drive the limo and Lynda and I will take everyone over to the impound lot to get the ambulances. Is that all, Mayor?"

"Yes Larry. I pass to Pete."

"Larry, I'll piggyback on what the Mayor said. The two military locations are moving right along. They'll open on schedule."

"I'm glad to hear that Pete. What else do you have?"

"You won't believe it, but we're still getting calls from our good citizens reporting mob members. Mostly the same names we already have. But they're telling us about different wrong doings. We're really getting a wealth of information."

"I love it when our people trust us enough to call us with that kind of information. What else?"

"Our real estate people are still putting together deals on the condemned properties around our new hospital."

"Good."

"Now Larry, what you're waiting to hear. My Hollywood friend found us a Presidential look alike back east. I think he said Dayton, Ohio. The man works small clubs and gets great reviews on his act."

"When will he be here?"

"I don't know. You'll have to ask Sam. I turned the man's name over to him."

"What's the F.B.I. have to say about it Sam?"

"We had two agents catch his act last night. Afterwards they talked to him. He was happy to do his patriotic duty. The $10,000 was also a great incentive."

"I thought that would help."

"Now, to answer your question Larry, he'll arrive this afternoon about four. Wade and I will pick him up at the airport and bring him here."

"Would you like to use the limo?"

"I'd rather not draw any extra attention to him."

"You're right. What else?"

"The F.B.I. is paying for his performance."

"That's good. We appreciate it. That's $10,000 that's stays in our slush fund. Do you think you'll be here a little after five from the airport?"

"That's about right."

"What have you told the man?"

"His country needs his help and special skills Sunday night."

"That's it?"

"That's it Larry. We thought we'd let you explain it to him."

"Thanks Sam. I knew I could count on you."

"Hey, we always try to give you the easy jobs. That's what makes us so nice."

"Cute Sam, real cute!"

Everyone started to laugh.

"All right, I'll take care of it. But I'd like everyone here at ten to five. We need to make sure he's good enough to pull this off. If that's all Sam, we'll get back to Pete."

"That's all. It's back to you Pete."

"I have the surveillance all set up at the hotel. Unless you know where it is, you'll never find it."

"You realize we need to know who the inside man is as soon as he appears on the screen?"

"Unless you need me somewhere else, I'll man the unit myself."

"That's a good idea Pete. I like it. For now, that's how we'll work it. What else?"

"I pass to Tom."

"I pass to Jim."

"Canada is getting close to going down sometime next week. I'll let you know when. I pass to Lynda."

"I talked to Sorrono the Great this morning. He said he'd be ready by Sunday morning. He also sent a special 'thanks' to you, Larry for the wonderful help you sent him."

"I'm glad they're working out for him, anything else?"

"No, I pass to Robert."

"I pass to John."

"And I pass to Yoto."

"Nothing to report. I pass it back to Larry."

"Can I say something I forgot Larry?"

"Go ahead Mayor."

"I did invite everyone to my wife's birthday – barbeque celebration tomorrow afternoon. Pete and Tom are the only two who have R.S.V.P.'d, would everyone let me know by six today? I don't want to be short on food. That's it Larry."

"Why don't I make it easier for you Mayor? Everyone put a hand in front of you so the Mayor can see it. Put the number of fingers into the air for you and your guests. Mayor if you'll count the fingers that'll take care of your problem."

"Thanks Larry. You can continue now."

"You're welcome Mayor. I think everything is being taken care of the best it can be done. So I'm going to change the subject to something new. Who can best describe the property we've just taken in down south?"

"That would be me Larry."

"Then Wade, I'd like you to tell us everything you know about the property."

He pulled out a small notebook from his inside coat pocket and flipped it open. "I had a feeling you'd want that information so I made notes about it."

"Please elaborate on it for us."

"The property has a main house with 6 bedrooms and 5 bathrooms. It's about 5500 square feet. There are also three bunk houses that can sleep about 20 people each with bathrooms and showers. Other buildings consist of two barns, two tack rooms, a work shop, and a tool shed. The place is in pretty good condition. It even has piped corral fencing. Everything I mentioned sits on 160 acres of deeded land."

"What you pointed out to us from the chopper looked a great deal larger than 160 acres."

"Larry, 160 acres is deeded land. The other 120,000 acres are B.L.M. (Bureau of Land Management) leased land for cattle grazing."

"Pete."

"Yes Larry?"

"Have our Real Estate Officers check out the leases. We have no use for them, but I'd be willing to bet we could sell or trade them for something of value."

"I'll get right on it Larry."

"Anything else, Wade?"

"No Larry, that's about all I know."

"Thank you, Wade. That was a good presentation."

"I'm glad you liked it."

"Now what's needed is an idea of what we should do with this property. If we all remember correctly John's a city boy so he can't help us."

Everyone laughed.

"Larry, are you picking on me?"

"No, just reiterating what you said earlier."

We all laughed again.

"All kidding aside, we need to think of something constructive we can do with the ranch."
"Do we need to follow 'Larry's theory'?"
I asked, "Which one is that Jim?"
"The one where if it doesn't make a profit it's not a good idea."
Everyone was laughing again, even me.
"Cute Jim, real cute."
When the laughing quieted down I made a short statement,
"Gentlemen, one, this is a serious problem and two, it doesn't have to make a profit."
We laughed again.
"If that be the case Larry, I'd like to make the first suggestion."
"Go ahead Jim."
"I'd like to see a nice ranch for the autistic, mentally handicapped, terminally ill I think you get the idea, type children."
"Lynda, make notes of the suggestions for me. With the show of hands, there will be a few."
"I'll take care of it Larry."
"Let's see, I think John the city boy put his hand up next."
We all chuckled a little.
"What about a place for boys out of lock up or borderline kids to help them adjust back into society?"
"I like it. Mayor, you were next."
"What about a camp for the inner city youths?"
"Tom?"
"What about a dude ranch for the rich and famous so we can show a profit?"
"Robert?"
"Can't we just sell it?"
"Pete?"
"How about a retreat for our own people?"
"Sam, you're next?"
"I'll tell you what it won't work as. That's a distribution point for drugs."
We all agreed.
"Looks like we've covered the subject."
Wade asked, "What about you Larry? Do you have a different idea?"

"You know, Wade, I haven't given it a whole lot of thought. I figured someone would have a good idea and we'd just do it. The trouble we now have is we have six good ideas. So if I did have an idea, which I don't, I'd only add to the problem."

Pete asked, "Larry, would you like me to form a committee of volunteers to figure out which plan is the best?"

"We don't need a committee for that. Six of you gave me a plan. If you think your plan of action is the best raise your hand."

All six hands went up.

"See how easy this is Pete?"

"That's why I figured a non-partisan committee could go through the ideas and pick the best one."

"That's the problem I have Pete. They're all good ideas. So what's needed is a supreme commander to make the decision right now without a bunch of hooey."

The Mayor asked, "I know you're versed on a lot of subjects but do you think you know enough to make a correct decision about this?"

"Yes Mayor, I feel qualified to make the right decision."

As I looked around the table I could see strange looks on six faces.

"By the looks on your faces I would say no one wants to lose. So being the fair and impartial judge that I am, I pick all six of your ideas as the winners."

"How're you going to do that Larry?"

"A lot easier than you may think Mayor. There are 12 months to a year. If we give each program a 2 month period it'll work."

"Two months seems awful short Larry."

"Mayor, look at it as eight to twelve sessions depending on the weather. The sessions will be five to seven days long. We need to make some changes and do some fix up at the ranch. Plus, add a pool, spa, weight room, commercial kitchen, and steam room. If everything is handled correctly, the money we make on the tourists should almost cover the rest of the year."

"How do we get staff out there in the middle of nowhere?"

"That's easy Tom. The boys we take out there who deserve a second chance will get one. The top 50 percent of each class may stay on to help teach the next class. If they wish to, they may also stay and take care of the kids who come down. When we feel they've earned the right to say their time is served they'll have the option of staying on and being paid while they continue to learn. Once again Mayor and Pete, there's a lot of loose ends, but I'm sure you can get a committee to help out with those."

"Now that we have the basis Larry, it'll be a snap."

"Thanks Pete. Oh Pete, before I forget, did you make the tape I asked for?"

"Yes Larry, but I left it in my car."

"When you leave take Coop with you and give it to him."

"You know I don't care for sex tapes Larry."

"Cute Coop, real cute. Hopefully this tape will keep you and Josh alive."

"What's in it Larry?"

"Pete, why don't you tell Jim, as well as the rest of the guys what's on the tape?"

"Larry called and explained how whoever has taken over the back east family would send someone out here to check with the only two survivors about what really happened in that office last night. So the tape shows the Don killing the nephew and the nephew killing the Don. It also shows Coop and Josh, unarmed lying huddled out of the line of fire. Then it shows a lot of smoke, and that's how our boys escaped. Everyone else must have killed one another."

"I love it! Thanks Larry and Pete!"

"You're welcome Coop."

I said, "That goes for me too, Coop. As of Monday I'm going back to my regular schedule. Mrs. Thompkin is already lining up luncheons for me. So we'll just work around things as always. Sam, when will you and Wade have a full report on our raid last night? We'd like to know what happened at the other locations. We'd also like to hear what Washington had to say."

"You'll get it as soon as I get it."

"The following morning meeting will be soon enough."

"Sounds good to me, I'll do it that way."

"Is there anything else?"

No one said a word.

"Then I suggest, gentlemen that we work together to see that the President has a safe visit to our city. Which leads me to one last quick question, Pete, when's the makeup woman coming in?"

"She'll be here Sunday. I'll bring her up to your place at that time."

"Approximate time?"

"She gets in at 11:15 A.M. Sometime after noon."

"That works for me. Now, if that's all gentlemen, let's get to work."

Yoto, Lynda, and I dropped the Mayor, John, and Jim off at the storage yard. Pete had called over to the yard before he left my office and told them to have three ambulances gassed and waiting for us.

Yoto pulled the limo up to the emergency entrance to the hospital and dropped Lynda and me off. He then pulled the limo out of the way of the entrance. We hadn't gotten too far into the emergency area when I could see Doc helping some other men move a large counter. So Lynda and I hurried to them and gave a hand. When the counter was in place I nodded at Doc.

"Commissioner, glad to see you!"

We shook hands. He also said 'Hello' to Lynda and shook her hand.

"What brings you to my hospital? Oh! Let me take that back. The Mayor said you'd be by today with my surprise."

"That's right. Have you figured out what it is yet?"

"I have a thought, but it's too wild for me to think."

I had asked the boys to turn on the sirens when they turn onto the side street going around to the front of the hospital.

I looked over at Lynda, "Do I hear sirens? Something must be happening outside."

Lynda replied, "Maybe we better go out and see what's up."

"Good idea Lynda. Doc, by the sounds of things you better come with us, someone may be hurt."

The three of us ran to and out the emergency room door. Lynda and I were in front of Doc. The minute we got outside my boys turned off the sirens but they left the flashing lights on. Lynda and I stopped and separated so Doc was looking right at the ambulances.

As Doc walked past us I patted him on the back and said, "Surprise!!"

He had a shocked look on his face. "Are you serious Larry? Three ambulances?"

"Well, not quite."

"I didn't think so. Ambulances cost a lot of money. What I mentioned earlier was I was hoping we could get one ambulance."

"We've done a little better than that for you. We got you 12 ambulances, three air-vac helicopters, and two air-vac planes. Surprise!!!"

He once again had that dumbfounded look on his face.

"Can I ask how you did it? Or maybe I shouldn't know."

"They're part of a raid. We'll also get you all of the office and dispatch materials. Will you be able to handle everything?"

"Not by myself, but I know someone who owned an ambulance service. He sold it and took an early retirement. The retirement's been killing him. I think I can hire him at a reasonable salary. He can make a few dollars and live a lot longer."

"Sounds like a winner to me. The vehicles will be kept in our storage yard until you need them. Just call Pete and he'll have the stuff delivered to you."

"Sounds great, Larry, and you have my permission to give me a surprise any time you wish."

"I'm glad I made you happy."

"Larry, you've made every wish I've ever had come true. You're more of a friend than any man deserves."

"It's easy to do things for someone who does things for you without asking for anything in return."

We shook hands and gave each other a hug at the same time. We spent the next half an hour touring the hospital. We took the ambulances back to storage and headed back to my office. It was a little after four thirty when we arrived.

"John, would you and Jim see if you can find a disguise kit in my armory?"

"We'll take care of it Larry."

Lynda and Yoto got ice tea for the conference table. Everyone arrived at a quarter to and milled around talking. At 4:55 P.M. there was a knock at my door.

Lynda answered the door. It was Sam and Wade with our actor. They walked right through the office to the lounge area. All three of them went through the door and Lynda returned to the table. About a minute later Sam came over and sat down.

"He'll be out in a few minutes. I told him he had to audition for the job. He said, "If that be the case, I need to get myself ready." That's what he's doing right now. Wade is keeping an eye on him."

"Sounds good Sam. What's the file you put in front of yourself?"

He opened it and slid glossy 8 by 10 photographs of the President around the table.

"This is what the real President looks like. Watch our actor, his movement and mannerisms. We'll check his voice out later."

"Sam?"

"Yes Larry?"

"Why don't we treat him like the President? Tell him to pretend it's a cabinet meeting."

Sam arose from his seat while he was saying, "I'll handle it Larry. I'll tell him to do his best. He usually tries to make people laugh."

"Have him do his best. Tell him he can make up the cabinet people's names."

"All right Larry."

After Sam left, I took another chair, leaving the head of the table for the President.

"Gentlemen, play it straight. Do a little acting. We have to make sure he can pull this off."

We sat quietly sipping our tea and waiting.

Soon Sam reentered the room, "Gentlemen, the President of the United States!"

I watched his every move as the President entered the office. He had the walk and maneuvers down pat. When he entered the room we all stood up at attention.

He walked to the head chair and looked at us, "Gentlemen, please take your seats."

We spent the next fifteen minutes asking and answering questions. When things seemed to slow down, I was impressed. He looked and talked like the President.

I stood up and said, "Mr. President, I'm impressed. Let me introduce you to everyone. Then I'll tell you about what we need you to do."

"Are you sure someone wants to kidnap the President?"

"As sure as you're sitting here Mr. Kennsington."

"Please call me Al."

"All right, we'll do that."

I spent the next five minutes explaining to Al what he'd have to do. After I finished we all sat quietly.

"You've had a minute to digest what I've told you. Is that enough time for you to make a decision or do you wish to sit and think about it for a while longer?"

"I always thought this kind of thing was a real hard sell. So far you haven't done that."

"Let's see Al, I could tell you how patriotic this thing is to do, but you already know that don't you?"

"Yes I do."

"I guess I could threaten you with the I.R.S. or tell you we have two other people who will do the job or that you'll be branded a coward. There's a lot more we could think up to say Al if it takes that to get the job done, I don't want you on our team. The F.B.I. is paying you $10,000.00 because we don't expect a man to work for nothing."

"I understand and I'm glad you asked me the way you did. I have only one question, make that two."

"Go ahead."

"Could I get killed doing this?"

"Yes, but we'll do everything we can to protect you. That's why it's so important for you to study your script and keep your mouth shut. They can't find out that you're not the President. Do you understand that?"

"Yes I do."

"What is your second question?"

"If I live through this will I get to meet the President?"

"We'll do one better than that for you. You'll have dinner with the President and the First Lady."

"You can arrange that?"

Sam spoke, "Believe me, he can arrange that."

"Did I convince you boys that I was the President?"

I said, "Let me have a show of hands of who was convinced."

Everyone raised their hand including me.

"I know I'm convinced that I can do it, and if you're convinced that I can do it…I'll do it."

Everyone applauded. I reached over and shook his hand.

"Sam, do you have a place for Al to stay?"

"I was thinking of a safe house but……."

"But you're afraid of a leak."

"Larry, we're talking about the President of the United States. We can't be too careful."

"I agree. Why don't we do this the easy way? Who would like a roommate for a couple of days?"

"You have all the room Larry."

"I also have the greatest amount of press exposure Jim."

Tom said, "I agree with you Larry. So if Al doesn't mind he can be my cousin for a couple of days."

Sam asked, "What about his looks? We got a lot of strange looks at the airport."

"John, do we have something we can loan Al that will correct this problem?"

"We sure do Larry."

He reached down by the side of his seat and came up with a small suitcase. He got up, walked over to Al and handed him the case.

I said, "It's a disguise case. Before you leave go into the bathroom with Tom and do something with your face."

"I will Larry. Thank you."

"Tom."

"Yes Larry?"

"You can bring your cousin to the barbeque tomorrow."

"Thanks Larry."

"Now, if there's nothing else, this meeting is adjourned."

We all left the office leaving Tom to lock up.

ABOUT Dinner with the Mayor and his wife Judy went well. We had a great time. Lynda and I were in bed by midnight.

"Larry, are you really tired?"

"No, and I take it you're not."

She was standing by her side of the bed. She slipped the straps of her nightgown off her shoulders and let it slide to the floor. I was watching her with a great amount of delight. She is a beautiful woman with an equally beautiful body. It still amazes me how she fell in love with me. The nice part is that when this town is cleaned up she'll marry me. As I was thinking she was crawling into bed next to me. I stopped questioning what she could see in a man old enough to be her father, and just thanked the Gods for sending her to me. We made love for about half an hour before we fell asleep in one another's arms.

We slept in Saturday morning, made love and then had breakfast. We cleaned up and headed downstairs. It was almost one o'clock. John was waiting with the limo.

As we entered the limo I said, "Good morning, John."

"Good afternoon Larry. Lynda."

Lynda said, "Good afternoon John."

We arrived at the barbeque about 1:15 P.M. and we left about 5:00 P.M.

As we were driving back to my place John said, "Larry, look in front of us at the pickup truck on our left and the car to the right of it."

It seemed the truck was trying to get away from the car. The driver and the passenger in the rear seat of the car extended their arms out the windows. In their hands they each had a gun. They opened fire on the truck. The truck driver applied his brakes and came to a complete stop. The car stopped and started to back up to finish the job.

"Lay on the horn John and head for the car."

The boys in the car stopped and fired a few shots at us. They ricocheted off our bullet proof limo. That was the last mistake they'd ever make.

"John, drop Lynda off at the truck."

"Okay."

As he came to a stop I asked, "Do you have your cell phone in your purse?"

"I do."

"The shooting scene is your baby. We're after the bad guys."

I jumped out of the car with her and got back in the front seat.

"Full steam ahead John. They have a bit of a lead on us."

I picked up my radio and called the main dispatcher at precinct one.

"Dispatch."

"Dispatch, this is the Commissioner."

"Yes Sir!"

"We're in my limo in pursuit of a car full of shooters. We're on

Central heading south. We need intercepts at Maple and Oak. The vehicle is a Mark IV black low rider with at least three occupants. They're armed and killers. They will be taken out in the combat mode. I want a road block on Oak. Have the units on Maple follow me when I pass them. The idiots in the Mark IV haven't even realized that we're following them. I'll stop the car and we'll all take out the cars' occupants."

As we rolled by Maple three cars fell in behind us.

I then heard the dispatcher, "The road block is in place Commissioner."

About that time the boys in front of us hit their brakes. At the same time I activated the weapons system in the limo. The boys did a u-turn only to be facing us. The three cars behind me spread out and put their lights on across the road. Before the boys had a chance to move I sent a small rocket out of the front of the limo. It struck their car in the front grill and exploded taking out their engine. We moved forward and the boys in the car opened fire on us. I then returned fire with one of the two machine guns in the limos' arsenal. Meanwhile the rest of the officers around the car also opened fire. When we finally ceased fire you couldn't even recognize the car.

"John, get out and make sure no one goes near the car."

John jumped out of the limo and shouted out my order. While he was doing that I called the Mayor.

"Get some of our reporters to Central and Oak NOW! I'll explain later."

We disconnected. I got out of the limo as John returned to it.

John said quietly, "Time for another lesson Larry?"

"John, you get smarter every day. The reporters are on their way. What do we know for sure?"

"Some mob will be shy three members tonight. One of the officers recognized the car as belonging to one of the mobs."

"Sounds good. Do you have someone running the car license?"

"Yes."

"Good. Will you get me Lynda on the phone?"

He jumped in the backseat and dialed Lynda's number and handed me out the phone.

"Lynda?"

"Yes. How are you?"

"I'm fine, what about your situation?"

"Don't know. The ambulance just left with a wounded pregnant woman. Her husband will be leaving in a minute. He has a bullet in his thigh."

"Which hospital?"

"General."

"Do you have backup?"

"Yes, I have three cars here."

"Have one of them bring you down the street to Oak. Have the other two rope off the truck until the reporters get their pictures of it. Make sure they know to stand guard."

"I will Larry and I'll see you shortly."

I handed John the phone and he put it back into its cradle. He got out of the car and closed the door. "Now what?"

"Now we wait for Lynda, also an officer to put in charge who knows what to say to the media."

John said, "Naturally we'll be gone by the time the media gets here."

"That's my plan. So pull the limo out of the street and into the alley over there," I said pointing to the alley. "Then give me a hand out here."

I walked by the officers roping off the area. They had already blocked off the street in both directions with their vehicles and flares. It wasn't long before a lieutenant I recognized showed up. I had John fill him in while I went to the limo to wait for Lynda. She arrived at the same time as the reporters. The black and white saw my limo and pulled over by it. Lynda got out of the patrol car and into the limo.

"I'm glad to see you made it."

"Where's John?"

"I think he's out there trying to get on T.V."

She laughed and said, "He knows better than that."

"I know. I was only kidding. Here he comes."

He got in the driver's seat and said, "It's all set. When they finish here the reporters will go down the street and then to the hospital."

"Lynda, call Pete so I can fill him in."

After I finished with Pete I called the Mayor. Then I settled back and got back into my conversation with Lynda. "Where were we before we were so rudely interrupted?"

""We were talking about how nicely mannered Doc's children were."

"That they were, the perfect little lady and gentleman."

"What I was wondering is what was Coop bending your ear about?"

"Remember yesterday we gave him the video tape in case someone from back east shows up?"

"Yes. What about it?"

"They were waiting at the house with Josh when Coop arrived home from the meeting."

"Guys from back east?"

"Yes four of them."

"What happened?"

"He said it went beautifully. He told them the same story that Josh had told them. Then he put the tape into the VCR. He told them he had to pay a lot for this copy and he hadn't had a chance to see it yet. If they wished, they could all watch it together. After seeing it they said they appreciated everything Coop and Josh had done for the family. The Don's son said he would honor his father's debt."

John asked, "Which means?"

"Very simple John, if Coop or Josh ever needs a favor from the family they've got it."

We all busted out laughing.

Lynda asked, "Larry isn't that what's called 'having your cake and eating it too'?"

"Something like that Lynda."

We laughed some more.

John asked, "Did you get a good look in the Mark IV Larry?"

"No John. Remember, we had just eaten?"

We all started laughing again.

"Like that would really bother you."

"Not really John, but you had looked at it and that was enough for me, how'd it look?"

"Really gruesome! They won't be able to use it in print."

"Look at it this way. By leaving things the way they really are the reporters now have a choice of how they wish to handle the situation. It's our job to make the news. It's their job to report it. If they don't tell me how to make it, I won't tell them how to report it."

"I agree with you Larry, but we've given them a hard way to go today."

"I hope someone has the guts to say it and report it like it is."

"I can report this Larry."

"What's that John?"

"You're home."

"Cute John, real cute."

"See you in the morning."

"See you then John."

Chapter 14

I had scheduled a special Sunday morning meeting for everyone. We needed to be ready for the President's visit. We met from 11:00 to 11:30 A.M. Everything and everybody was set and ready to go. We even had two matching bullet proof suits for the President and his imposter. We even had a duplicate pin that the President would be wearing in his right lapel. We had his outfit down to his undershorts. Our man would definitely look like the President. We had memos of everything the President had done in front of his security for the last 24 hours.

The F.B.I. would handle the clearing of the hotel suite for the President. Naturally Sam and Wade were in charge. The suit of clothes for the President was hooked onto the bottom of the mattress with plastic hooks. The reason for that was no matter how well they do their job the Secret Service always sweeps the area with a metal detector.

It was almost one o'clock when Pete arrived with our makeup lady, Judy Peters. Tom was already there with Al.

After the introductions Judy asked Al, "Who did your lousy makeup job?"

"I did it myself. I'm afraid I'm not that good at it."

"You can say that again."

I winked at Al without Judy seeing me, "Why don't you take off your makeup so Judy can see who she's addressing?"

Judy watched as Al removed his hairpiece and sideburns, then his moustache and goatee. Next came some cold cream and a towel that Lynda had gotten him. As he wiped away the facial makeup Judy looked in shock, "I can't believe it! I'm sorry for insulting you Mr. President."

"It's all right Judy. You had no way of knowing who I was under all that makeup."

"I have to ask, why do you need my help Mr. President?"

"Because he's not the President of the United States."

"If he's not he sure fooled me."

"Yes, he fooled you. But we didn't bring you here to be fooled. I'll tell you what we need done. You'll tell me if you can do it by seven o'clock tonight."

I handed her a thick folder. "Inside you'll find 24 photos of the President from every angle. We need Al to look like those photos."

She opened the folder and looked at a few of the pictures. She then turned to Al, grabbed his hair lightly and rubbed it between her fingers. "The hair color will be the tough part but I can do it."

I explained to Judy why we needed Al to look like the President. Then I left it up to her if she wished to do it. Once she had a handle on what we were doing she was more than happy to help out. I put the two of them in a back bedroom with Tom.

"You need anything you ask Tom and he'll get it."

"I should have everything I need."

I believed her. She had two large heavy suitcases that she had brought with her. I left her to do her thing. While they were working another fax came in with more presidential information on it. I had Lynda take it back to Al. Pete had returned from the hotel where he was supervising our local police support.

"Pete, I watched the news and looked through the paper and I was impressed at how well the paper covered yesterday's takedown. I especially liked how the newspaper put some photos on the front page and then a warning not to open the paper if graphic photos disturb you or if you have a weak stomach."

"That's the same thoughts I had. I even called and talked to some of the reporters. I faxed them the rap sheets from the shooters. I also asked if they thought we needed a press conference about this incident. They told me not to waste the Commissioner's time or my own with such nonsense. Just keep on doing the things we're doing. Your friend Mrs. Basil of the Morning News asked me to tell the Commissioner, 'we're getting closer everyday to making our streets safe to walk on at night'."

"I do like that lady. She has a lot of spunk. And she's right. Every day we get a little closer to a clean, safe town. Now I'd better let you go. You have the airport to check out and the hotel."

"I'll do the airport and then the hotel."

"Did Sam give you a photo file of everyone on the President's staff who will be here today?"

"Yes it's in my car."

"Good. You better get going."

"All right, but a quick question, how are you getting Judy and Al into the hotel?"

I reached into my pocket and pulled out two clearance photo I.D.s. "Plus Sam or Wade will accidently be at the door when they arrive."

"Do they know where they're going?"

"They've studied the layout, but to help them out Sorrono the Great and Officers Weeks, and Counker will arrive at the same time. All the materials needed are already there including Judy's extra makeup kit."

"Is Sorrono also a cop?"

"Yes."

"Sounds like a good plan."

"We'll know for sure when it works. Now get out of here."

"I'm going! I'm going!"

Lynda came back as Pete left. I asked her, "Is everything under control?"

"Just fine."

"How are they doing back there?"

"She's meticulous and slow but she wants his hair and eyebrows perfect."

"That's good......"

The phone rings and Lynda answers it, "Hello?"

"Hi Lynda, this is Sam. Is Larry there?"

"Where else would he be? You know he's too young to go out and play by himself."

When I took the phone from her she was laughing and so was Sam on the other end.

"Hi Sam, don't laugh, next week they're going to fit me for long pants."

Now we were all laughing.

"What do you need Sam?"

"I got word from the President that he'd like to see you at eight o'clock sharp."

"In his suite at the hotel?"

"Yes. I'll meet you in the lobby a few minutes before and escort you to his room."

"Sounds good, I'll see you at 7:55 P.M."

"See you then."

I hung up the phone.

"Are you going to meet the President?"

"At eight o'clock sharp."

"You lucky dog, some day I'd like to meet the President."

"Then I suggest you wear something nice tonight."

"What do you mean?"

"Lynda, I love you and I'm going to marry you. Is that right?"

"Yes it is."

"At times you let that cloud why you're really here. As I remember it, 'your life for mine'. You are my primary bodyguard. That means, young lady, you must go everywhere I go. Tonight is no exception."

"What about the President?"

"The way he's protected, he'll be the first to understand. If not, he'll have to learn to live with it. Plus, I want General Hatchaway to meet you. I have a great deal of love and respect for that man."

She came close to me all beaming and smiling. She put her arms around me and asked, after she kissed me, "How do I thank you?"

"Go tell Tom and the others that we're getting ready and not to bother us. When you return, meet me in our bedroom and I'll think of some way you can thank me."

"I can't wait to see what you have in mind."

The rest of the afternoon fell into place. We all had something to eat. Then we got ready and Tom took Al and Judy to the hotel. Yoto drove Lynda and me to the hotel. At 7:55 P.M. the hotel lobby was already a buzz. Sam found us and escorted the three of us to the elevator. Wade was holding the door open and directing people to use another elevator. We stepped aboard and the doors closed behind us. When the doors reopened we followed Sam out of the elevator. Wade picked up the rear. It was eight o'clock sharp when we stopped in front of the President's door. It took about 20 seconds before we walked into the suite. There were four people milling around the suite but there was no President or General Hatchaway. I saw what I figured to be a bedroom door open and out stepped General Hatchaway.

"All right people! The President wants everybody out of the suite so he can converse with his friends."

They hesitated a little but then moved out into the hallway. After the door closed I walked over to General Hatchaway. "General!"

"Colonel Towers! God you're a sight for sore eyes!"
We shook hands.
When he let go of my hand I said, "You remember Sergeant Yoto?"
"Yes I do."
At that time the bedroom door opened again. As a figure walked through it General Hatchaway said, "May I present the President of the United States!"
Yoto and I snapped to attention and so did Lynda and the General.
"At ease, people, and General Hatchaway please introduce me to our guests."
Sam and Wade had waited outside the room.
After introducing Yoto and me, General Hatchaway said, "I'd like to introduce you to this beautiful creature, but I haven't met her yet."
"If I may, Mr. President, may I introduce you to Sergeant Lynda Stalls? She's my body guard as well as my fiancé."
She shook hands with the President, "This is a great honor Mr. President."
"For me as well Ms. Stalls, I have a feeling that the man you're protecting will someday change this whole country. Won't you Commissioner?"
"Sir, we're just cleaning up one town. But if what we do here can carry over to other towns, cities, and states I'll be very happy. It takes a lot of dedicated people to make this happen, and we want to thank you for giving us military support with our school project."
"You're more than welcome Commissioner. Are you sure about tonight?"
I pulled a card out of my pocket. On it I had printed 'the room may be bugged. Let's walk into the bathroom'."
We walked into the bathroom and I turned the water on. Pete had called me earlier to tell me who planted the rifle. I turned over the paper in my hand. I had written the name of who had planted the rifle.
"My God! He's my second in command of my secret service agents."
"I know Mr. President. That's why I would like my people to protect you."

"General, what do you think?"

"Mr. President I'd trust my life and the security of our country to Larry Towers in a minute."

"That's good enough for me."

"Thank you for the compliment General."

"You deserve it Larry, for all the lives you saved during the war and after it. As well as the time you saved both me and my command from capture. I owe you a lot Larry. With the help of the President we'll try to repay you any way we can."

"Thank you General. You know I'll take advantage of your offer."

"Yes I do Larry."

I quickly explained to the President what was expected of him. I showed him the plan of the door trick and how it worked so he'd be ready for it. While he was studying the plan Yoto brought in the suit that we had hidden under the mattress. It was pretty close to the one he had on.

"I really need to change my suit?"

"Yes Mr. President. Two reasons; one it matches the one your double is wearing. Two; its bullet proof. Who knows? They may be using a real bullet and bullets do ricochet."

"I guess it was a dumb question."

"The only dumb question I know is the one someone doesn't ask."

The President changed and then conversed with us for about five minutes.

As we were getting ready to leave the President motioned us back into the bathroom. He turned on the water and spoke, "I've asked this before General and I really don't understand why we have to go through all of this. Why can't we just arrest our traitor and move on?"

"May I answer him General?"

"Sure Larry."

"Mr. President, would you agree with me that these people do not want you dead?"

"I'll agree with that. If that's all they wanted they would have done that a long time ago."

"So now they want to kidnap you. Why?"

"I don't know."

"General?"

"I don't know either Larry."

"Gentlemen, I hate to admit it but I don't know either."

General Hatchaway said, "That's why we're allowing them to kidnap the President's double?"

"That's one reason."

The President asked, "Are there others?"

"Yes Mr. President there are, and I'd like to get everyone of the local people involved. I'd also like everyone on your staff that's involved. Lastly, if there is one, I'd like the country that hired these boys to be recognized."

"Wait a minute Larry, country?"

"Yes Mr. President, country. This plan has been a long time in the making. I feel it's directed at the Presidency, Sir, not you personally."

"Am I hearing you right over this running water? I'm not the target?"

"No Sir. Not personally. You just happened to be the President when their plan came together."

"God! How lucky can I be?"

"To have Larry here? Quite lucky."

"I have to agree with you General."

"Gentlemen, I'll agree with both of you when this plan has succeeded. Now I think it's about time that we get out of here so that the President can make sure he's ready for his speech."

The President said, "Thank you Larry. Let's go out to the other room so I can say goodbye to my other guests."

As we rode down the elevator I could tell that Lynda was bubbling over with pride. She had a personal meeting with the President of the United States. Not many people can say that. When we arrived downstairs we made our way to the ballroom so we could listen to the President.

The speaker at the podium was just finishing when Lynda, Yoto, and I took our seats.

Then we saw a couple of secret service men enter the room. From the podium I heard a clear voice announce, "Ladies and Gentlemen! The President of the United States! Everyone stood up applauding. We joined right in. I looked at my watch. It was eight thirty P.M.

The President was to speak for 40 to 45 minutes. At 9:00 P.M. a shot rang out from a rifle on the mezzanine. The shot was overly loud, and I didn't see a projectile hit anywhere. Like I had suspected, it was a blank.

It did what the bad guys wanted it to. It caused panic in the room, also on the stage. The secret service was all over the President. I heard shouting, "GUN! Gun!" After a few seconds delay the secret service men had the President well covered and they ushered him out the side of the stage. They were following our escape path to a tee.

While all this was going on things were also happening in the parking garage. There were three black limos in the underground parking garage. There was the President's limo, his decoy car, and a limo to carry local dignitaries to the airport to see the President off.

This is the area the guy in the night watchman's uniform was to handle. The third limo was parked behind the President's limo, and over a manhole cover. The night watchman pushed up and opened the manhole cover. He then put a small remote controlled car loaded with nitroglycerin type explosives on the pavement. He ran the car remotely to the rear wheel of the front limo. He ran a second small car under the front of the front wheel of the second limo. He lowered himself and replaced the manhole cover as he went. He then returned to work. He knew when all the confusion started he could easily get away.

As the President moved down the hallway toward the parking garage door, as well as our rigged door, it was now up to General Hatchaway. He stopped the party and President in front of our door. The General was holding one arm of the President which he let go of. He pushed three of the six secret servicemen closest to the outside door to check outside. As they left he grabbed the man who had a hold of the President's other arm and pushed him toward the other end of the hall, "Check out our back! Quickly!" The three men ran toward the other end of the hall. The second they turned their backs the President faded through the door and his double, Al Kensington, appeared and the General grabbed his right arm. He then yelled at the three guys heading back down the hallway.

"Does it look all right?"

They stopped dead in their tracks and one of them yelled, "It's all clear!"

"Then hurry back and let's get the President out of here!"

As they headed back one of the other agents from outside held open the exterior door. He said, "Let's move! It's all clear out here!"

They hurried the President out of the hallway and stuffed him into the second limo.

Our second in command for the Secret Service was yelling out orders. Once he had the President secure he said, "The first limo will be the decoy. I want a couple of you boys in the back seat and one in the front. I want the same thing in the President's car. General Hatchaway! Will you get into the back seat of the decoy car?"

The General moved quickly and got into the car with the other men. He wanted the kidnapping to go as smooth as possible.

The limos were already running. The other agents and our bad guy, Eric Turnser, got into the President's car. Eric got in on the driver's side and spoke on his radio. "All right! Let's move out!"

Both cars rolled forward at the same time. The two explosions sounded like one. The tires were blown apart and smoke was everywhere.

Eric opened his door and pulled the President out of the limo by his left arm. While he was doing this the third limo pulled up beside him and he opened its rear door and pushed the President inside. There were two D.P.S. Officers on motorcycles in front of the limo.

Eric said over his radio, "I'm getting the President to Air Force One before anything else happens." He was already rolling out of the underground garage with the police escort, so there was nothing anyone could do.

The limo headed toward the airport. It went for about a mile before it turned and headed toward the industrial part of Pertsville.

When the limo turned off in the wrong direction our President asked, "Eric, this isn't the way to the airport is it?"

"That's right Mr. President. As of now you can consider yourself my prisoner, so lean back and you won't get hurt."

Our imposter, Al, reached for his watch as we had taught him to do. His watch contains a homing device.

"Mr. President, why don't you give me your watch, we don't need anyone following us."

Al handed over his watch and Eric put it in his pocket.

"Now sit back and keep your mouth shut and everything will be fine."

Al did as he was instructed.

We knew that Eric would take away the watch so we sewed homing devices into Al's coat and pants. We also put a unit into a false tooth. The devices in his clothing were activated before he left the hotel. Our boys were in the air in two different directions to cover the kidnapping. Once they picked up the signal they kept their distance and followed the car. All of a sudden the signal got very weak so they immediately closed the gap between themselves and the limo. Because they didn't have visual contact they had no way of knowing that the two motorcycle officers had pulled into a deserted alley with tall buildings on both sides and right up a ramp into a large semi box. The limo followed them. The truck was closed up and driven away in less than thirty seconds. They had to have practiced a long time for it to go so smoothly. The semi truck drove to the far southwest side of town. The truck was marked up like a furniture van line which is a common sight on the road. Most people are oblivious to them. The truck drove to a ranch with a big barn. It was a normal type of barn you drive in one side and out the other. The truck drove into the barn and the barn doors were closed to the rear of the van. In order to have enough room to remove the limo the cab of the truck stuck out the far side of the barn. When the vehicles were unloaded the van was closed up and sent on its way.

Realizing that Al and the bad guys were now stationary, my boys radioed the coordinates to Pete. When Pete called me on my cell phone I was in the President's suite at the hotel where all his staff was waiting. Besides my team members General Hatchaway was the only other person to know what was happening.

The hotel was getting back to order. In all the confusion our makeup girl had put a disguise on the President and a couple of my boys slipped him out of the hotel. They took him to my penthouse. Lynda had gone with them, as well as Sorronno the Great and the makeup lady. They used my limo so I knew they were all safe. Before they left the hotel Sorronno the Great had done a couple of adjustments to his trick door to make it like a real door. I didn't want anyone the least bit suspicious of what really happened.

I hung up the phone and gave the General the high sign. "That was my Chief of Police. He checked with everyone and they can't find a shooter."

General Hatchaway said, "In all the confusion he'd have no problem getting out of here."

"I agree. It's a good thing the President is safe."

"That worries me a little Commissioner. We should have heard something by now."

He yelled at his aide, "Get me Air Force One!"

As his aide reached for the phone, it rang. He picked it up. "Hello?....Yes, he's here. It's for you General."

"General Hatchaway."

"General, this is Air Force one. We were radioed that there was a problem and that the President was on his way. Was there a change in plans Sir?"

"I don't know yet. But I want you to stay where you are, and do nothing without my direct order. Do you understand what I just said?"

"Yes Sir, I do."

"Good. Then I'll say it again. That plane does not move an inch without my direct order."

"Yes Sir. Understood Sir! If the President of the United States gets on this plane it won't move without your order."

"Now you understand me! I'll speak to you later."

"Yes Sir."

General Hatchaway hung up the phone. There were about a dozen agents in the room besides the General, his aide, Yoto, Sam, Wade, and me. I still had an uneasy feeling.

The General spoke, "Let me have your attention." Everyone quieted down. "The President has not arrived at Air Force One."

Now there was a real hush in the room.

The General's aide asked, "Shall I get Washington on the phone Sir?"

"And tell them what? The President is somewhere with one of our best agents? We need to hear something before we tell the world we lost our President. He may not be lost at all. So let's wait a little. If he's dead, wasting a little time won't matter. If he's been kidnapped his captors will call us, so we will wait."

We waited for about 25 minutes when the phone rang. The General answered it.

"This is General Hatchaway."

"And this is the terrorist who has your President and his body guard."

"Are they all right?"

"Yes. But if you don't do as we ask, they won't be."

"Can I speak to the President?"

"Yes. Here."

"Mr. President?"

"Yes General?"

"Are you all right?"

"Yes, I'm fine."

"Hang in there Sir and we'll get you out!"

The minute General Hatchaway said, "Hang in there." Al knew that we knew where he was.

"General, we don't give in to terrorists."

The terrorist grabbed the phone and got back on the line. "I would think twice about obeying that last order. General, I'll call you back in ten minutes to give you our demands. While you're waiting General, I want you to call Air Force One and tell them that the President will be there shortly and they should follow his orders to the letter. Do you understand me?"

"Yes I do, and I'll take care of it."

"And General, if you don't inform Washington or the press, I'm sure we can handle this whole situation between ourselves."

"I won't tell a soul, at least until I hear your demands."

"That's good General. I'll talk to you in ten minutes."

He hung up the phone and said, "Gentlemen, gather around. The President has been kidnapped."

The General's aide reached for the phone and the General covered his hand with his own. "What are you doing?"

"Getting you Washington D.C.."

"I told the terrorists I wouldn't tell a soul. I've told you folks because you're all here and here you'll stay until we decide what to do."

He released his aide's hand. "You may get me Air Force One again."

He made the call and handed the General the phone.

"This is General Hatchaway."

"Yes Sir!"

"The President will be coming aboard soon. Follow his orders to the letter."

"Yes Sir."

The General put the receiver down and said, "Now we wait."

I moved as far away from everyone as I could. I nodded to Yoto and he followed. When General Hatchaway looked my way I beckoned him to my side.

"What do you think Larry?"

The tone of our voices was so low that no one else could hear us.

"Two things, One; you're playing your role beautifully. Two: I was right. We have a mole among us."

"Are you sure?"

"Yoto, tell the General."

"How did the terrorist know that you controlled Air Force One? That's the President's plane and he controls it as Commander and Chief."

"You're right! I've been trying to keep up appearances and it slipped over my head. Any ideas Larry?"

"Yes. We have four choices."

"Four?"

"Yes. Four different people used the bathroom during our first 25 minute wait."

"I bet you have it narrowed down."

"You're right General. My money is on your aide."

"May I ask why?"

"I saw him earlier today and he was meek and mild. Now he's aggressive and trying to do your job. He's seeing if you'll go against the terrorists."

"Now that you say it I do notice a big difference. What shall we do?"

"All I can say is follow my lead. I think I know what they want and who they're working for. You better get back by the phone. Repeat their demands out loud so we can hear them. Then tell them you need ten minutes to be sure you can do what they want without getting Washington involved. Have them call you back."

He walked away and back to the phone.

"Yoto, in the bathroom. Walk Silent and Walk Deadly recon."

Yoto was near the bathroom door when the phone rang. We all watched the General as he picked up the receiver. I looked back at where Yoto was and he was gone.

"Hello?"

"Hello General, are you ready to make a deal?"

"What are your terms?"

"We want ten tomahawk missiles with nuclear warheads and two hundred million dollars in cash."

"I can do that if you can follow my ground rules."

"I'll listen."

"We get the President back unharmed along with his bodyguard. We will not pursue you for this crime. No one will ever know that this took place."

"If I don't agree?"

"If you harm the President of the United States there won't be a place in the world that you can hide. You will be hunted down and tortured until you die."

"You make my choice easy. You'll get your President back in one piece."

"Before the final exchange I'll want to speak to him as well as see him."

"It'll be done. Now, we're agreed?"

"We are."

"Good. I know you have a ship not too far from Saudi Arabia that is carrying more than ten missiles. I want you to direct the ship to head at full speed toward Saudi waters. A freighter will be heading toward it. They will rendezvous and unload the cargo. Can you handle all that?"

"I don't know. But I think I can. Will you call me back in ten minutes and I'll confirm everything."

"All right, you have ten minutes."

After the General hung up the phone I started in. "General. With one phone call I can have the money for you in about an hour or so."

One of the agents spoke up, "That won't give us much time to mark the money."

I shook my head 'no' at the General but he was way ahead of me. "We're not marking the money. That's my order and you'll follow it."

I started back in, "We don't have to worry about the tomahawks, do we?"

"What are you getting at Commissioner?"

"Well General, I happen to know that without the launching and arming codes the missiles are worthless. If you try to manually make them work they will blow up in your face."

"That's right Commissioner, seeing that he didn't ask me for the codes I couldn't see any reason to offer them."

"I see your point. That was good thinking General."

"Now all we have to do is wait for his call."

The General's aide excused himself to use the bathroom. A few minutes later he returned. A couple of minutes after that Yoto returned to me.

Yoto gave me the high sign, which meant the aide was our mole. I, in turn gave the General the high sign. At that moment the phone rang.

"Hello?"

"Hello, General. What have you decided?"

"I can have the money at the plane in two hours."

"Good. The missiles?"

"I'll make that call when we hang up. You'll have your missiles."

"That's good General. And don't forget all the codes that go with them."

"You'll get everything."

"Good. I'll see you at the airplane."

"Would you answer one question for me?"

"What's that?"

"What country do you work for?"

"General, if the tables were turned you wouldn't tell me that would you?"

"I have to agree with you. Now look at your watch. I have close to ten thirty. I'll have the money at the plane at twelve thirty and I'll leave it with the pilot. You get there whenever you get there. You have a complete communications center on Air Force One. Please contact me when you're in the air."

"I will General and thanks for your cooperation."

The General hung up the phone.

I quietly said, "Yoto. Walk Silent and Walk Deadly, combat."

Yoto disappeared behind the curtains. I walked closer to the General and his aide.

"General? I think it's time we told everyone our little secret."

"Go ahead Commissioner. You have the floor."

"We know where the terrorists are holding the President. I only have to make one call to my Chief of Police and he will take them down."

The General's aide asked, "Are you sure you know their location Commissioner?"

"Yes I do. It's a ranch with a large barn on the southwest side of town. Now I better call and get this thing over….."

The General's aide pulled out his gun and pointed it at the General. "Unless you want to see a dead General you better do as I tell you. Everyone drop your guns!"

The General spoke, "Do as he says."

Everyone dropped their guns.

"That goes for you too Commissioner!!"

I grabbed my coat by the lapels and pulled it open wide and said, 'I don't wear a gun. It makes my coat bulge and looks funny."

"An unarmed Commissioner, that's rich. Now everyone but the Commissioner move over there." He pointed to the open side of the room. He had the General to his left and his gun in his right hand. He had his left hand on the General's right shoulder.

"Now Commissioner, you're going to make a phone call, and not to your man but to the bank."

He watched as I reached across the table for the phone. It was a little out of my reach so he leaned over and pushed me the phone. As he went back to his upright position he had Yoto with his left arm around his neck and his right hand on his gun hand wrist. He snapped it quickly in the direction of the ceiling. This completely opened the man's chest to me. I slipped out my sleeve knife and threw it at the man's chest. You could hear the 'thud' as it went deep into his chest. He slumped to the floor. Yoto removed my knife and picked up the gun. He wiped my knife off on the man's suit jacket; he handed it back to me and put the gun on the table.

"General, you may want to stick that gun in your belt. You may need it later. Gentlemen, retrieve your weapons and get ready to move out."

Everyone picked up their weapons, and the General put the gun from the table into his belt.

"With your permission General?"

"Men, the Commissioner is now in command."

"Thank you Sir. A couple of you guys pick up the body, put it in the bathtub, and cover it with something."

When they finished I had everyone gather around me. "I'm going to tell you what you need to know and what I expect you to do. First; what we know. The gang consists of ten mercenaries, not terrorists as they wanted us to believe. Now we have one dead, which leaves us nine. My boys have all of them under surveillance. They'll call me the minute they move. I'm figuring we'll take them down at the airport."

One of the Secret Service men asked, "How do you know they're mercenaries and not terrorists? And how did you get the count of nine?"

"First things first; terrorists don't care about money. The people behind them have more money than they'll ever use. But these boys want 200 million dollars. The second part of your question has a longer explanation. To do a successful job, I know the bad guys would have to have two inside people."

Another voice said, "You've killed one, now how can we find out who number 2 is?"

"We already know."

Same voice, "Who?"

"Secret Service Agent Eric Turnser."

There was a bunch of 'it couldn't be!' 'you're kidding!' 'he would never!'

General Hatchaway spoke, "Gentlemen! Please quiet down! If the Commissioner said Santa Clause was our second man I'd believe him. So gentlemen he's in charge and he's one of the best in the world at retrieving kidnapped people alive. So follow his orders to the letter. Commissioner..."

"Thank you General. Enough said about me. Let's get back to the question I was answering. We have the two inside men. Next, they had an outside man in the garage area to rig the two limos. Then there's the driver of the third limo and the two pretend D.P.S. motorcycle officers. The driver drove the limo and the two cops followed him into a waiting semi. Two men were needed at the truck to open and close up the van and handle the ramps. They needed two more men at the ranch to open the gates and close the barn doors. Add them all up and you get ten. One dead leaves nine. There could be more but I don't think so. These boys are born greedy. Less people equals more money for each person. Now back to our problem. We need to separate the President from his captors. We'll do this at the airport."

Someone asked, "How Sir?"

"Easier than you may think. I have six sharpshooters who have killed under fire. That will take care of six of the bad guys. I can get the closest one to me with my knife. That leaves two still alive."

"Commissioner, Jake and I were snipers in Nam. The VC had a price on both of our heads."

Jake spoke, "To tell the truth Sir, we were a couple of the best."

"Are you still?"

"We constantly work at it Sir."

"That works for me. Everyone else will be back up. So I want everyone to relax while I make a few phone calls."

Next I called our banker. I had explained to him earlier what I had in mind so he was already to leave when I called. I asked him to go to our safe deposit boxes and fill a couple duffle bags full of large bills. I then called Lynda and gave her instructions.

When I finished my phone calls I asked, "Does anyone have a question before we move out?"

One of the young secret service Agents asked, "Sir, not saying I disagree with you, it's just a question."

"Then ask it. The only dumb question is the one you don't ask."

"You killed a man in front of us. Now you're ordering the deaths of at least nine more people. No trial or due process of law. How can you do that?"

"Very easily."

Everyone laughed.

When things quieted down the young man retorted, "I was serious Sir!"

"I know you were. But I thought a little humor would be good for everyone. So now I'll answer your question if you'll answer mine."

"What is it Sir?"

"You're awful young. Have you ever been in a war?"

"No Sir. But......"

"Hold the buts. Have you even killed anyone?"

"No Sir. I hope I never have to."

"Don't we all? But real life isn't like that. Tell me if I'm wrong. There's no sense in us killing these boys if when this is all over they're going to release the President. Correct?"

"I have to admit, it's crossed my mind more than once."

"Show of hands! Does anyone think the President will be returned alive?"

No one raised their hands except the man I was talking to.

"But I heard the General say that they would deliver the President in one piece."

"They will. He'll be dead but he'll be in one piece."

"Are you sure of that?"

"As sure as you have blood running through your veins. If we allow the President to get on Air Force One we'll never see him alive again."

"You've convinced me. What's our plan?"

"We're dealing with professionals, which means our job is going to be easy but not simple. The limo will hold everyone. If I was ram rodding the job I'd drop off a few of my men within rifle range to make sure no one would be in range to kill us. The two pretend motor cycle cops would flank the car. They would stay on the move and constantly make wide circles until they got close to the plane."

A voice asked, "How are we going to get around that?"

"That's why we're heading to the airport right now. If I was them I'd arrive at the airport at 12:35 A.M. I wouldn't want to spend one minute longer than necessary unprotected. Air Force One is a flying fortress. That's where I'd like to be."

We left the hotel and headed to the airport. We arrived at 11:20 P.M. Air Force One was parked on a back runway all by itself. I explained to everyone that six of my sharpshooters are hiding around the plane. "Pretend you're the kidnappers looking for them. Try real hard to find them."

The reporters were in a special briefing room awaiting the President's arrival.

The guards for the plane were moved back out of firing range.

I was in a car with General Hatchaway. We slowed down and the General rolled down his window. The guard recognized him and saluted. He saluted back as we continued on toward the plane. Pete got out of his car as we approached. To Pete's left was the SWAT van. The driver got out of it and headed over to Pete. We got out of our car and headed toward Pete.

We all sort of converged in the middle.

"Chief."

"Commissioner."

"Would the SWAT Captain take these two boys and have them changed and hidden? Would you also brief them on how we're handling things here?"

The three of them walked away together and I continued to talk to Pete. "Do you have your people deployed?"

"Yes I do. Did you see anyone?"

"No one saw anything."

"I have to agree with Larry. You've done a great job."

"Thank you General."

"My boys know what they're going to do. What I'm worried about is what are you going to do Larry?"

"Pete, nothing dangerous."

"Would you mind telling me about this 'safe thing' you're going to do?"

"I'll come down the ramp of the plane as the crooks limo pulls up. I'll have a duffle bag on my shoulder. He'll ask, 'you did bring the money didn't you?' 'As you requested.' I'll show him the duffle bag full of money and point out the ones stacked by the door of the plane which are mostly full of paper with some money on top."

Pete said, "The full one is sitting by itself and the others are stacked together. They're all at the top of the ramp just inside the plane."

"You told your boys to open fire the minute the President is clear?"

"I did. And they're all using noise depressors. Half of them will be dead before they know what's happening."

"Good. I'll take care of whoever comes to check the money."

"That's what I told the boys."

"How will they know who their target is?"

"I have them on a static beeper type communication."

"Could you explain that?"

"Yes General. I figured the mercenaries will probably have a scanner going when they approach our area. So they'd have no problem at all picking up our voice commands. But by using static no one will pick it up. It's like Morse Code using static. Everyone has a number. First person out of the car belongs to number one and so on."

"What about the two guys on the motorcycles?"

"I have two guys designated just to them. Each man gets the closest guy to him."

"What do you think General?"

"It sounds like he has things well in hand Larry."

"I feel the same way. Where have you hidden the men Pete?"

"Do I have to tell you Larry?"

"Not if you don't want to."

"Let me say this about that. We have people in the wheel wells, on the wings, in the jet ports, and underground between the runways. We used color masking to hide the people on the plane. The others are almost buried alive. When signaled, everyone will come out of their camouflage shooting."

"I couldn't have asked for more."

Pete asked, "Should the General and I pull back to the guard area?"

"That's a good idea Pete. On your way out tell the SWAT Captain to join you as soon as he's finished."

"I will Larry. I'll see you later."

"See you later gentlemen."

As they left I thought the moonless night won't hurt us either.

I walked up the boarding ramp and found the bag full of money. I wanted to be prepared for later. After relaxing for a while I looked at my watch. It was almost midnight. I walked over and looked out the open door. Everything looked quiet and peaceful. I then took a second look. There were headlights heading to the plane. They were moving slowly and cautiously. I could also see two motorcycles driving erratically about the car. I looked at my watch again, still a little before midnight.

This guy is sharper than I thought. He's over a half an hour early. This means he wanted to secure the plane before I could arrive with the money. I hope my element of surprise would at least disturb him a little. I knew it wouldn't make him mad. In his business he can't afford to get mad. That would only take away from his ability to do his job. I did feel good about one thing; he didn't have two guards on the outside walking to the plane. He probably figured being early he'd take us by surprise. Boy! Was he wrong!

Knowing how uncomfortable it was for my men hiding in the camouflaging, I was happy he was early.

I walked out on the ramp with the full duffle bag in my right hand. A motorcycle drove by the stairway and stopped. The limo pulled up slowly and stopped with the front passenger door even with the stairs. The second motorcycle pulled up to the right rear of the limo. The men on the motorcycles were carrying machine guns on straps which were around their bodies. I hoped my boys got them with the first shot; otherwise those machine guns would do a lot of damage to me and our President. The boys with the machine guns had them in their hands and were looking around for anything that moved.

As the front passenger door opened I started to descend the stairs. I swung the duffle bag to my left and grabbed it with my left hand. With both hands I hoisted it above my head. My jacket came open showing I didn't have a weapon. By the time I had gotten to the last two steps, Eric, the traitor, was out of his side of the car and the driver was out of his.

Eric looked at me and said, "So we meet again Commissioner."

"It looks that way Eric."

"I hope that duffle bag is full of money."

"It's not my laundry. Plus there's three more bags just like this one at the top of the stairway."

The driver spoke, "He's telling the truth. I can see the bags from this angle."

"Can I look in your bag?"

"If I can see and talk to the President."

"Everyone out of the car and bring that numbskull with you."

"I take it you didn't vote for him?"

"You got that right! If he should be President then I should be God."

People were getting out of the car. The President was pulled out by the last man who had a pistol to the President's head. The shooter stood leaning against and inside of the open door on my side of the car. He had the President's arm and was holding it tightly.

I walked down the remaining steps. "Would you have your men move out of the way so I could at least see the President?"

They moved away and scattered out a little more. If nothing else it gave my people clearer targets to shoot at.

"Mr. President. Are you okay Sir?"

"Yes I am Commissioner."

"Have they treated you all right?"

"Yes they have."

"Good. They should be releasing you soon."

"Thank you Commissioner."

"Eric, here's part of your money." I tossed the bag at his feet. I was less than six feet from him.

He bent down to open the bag and he froze when he saw me backing up. He came back to a standing posture. "Commissioner, there wouldn't be a bomb in this bag would there?"

"No, just money."

"Then you wouldn't mind helping me open it would you?"

"Not at all."

I moved in closer to Eric. We were almost face to face.

"Shall we do this together?"

"Sure Eric."

I squatted down on my side of the bag and he did the same on his. I put my hand on the zipper and slowly started it and then yanked it all the way open. "See, lean, green, unmarked cash."

"So it is." He was running his hands in the bag to feel the money. When his hands came out of the bag each one had packets of bills in them, he put his hands into the air so his men could see the money. I figured this was as good a time as any to make my move.

I reached in my left sleeve and brought out my knife. I lunged it at Eric's chest only to feel a bullet proof vest slow it down. It stopped me long enough for Eric to throw the money into my face and swipe down with his left hand which dislodged my right hand from my knife. He sprang over the money bag on top of me. Every one of his men had their eyes on us when all hell broke loose. As I struggled with Eric I could hear gun shots coming from the bad guys.

I found out later that the man next to the President was the first one shot. At that time the President did what he had practiced. He dove head first onto the floor of the limo.

I really had my hands full with Eric. I had read his dossier earlier and he was one well trained individual.

I knew he had a gun in the rear of his waistband and one I could see in the front. I had to keep his hands away from them. Another thing that made it a tough fight was his size. He was about my size and fifteen years my junior.

We rolled on the ground until he hit the stairs. I had his hands at the wrists. When he hit the stairs his back was against it. I wedged my right shoulder against his left shoulder. I knew I wouldn't be fast enough to get his gun out of his belt so I could use it. If I drew it out he'd knock it away. And that would make our fight a little more even. I reached, we struggled, and he forced the pistol to fly away. Now it was my skill against his. As his hand forced the gun to fly into the air away from us I was able to hit him under his jaw with my right hand. He recoiled upward from the punch. While going upward he forced his whole body to continue in that direction. He twisted to his right and managed to roll over on top of me. But he didn't stop there. He rolled another three times and scrambled to his feet. By the time he finished I had gotten to mine and faced him.

"Give it up Eric!"

He looked around at his men. There were none of them alive. "You killed them all!"

"Death begets death, Eric. So give it up!"

"Commissioner, I'm going to kill you. Then Air Force One and I are getting out of here."

I was standing about six feet from Eric. What I didn't know was that Pete had broken radio silence after the last man was killed. He informed all his sharp shooters "If you have a clear shot, take it!"

After the last word came out of his mouth Eric reached his hand behind himself waist high. I knew the next time I'd see that hand it would have a gun in it. There was only one thing I could do. I fell down on my fanny and brought my right knee to my chest to draw out my two shot derringer. I hadn't cleared leather when Eric was pointing his gun at me. Before he could shoot bullets hit him from every angle. His head seemed to explode from the multiple hits from every direction. His gun fired into the ground as he slumped into a headless heap. While I stood up my people were walking toward me guns in hand.

I yelled out, "Check the bodies!"

Looking in the distance from the direction of the perimeter guards I could see headlights heading our way. While I stood waiting for Pete I thanked the Gods for another successful mission.

I walked over to the crooks' limo. The two sharpshooter secret Service men were helping the President out of the car. As they brushed him off and asked him how he was doing General Hatchaway's limo pulled up. Everyone got out and headed to the President except the General. As they were paying their respects to the President my limo arrived. John pulled it up as close to the crowd as possible.

As one of the rear doors facing the crowd opened General Hatchaway spoke in a loud, clear voice, "Gentlemen, may I have your attention?" Everyone looked at the General as he stood by the open door. As a figure emerged from the car the General said, "May I present the President of the United States?"

You've never seen so many dumb-founded and confused looks in your life!

The men left our imposter and walked over to the President. One of them said, "I don't understand!"

I answered him, "You don't think we'd expose the real President to this kind of danger do you?" They all still had confused looks on their faces. "General Hatchaway will explain it all to you on your flight back to Washington."

I walked over to our imposter. "Al, you've just finished the performance of your life. I want to thank you from the bottom of my heart."

The President had followed behind me. "That goes for me as well." As he spoke the President went right up to Al and shook his hand. "I look forward to having you and your wife visit me at the White House. My people will be in touch with you soon. Thank you again."

"I'm glad I could do it for you and my country Sir."

With that said the President turned to General Hatchaway, "Are the reporters next on the agenda?"

"Yes Sir. Right this way."

The President was escorted inside where the reporters were being held. He explained to them, using our pre-arranged speech, how we had just done a top secret mock-up of a terrorist kidnapping of a President. They bought the story and the President was soon on his plane heading back to Washington D.C.

Al joined my boys and me for a late night snack. We then dropped him off at the Airporter Hotel. To make things easier on everyone I had his belongings moved to a room at the hotel. It would make it easier for Al to catch his plane later in the morning.

On the drive back to my office I informed everyone that we'd have our meeting at two o'clock. "Everyone is to go home and not return to work until after one o'clock." The Mayor and Pete looked at me strangely. "Don't look at me like that. That order includes you two."

They nodded their heads in the affirmative. "I want everyone to know I won't be in my office until two. So don't bother me!"

Chapter 15

Lynda and I felt fresh as a daisy when we entered the reception area of my office at two. "Good afternoon Mrs. Thompkin! How are you today?"

"Just fine Commissioner."

"Do you have everything under control?"

"Yes Sir. Your team is inside waiting for you. I got your message when I got in and I cancelled your luncheon. Other than that your office is running as normal."

"That's very good. Thank you." Lynda and I turned and entered my office.

As we walked over to the conference table I could see my whole team. "It's nice to see everyone so bright eyed and bushy tailed this afternoon. I hope everyone got plenty of rest."

Everyone was smiling so I continued on, "I hope things are somewhat back to normal. If no one has any kind of an emergency we'll handle our meeting as always. Which means... Sam, you're up."

"We're coming to a head with the Canadian truck smugglers. We should be moving on them sometime this week."

"That sounds good. Anything special you need from us?"

"No. Pete and Jim are coordinating with us beautifully."

"Glad it's getting handled."

"Oh. There is one thing."

"What's that?"

"I have seats for four people in the plane if you'd like to help us with the raid just south of the Canadian border."

"Sounds like fun. Can I give you my answer when you have a definite time set?"

"Sure."

"How's the operation here coming?"

"Tentatively I have Wade, Pete, and Jim handling the bust here. I'm going to handle the border operation. Other agents will take down the two other American cities they are working in. My friend, Charles Winlock of the Mounties will handle the three hits in

Canada."

"Sounds like you have everything in order. Do you have anything else?"

"No. I'll pass to Wade."

"Sam covered it all. I'll pass to the Mayor."

"I have a couple of things. One; the hospital is coming along fine. Two; I'm arranging a meeting with all school principals Saturday morning at 10 o'clock."

"Where will we meet?"

"The Council Chambers, Larry."

"I like it, anything else?"

"No. I'll pass to Pete."

"Let me piggyback on the school situation. The two school campuses will be ready in a week. The army has everything from surplus clothes to barracks and food if we want to keep the students at the schools."

"I've thought about housing the students a couple of times, but I figured the cost would be enormous."

"Thanks to the army the cost will be nothing."

"Good job Pete. Let's play it as it comes. Pass on a 'well done' from me to the people you're working with."

"I will Larry. Next, the media is still bombarding the public with the idea of turning gang members in. We're still getting a large amount of calls. We're also getting calls about everything from meth labs, car thefts, food stamp black market, and drug deals."

"I told you at the beginning, we'll know when we're doing a good job when the people of our town start to trust us and turn in the bad guys. I'm happy to see it happening Pete. What else do you have?"

"The last thing is the rundown properties around our hospital. I've had some of our people working with the Mayor on getting most of the properties condemned. Some of the properties need a bulldozer."

"To go along with my ideas that's what they will get."

"Our boys have some contracts they've written on the properties that they'd like to run by you."

"I trust the intelligence of the people we have on that committee. Make sure you remind them it's their money they're spending. If they feel they're spending a fair amount of money for a parking lot tell them to do the deal."

"I understand Larry. I'll relay your message and I'll also pass to Tom."

"I'll pass to Jim."

"Everything's been said on my subject. I'll pass to Lynda."

"I had a nice long chat with the President last night. He wanted me to thank everyone for what we had done for him. If you'd like commendations for your men Larry, contact General Hatchaway."

"A show of hands, who would like a commendation for doing something that according to history, never happened?"

No one raised their hands.

The Mayor said, "I remember our leader saying 'We're not here to impress anyone. We're only here to clean up our town.'"

We all laughed.

"Anything else Lynda?"

"No. I pass to Robert."

"I'll pass to John."

"I'll pass to Yoto."

"I'm happy the Gods are still protecting us. I'll pass it back to Larry."

"Pete, how many of our force have we lost in the past ten years due to a disability?"

"I'd have to check Larry. I'd guess 30 to 50. I can have a better count for you at Wednesday's meeting. May I ask what you have in mind?"

"It's kind of simple. Due to standards that we made up, a man's career can be destroyed in a heartbeat while doing his job. I don't like it. When someone puts his time and dedication into being a cop that's all he wants to do for the rest of his life. I feel it's our job to make sure he's able to do just that. Unless the person is dead or a vegetable we can retrain him to do something useful around here."

Everyone around the table seemed a bit misty-eyed.

"What's the matter with everyone?"

Pete spoke first, "You never cease to amaze us. Your compassion and willingness to help people you don't even know is unbelievable."

"Thank you all for your good thoughts. We're all family and family takes care of family. Just because your brother gets hurt you don't throw him out of the family. But in today's society we push these people out because it cost too much to make a place for them. By being self sufficient we can take care of our own without having to answer to anyone but ourselves. Here I am on my soap box again! Time to get back to work; I know everyone has plenty to do. If there's nothing else, let's get to work."

What was left of Monday and Tuesday went by uneventful. Wednesday's meeting started the downfall of the Canadian smugglers.

"You have the floor Sam."

"It's time Larry. We're flying out tomorrow. The raids are set for sunup Friday. Communications are the first things we'll cut. By 6 to 7 o'clock Friday morning everything should be over. Are you coming with us?"

"No. I appreciate the thought but I feel the need to stick around here."

Jim asked, "What's the matter Larry? Don't you think we can handle it here?"

"Jim, you know better than that. Something in my mind says 'Stay here! Don't go!'."

Sam said, "Well you know better than I do. I'll see everyone Saturday if we're having a meeting."

"Make it Monday."

"All right, I'll pass to Wade."

"I'm going to spend a lot of today and tomorrow with Pete and Jim coordinating our local take downs. The crooks have a car lot, house, condo, storage units, and bank accounts. As usual we need to hit them all at the same time so it will take a little planning."

"That's our motto 'Be prepared!'."

"We will be Larry. Will you be with us?"

"I don't think so. I'll let you know later, anything else?"

"No. I'll pass to the Mayor."

"Nothing new, I'll pass to Pete."

"The schools will be done sometime next week. All the call in names we're getting of mob members is now in our computer."

"That's great. I want to take the mob members names we get from the schools and cross reference them with our names to see what kind of kids we have."

"Larry, aren't we going to have trouble trying to relocate kids to our schools?"

"I'm not totally clear on the law. I asked the Mayor to run it by his Judge friend and have it researched."

"I did just that Larry. It took a lot of man hours to cover every possible complaint. But we did it. The thing that saved us was the fact that we made all the school type changes without legislative vote. Seeing we've done it we can undo it."

"What would have been our biggest problem?"

"That's easy Larry. Kids ability to attend any school they please."

"How are you getting around it?"

"Easy. We're changing the granting to, 'By invitation only'."

"Which means?"

"The student wanting to attend a particular school sends a letter for review. At which time he's admitted to that school by invitation."

"Sounds good and simple."

"It is. Plus there are a lot of other things we can get around. When the trouble makers are weeded out they'll have two choices. One; go to school our way and get an education. Two; quit school and live on the streets. Whichever one they choose we'll be there to watch them."

"That we will Mayor. That we will. Anything else?"

"No Larry."

"Did that answer your question John?"

"Yes it did Larry."

"Good. You may now continue Pete."

"The buying of the condemned property around the hospital is going forward. The men thank you for your vote of confidence. They said they'd get the properties for next to nothing."

"I knew if I gave them their head they'd run the race and win. What else?"

"You gave me another pleasurable task. If there was anyone who doubted your sincerity and love for your men, they no longer do. When I explained what you wanted to do to my ranking officers, they were in shock. That's a good shock….not a bad one. After our special meeting they passed on the assignment to their men. Everyone's been talking about nothing else since. I've never seen so many people working on a single project before."

"I'm glad they liked my plan."

"Well Mr. Modesty. It goes a little deeper than that."

"What do you mean?"

"Well you got a lot of the usual responses, but one sticks out in my mind. I won't tell you who said it but I'll tell you pretty much what they said. In a nutshell it went something like this. 'I told you if we were in war he was the kind of commander not to leave anyone behind.' His friend said, 'You're right. If you had to put your life on the line for someone, he'd be it.' That's all I heard before they walked away."

"Pete, thank you. It looks like our family has finally come together. Did you get the job done?"

"Yes we did. We have 64 officers who've had to quit or retire on disability compensation."

"All right Pete. Here's what I'd like you to do. Set up a committee to meet with and talk to these men individually. The men will be asked to come in for an evaluation. Promise them nothing. I want them to show us their willingness to be back on the force. Please have our psychologist on the committee."

"I understand what you're saying and it shall be done."

"Thanks Pete, anything else?"

"One thing, the meeting with the school principals…do you want me there?"

"Yes I do. I see you, Lynda, the Mayor, Yoto, and me attending. I'd like everyone there, but I think we'd scare them to death."

"Should we meet here at 9:45 A.M.?"

"Make it 9:30 A.M. Pete. We'll have Yoto bring the people upstairs at 10 A.M. That should work for everyone. Is that all Pete?"

"Yes. I pass to Tom."

"Tom, before you speak, does anyone have anything else to say?"

Yoto asked, "Will you need me to drive on the weekend?"

"Yes I will Yoto. We'll decide when and where after the Saturday morning meeting."

"Sounds good to me, I pass it back to you Larry."

"Pete?"

"Yes Larry?'

"Have you been raiding the mobs around town?"

"Every time we hear about a meeting we raid it. We usually allow them to get started then we hit them and hit them hard. We've had arrests from weapons violations to curfew violations. We run them in and keep them for as long as we can. We talk to their parents to get all the information we can about them and the kid. Most of them are at their wits end. So whatever we do to their kids to make them better, they'll be on our side."

"Sounds good Pete, I like when you stay one step ahead of me. Keep it up. Also get me a list of the properties around the hospital as we own them."

"When will we start working on them?"

"Tom, I thought the best idea would be when we own all of them."

Jim asked, "Why is that Larry?"

"Kind of simple really, I wouldn't want anyone to know what we're going to do with them."

Tom asked, "May I ask what we're going to do with a bunch of condemned buildings? Besides making a lot unneeded parking lots?"

"I know what I have in mind Tom, but before I answer you I'd like to hear from the Mayor."

"Anything in particular, Larry?"

"Cute real cute, Mayor."

"I'd like to hear what the inspector had to say about the buildings."

Everyone was chuckling.

"Most of them are old but very stable. They need all new electrical and plumbing and things like that. Otherwise, structurally we can use about 70 percent of them."

"Sounds like what I was thinking. Now I'll answer your question Tom. I see two choices. One; convert the buildings into apartments to be rented out. I think one of the buildings is ten stories high. We can make a lot of apartments out of it. Two; do the same thing, but rent them out to low income families."

"I like the second version Larry."

"I'm glad you do Tom, but before we do anything, we need to control all the properties. Then we can weigh the best approach. We need to show a profit. Not a large one but still a profit."

Everyone laughed.

The Mayor said, "You'll never change Larry."

"You're right Mayor. Do I have to?"

"No. We like you just the way you are."

"Good. Unless there's something else I'll see everyone in the morning at nine."

The rest of the day went by without a hitch. Lynda and I ate out and enjoyed a relaxing evening.

Everyone was on time except Wade. At 9:05 A.M. we were just getting ready to start the meeting when Wade walked in.

"Just because the boss is out of town doesn't mean you can be late."

Everyone started laughing.

"Come on guys! I had to drop Sam off at the airport."

"What do you think guys? Should we forgive him?"

Everyone said, "Yeah."

"I guess you're lucky this time. By the way, how's he flying?"

"He's taking a small commuter plane to Denver. He's the only passenger on the plane, but it makes three stops on the way and it will be full when it gets to Denver."

"Sounds like fun to me. Now, shall we get started?"

Wade said, "I told you about Sam. What's left is the raid in the morning. I'll continue to work things out with everyone. Other than that there's nothing new. I'll pass to the Mayor."

"The meeting with the school principals Saturday is all R.S.V.P.'d"

"You sent them invitations?"

"Larry, we wanted to invite principals and assistant principals only. We didn't want this meeting to be public so I sent each person an invitation to their home address. Everyone I sent out to has responded and will be here."

"At least I won't be speaking to an empty room."

"No you won't Larry. They'll be packed in pretty tight."

"Job well done. Anything else?"

Before he could answer the hotline phone on my desk rang. I don't know why, but I sprang out of my chair and ran to the phone. I picked up the receiver. "This is the Commissioner!"

"This is the Mayor's secretary. Put on your T.V. to channel 12. There's been an accident and an explosion at the airport."

I said, "Thank you!" as I hung up the phone. I yelled over to Robert who was closest to the T.V. "Robert! Turn the T.V. on channel 12! There's an emergency at the airport!" He jumped to his feet and moved to the T.V. He grabbed the remote off the top of the set. He pushed the on button and the 1-2 button to make sure it was on channel 12. As the T.V. tuned in he made sure the set was facing us.

We could hear the voice a second before we could see the picture.

"......Commuter plane has somehow turned over while trying to take off. You can see the flames in the distance. This reporter can't see how anyone could have survived this crash!"

We watched the reporter as someone handed her a white piece of paper. The paper was folded in half. She opened it and said, "The piece of paper I was just handed has the flight number on it." As she read it, it was flashed on the screen.

Wade said, "Oh my God!"

By the look on his face I didn't have to ask the question but I did anyway, "What is it Wade?"

"That's Sam's flight!"

A saddened stillness came over all of us. Sam was family and it looked like he'd been blown to bits.

"Robert, turn off the T.V. and let's get out to the airport."

We all headed out the door together. I was in the lead and Robert was bringing up the rear. I opened my office door and got the shock of my life. Sam was standing in front of me. Sam said, "You guys look like you've seen a ghost!"

I threw my arms around Sam and hugged him as I pulled him into my office. Everyone else was greeting and touching him to show how happy they were to see him.

After I let him go he spoke again. "I'm glad to see everyone missed me, but I've only been gone a few hours."

"Then you haven't heard the news?"

"What news Larry?"

"Let's go back to the conference table. Robert, put the T.V. back on."

It only took Sam about 20 seconds to realize what had happened. "That's the plane I was supposed to be on!"

"That's why we were all heading to the airport."

"Boy I'm glad I listened to you Larry."

"What do you mean Sam? I didn't tell you anything."

"You sure did. You told me you didn't know why but something told you not to go with me. I tossed and turned all night. I didn't sleep worth a darn. After Wade dropped me at the airport I called our boys in Denver and asked if they could do the raid without me. They said 'no problem'. Then I went outside and hailed a cab and here I am!"

"We're very glad you are. We're also glad you listened to me."

John said, "What a great leader we have! He's now giving orders without giving them."

"Cute John, real cute."

Chapter 16

"Sam, we're glad you're here and safe. Now we need to get back to the meeting. Mayor, you were up. Do you have anything else?"

"No Larry. I'll pass to Pete."

"We're all set with Wade for the bust tomorrow morning."

"Sounds good, will you have a drug dog there?"

"Yes. We discussed it and thought it was a good idea."

"So do I. Keep up the good work."

"We still have the mobs on the run."

"Pete, I think once the new schools get cranking the mobs will dry up. Some of the hard core boys will stay to shoot it out. But there won't be many."

"You could be right Larry. It's amazing how their boldness has started to fade. Very few of them are wearing their colors. I think they're afraid they may be shot on sight."

"That's not far from the truth Pete. Keep the heat on them."

"I intend to Larry."

"Good. What else you got?"

"The disabled officers you had us checking out."

"Yes. How's it going?"

"I think we can put about 40 of them back to work part and full time."

"Now that's the kind of news I like to hear. I'm glad it all worked out."

"So is everyone I've talked to about it. I have to give you a hand for what you've done."

As he started clapping his hands everyone joined in.

I did the only thing I could, I said, "Thank you for the praise. Now it's time to get back to work. What else Pete?"

"The hospital is going great."

"Good."

"Did I mention our citizens are still calling us about the mobs? And we're also getting other crimes reported."

"Yes you did but I enjoyed hearing it again. Pete, the raid in the morning ...who's taking down the car lot?"

"Wade are you handling that?"

"I don't know Pete now that Sam is back."

Sam said, "Everything is the same. I'll help oversee the take down of the main house."

"Wade, if you don't mind, Lynda, Yoto, and I would like to join you."

"I'd be happy to have you."

"What's the agenda?"

"We're meeting at the shopping center parking lot at 20th Street and Adams at 6:30 A.M.. We should do the raid between seven and seven thirty."

"That seems pretty late in the morning."

"It is but we have a time difference. Soon as we get the call that the northern raids are done, we'll move."

"Sounds like a good plan to me. Are the local storage units being hit at the same time?"

"Yes they are Larry. I have a couple of small teams doing that job. I don't expect a lot of resistance from the storage units."

"I agree with you. Are the mini-storage locations themselves clean?"

"We checked out the ownership of the two locations. They're as clean as a whistle."

"Then there shouldn't be a problem. We'll meet you in the parking lot at 6:30 A.M. Unless you have something else, I'll return the floor to Pete."

"Thanks Larry. The last thing I have is; I'll be with you in the morning and Jim will be with Sam. I pass to Tom."

Before Tom could say anything I interrupted. "Does anyone have anything new?"

No one said a word.

"Then gentlemen, it's time to get to work."

Everyone left and Lynda and I settled in to catch up on our paper work. No matter what else there was in town, there was always an adequate supply of paperwork. I thought we could get caught up seeing that we didn't have a luncheon to go to.

It was a few minutes after eleven when my hotline from the Mayor's office rang. I picked up the receiver, "Hi Mayor. What's up?"

"I have Mrs. Ruth Baker in my office. She would like a private audience with you."

"And Lynda?"

"Yes both of you."

"I take it she doesn't want to come to my office?"

"That's right."

"Lynda and I will go out to the elevators. Send her up to my floor. When the doors open we'll get on the elevator and take her up to the penthouse for tea."

"I like it."

"Good. Look at your watch. Wait four minutes and walk her out to the elevator. That will give Lynda and me time enough to get there."

"When I hang up the phone I'll start counting." Click.

I hung up my phone and turned to Lynda who was standing beside me.

"It sounds like someone is having a problem."

"That someone is Mrs. Ruth Baker."

"You mean the late Senator's wife and council woman?"

"The same one. She also owns the Baker Department Stores across the country, as well as our two largest malls, and a lot of other businesses."

"I wonder what she wants."

"If we head out to the elevators we may find out."

As we were walking she smiled and said, "As usual your great mental ability has answered my question."

"Cute Lynda, real cute."

We walked out of my office and passed by Mrs. Thompkin's desk. "We're taking an early lunch. We'll be back around one."

"Yes Commissioner. Have a good lunch."

We walked out of the reception area and down the hallway to the elevators. We were there about thirty seconds when Mrs. Baker's elevator arrived. After the doors opened we stepped on without saying a word.

After the doors closed I spoke, "Mrs. Baker, this is Sergeant Lynda Stalls my bodyguard and fiancé and a member of my personal team. You may speak freely in front of her."

"I know. The Mayor told me all about her."

The elevator doors opened at my penthouse. We got off and proceeded inside. We walked into the living room where I offered my guest a seat.

"Mrs. Baker would you like something to drink?"

"Yes Commissioner. Would hot tea be too much trouble?"

Lynda answered for me, "No trouble at all Mrs. Baker. I'll be back in a few minutes."

Mrs. Baker had sat down in one of the chairs across from the couch, so I took a seat on the couch. We were almost face to face with only the coffee table between us. She set her soft sided leather brief case on the table. She opened it and slid out a file about five inches thick which she laid on the coffee table.

As she pointed to the file she spoke, "In here you'll find almost two years of information about my daughter and son in law. I've had some of the best in the business work on this matter. They've all come up with the same conclusion. My daughter is dying but they don't know how. All the Doctors say almost the same thing. I know in my gut that her husband is killing her but I can't prove it. Can you help me Commissioner?"

"Mrs. Baker I'll do my best."

"Knowing your experience, I hadn't even thought about you until the Mayor suggested and then convinced me to see you. But I still have my doubts."

"I can tell by the size of your file and what you've said that I'm not your first choice. What I want to be is your last choice. That will mean I've solved your problem."

"I hope you can Commissioner, for two reasons. One; you're my last hope. Two; she's my only child."

At that point in our conversation Lynda returned with the tea.

I turned the file around so it was facing me. "Do you have time to go though the file with us?"

"I'm out shopping until five o'clock. I'm dropping by my daughter's house on my way home."

"Why are we being so hush- hush?"

"If the wrong person was to see me and accidently tell my son in law….who knows what would happen?"

"I see what you mean. He'll either bring an end to your daughter or stop altogether just to start again later. Don't worry. He'll never see us coming."

"The way the Mayor talks about you. He thinks you are some kind of crime fighting God."

"He always does exaggerate a bit. I have an excellent staff and a lot of luck. But enough about me, let's look at this file." As I opened the folder I asked, "Is the file in any kind of order?"

"Yes. The latest happenings are on top."

"Then in order to get the complete picture I should start at the rear of the file."

"That would be my suggestion."

I picked up my glass of iced tea off the coffee table and leaned against the back cushion of the couch. I took a relaxed sip of my tea.

Mrs. Baker picked up her cup and saucer and leaned back in her chair. For about two minutes no one said a word.

"Mrs. Baker."

"Yes Commissioner?"

"This is not a matter that I can handle."

"I'm sorry to hear that Commissioner. The Mayor said……."

"I cut her off in mid sentence. "Let me rephrase my statement. I can't handle your situation alone. I'll need the help of all my team, as well as the F.B.I. Is that okay with you?"

"As long as they're discreet."

"No one will know they are there except you if you recognize them."

"I understand Commissioner."

"Then may I call them up here?"

"Yes you may."

"Would you like me to make the calls Commissioner?"

"Yes Sergeant. Also call Mrs. Thompkin, the Mayor, and the Chief."

"It shall be done Sir."

As she left the room I continued to relax and so did Mrs. Baker. I knew she was nervous and a twenty minute wait wouldn't make her feel any better. I thought it best to change the subject to help her relax. "Mrs. Baker, how are your department stores doing?"

She seemed to get a little spark back into her movement and voice. "Not as good as we'd like it to be. It's so hard today to compete with all the discount operations out there."

"Your stores have a good quality of retail merchandise. You probably still use a keystone markup." (If the store pays $5.00 for an item they sell it for $10.00)

"That we do, it's the only way we can survive."

"How much business do you lose to these other stores?"

"About 40 percent, if it wasn't for sales bringing people in I'd probably have to close the stores."

"I bet you've checked it out thoroughly and there's no way you can compete with these other stores."

"You're right Commissioner. There's no way we can compete. I've had some of the most knowledgeable people in the business try to figure out a way. There isn't one."

"Do your stores back east have basements?"

"Yes they do."

"And what merchandise do you keep there?"

"Housewares."

"May I suggest something to you?"

"Sure. Go ahead."

"You need to stop trying to compete with the discount operations and join them."

"I'll close the doors before the Baker Department Stores become a discount house."

"You got me all wrong. The store will stay the same, but just like the old days, you'll have a Bargain Basement! One half with all merchandise priced a dollar. The other half with close outs and mark downs. This will generate a traffic flow of people who will in turn spend money all over the store. You'll have the best of both worlds without degrading your store. It's important to keep enough help in this area to keep it up to your standards. What do you think?"

"The Mayor was right. That's a problem we've been working on for over three years and I've spent over two hundred thousand dollars on studies and projections. You sit here for ten minutes and solve the whole thing! I can't believe it!!"

"Then you think my idea has merit?"

"Not only merit Commissioner. It's Brilliant! I'll capture both ends of the market."

"I think you'll find the profit structure from the basement will surprise you."

"I agree. I'll get to work on your idea Monday. Thank you for your idea."

"You're welcome."

As we finished speaking Lynda walked in with a pot of hot tea and pitcher of iced tea. "The boys are on their way."

"Thank you Sergeant. While you finish in the kitchen I'll get more chairs."

The boys, the Mayor, and Pete all arrived together.

After the introductions and before I got started I asked, "I know we have a major raid in the morning. Is there anyone who is not ready? If so you have my permission to leave. We'll be here until five."

"Commissioner."

"One minute Sergeant. Mrs. Baker, when my team and I are together we address one another by our first names. Since I consider all the council people as part of my team I would like this meeting to be informal."

"Sounds good to me."

"Thank you Mrs. Baker." (I had too much respect for this lady to even think of using her first name!) "Now Jim, you had something to say?"

"Yes. I called Sam and Wade and told them if they needed us for anything we'd be here."

"That's good. Mrs. Baker, Sam and Wade are our connection to the F.B.I."

She nodded her approval.

"I think everyone has noticed the thick file in front of me. I'm not going to tell you anything about it. We'll start at the beginning and go through it page by page. Mrs. Baker will answer any and all questions."

I reached down and opened the file again. This time I picked up all the papers inside and turned them over again. I placed them on the left side of the manila folder. I was looking at the first item upside down. It was all white and about 8 inches by 10 inches. I knew without turning it over that it was a photo. I picked it up and turned it over. I was looking at a wedding photo. There was a small post-it note on the lower right side that gave a date of almost two years earlier. I looked at Mrs. Baker, "Your daughter and son in laws' wedding?"

"Yes it is Commissioner."

"He's a very good looking guy."

"What you're trying to say is he is too good looking for my homely looking daughter."

"I didn't say that."

"No. But that's what you were thinking."

"I can't lie to you. That is what I was thinking. The two of them just don't go together."

She looked over at the Mayor. "You were right Mayor. He's the man for this job. Commissioner, I know she's homely. I spent my life being over protective and overly sheltering of her. She was 28 when she married. I had her late in life. She's not dumb, but she is a little slow."

"If being slow is a fault we all have a problem."

Everyone laughed.

"I guess you're right Commissioner. We all have problems."

"Yes Mrs. Baker we do. We're now going to jump into your file and find out what's really happening."

We spent the next hour and a half going over about a third of the file thoroughly. "Gentlemen, let's take a break. Lynda and John will go out and get us some pizza. That's the least I can do seeing that I made everyone work through their lunch hour."

Mrs. Baker offered to pay for lunch. I assured her it was not necessary. She was our guest.

We kept going over the part of the file that we had already finished. I was proud at how well everyone had followed my original order. No one attempted to get ahead of the information in front of us. I could also tell that Mrs. Baker was impressed.

We had lunch and continued to finish the file. At 4:35 P.M. I had a few piles of paper on the table. One large pile and a few small ones. "Mrs. Baker, are these files for us to keep?"

"Yes Commissioner."

"Good. As I read off the piles of papers and tell you what I want, whoever can handle it best.... take care of it."

I grabbed the closest stack to me and held it in my hand. "The large stack of papers we can use for reference. I'll condense it and put the information in my safe. Now let's scc what I have here. I need someone to check out Charles T. Winder. I need you to do a deep and thorough checking. Get his fingerprints from him and work with the F.B.I. I want to know everything he's done since he was

16 years old. And something tells me I want to see photos of him throughout his life."

Tom asked, "May I handle that?"

"I'll help him Larry."

"All right Jim. You two have it. The next pile is easier. It's Mrs. Baker's daughter, Tammy. Now we already know that she has always had bronchial problems. But has she been somewhere, or is she doing something differently, that could be causing this illness?"

Robert spoke up, "Larry, may I take care of it?"

"Sure."

"I'll give him a hand."

"Okay John. Now this pile is everything about the house. When and how it was built, who goes in and out of the place; maid, the gardener, ….you get the idea."

Lynda and Yoto spoke at the same time.

"I need the two of you with me."

Pete said, "That only leaves the Mayor and me."

"Glad you two volunteered."

"Larry?"

"What's the matter Pete? Not to your liking?"

"I was holding out for a shot at the inside of the house. I guess you, Yoto, and Lynda will handle it."

"Not all together. We have twenty snapshots of the inside of the house. Eight of those are shots of Tammy's room." I picked up the packet of photos and handed them to Pete."I want you to blow them up to eight by tens and make a set for everyone. What I want everyone to do is go over them with a fine tooth comb and see if they can find anything amiss. When we physically check out the inside of the house everyone will be there. First we'll compile all of our information to make sure we know what we're dealing with. Then we'll set a trap and put an end to this man once and for all."

"Then you believe I'm right Commissioner?"

"I never doubted your intuition for one moment. Does anyone think she is imagining her daughter is being murdered?"

No one said a word.

"Does that answer your question Mrs. Baker?"

"It sure does Commissioner. Thank you."

"I want everyone downstairs and back to work. You can go home when you feel like it. I need Mrs. Baker, the Mayor, Yoto, and Lynda to stay here with me. Mrs. Baker? I know the Mayor is a dear friend of yours. Anytime you wish to speak to us do it through him. Also to answer the question you're about to ask. I'm allowing Robert to check on your daughter, because from the first moment he saw her picture he wasn't able to take his eyes off her."

Yoto added, "I also noticed how he kept her side of the large wedding picture uncovered so he could see it."

"Should I be worried?"

"No Mrs. Baker, Robert's harmless. He knows his job and he'll do his best."

"May I speak freely Commissioner?"

"Always Mrs. Baker."

"As you already know the Mayor had to almost twist my arm to get me to see you. I remember not long ago when we hired an inexperienced man to clean up our town. It's hard to explain how I feel right now. Out of all the late Senator's friends I haven't been able to convince one of them to help me. Yet, at a snap of my fingers you're right here to not only try to understand what is happening but to get right to doing something to try to put a stop to it. The Mayor told me about the big raid you're doing in the morning. How you've been working on it for months. Yet, you stopped everything to help me."

"Mrs. Baker you're family. Don't ever forget that."

"I won't."

"Is there any way to get your son in law out of town overnight?"

"As you know by the papers you just read I made him a Vice President of Baker's Stores when he married my daughter. I'm sure I can send him across this lovely country of ours whenever you say."

"Good. I'll give you as much notice as I can. Now, if no one else has anything I think we should call it a night."

No one said a word.

"Mayor, would you see Mrs. Baker to her car?"

"I'll take care of it Larry, and I'll say 'goodnight'."

Mrs. Baker said, "That goes for me too. Goodnight."

We all said our goodnights and they left.

"I'm hungry."

"So am I Lynda. Yoto?"

"Very much so."

"Why don't we wash up and get out of here. We'll decide where we're going when we get in the limo."

We got off the elevator and walked to the limo. Lo and behold the Mayor was leaning against the car.

I asked, "Did you miss something?"

"Yes, a free dinner."

"I thought for sure we'd fooled you."

"Never! Let's get going. I'm hungry!"

Lynda and I were back in our penthouse a little before eight. The Mayor had told us over dinner how Mrs. Baker couldn't stop talking about us. This made me happy. I had a feeling that things would work out okay for her and her daughter. As we were getting ready for bed I put everything out of my mind except Lynda. It was a little before nine when we crawled into bed. We made love until after ten. Lynda curled up in my arms and we fell asleep.

We met Yoto in the parking garage at 6:10 A.M. At 6:28 A.M. we arrived at our meeting place. Wade was there with his men and ours. He was standing around talking to his team. We got out of our limo and walked over to his group.

"Good morning Special Agent Brewer!"

Wade responded, "Good morning Commissioner, Sergeant Stalls and Officer Yoto. Glad to see you made it."

"Would you bring us up to date?"

"Sure Commissioner."

We followed Wade as he walked away from the group. We stopped at the front of a car. On the hood was a large flat piece of paper. The corners were weighed down. As Wade pointed to it, he explained what we were looking at. "This is a large diagram of our mission. You can see how I've deployed our men. What do you think?"

"Looks good to me. Who do you have on the inside?"

"What do you mean Larry? The lot is awful small."

"It's large enough if someone, for some reason, is there this early in the morning they'll be able to draw and fire before your men can take them."

"I agree with you, but we'll have the lot secured before anyone arrives at eight."

At that point of our conversation a car pulled up and parked by my limo.

Wade rhetorically asked, "Who could that be? Everyone's here!"

"Not quite Wade. It's half of your inside team. Yoto!"

While we stood waiting Yoto went over to get whoever was in the car. He brought an Oriental woman over to our group.

Yoto asked, "Wade, you remember Lyn-Yhi?"

"Oh yes. She's the special member of our team."

I said, "That's right Wade. She and Yoto are going to be our inside people."

"Sounds good to me, I'm glad I thought of it."

We all started laughing.

I said, "Wade, I can always count on two things with you. You'll either get the job done or at least take the credit for it."

We all continued laughing until we were interrupted by Wade's cell phone. We quieted down and listened to his conversation.

"Hello. This is Wade. Are you sure? Everything's locked down? Then we can move? Sounds great, I'll let you know later how things went here." He pushed the button on his phone to disconnect. "Did everyone hear?"

I said, "Yoto and Lyn-Yhi get going! You have ten minutes to get into position."

It seemed Yoto wasn't gone for a couple of minutes when my cell phone rang.

"Yes, this is the Commissioner."

"Yoto here. Recon. The lot is crawling with people. There's a semi full of trucks being unloaded. What do you want us to do?"

"Hold fast until I get a look at the situation."

"Anything else?"

"Yes. How many trucks are left to be unloaded?"

"Two."

"I'll be back to you in a few minutes. Wade?"

"Yes Larry?"

"Do you have someone watching the lot?"

"Yes. I have two people there on radio silence until I call them, which I was getting ready to do."

"I'd suggest you don't."

"What do you mean?"

"Yoto just called me."

"I heard your phone ring. What did he say?"

"Your empty car lot is full of people. They're just receiving a shipment of trucks and they're still unloading."

"Then what're Yoto and Lyn-Yhi doing?"

"I have them in a holding pattern. The lot is too small for the semi and us. You need to get two two-man units close enough to follow the semi when it leaves the lot. Allow it to get a few miles away before they pull it over. They need to detain the driver and take his truck to our impound yard to be searched."

"We've checked out all the companies they have doing their hauling and they all seem to be okay. But I'll get two of your black and whites to do as you say. I'll be right back."

While he was gone I called Yoto and filled him in on what was happening. As we were talking Yoto said, "I hope they're on their way."

"Is the truck leaving?"

"That's what it looks like from here. They're helping the driver back his unit into the street. Hold on! You said you were sending two units, right?"

"Yes."

"I just spotted them."

"Good. I want you to call me when the lot settles down. We're ready to move on your call."

"Okay, I'll let.....Larry!!"

"Now what?"

"Is there something about this take down you haven't told me?"

"Not a thing. What's happening?"

"You know that pretty sports car that Pete got for Coop and Josh?"

"Yes. What's that got to do with this mission?"

"I don't know, but they just pulled up in it."

"Onto the lot?"

"Yes. And they're now getting out and meeting all the people, of which I count five. Coop and Josh make seven."

Wade walked up to me, "Are you talking to Yoto?"

"Hold on a minute Yoto. Yes I am Wade."

"What's the lot look like? Are we ready to move out?"

"The lot looks like a New Year's Eve party."

"You're kidding!"

"No. Do you by chance have Coop and Josh helping you?"

"No, why do you ask?"

"Because they've just pulled onto the lot."

"Larry, I hope you'll believe me! I've never had a bust like this go so wrong!"

"The way I see it the Gods have put all the rats in one place for us. So don't feel bad. Get your boys ready to deploy."

"What about Coop and Josh?"

"We can't hold customers who are shopping for a truck can we?"

"No we can't."

"Good. Now get your men set. Yoto!"

"I'm still here Larry."

"Continue with the original plan. Warn Coop and Josh if you can. They have to be there on drug related business."

"Do I still have 10 minutes?"

"Yes. Look at your watch. In 10 minutes we'll start moving in."

"We'll see you then."

"See you then."

I hung up as Wade returned. "The boys are ready to move."

"Have them get into their assigned positions around the lot. They only move on your command."

"I'll be back in a minute."

He returned as our people were moving out. "Now what Larry?"

"Now I'll call Coop on his cell phone and see if I can get him out of there."

I dialed Coop's number and he answered on the second ring, "Hello?"

"Coop? This is Larry. You don't have to talk, just listen. We're about five minutes away from raiding the lot you're standing on and I need you out of there. Now you can say whatever you want to get out of there."

He started to yell and shout so I hung up. I knew he'd get the job handled.

I had Wade drive the limo. I thought it might look funny with Lynda behind the wheel. As we neared the lot I could see Coop's car pulling away. I could see Yoto and Lyn-Yhi. They had two of the guys helping them look at trucks.

"Wade, let's really surprise them. Pull right on the lot as close to the small office building as you can. When they see our car I'm sure the three of them will come out to greet us. We'll alight from the car when they get close. Lynda and I will get out first at which time you'll tell the boys to move in. Then you'll get out, pull out your gun and arrest these boys."

As Wade pulled onto the lot, he said, "I got it Larry!"

Sure enough it went down just the way I said. When Wade got out of the car I was a little bit in front of him, seeing we got out of the same side of the car. Lynda was on the other side of the car with her hand in her purse.

As Wade walked up towards me, one of the bad guys asked me, "Can we help you sir?"

"You can't help me but you can help my friend."

They looked at Wade who flashed his badge and said, "This is the F.B.I.! Put your hands in the air! You're all under arrest!"

Out of one corner of my eye I could see Lynda dropping her purse leaving her gun in her hand, pointed toward the trio. Out of the other corner of my eye I could see Yoto knock the support out from the hood and slam it down on the guy who was under it showing Yoto something. As all this was going on the three men in front of us were reaching for parts of their bodies that would only produce a gun in their hands. The man closest to Lynda had his gun out first and pointed it at Wade. I had explained to Wade many times before that when doing this type of situation each person is responsible for the person even with or closest to them. This meant the first shooter was Lynda's responsibility. Wade could watch him out of the corner of his eye but he wasn't to act on him. Instead his man was in the middle and that was his target. When Wade saw the gun pointing his way he moved his gun and pointed it at Lynda's man. Before this man could fire at Wade, Lynda put two slugs in his head. Now we had a problem. The other two shooters now had their guns out. I had only one knife and two targets. I knew Wade's target would fire and get Wade before he could get his gun back around to the shooter. As I pulled out my sleeve knife with my right hand from my left sleeve I kept my hand moving with enough force to knock Wade off his feet as shots were fired at him. After pushing him over I recoiled in the same motion and flung my knife into the upper chest of my man.

He dropped his gun before firing and grabbed at the knife. I jarred Wade so hard that his gun left his right hand and flew in my direction. I grabbed it out of the air. I squatted down and opened fire at Wade's man. While I was filling him full of holes he fired twice in the direction he thought I was standing in. This guy stood about 6'4" and weighed about 280 pounds. So it took more than one bullet to bring him down. This whole sequence of events only took a few seconds. I stood up to see Lynda with gun in hand moving to check out the bad guys. Wade sprang to his feet and went to give her a hand. I looked over at Yoto and watched as he attempted to get Lyn-Yhi's man off her. The guy was three times her size and twice Yoto's size. As Yoto removed one of his hands Lyn-Yhi brought her leg up and smashed downward on her captor's instep as hard as she could with the heel of her shoe. The pain made him lift his foot off the ground which left him off balance. She had smashed his right foot. Yoto had pried loose his left hand, so the minute he lifted his right foot Yoto stepped back a little and smashed the man's left knee with enough force to make the man let go of Lyn-Yhi and hit the pavement like a ton of bricks. Yoto moved in and kicked the man in the head. That was all I could see from my position. Our back up was now all over the place. They were helping Yoto with his two prisoners.

"Wade."

"Yes Commissioner?"

"I want you to form all the men around me and the dead guys. I want the men facing away from me to make sure we're not attacked."

When he was done I was standing over the man with my knife in his chest. I knelt down so he could see and hear me.

"I need help."

"I know you do and I need information."

"I want a doctor and a lawyer, and I'm not telling you a thing."

"Then you're going to die, the minute I pull my knife out of your chest you'll start bleeding at a fast rate. You'll bleed to death before and ambulance can get here."

"You can't do that!"

"Watch me!"

I reached down and worked at prying his hands away from my

knife.

"You're really going to do it aren't you?"

"Scum like you is better off dead."

As I pulled at the knife he asked, "What do you want to know?"

"Where do you keep all the drugs and loot?"

"That's all?"

"Yep."

"Back wall of the office has screw on paneling. The stuffs back there."

"How about the house?"

"Same way in the garage."

"The storage units?"

"You know everything don't you?"

"I try. Now again, the storage units?"

"All right, inside the old T.V.'s. And turn over the couches. They're hollow underneath. And before you ask, the four old cars have their trunks full."

"That was two at each storage unit, right?"

"Yes."

"Did I miss anything?"

"The units we got in today."

"No, I know about those. Thank you anyway. Agent Brewer, call this man an ambulance, he's still alive."

The man looked up at me from the ground and asked, "Mr. would you have let me die?"

"Yes I would. It's a lot cheaper than putting you in jail."

"What did I ever do to you?"

"You were born."

I turned and walked away. I stopped at a clean looking truck and leaned on it waiting for my people. Wade worked his way over to me as well as did Lynda, Yoto, and Lyn-Yhi. Wade said, "Larry, I divided the men into teams to tear this place apart."

"Good thinking Wade. You're only using our hurt friend's information as a guideline."

"That's right."

"How many men are you sending to the hospital with our friend?"

"Two."

"Would you go over there and put one of them in charge of my knife?"

"Why don't I have the medics remove it?"

"If you do that he'll bleed to death before you can get him to the hospital."

"Then you were serious when you told him that."

"Very much so. I knew where I wanted my knife to go and it hit its mark."

Yoto said, "Larry's the only person I know who takes a knife to a gunfight and wins."

"That I am, Yoto that I am."

Wade walked away to talk to the officers.

I asked, "Lyn-Yhi, are you all right?"

"Yes Larry, thanks to Yoto."

"I'm glad to hear that. We're having a meeting in my office at five tonight. Can you be there?"

"Yes Larry. I'll be there."

"Yoto."

"I'm okay Larry and I'll be there."

"I know you will. How are you doing Lynda? You look a little upset."

"Our part of the mission didn't go down according to plan. Did I do something wrong?"

"You know what you did was correct but someone else made a mistake. He knows it and I'll take care of it tonight. That's all we're going to say about it for now."

"I understand Larry."

"Good. Now, if you guys want to have some fun, find the keys to the truck I'm leaning on and tear it apart. Nicely of course, we do have to sell these units. Let's see what these boys are smuggling."

Before we could move Wade returned with keys in his hand. "I got these keys off the desk in the office. They must be for the units that just came in."

"I think you're right Wade. See if one of the tags has the numbers 31427 on it."

"Here it is." He handed the keys to Yoto who used them to unlock the cab door.

"Wade, I hoped you informed everyone that we're not here to destroy the place or what's in it. We need to sell everything that's here. Which means when I walk into that office it better look like no one has been in there."

"I told them Larry. But I'll go reiterate the point to everyone. You know you don't really get this place unless you find drugs here."

Yoto said, "I don't think the white powder in these bags under the seats is flour or sugar."

"As usual Larry, you were right."

"I'm just lucky Wade."

After Wade walked away to talk to his men I joined everyone at the truck.

Yoto asked, "Larry, do really think anyone believed you when you said it was a lucky guess?"

We all started laughing.

"Cute Yoto, real cute."

When we finished laughing we went back to searching. There wasn't very much room under the front seats. We asked Lyn-Yhi to slowly and carefully use her thin arms and small hands to feel the underside of the front seat.

"What do you feel Lyn-Yhi?"

"Larry, there are springs and enough other things to warrant pulling out the seats."

"Thank you Lyn-Yhi, if that's your suggestion that's what we'll do. Was there anything in the glove compartment or in the ash try?"

Lyn-Yhi said, "The glove compartment is empty and the ashtray is full of trash." Lyn-Yhi opened and shut each area as she answered my question. "Any other questions Sir?"

"Just one little one Lyn-Yhi. Why in a clean, detailed truck would the ahstray be full of cigarette butts and whatever else there is in there?"

Lyn-Yhi was not a dummy. She looked at me and said, "To keep people who are not as smart as we are from looking inside the ashtray."

"I think you may have something there. Yoto see if you can pull the ashtray out. I'll put the tailgate down and we'll empty it out there."

Because of the truck's name across the tailgate, when I put it down, it formed a shelf and the reverse of the letters formed pockets. The tailgate was now parallel to the ground and even with the bed of the truck. Yoto brought me the ashtray. It was larger and deeper than ones you see in a car. In one indenture of the tailgate I poured out the trash. It contained what I expected, cigarette butts and a gum wrapper.

"Was I wrong Larry?"

"No, Lyn-Yhi. The ashtray only looks empty. Yoto, your knife."

"I thought you had one."

"It's sticking around here somewhere."

Lynda added, "You must be getting old when you can't remember who you left your knife sticking in."

We all had a little chuckle as Yoto handed me his throwing knife. I slid the blade inside the ashtray following one side down until I hit bottom. I marked the blade with my thumbnail and pulled it out of the ashtray. Next I put the blade, while still holding my thumbnail in place, along the outside of the ashtray. The blade went down about halfway. I showed it to everyone. "What do you think people?"

Lyn-Yhi and Lynda said, "False bottom!" Yoto nodded his head in agreement.

"What a smart team! They can all see the obvious!"

Everyone laughed.

I held Yoto's knife in my right hand and slid my thumb and index finger down the blade. I detected something on the tip of the blade. I slid my thumb and finger off the blade and rubbed them together.

"What is it Larry?"

"Lynda these boys went to a lot of trouble to hide what's in this ashtray. It's got to be something really valuable."

"Why do you say that?"

"They sealed the bottom of the ashtray with paraffin. What I feel on my fingers is wax. What I'm going to try to do now is cut along the outside edges of the wax and bring it out in one piece."

The task wasn't hard to do. Yoto's knife was razor sharp. After the wax broke free I poked the knife gently into the center of the piece. I drew the knife up and out came the paraffin. I set it aside and handed Yoto back his knife. He wiped it off and put it away. Next I turned the ashtray over with my hand covering the open end. A black velvety feeling bag came to the opening. I got a hold of it with my finger and my thumb and wiggled it around until it fell out into the palm of my hand. I put the ashtray to the side and held the black bag by its tie string. "Should we see what's inside?"

Everyone had a look of anticipation on their face.

I set the bag on the tailgate and untied the one knot holding the bag closed. I reached in my pocket and pulled out my hanky. Lynda helped me spread it out on the tailgate. I then proceeded to empty the contents of the bag onto my hanky. As I had figured the bag was full of diamonds. A quick count gave us twenty five, some with settings and some without.

Wade came back over to see what we were up to. "Wow! You hit the jackpot!"

"If all the trucks that came in this morning are gone over like this one was everyone will hit the jackpot. I think we've had enough fun with the trucks for right now. You need to get the hauler back here and have him take these units to our impound yard. I want our boys to take them apart and find everything there is to find."

Wade got on his cell phone and had our boys holding the truck and driver to bring them back to our location.

I said, "Let's go look at the office before we get out of here. Lyn-Yhi, if you'd like to leave, I know you have to go to work. We'll understand."

"Thank you Larry. That would be a good idea."

"Yoto, walk her to her car. We'll see you tonight."

She said good bye to all of us and left with Yoto.

As we walked into the office I watched four of our boys searching through everything in sight, which wasn't very much. The office was a small frame building that had two steps up to a small porch and four steps forward into the office. The office size was about 20 by 20. It was semi divided into two offices. Nothing fancy, just a place to write up sales contracts and credit applications. The boys had unscrewed and removed the back wall panels. I could see on the top of the rear desk the start of a pile of stolen contraband.

I asked so everyone could hear, "What's in the refrigerator?"

One of the men answered me, "Six cans of coke, two cans of beer, and four ice cube trays."

"Thank you officer, are you finished with it?"

"Yes we are Commissioner."

"Does anyone besides me want a coke?"

Lynda asked, "Isn't it a little early for coke?"

"I'm thirsty and I didn't hear orange juice on the menu."

"Do you want me to get it for you?"

"No Sergeant Stalls. I'll take care of it. But what I'd like to see everyone do is go over everywhere our boys have already searched and see what you can find. I have a feeling these boys hid a lot of jewels here and everywhere else."

I opened the refrigerator and looked inside. Sure enough, the boys had the contents correct. I grabbed a coke and looked for something out of place. If my feelings were correct these boys were stockpiling stolen diamonds. The ice cube trays seemed tidy just like the rest of the refrigerator. Clean and tidy. I could only see one small problem. Where the ice cube trays sat in the freezer area there was about a half an inch of ice accumulated under the trays.

"Sergeant Stalls see if you can find a bucket and some rags. Then fill the bucket half full of water and bring it here."

One of the other officers said, "You'll find that stuff in the bathroom."

"Agent Brewer, while she's doing that will you remove the back of the refrigerator?"

"I'll take care of it Commissioner."

Wade looked at the back of the refrigerator. He then went to the bag of tools on the floor near the front door. He got out a Philips screw driver to do the job with.

"Everyone listen for a minute. You already know not to be destructive. What you don't know is that these boys are into other things than drugs. As a matter of fact I think drugs are something they just thought of recently. They started off with stealing trucks in Canada. They changed serial numbers and speedometers so they could sell them. With their limited overhead they had a great profit. But like all crooks they got greedy and added jewel theft to their resume and now they're also doing drugs. So gentlemen, you're looking for everything from items as small as a diamond, and who knows how large an item could be? If you feel you need to reexamine something ….do it! Remember, everything inside this office is ours."

"Commissioner!"

"Yes Agent Brewer?"

"I found out this morning, after my people had gone through two different corporations that our bad guys owned this lot, which means you now own this building and the lot it sits on."

"Thank you. That's great to know. We're now in the used vehicle business. Looks like more work for volunteer time. I like how the Gods help to bring a good plan together. Now, we better get back to work. I wouldn't want our boss to fire us."

Everyone laughed as we got back to work.

As Lynda was bringing me the bucket of water Yoto rejoined us.

"Did you get her off all right?"

"Yes Commissioner."

"Good. I need you to get the screw gun and get all the panels off the walls that have screws in them. The back wall has been done for you."

Yoto turned and walked to the back wall and picked the screw gun up off the floor. He proceeded to start in the corner of the room examining the panels.

Lynda had put the bucket down by my feet in front of the refrigerator and handed me a dry rag. I opened the freezer section and moved the ice cube trays to the other side of the freezer.

I spoke almost in a whisper, "If you wet the rag and rub on the ice you may find diamonds when the ice melts."

She replied, "Do I get to keep them? You know they are a girl's best friend."

"Cute, real cute."

I left her to her task and walked around to the back of the refrigerator, "What's it look like Agent Brewer?"

He'd just set the back of the refrigerator against the wall. "I guess it looks like the inside of a refrigerator."

I chuckled and said, "Another comedian."

Wade took his penlight out of his pocket and flashed it into the back of the refrigerator. "Well, what do we have here?" He reached his hand into the back of the refrigerator and came out with a little black bag. It looked just like the one in the truck. He handed it to me and said, "I wonder what's inside this little bag?"

As I felt the weight of it in the palm of my hand I said, "Twenty five diamonds in and out of settings."

We walked over to the rear desk and I opened the bag. On a spot I cleaned on the desk, I slowly poured out the contents. I reached out and separated the pile and gave half to Wade. I took half and we both started counting.

When I finished counting I said, "I have twelve pieces."

"And I have thirteen, which makes twenty five. How'd you know?"

"Lucky guess?"

He whispered, "You can do better than that."

"All right, the bag outside also had twenty five pieces. I thought if I was a bad guy hiding caches of diamonds I'd need to know two things. One, where they are and two, how many do I have. These boys are smart enough to know that a large shipment of unidentifiable diamonds would demand a much higher price from a fence here, which leaves another point for discussion."

"What's that?"

"Somewhere there's a list of all the hiding places. It would be in the head of the lead player or in one of the many books around here or, if it was me, both places."

Wade asked loudly, "Did everyone hear that? If you came across something strange in writing we want to know about it."

One of the officers going through the books said, "I saw something strange in one of these books earlier."

Wade said, "Check until you find it again and bring it to us."

"Yes Sir. I'll do that."

I said, "Wade you can close up the refrigerator now."

"Do you think that's all we'll find Commissioner?"

"Yes I do, in this spot. But there's a lot more places you can hide twenty five little diamonds."

"Where else do you want me to look?"

"See the shadow box type car pictures on the walls? Take them apart and see what you can find."

"I'm on it."

I raised my voice a little, "Who searched the back wall?"

"We did Commissioner." Two of my men raised their hands.

"Is that all you found…a half a dozen guns?"

"Yes Sir. I'm sure we would have noticed a little black bag."

"Commissioner! I found the book!" He came over and handed me the book open to the correct page.

"Thank you Officer."

I walked over and sat down in a chair in front of the desk.

"Everyone continue to do what you're doing while I try to figure this book out."

The page looked like this:

L.C.	H.M.	U.S.	U.S.S.
3WVI	WGII	DV	DV
RII		TV	TV
3PFIII		C	C

I kept going over every known code that I'd read about. This didn't fall into any of those categories. I thought this has to be a simple code for an absent minded crook. Using what we knew it came to me.

"I got it! Would everyone gather around this desk? I'll explain it to you." I got up and walked behind the desk as they all approached it. I left the coded page open for everyone to see. "Take a look at it and give me your comments if you have any."

After everyone had a minute to absorb it I asked again, "Does anyone have an idea for me?"

Wade spoke first, "Commissioner you've been looking at it for less than five minutes and you figured it out. I could look at it for five hours and not see anything more than what I'm looking at now."

"What about the rest of you?"

"Commissioner I'm the one who stumbled on the book originally. I'd sure like to know how you broke the code."

"I'd be happy to explain it to everyone. When I was younger I used to study codes. Remembering them and looking at this one I knew it was a simple home-made code. Now, what do we know for sure? First we know the crooks have four hiding places. Look at the code as I explain it. There's the car lot, the house, and two mini storage units. So let's make it easy and reverse the letters of the headings, L.C. to C.L. which stands for car lot. The next one threw me so I went on to the last two, U.S. to S. U."

Wade blurted out, "Storage unit!"

"That's right and U.S.S. to S.S.U., any takers?"

One of the officers asked, "Could it be the name of the storage unit?"

"You're making it too difficult. S.S.U. stands for second storage unit."

Everyone laughed.

"Now that I had the three places that we knew about I needed the last one. His home, H.M. reversed is M. H. I knew the H was for home. Knowing it was his home I came up with 'my home'."

"What about the next part?"

"Agent Brewer, that was a little trickier. But by using the information I knew it fell into place. The only place we knew about was here. So I used that. Let me back up. I hope everyone is following my thinking. This man is worrying about misplacing diamonds. A small item easily misplaced. Now I looked at the car lot column to see if anything made sense. 3WVI and 3PFIII made little sense, but RII could stand for refrigerator two bags. If that's correct 3WVI means 3 walls and six bags. 3PFIII should yield three bags of diamonds in three of the many pictures on the walls. So gentlemen get back to work and don't make me out a liar!"

Yoto had two walls uncovered. They were full of firearms and other weapons. Yoto and one of the other officers removed everything and continued to fill the other desk and everything around it. While they were doing that one of the other officers was taking down the back wall for the second time. Everyone kept looking but no one could find the diamonds.

"Commissioner they're not here," I heard an officer say. I looked at the two walls that Yoto had opened up. I then went over to the rear wall where the officers and Yoto were standing, "What's the matter boys? Are you having a problem playing hide and seek with the diamonds?"

I started to laugh.

One of the frustrated officers said, "I don't think its funny Sir. We can't find them."

"Relax! It's only a job. No one's going to die if we don't find them."

"I'm sorry Sir. What frustrates me most is you said they're here and you're not usually wrong!"

"That includes this time."

"Then you know where they are?"

"Yes I do. So does Officer Yoto."

"I do?"

"Remember 1964? Top secret combat center, instead of messages?"

"Diamonds!"

"Right!"

Lynda asked, "Could you explain all that to us youngsters?"

"Yes Sergeant Stalls. During the war if you went on a secret mission and there was a change or extra instructions at a designated area there would be tape on a post, door, or wall. It would be out of the way and nothing anyone would pay attention to. You'd carefully pull it off the wall and the message would be on the reverse side. All through the war the enemy never found out about it. Now for the people here who don't know about construction you don't use tape to put up walls. You see all the tape on the wall? It's not supposed to be there."

"Sir, there's got to be over a hundred pieces of tape on the rear wall alone. Is there an easier way to do this?"

"Yes there is."

"Can I tell him how to do it Commissioner?"

"Yes Officer. Go ahead."

"Just feel the tape until you feel the diamonds."

"Will that work Commissioner?"

"No. But it's a good idea."

"Then I'll ask again Sir. How do we find them?"

"The guy looked to be about 6 foot three which puts his eyes at about 5 foot eleven so I would look for the only piece of tape that's about that high off the floor."

Wade said, "Commissioner, I'm six feet tall."

"Good. Go stand by the tapes and everyone else watch for one about an inch from the top of his head."

He walked up to the furthest stud to his left. As he went from stud to stud he was stopped at the third and fourth one.

"Commissioner what was wrong with my idea of feeling the tape?"

"Reach over and feel one of the tapes we marked."

He ran his fingers over the tape and felt it. "There's nothing here Sir."

"Officer Yoto, remove the tape he just touched."

Yoto removed the tape slowly and carefully. When he turned

around he laid the tape upside down on his hand holding one end in his finger tips. As he showed everyone the tape they could see the sparkling diamonds.

"Why couldn't I feel them Sir?"

"Two reasons; one; the tape is thick and spongy. Two; there is an indentation on the two by four. When you'd push on the tape it had room to give. Someone count the diamonds. There should be twenty five of them."

Wade said, "I've already done it and there are twenty five Sir."

"Good. Put them in the black bag and let's get back to work."

They easily found the rest of the diamonds. Wade found the other three black bags behind the pictures on the walls. I had Wade call the boys at the house to go into the walls in the garage. He told them what to look for and how to find them. He also called the people who took the storage units and told them what to look for and where to find it. Yoto, Lynda, and I left Wade in charge and headed back toward my office.

Chapter 17

"If everyone would like breakfast I'll buy!" I ordered a stack of hot cakes and everyone followed suit. "You guys know you don't have to order what I'm having."

Lynda said, "We know that. I just feel like pancakes."

"Me too."

"All right, you win. I'm not fighting both of you."

After the waitress left we discussed our morning.

"I think we made quite a haul Larry."

"I agree Lynda. It was a very profitable morning."

"Larry, I've got a question for you."

"What is it Yoto?"

"How long have we been here?"

"Since we pulled into the parking lot?"

"Yes."

"Twelve to fifteen minutes. Why?"

"How hot is it out?"

"It's about 90 degrees. Why?"

"That's what I'm wondering. Why?"

"You're going to have to do better than that."

"Look across the street."

"All right," Lynda and I looked.

"See the woman pushing the open baby carriage?"

"Yes what about her?"

"She's been there since we've arrived."

"Maybe she's waiting for someone."

"If so Lynda wouldn't it be better to keep the baby in the shade of the building?"

"You're right Yoto. Something stinks and it's going to ruin our breakfast."

Yoto said, "You're right Larry. Look what's coming up the street and it's going to make a right turn in front of our lady and her baby carriage."

Lynda responded, "It's a Brinks Armored Truck."

"We better get moving. Yoto give Lynda the car keys. Lynda, give me your gun. You get one out of the car. Play it by ear, Lynda. Put the car where you think it will do the most good and radio for back up. Yoto you take the right and I'll take the far left and center. Walk Silent and Walk Deadly." As we walked by our waitress I flashed her my badge and said, "Hold our breakfast. Get your customers away from the front windows. We'll be right back."

Yoto was gone before I hit the door. I walked as fast as I could. I covered about half the distance when I heard the crash. You could hear the lady yelling and crying, "My baby! My baby! It's trapped under the truck!"

The driver of the truck jumped out along with his man riding shotgun. While they went back to help the lady with her baby the rear guard stayed locked in the truck. As the men pulled the baby carriage out from under the front wheels of the truck I was close enough to hear one of the guards say, "Where's the baby?"

At that point the lady pulled out her gun and said, "Here's Baby gentlemen. If you cooperate no one has to die. I want the keys to your truck."

As the other guard started to reach for his gun a man in the crowd pointed a gun at him and said, "Not a good idea Mister!" The guard handed her his ring of keys.

"Now you two guards lay flat on your stomachs on the sidewalk and stay there until we're out of sight."

They did as they were told. The young man walked up to them and pulled their guns out of their holsters and tossed them in a nearby trash can.

The woman said, "Cover me while I unlock the passenger door." She moved to the door and he moved with her facing the crowd while he walked backward.

"Excuse me folks."

"What do you want old man?"

"I happen to be Commissioner Towers and I'm going to have to arrest the two of you."

With this said the woman turned around before opening the door. "Do we have someone making a joke?"

"Let me assure you this is no joke. Put down your weapons and come peacefully or we'll kill you where you stand."

"I heard a 'we' Commissioner. But you're the only one I see. I haven't got time for games. The police are on their way. Kill him

Mike."

Mike started to aim his gun when Yoto put a bullet in the back of his head. The woman started to draw her pistol from her belt when I pulled my hand out of my jacket pocket with Lynda's gun in it. As I fired so did Yoto. She died in the cross fire. I helped the guards up as backup arrived.

"Officer Yoto, take over and make it short. I'll be waiting in the car."

It took Yoto about five minutes to bring the Sergeant in charge abreast of the situation. He then returned to the car and we returned to the restaurant for our breakfast.

Chapter 18

It was close to twelve when Lynda and I walked past Mrs. Thompkin. "How's everything going Mrs. Thompkin?"

"Fine Commissioner, I have everything under control." As she was talking she handed me a couple of messages.

"Glad to hear that. There's one thing I know for sure Mrs. Thompkin, I can always count on you holding down the office."

"Thank you Sir."

"You're welcome."

With that said Lynda and I walked into my office.

"Who called?"

"I don't know Lynda. Let me take a look." I unfolded the papers that were folded in half. "The Mayor wishes to speak to us as well as Coop and Josh. I think I'll call Coop and Josh first."

I sat down at my desk and dialed Coop's number. He answered the phone, "Coop."

"Larry. Over."

We both laughed.

"It's been a long time since I heard that response."

"I know Coop. It just slipped out."

"I enjoyed it."

"I'm glad you did. Now what were you guys doing, need I ask, at our bust this morning?"

"Our job, as I remember it, we're undercover drug lords."

"Wow. That sounds impressive!"

"I knew you'd like it."

"Now back to my question."

"We were contacted through some people that these boys were bringing in drugs and diamonds for disposal here. We had an appointment to meet with them, talk terms, and see the merchandise. But we got interrupted by the cops."

"We've been working on this bust for months. We hit four states and Canada this morning."

"Then our little bit of information will be worthless to you."

"That's right. Pretend you weren't there."

"We can do that."

"Good, anything new happening?"

"We're hearing a lot of different rumblings on the streets but nothing worth reporting. It's mostly about no drugs. The person they blame for this is the new Police Commissioner. I'm afraid the word's out."

"That's all right Coop. I knew we couldn't keep me a secret forever. If that's all you've got I better get going. Talk to you soon."

"Yeah Larry, talk to you soon."

I pressed the receiver button down and dialed up the Mayor.

"Hello. This is the Mayor."

"And this is the Commissioner. I got your message. How can I help you?"

"Just wondering how things are going."

"The raid this morning went great. The armored car robbery that Yoto, Lynda, and I foiled on our way back to our office also went great. But what you'd….."

"Wait a minute!! What armored car robbery?!"

"It's almost noon. If you put on channel four they'll tell you all about it."

"I'll do that and call you back."

"Bye."

I hung up the phone and buzzed my team's office and told them to tune in channel four. I hung up my phone and sat back in my chair and relaxed.

We must have made the top story of the day because by five after twelve my private line was ringing. "Hello Mayor. How'd you like the report?"

"If you were one of the two undercover officers who stumbled onto this crime, you got good coverage."

"Does that mean Yoto and I did a good job?"

"Two dead bad guys, no one hurt, and no money missing? You did great."

"Thank you. Now about the other thing you wanted to ask me."

"Well now that you brought it up, how are we doing with Mrs. Baker's daughter's problem?"

"I don't know, but if you show up for the five o'clock meeting we'll both find out together. How does that sound?"

"Sounds great, see you then."

"Lynda, make sure all the boys know about the five o'clock meeting."

"I'll take care of it."

"Good. Why don't you use my desk? I'm going to take the packet of photos that Pete sent over of Tammy's room and house and lay them out on the conference table. Join me when you're finished and we'll look at them together."

As I walked away she said, "I'll be there in a few minutes."

After laying out the pictures I looked at them as you would any photographs someone was showing you of their house. Boy, I thought, this place is a small mansion. From what I could see it was a large two story colonial style house. Being an ex real estate broker I figured the house to be over 6,000 square feet. There was a beautiful stairway to the left side of the foyer as you entered the house. From the front door the foyer was a large semi circle of white imported marble. It allowed you access to the sunken living room to the left of the stairway. Next, was a hallway leading into the house. Next, on the wall came an opening to a great area, then another wall, and just before the front door is a door to the library. Like I said, it is a very large foyer. I could also see part of a huge crystal chandelier hanging down from the center of the foyer. The ceiling had to be 15 to 20 feet from the floor. I was impressed with the first photo, but no closer to solving our problem. There were a couple of shots of the outside of the property, but they also told me nothing. The next thing I did was try to put the photographs in order of importance. I noticed out of the corner of my eye Lynda was getting up from my desk. "Lynda."

"Yes Larry?"

"Would you bring me some small post-it tabs?"

"All right."

I went back to the photos and a couple of minutes later I was marking the photos and explaining to Lynda what I was doing. I marked the photos around and outside of the house 1 through 12. I randomly numbered the last eight photographs of Tammy's room. I would have sought some kind of order but I couldn't find anything amiss in them. At this time one photo was as important as the other.

Lynda and I sat going over each photo until three o'clock. We tried to cover every photo from every conceivable angle. We even discussed the home's interior decorating.

"I hope the boys can see something we're missing."

"So do I Larry. As you always say, 'it's there; you just have to see it'."

"That's the part that bugs me so. I know as sure as there is life in my body it's there!"

"Don't worry. We'll find it."

"I agree with you Lynda. I just hope we'll be in time."

"We will be Larry. Why are you picking up the pictures?"

"You know I only need four to five hours sleep a night."

"Yes I do."

"For some reason I'm tired and need a little nap. Hopefully after resting my mind I'll be able to see things more clearly."

"Sounds good to me."

We went up to our penthouse. After a snack, some relaxing and a twenty minute nap I felt great and so did Lynda.

It was twenty to five when we walked past Mrs. Thompkin. "Mrs. Thompkin, if you're not doing anything pressing why don't you head home?"

"That's a good idea Commissioner. I will. Good night Sir."

"Good night Mrs. Thompkin."

We went inside and got the pictures out of the safe. "Lynda, while I lay these out why don't you get a couple of pitchers of iced tea?"

While she was gone I started to compare the bedroom photos. I knew there was something amiss but I couldn't put my finger on it. That's it! Finger! I walked to my desk and picked up my direct line to the Mayor.

"Hello, this is the Mayor."

"Larry here."

"Yes Larry. What do you need?"

"I need Mrs. Baker's son in law's finger prints. Could you call her and ask if she could meet you in the lobby at six tonight? Then we could figure out a way to get them."

"I'll take care of it. And I'll see you in a few minutes."

Lynda came in with the boys carrying drinks and glasses.

"What's up Larry?"

"What's the matter Jim, can't a man make a phone call without something being up?"

"Normal people can. But that leaves you out. Now what's new?"
"I called the Mayor to invite Mrs. Baker to our meeting at six."
John said, "Then we better be done by that time."
"We will be John, unless you boys have something that I'm not aware of."
I got no sign of anything new so I knew we'd be right on my schedule.
By the time we all settled in at the conference table everyone had arrived. Almost everyone had notes in front of them. It was two minutes to five when I called the meeting to order.
"For those of you who didn't hear Mrs. Baker will arrive at six, so we better get started. Sam, tell me something nice."
"Well, you were there for one of the raids and searches. Our part went as good as yours. After Wade called me we took off all the screwed on panels in the garage. Also the family room had some."
"Were there any diamonds in the family room?"
"No Larry. As a matter of fact we didn't find anything there."
"Good. That's what the secret code said. What did you find in the garage?"
"Two black bags with twenty five stones in each."
"Nice, anything else?"
"Some guns and drugs, just the normal stuff."
"Any arrests?"
"Just the owner's wife, she claims she knows nothing of her husbands' business activities."
"Check it out thoroughly. She could be telling you the truth."
"We will."
"What else?"
"The boys who raided the storage units found all kinds of new merchandise, drugs, and weapons of all kinds. The cars you found out about, the trunks were full of drugs. So considering how everything worked out, we had a very successful day all around. I pass to Wade."
"For everyone who didn't make it this morning, we had a great time. We have a lot of bad guys off the street and a large profit. I pass to the Mayor."
"Before you do we have something we must discuss."
"Can I tell you I'm sorry and it won't happen again?"

"No, you almost got you and me killed. I think you should tell the group what happened. I'm not mad at you, but this is a great learning tool for everyone. You don't think for yourself when the situation is one that I've described to you. You only do as you're supposed to because the rest of your team is counting on you. Now, explain to the group what happened."

"Yes Larry." He commenced to tell the group the error of his ways. "And in closing I want you to know if it wasn't for Larry and Lynda I wouldn't be here. Now after going through the whole thing again I see where I was wrong in asking you to accept my apology Larry. I need to ask both you and Lynda to accept my apology."

I looked at Lynda and said, "I think he's learned his lesson Lynda."

She nodded her in agreement and we both faced Wade and said together, "We accept your apology."

"Thank you, both of you."

I said, "You're welcome. I hope everyone was paying attention. Today we were lucky. We need to be smart not lucky. The two men I knew would have the most trouble following my orders to the letter were Sam and Wade. No offense gentlemen. I know how hard it is to reprogram years of F.B.I. training. I'm not saying my way is better than yours. All I'm saying is that when we get in a tight spot I want us all on the same page. So I hope you get it straight before you get one of us killed. Now, if I remember it correctly Wade had passed to the Mayor."

"That he had Larry. We have our meeting in the morning with the school principals at 10 A.M. Are you ready Larry?"

"No I'm not. I need a speech right?"

"You haven't written a speech yet?"

"No but I'll get on it tonight."

"That would be nice. Are we going to meet here tomorrow at 9:30 before the meeting?"

"That's right. Seeing no one can use the elevators on the weekend without a key I need two volunteers to shuttle people up to the council chambers on the third floor."

Tom and Jim raised their hands.

"Thanks boys. Be here at 9:30. Back to you Mayor."

"I talked to Doc and things are still ahead of schedule at the hospital."

"That's great. I'd like to drop by next week and see Doc and check on his progress. Keep in mind, anyone with a spare minute can drop by themselves."

Pete asked, "What's a spare minute?"

Everyone busted out laughing.

As I was laughing I shook my head and said, "I guess I do keep you guys busy."

When the laughing and joking subsided I turned it back to the Mayor.

"Larry I pass to Pete."

"We're raiding the mobs with good results. People are still calling in tips about potential crimes. I'll be here in the morning. There are four more properties we need to tie up around the hospital and then we'll own everything in a two block area."

"Weren't there some empty lots in that area?"

"Yes Larry. We were able to buy some cheap and the city helped us to get the others."

"You did pay a fair price for them didn't you?"

"Looking at the area they were appraised for next to nothing. So we offered the owners the appraised value and they were happy to get it."

"I'm glad you handled it that way. I don't want anyone thinking we're misusing our powers."

"No way Larry, everything is on the straight and narrow."

"Good. Keep it that way. What else?"

"I've checked locally and Sam and Wade used the F.B.I. to check nationally and everyone on Mrs. Baker's list of employees in or around the house are clean."

"How'd I know that was the answer I'd get?"

Everyone chuckle and smiled.

"By the reaction of everyone Larry, we're all thinking alike."

"That we are Pete. Please continue."

"I haven't had a chance to get some experts on fauna and flora to visit the house to see if there is something that is causing her problem."

"Maybe we could save you some time and money."

"How so Larry?"

"Pete, let's go over what we know. Let's do a comparison to the time she's lived in the house to the time she's been sick."

"She's been sick about half the time."

"I think that would rule out any outside problems. That takes care of flora. Now let's look at fauna, which are the animals in the house. There are two guard dogs outside."

"They were brought over from her mother's house when they moved into their house."

"The dog inside?"

"She has had him for eight years."

"The cat?"

"Six years."

"I think we can rule out fauna. She has had all the animals much longer than she's been sick."

"I see what you mean Larry. The help and the outside of the house are squeaky clean."

"I agree. Is there anyone who has a different thought about this?"

No one said a word so I told Pete to continue. Before he could Wade interrupted, "Larry, I almost forgot." As he was speaking he was taking something out of his inside jacket pocket. It was wrapped in a white men's hanky. It was a long item. As he unrolled the wrapping from it I knew it was my sleeve knife. He slid it down the table to me.

"Thanks Wade. I've missed my little baby." I slid it back into its case on my left arm as Pete continued to speak.

"We haven't compiled everything yet on the raids this morning. It'll take a couple of days to figure out. A guess-timation of properties, diamonds, vehicles, personal property, we should hit over two million."

"That's a good day's work Pete. Sam, what about the condo they owned?"

"We couldn't touch it until we arrest the leaders' wife. The unit was in her name alone. The boys got a warrant and hit the place about one o'clock."

"Good. If we can tie her into this mess we'll own the unit."

"Even if she walks you'll own it."

"Why is that?"

"The boys found a hundred thousand dollars worth of heroin in one of the bedroom closets."

"Hooray for our side! Anything else?"

Everyone was smiling. It's really a good feeling knowing you're making a difference.

"One thing Larry, I hope you don't mind but our boys have taken the initiative and I didn't have the heart to say anything but 'a good job'."

"What radical change did they make now?"

"You remember how you had them call in all our disable officers for re-evaluation?"

"Yes I do."

"After deciding that we could hire forty of them back to work they set up a volunteer board to review each man. The board wanted to see if they needed a refresher course at the academy or if they can work without retraining. Also they needed to figure out what job or jobs each person can do. I made it easy on them. I told them that they were in charge of hiring the men and assigning them their positions. What do you think?"

I sat thinking for a few seconds while Pete seemed to squirm in his chair a little. As I scratched my head I asked Pete, "Where is the part I'm supposed to mind?"

Everyone started to laugh.

"Then you don't mind?"

"Pete, you know I love to see our boys take charge. Send them my blessings. Was that everything?"

"Well, just another little thing. Our civilian volunteer force has tripled since you took over. Our ability to pay them a little money enables them to afford their uniforms and supplies."

"Glad to hear it."

"Now I pass to Tom."

"Larry, Jim and I have been using every available resource to us to trace Mr. Charles T. Winder. If you follow his surface trail, he's a really smart and nice person. But if you dig deeper, he died six years ago, if we have the right guy."

"I have a feeling you do Tom. I also have a feeling that he's done this before, and will do it again if we don't stop him. That's the reason I've invited Mrs. Baker to our meeting. This guy can change a lot of his features but he can't change his fingerprints. With her help we'll get a set of them and Sam, you'll run them for us."

"Be happy to Larry. Scum like this turns my stomach. I agree with you. He must have done this before. That's why we can't figure out how he's doing it. As you said Larry, as long as he can get away with it he'll keep doing it."

"You're right Sam, anything else Tom?"

"I pass to Jim."

"You heard my reports from everyone else. I'll pass to Lynda."

"As you know I was at the bust at the car lot and I think we owe a round of applause to Lyn-Yhi who helped out this morning."

We gave her a big hand. I could tell it made her happy.

"With that said, I pass to Robert."

"John and I have been checking out Tammy. Nothing to report, she had the usual childhood diseases, nothing worse than braces after her twelfth birthday. While you folks were doing the bust this morning I was over at our new hospital visiting Doc. I took the part of the file that you had given me which had a bunch of doctors and hospital tests and reports, most of which I couldn't understand."

"Did Doc help you out?"

"Larry, he stopped what he was doing and gave me his full attention. After he realized what I needed to know he gave me a pair of coveralls and put me to work sanding and patching. He said, 'Larry wouldn't like it if I lost two hours of work. So you'll take my place.' I did his work and he did mine."

We all laughed.

I said, "I love Doc's work ethics. What was he able to tell you?"

"This lady has been tested by the best. If she has a disease it's one that no one else in the world has. As Doc put it, 'you have a lady dying, but she's not really sick.' Larry I sure hope you can help her."

"Robert, we're all helping her and we won't stop helping her until she's well again."

"Thanks Larry. I pass to John."

"With the help of my computer and a couple contacts of mine I found out that Mrs. Tammy Winder has an 18 month old insurance policy for the sum of one million dollars."

Tom asked, "And it's payable to her husband right?"

"Yes it is Tom. But that's not all. It pays double indemnity for accidental death."

After looking around at everyone I said, "Why is it we're not surprised? I don't think I have to explain to anyone how she's going to die, do I?"

They looked at one another and then back at me and then altogether they said, "Accidently!!"

"I like a group that stays on top of things."

The Mayor said, "Talking about that, I'd better get downstairs to meet Mrs. Baker. It's five to six!"

"We'll be right here waiting for you Mayor."

As he left my office I asked John if he had anything else.

"I pass to Yoto."

"Good mission today. I pass to Lyn-Yhi."

"I enjoyed working the mission today. I found out more things about myself. One, I need more training from Yoto. Two, I had trouble holding up my part of the mission."

Wade asked, "Did you at least get the correct guy to fight?"

"Yes I did that."

"Then you did a better job than I did."

We all laughed including Wade.

"That's one thing about you people. You never harshly criticize or punish one another."

"If a person is sincere and loves who he's working with he feels worse about the thing he's done wrong than you ever could. I'll use Wade as an example. The only reason I brought it up was as a training tool for everyone else. If there was no lesson to be learned I would have pulled Wade aside and talked to him. Did you finish your report Lyn-Yhi?"

"I have only one other thing. I'm happy to be a part of this team."

"And we're happy to have you. Now, does anyone have anything else before Mrs. Baker gets here?"

No one said a word.

"Has everyone had a little time to spend on the photos?"

They all nodded in the affirmative.

"Does anyone have any ideas?"

"Larry?"

"Yes Tom."

"I've spent over three hours going over all the photos. I've narrowed the important ones down to the eight of Tammy's room."

At that moment we could hear the office door opening. "Hold on a minute Tom."

The Mayor escorted Mrs. Baker over to the conference table. He took a minute to introduce her to the people she hadn't met.

Mrs. Baker said, "The F.B.I.! Larry once again I'm impressed."

"Mrs. Baker these are the men we work hand and hand with. Also they're a part of our team. We've also made Lyn-Yhi a part of our team out of necessity. It's a long story that I can tell you some other time. Right now I'd like to get to more important matters regarding your daughter Tammy."

"I definitely agree with you. The Mayor told me on the phone that you needed my help."

"Yes we do. We don't think that Charles is really 'Charles'. What we need to do is arrange to get his fingerprints as soon as possible."

"The Mayor also mentioned that when he called. What the Mayor didn't know was Charles was in my office explaining how successful his new local ad campaign was. So I pulled out two high ball glasses and we toasted his success with a cocktail. Then I sent him home to be with Tammy."

"Don't tell me!"

She opened her large handbag and pulled out a plastic bag with a cocktail glass in it. She held the bag up between her index finger and her thumb so everyone could see it. "Will this help out?"

"Sam."

Sam got out of his seat and walked over to Mrs. Baker to relieve her of the glass. He then returned to his seat.

With a smile on my face I said, "Mrs. Baker, I could kiss you! You've saved us 24 hours or more."

"Larry, you've found something out haven't you! Don't hold out on me! I have a ……..''

"Mrs. Baker I hate to interrupt you but I told you last night that you are a part of this team which means everything we know you know. I just haven't had a chance to bring you up to date yet."

"I'm sorry Larry. I should know that you are different from all the other groups I tried to get to help."

"Let me fill you in." It took about five minutes to bring her up to speed.

"So you think he'll try for the 2 million dollar accidental life insurance policy?"

"Wouldn't you?"

"In a New York minute!"

"If Tammy died how would Charles fare without the insurance?"

"Cars, the house and furniture, things like that, no real cash to speak of."

"That's what we thought."

"It looks like the fingerprints are all we have."

"Don't look so disappointed Mrs. Baker. We actually know quite a bit."

"Like what?"

"Let's use the 5 W's of police investigation: What; Who; Where; When; Why. Now so far we know who; Charles. What; to murder your daughter. Where; at their house. Why; for financial gain. There's only one W we don't know and that's when. Does that make you feel better?"

"Yes it does. You boys do impress me. How will you find out the When?"

"That's where your fingerprints come in. If my thoughts are correct he's done this before. We need to find out where, when, and how they died."

"When you say 'they', you mean he's done this more than once?"

"That's right. I would say he's done it at least twice which makes your daughter number three."

"Is there a reason you think this way?"

"Yes. This type of an individual is made not born the way he is."

"Would you explain that?"

"The scenario went something like this: He's a good looking man who was forced into his first marriage. The woman was probably pregnant. Somewhere along the line she lost the baby. All he could think about was getting rid of his wife. For some reason divorce didn't enter his mind. He bought a life insurance policy on both of them and proceeded to find a way to kill his wife so it looked like an accident. I would say it took over a year to do but he got the job done. After getting the insurance money he moved to another state and looked for another victim. He thought, 'if the police are too dumb to figure out what I'm doing I can keep doing it'. This time he finds a woman who is alone and vulnerable. Two years later she dies leaving him everything plus a good size insurance policy. Now he's ready for the big time. He moves to Pertsville, rents a nice place, joins a country club and waits for his next victim. Along comes Tammy and the rest, as they say is history."

"Are you sure it happened that way Larry? It sounds like a script for a Hollywood movie."

The Mayor piped in, "If Larry thinks that's how it happened, I'd put my money on it."

"So would I" said Pete.

Everyone else nodded in the affirmative.

"God, what a fool I've been!"

"Not really Ma'am. You had the man checked out. Which is a lot more than anyone else would have done. So relax. Everything will be okay from the point of your daughter being alive. We can't do very much for her emotional scars. Do make sure you get her someone to talk to when this is over."

"I already have someone in mind."

"Good. We're going to need to get into the house Monday or Tuesday."

"Let me know which day you want as soon as possible. With his new ad campaign I can send Charles around the country with no problem."

"Let's see if I can get you an answer right now. Sam, you know how important this is to me. When can you have the prints done?"

"Larry when I leave here I'll go back to the office and call in a favor or two and I'll have something for you tomorrow."

"Thanks Sam. Mrs. Baker, send him out of town by noon Monday and I don't want him back until Tuesday evening. Can you do that?"

"That's about all I can do. He hates to be gone two evenings in a row."

"You mean overnight, two nights in a row?"

"That's right."

"What does that tell us boys?"

Jim was the first to answer, "He's doing something every night that's causing her a slow and agonizing death."

"I don't think you had to be that descriptive. But you answered correctly."

"I'm sorry Mrs. Baker."

"It's quite all right Jim. It's the truth and we have to face it if we're going to put an end to it."

She looked away from Jim and back to me. I looked her straight in the eye and said, "Before next week comes to an end your situation will be over. That's a promise Mrs. Baker."

"Thank you Larry. I'll hold you to it. Oh by the way Larry, I don't know if these will help…" She had her hand in her handbag again. "But I brought you all the photographs I have of my daughter and her husband. There's also a real good shot of him by himself."

She handed them to me. There must have been at least 50 of them. "If you don't mind Mrs. Baker, something tells me to go through these photos now with you here. Will you take a break with the boys for a few minutes while I go though the photos and separate them? Afterwards we'll all go through them."

"I don't have a problem with that Larry."

It took me less than five minutes to separate the photos in some kind of order. My main concentration was on the inside of the house and particularly the bedroom. She had half the shots of them at the office, park, on a boat, in a car, and a few places I couldn't place. The other half is what excited me. It was them in the house and some of both of them in their bedroom. There were a half a dozen shots in the bedroom. One even had the couple in bed together. I put three pictures to my left and three to my right. I asked everyone to retake their seats. As Lynda sat down I handed her three of the photos. Then I turned and handed the Mayor three.

"I'm sending around half a dozen photos of the bedroom. I feel, along with everyone else in the room, that our problem is in this area." While I was talking Lynda was looking at her batch of photos.

"I hate to say it in front of the group Larry, but Charles has the same problem you do with the funny shape of his hair in the morning."

"Let me see." I took the photo back. It was the one of the couple in bed. I held it over so Mrs. Baker could see it. "Can you tell me when this was taken?"

"Yes, about six months after they were married. They had me stay over Christmas Eve so I snuck up on them Christmas morning and got a candid shot."

"Let me guess. Your daughter at this time had a cold or bronchial type infection she hadn't been able to shake. She probably had it for at least a month."

"That's right. That's why I went to their house so she wouldn't have to travel. How did you know she was already sick?"

"Lynda told me."

"I did?!"

"Yes you did. You're brilliant." I squeezed her hand as I said it.

"Thank you. Now will you explain to me why I'm so brilliant?"

"Mrs. Baker would you mind going out in the reception area with the Mayor for a minute?"

"Not at all, if it'll answer Lynda's question."

"It will."

She left with the Mayor. They had no sooner closed the door when John and Robert got out of their seats and headed for my secret arsenal, which is located behind a big painting behind my desk. As I arose from my seat I said, "If everyone will relax for a minute we'll be right back."

As I walked into the arsenal Robert asked, "What are we looking for Larry?"

"I remember where it used to be, but we've added so many things." I was looking as I was talking, "Here it is! Come over here Robert and put this on."

We left the arsenal and closed the secret way in. "Robert, wait inside the lounge door for John to come for you. John, you wait outside the door. When I call you bring Robert to the table."

"I'll take care of it Larry."

I left them and headed for the office door. I opened it and asked Mrs. Baker and the Mayor to join us.

Mrs. Baker asked as she sat down, "Do you have an answer for Lynda?"

"You women sure stick together."

"That we do Larry."

"Before I give you my explanation I want everyone to take a look at the photo in question. Pay particular attention to the side of his hair." After the photo returned to me I called to John, "Would you bring Robert here?"

I could hear the lounge door open and shut and a few seconds later John and Robert appeared. Everyone was looking at Robert and quietly laughing.

Wade said, "Don't tell me! We're going to play spaceman."

"Cute Wade, real cute. Robert, face the table so everyone can see the side of your head. John, very carefully pull the elastic strap out from his head without messing his hair."

"As you can see, when the mask is removed you can see a faint line in Robert's hair just like the one in the photo of Charles."

All the kidding and joking around the table had stopped and everyone had a very serious look on their face.

"What is the apparatus Larry?"

"Mrs. Baker, it's an air filtration mask. It does make you look a little like a spaceman Robert."

"Thanks Larry. I needed that."

"I'm only kidding. Does everyone get the picture?"

"I think so Larry. But I'd feel better hearing it from you."

"When your daughter first got sick the two of them were sleeping in the same bedroom together."

"I would say so. They were married!"

"Yes they were Mrs. Baker. But now she sleeps alone and her husband sleeps in a different room, right?"

"Yes in case what Tammy has is contagious."

"Whatever he's doing to Tammy, he's doing during the night. According to the medicine she's taking one of them is a sleeping pill."

"Which means?"

"It means he can enter and leave her room at will without bothering her, which means he can do whatever it is he's doing to kill her and never have a witness."

I knew I shouldn't have talked so lightly about Tammy's death. I knew by the way Mrs. Baker looked when Jim had made his remarks that she was ready to collapse. "Mrs. Baker said, "My baby!!" Then she broke down and started to cry. The Mayor held her and lightly patted her on the back. I never understood why people pat grieving people on the back. Anyway the next thing I did was reach into my pocket and get out a clean white linen hanky and handed it to Mrs. Baker. After she cried for a minute or two she wiped her eyes, blew her nose, and regained her composure.

Mrs. Baker said, "I ask everyone to forgive me for my outburst."

"It is I who will ask for your forgiveness Mrs. Baker."

"Why would you do the Larry? I'm the one who made a spectacle of myself."

"Yes Ma'am but I'm the one who purposely drove you to it."

"May I ask you why?"

"My reason is simple. It's to keep you and your daughter alive."

"Would you elaborate please?"

"The first time we met I could tell you were a time bomb waiting to go off. If by chance you went off at the wrong time in front of the wrong person you could destroy everything we are working on. So I figured it would be better to have you go off in front of friends who love and care for you. So I did."

"Once again you were right Larry. I feel a lot better and stronger. I don't think I'll have any more of a problem with the situation."

"I know you won't Mrs. Baker. Everything from now on will be just fine."

"Pete, take the bedroom shots and blow them up. Get everyone a copy by morning."

"It'll be done Larry."

"Good. The only other thing that we can accomplish this evening is for me to take everyone out to dinner."

"Larry, would it be wrong of me if I offered to buy dinner for everyone?"

"No Ma'am. From time to time everyone buys dinner. You may even pick the restaurant."

"I can't make it this time but I'll join you next time. I have a charitable meeting I have to run at 7 P.M."

"Seeing we never turn down a free meal I will thank you for the men."

"Please enjoy yourselves. I'll wait to hear from you."

"Mayor, will you and John escort Mrs. Baker to her car and then meet us at the limo?"

After they left I kept thinking about Tammy. "Lynda, see if you can get Doc on our cell phone so I can talk to him as we walk to the limo."

"Should I try his home number?"

"Where do you think you'll find him and his friends on a Friday evening?"

"At the hospital."

"That's right. If I have him help with this case maybe I can get him away from there for a few hours. He's working too hard."

"I know with your total recall you know the number at the hospital."

As I gave her the number she punched it into the cell phone. In a few seconds Lynda said, "Hello. This is the Commissioner's office calling Doctor Kaplin." As we were walking toward the elevator she said, "Doc this is Lynda. Larry needs to speak to you. Hold on."

She handed me the phone, "Hi Doc."

"Hi Larry, what's up?"

"You have a chance to be a hero."

"If I can help you Larry you know I will."

"I know that. I was only kidding around."

"What's the problem?"

"We're on our way to dinner and I have a big meeting in the morning. You'll probably be in Shul in the morning."

"That I will. I have to thank God for my life, family, and friends. But I'll be here after one."

"Good. We'll drop by in the afternoon tomorrow."

"See you then."

"Yeah, I'll see you then."

I disconnected the phone and handed it back to Lynda. She held onto it until we got into the limo, then she put it back into her purse.

We proceeded out to have a nice meal. We went to our favorite Italian Restaurant. The Mayor called ahead and asked if we could have our usual meeting room. We ate a good meal and continued to discuss the case. We all seemed to agree on one point. There was something in the pictures doing the killing and we were looking right at it. That was the part of this case that was driving us all nuts.

After dinner John dropped us off at the elevators. Everyone headed to their cars while Lynda and I took the elevator upstairs. After six o'clock the elevators won't move unless you have a key. As I started to slip my key into its hole I noticed scratch marks around the hole. With the door closed I looked around the inside of the elevator. Lynda knew something was wrong so she opened her purse to make it easier to get her gun.

"Let me have the cell phone."

She handed it to me as I slipped my keys back into my pocket. As fast as I could I dialed the limo. John picked up the phone. "Hello?"

"John this is Larry. I forgot you wanted me to call so as I'm standing in my elevator to go upstairs I thought I'd give you a ring."

"You don't forget anything. You're in trouble right?"

"Yes it is."

"You can't talk?"

"No I can't."

"Well stay on this floor. I've got Jim and Yoto with me."

In the phone I could hear the limo burning rubber as he was trying to speak and drive. Yoto must have grabbed the phone from him. "Larry. Yoto. John's driving. I need to know how many."

"Don't know yet."

"If you're in the elevator and you don't know how many they have to be ......wait a minute! There's no one outside."

"That's right."

"Then they're above you."

"That's right John."

Yoto understood that the person I'm talking to shouldn't have changed.

"How do you want to play it? Should we break in?"

"No. Not right now."

"Then you want us to be back up?"

"Yes that's a good idea."

"Are you going to take them to your office?"

"I could try that. But you're no good in the kitchen."

"Do our keys also open the secret entrance to your office through the kitchen?"

"You better watch what you're cooking. Make sure you know what you're doing."

"You want us to watch the elevator to see what floor you get off on?"

"That's right John. Now I've got to get going. I'll talk to you tomorrow."

I hung up the phone and handed it back to Lynda. She had read through the lines and knew we had company. I looked at Lynda and at the same time at the ceiling of the elevator. I could see movement above the light fixtures. I knew who ever they were it was time for them to spring their trap. So I figured I'd tell them where we were going. "After we get the numbers from my office we'll head on home."

"That's good. I'm tired."

As the lines finished leaving her lips we heard the light fixture being quickly removed from the ceiling.

"Everyone please stand still and don't move!"

I thought his statement was a bit redundant. But I said nothing seeing he had a gun pointed at us. When we heard the noise Lynda and I looked up at the ceiling trying to act surprised.

Lynda said, "Oh my God!"

At almost the same time I said, "What the heck?!!"

The guy with the gun said, "Joey jump down and cover them until we can get down."

Joey lowered himself about halfway down and then jumped down to the floor of the elevator. He pulled out a gun and pointed it at us. He stood there watching us as the rest of the mob joined us. We had a total of 8 mob members.

"Mr. Commissioner. We've been waiting for you. Would you put your key in the lock and take us to your office? We need to have a word with you."

"Business hours are from 9 to 5. You could have talked to me at that time with a lot less problem."

"Commissioner, I have at least three warrants out for me. All the rest of my boys are also wanted. So we don't do too much during the daylight hours."

"I can see your point of view. I wouldn't go wandering around during the day myself if I were you."

I stalled them as long as I could. I was giving my boys time to get weapons and communication gear from the trunk of the limo.

Jim took charge at the elevator door while John and Yoto went upstairs to the second floor. They waited outside the door on the staircase for Jim's directions. While Jim was waiting he made a phone call to Pete and told him the news. It went something like this:

"This is Pete."

"Jim here, we didn't get out of the parking garage. Someone or a group was waiting for Larry and Lynda in the elevator. I need you to seal off the building quietly."

"Can you handle the inside?"

"I have John and Yoto helping me. We can handle it but just in case someone slips through our fingers I want backup."

"I'll handle this end. In five minutes city hall will be sealed tight as a drum."

"Sounds good, gotta go, the elevator is moving."

After turning my key I pushed floor two on the elevator panel. It was silent on our trip up. For some reason people are afraid to talk on the elevator. When the doors opened on the second floor our captors nudged us off the elevator. As we walked down the hall I knew my boys were close at hand.

"I hope you don't mind me asking but does it take 8 of you to talk to me?"

"No. They're here because the first thing you're going to do for me is tell my boys where to find things like laptops, ..."

"I interrupted him, "You mean laptop computers?"

"Yeah!"

"You must have a great source for information. Yesterday we got 50 units in. They're still in there boxes upstairs in the storeroom."

"Give Joey the elevator key and the storeroom key."

I pulled out my key ring and gave Joey my old condo key that I never took off the ring. "You don't need the elevator key unless you're on the first floor or in the basement. Joey, you'll go up one floor and get off the elevator and look for the second door on your right. I'd suggest four of you could load the elevator in two trips each. If the boxes are too heavy don't kill yourself lifting them. Make another trip."

"Thanks for the advice Commissioner." He pointed to three of his boys, "You guys go with Joey."

Yoto whispered into his head phone, "Larry wants them all dead. Combat mode!"

The way Yoto explained it to me later was like this:

They hurried upstairs to the third floor. Yoto moved into the second office on the right and John stayed in the stairwell. They wanted to hit the boys from both sides. While John was waiting Jim joined him. John whispered, "Yoto, Jim's with me."

As John finished speaking he could hear the elevator doors

opening. They could hear the boys walk by. They were talking and laughing about how slick they were. And later on everyone would know how great they were because they broke into City Hall, robbed it, and capped the Commissioner.

John looked at Jim and nodded. Jim nodded back. Now they knew why Larry wanted all of them dead. They came here to kill him. Never give your enemy a second chance to do that.

John quietly opened the door a little and looked at the boys. Yoto had left the office door unlocked. That way you could put any house style key into the lock, turn it and it would open. That's what Joey did. He turned the handle and pushed the door open. As he stepped across the threshold to enter the room he was hit in the throat by Yoto. Yoto hit him so hard that he broke everything except his neck. The boy dropped to the floor. While this was going on John and Jim, with guns in hand, were running the short distance toward the boys. The two boys still in the hall drew out their guns. Before they could pull a trigger they were dead. The fourth boy was grabbed by Yoto. He was pulled by his hair around backwards. He tried to get his gun out of his belt to no avail. Yoto grabbed his chin and the back of his head and gave it a violent twist, breaking the boy's neck. Yoto grabbed each boy by the collar and dragged their limp bodies out into the hallway. He then tossed them on top of their friends. He took my key out of the door, manually relocked it and pulled it shut.

Then Yoto said, "Let's get downstairs boys." He moved at double time and everyone followed.

While the boys were upstairs Lynda and I were being intimidated by the mob leader.

"We had a nice town until you got here. Now all the pressure makes it hard to make a living."

"You know I'm only the Commissioner. If you're having problems you ought to take your complaints to the police department. You should talk to Peter Fortney he's the Chief of Police."

"Don't worry. He's the next one me and the boys will talk to."

"That's good. He's a fair man and I know he can help you."

"I bet he can, right boys?" His three cohorts started to laugh."Is it true you don't wear a gun Commissioner?"

"Yes it is. It makes my suit jacket look funny." I pulled open my jacket by the lapels as I spoke.

"How about your secretary?"

"She doesn't need a gun. She handles most men with her beauty and her charm."

One of the boys said, "I do like the looks of her charms."

They all laughed like young kids do when they say something wrong in front of adults.

"Well that's good to know. I'll put my gun away." He raised his black t-shirt and stuck his gun into the waist band of his Levis. "My boys should be back by now."

"That storage room is only known by a few people in the building. It only contains new things. It also has a few thousand dollars in postage stamps. Your boys are probably loading the elevator. Why don't you go upstairs and give them a hand?"

"Not me. Mike, you and John go check it out and tell them to hurry."

Yoto told me how he had waited in the stairwell while Jim and John had entered my office through the secret door in the kitchen that led into my bathroom lounge area.

After hearing the conversation Jim moved a safe distance from my office door and whispered, "Yoto."

"Yes."

"Two coming your way, do you need help?"

"No."

As the two boys walked by the fire escape door Yoto flung it open as far as it would go. He took two steps out and snatched the boys by the back of their shirts at the neckline and dragged them into the stairwell. The guy in his left hand he smashed into the heavy closing door. The other boy he threw like a sack of potatoes down the flight of stairs in front of him. Yoto pulled the unconscious boy he still had in his hand into the stairwell. He dropped his limp body to the floor. He proceeded down the steps to check out the boy on the lower landing. He squatted down over the lad and pulled his left shoulder toward himself, allowing the boy to roll over flat on his back. He felt for his pulse in his neck and he didn't have one. Yoto sensed a problem and spun around without standing. The boy on the upper level had come to and cleared his head enough to stand up. He looked down and saw his buddy lying by Yoto. He reached under his shirt and that was the last thing he did. Yoto pulled out his throwing knife, which was strapped to his calf and gave it a throw. It sank into the boy's chest and he fell forward down the stairs. As he was falling Yoto stood up. The boy almost landed at his feet. The boy was face down. Yoto pulled the body over by his friend and flipped him over. He removed his knife and wiped it off on the dead boy's shirt. He raised his right foot and put it down on the second step going up. He slid his trouser leg up and put his knife back into its sheath.

"Jim, John, you don't have to speak. The two boys joined their friends upstairs. I'll wait here to hear from you, out."

As everything was happening outside I was still working on the leader inside. "You know I'm the Commissioner and this is my secretary, Lynda, but I don't know what to call you."

"I'm Big Jake, leader of the Southside Hornets."

He was big. About 6 foot 2 and about 185 pounds. He looked to be about 21 to 23 years old.

"I haven't paid that much attention to the gangs around town. I didn't know there were white gangs around."

"Yeah there is and we're the baddest."

His friend agreed.

"Lynda, I wonder if Big Jake would like to go downstairs with us and clean out the Mayor's special fund he keeps in his safe. It's only five thousand dollars."

"I knew you guys kept cash here!"

"I figured you did. Should we go? We could be back before your boys return."

"Jamie, can you watch the broad?"

"No problem Big Jake. Take your time this is one job I'll enjoy."

I thought to myself 'That's what he thinks'.

"Lynda, combat mode is out of the question without help. So be cooperative and I'm sure these boys will let us go later. Isn't that right Big Jake?"

"Sure Commissioner. We don't want to hurt anyone. We just need to make a living."

"Be cooperative Lynda. I'll be back soon."

When Lynda looked at me and nodded I knew she had gotten my real message. 'Combat mode' and I'll be back....not we. She knew she had to take care of her boy before I returned. Jim notified Yoto that we were coming out. As we walked through the reception area Jake reached under his shirt and pulled out his gun.

"Big Jake, you don't need the gun. I don't have one. And you have my secretary and my word that I'm not going anywhere."

"I know that but I don't know if there is anyone else in the building. I hate surprises."

"Listen, I'm in no position to complain. If you feel safer with your gun out then keep it out. Just don't point it at me."

Jim and John were close enough to hear my last statement. They were in the kitchen.

Jim whispered, "Yoto, one bad guy with Larry. Has his gun in hand. I'll follow them."

Jim turned to John, "Return and see if you can help Lynda. She's alone with one of these scum bags."

Not knowing what my boys had in mind I asked Jake, "Do you want me to walk in front of you?"

"Yeah."

I opened the reception room door and we walked out into the hallway.

"What I don't understand Big Jake is why didn't you bring the rest of your gang with you?"

"These were the only boys I could get. The rest of them seemed to be scared of the new Commissioner."

"And you're not?"

"I'm brave enough to be here."

At that point in our conversation we had just passed the door to the stairway and I sensed Yoto there. I stopped turned around and faced Jake. "You know Big Jake some people wouldn't call you brave they'd call you stupid for attempting to kill the Commissioner."

"So you know the real reason we're here?"

"Yes I do."

"Then you're not going to take me downstairs?"

"That's where you're wrong Jake. You'll be going downstairs. Waaay down."

At that point Yoto was behind Jake. He reached forward and grabbed Jake's gun hand tightly and swung it upward to the ceiling. The gun went off. Yoto grabbed Jake's long hair with his left hand and literally threw him against the wall. Jake was still holding his gun in his right hand which was extended towards the ceiling. While Yoto was pushing Jake's face into the wall with his left hand he was pulling Jake's right hand away from the wall and then brutally smashing his gun hand against the wall. The third time he smashed it Jake dropped the gun. Yoto then used his left hand and by the hair pulled Jake's head back and smashed it into the wall twice. He then stepped back and kicked the back of Jake's right leg. This caused Jake to spin around about a quarter of a turn and land on his knees. His body was now leaning to the left resting on the wall.

Yoto turned to me and asked, "Are you okay Larry?"

"Yes Yoto. I'm just fine."

While we were speaking Jake, who we thought was unconscious was slowly reaching his left hand to the small of his back. He slipped it under his shirt and came out with a gun in his hand. As Jake pointed the gun at me he said, "You're not fine for long Commissioner. I told you I didn't like surprises."

As he raised his gun a little higher to aim I heard two puffs. Jake fell forward on his face with the gun still in his left hand. Somehow his right hand laid next to his other gun.

As Yoto and I looked down the hallway we could see Jim walking our way. "You looked like you needed my help."

Yoto said, "That's why we have backup. Thank you."

"Yeah Jim, thank you."

"You're both welcome."

I asked, "What about Lynda?"

"I don't know Larry. I haven't heard anything, but I'll check. John, do you read me?"

"Loud and clear, Jim. Lynda took care of everything here. It's all clear."

"Stay put. We're on our way there."

I said, "Jim go down and help Pete get started on clean up. Tell him we need to get this garbage out of here."

"I'm on it Larry."

As Jim waited for the elevator Yoto and I headed for my office. When we entered my office Lynda was sitting talking to John.

"Everyone okay?"

Lynda answered, "Yes Larry. We're just fine."

As I walked over to her she stood up. I gave her a hug and a kiss.

"I'm glad to see the Gods kept you safe."

"Were you worried?"

"Yes Lynda I was worried…..for the poor defenseless boy I left you with."

"He had a gun!"

Lynda looked seriously at me and I broke out laughing and so did she. Yoto and John joined in. I gave her another hug and said, "I always worry about you."

"I'm glad."

"Why don't you tell us what happened? I see your garter belt derringer on my desk."

"It's cooling down and needs to be reloaded."

John said, "I'll get her a bullet from the armory before anyone else gets here."

While he was doing that Lynda told us what happened. "It was really kind of simple Larry. It was almost the same way I took out Mr. Slider of the Slider Gang.* The young man was fascinated with my body. So I used that to my advantage. The whole ordeal went something like this: Jamie said, "Remember your boss said to cooperate with me." I sat down in this chair, it was one of the two chairs in front of your desk. He was standing in back of the other chair. I asked him, 'Is this what you mean by cooperative?' I slowly started to slide my skirt up. He went bug eyed and put both of his hands on the top of the chair in front of him. His right hand was holding his gun. As my skirt got up to my thigh he could see the start of my garter belt. He asked, "You're wearing a garter belt?" "Yes, would you like it?" "Oh would I ever!" As I started to slide it down I pulled out my derringer from it. "Now young man unless you want a slug in the head I suggest you drop your gun." He started to laugh, "There's two things wrong with that statement. That little gun can't hurt me and you're too chicken to use it. So now what I'm going to do is kill you. I've already killed three people and you will be number four." As he raised his gun off the chair I put a slug right between his eyes."

Yoto said, "He had you figured wrong didn't he?"

"Yes Yoto he did."

*Read about the Slider Gang in 'Our Town ~ The Mystery Series'

"Did he die instantly?"

"No he had time enough for a shocked look on his face. Other than that he fell to the floor like a bag of dirty laundry."

John came out of our secret armory and closed it all up. He picked Lynda's gun off my desk, loaded it for her, and handed it back to her.

"Thank you John."

There was a knock at the door. "Yoto, let Pete in."

Yoto opened the door and the Mayor walked in with Pete with some uniformed officers in tow.

The Mayor asked, "Is everyone all right, Commissioner?"

"Yes Mayor. Everyone's fine. How'd you get here? Never mind. The Chief called you?"

"Yes he did."

I looked over at Pete and made a hand motion for him to have two of our officers take the body on the floor out into the hall until the coroner arrived.

Pete said, "A couple of you boys take the body out of here and down the hall. Put him next to his friend."

There were three other cops standing there doing nothing.

"Why don't you three give them a hand? Then see what else you can do. There's nothing left in here to be handled."

They left and we relaxed.

The Mayor gave a quip of immeasurable proportions, "Larry, through your relaxation of the evening, have you put your speech together for tomorrow?"

Everyone started to laugh.

"Cute Mayor, real cute."

After things quieted down we explained to one another what had transpired through the evening. I asked Pete if he could handle things here so I could go upstairs and finish my speech writing. We all said our 'Good Nights' and Lynda and I headed upstairs.

As we stood in our bedroom taking off our clothes I asked Lynda if she'd like to unwind in the hot tub for a while. She looked over at the clock.

"Seeing it's only 10:15 P.M. that's a great idea, what about your speech?"

"The Mayor was being funny with his statement. If he only knew how true it really was. The Gods and I wrote the body of my talk tonight. So we can relax and love the evening away."

"You'll get no argument from me."

It was 11:30 P.M. when we crawled into bed. Lynda cuddled up next to me and went to sleep. I laid awake for a couple of hours putting the finishing touches on my speech for the morning. That's the nice part of having almost total recall. You can lay things out in your mind without using paper.

Chapter 19

It was 9:25 A.M. when Lynda and I walked into my office. Tom, Jim, and Yoto were in a heavy conversation.

"Larry, how come I missed all the action?"

"What can I say Tom? You went home too quickly. If I say we missed you will you feel better?"

We all had a laugh.

"It's nice to know I have a funny boss."

"That you do."

About that time my office door opened and the Mayor and Pete walked in. "Good morning gentlemen."

They said 'Good morning' and joined us at the conference table.

"Pete, how'd everything go last night?"

Both he and the Mayor had a newspaper under their arm, "Let me show you the nice job the Republic did." He laid the paper out on the table in front of me. While he was doing that he explained how smoothly he finished everything last night.

I said, "Pete, I like the headlines," as I read them out loud. "Eight Dead - Attempt on Commissioner Towers' Life Foiled."

Pete came back with, "When you read the article you'll see how nicely they covered the whole story. They ran the records of the scum who got killed. They also mentioned how stupid they were."

"What about yours Mayor?"

"I have the Sun Progress and they did the same kind of a job."

"That's good to hear. Scum is scum. No matter the age it needs to be dealt with."

"I bet you get some flack about it at the meeting."

"We'll see Mayor. We'll see."

Tom asked, "Is there anything special you want Jim and me to do?"

"Before I answer that Tom I'd like to mention how nice everyone looks."

They all smiled.

"Now here's what I'd like you to do. Mayor, is the Councilmen's chambers set up?"

"Yes it is Larry."

"Tom, you and Jim will leave here in about (I looked at my watch and it was quarter to ten) five minutes. You'll go upstairs and check out the Councilmen's Chambers to make sure everything is in readiness. Leave the double doors open when you finish. I want one of you on the elevator with your key in position. The other one will keep people in order waiting for the elevator."

Lynda interrupted me, "With the amount of people we're expecting, why don't I go down with the boys? I could keep the people in order while they shuttle them to the third floor."

"You heard the lady. That's how we'll do it."

Pete said, "Lynda I have a list of everyone who will be here." He handed her the list.

"Good work Pete. You even alphabetized it for me." Lynda grabbed a clipboard out of the desk on her way out. "I'll see you all at the meeting."

As they got up to leave I said, "Tom, you and Jim will sit by the doors after everyone has arrived."

Tom said, "All right Larry."

The three of them left.

"Pete you look a little tired."

"It was 2:40 A.M. when I finally got to bed. As long as you don't start world war three this morning I'm going home after the meeting to get some rest."

"I'll try to be very careful of what and how I say it."

They both started to laugh.

The Mayor said, "Tell us another one."

"Cute Mayor. Real cute."

"I thought you'd like it."

"What I'd really like to hear you say is that you have the elevator company coming out Monday to fix our problem."

"It wasn't easy getting a hold of them on a Saturday morning but I did it. They'll have someone out here Monday afternoon to assess what they can do."

"That sounds good. Now that I know Pete's going to bed after the meeting and the rest of us are all going over to the hospital to see Doc, Mayor would you like to join us?"

"I haven't anything planned. I'd love to. That does mean you're going to feed us?"

"Yes it does. We'll also take a look at some of the old buildings we've obtained. That way we can try to get some idea of how to utilize them."

"Sounds like fun."

"Okay. You two talked me into it."

"Into what Pete?"

"Going with you of course."

"Would you like to join us Pete?"

"Larry, you're a sly old dog, you are."

"All kidding aside Pete, you don't have to come along."

"I want to. It does sound like fun. And if you spend too long at the hospital I'll take a nap there."

"It sounds good. IT's 9:55 A.M. I think we'd better leave."

"I'll get the elevator while you lock up."

"For some reason Pete, I'd like to take the stairs."

"Then I'll walk with you."

"The thought is appreciated Pete." As we walked we talked. "Mayor you'll open in one minute or less. Pete, you get thirty seconds. The rest is up to me."

The Mayor said, "I noticed how long your speech is by the papers you're carrying."

"I have some papers in my inside jacket pocket. It's an old trick I learned from you Mayor. They have nothing to do with my speech but they make good window dressing."

As I opened the stairwell door I heard voices. I put my index fingers to my lips and looked at Pete and the Mayor. They stopped dead in their tracks saying nothing. I shut the door quietly. "It seems we have uninvited guests. Yoto. Walk Silent. Walk Deadly."

He opened the door very carefully and then slipped into the stairwell. While he was doing that Pete was down the hallway pushing the button for an elevator. The elevator arrived empty. The three of us entered it and headed upstairs. When we got off the elevator Yoto was standing there waiting for us.

"Yoto. Report."

"I know who they are. They followed the last group into the meeting room."

"Good work. Mayor, you and Pete enter the room and take your places. Yoto, you follow them and tell Tom and Jim who our visitors are. Then the three of you go up to them and ask to see their invitations. When they don't produce one ask them to step outside. I'll take it from there. Close the doors on your way out."

In a few moments I had two strangers standing in front of me in the hallway.

"Gentlemen, I'm Larry Towers Commissioner of Police for the town of Pertsville. May I ask who you are?"

"We really don't have to tell you our names."

"No you don't gentlemen. This is not a police state. Lieutenant Harden and Sergeant O'Riley would you please search the two gentlemen, cuff them, and book them for breaking and entering and criminal trespassing."

Tom grabbed the taller of the two boys and Jim put his hand on the other guy.

Mr. Bigshot all of a sudden changed his tune and attitude.

"Commissioner, this isn't necessary. Please let us explain."

"Gentlemen, there are a lot of people you are inconveniencing. You have exactly two minutes to explain yourselves."

"I'm Joe Fisher and this is my younger brother Bobby. I can explain ourselves and our actions in one word. STUPID!"

"Continue."

"My younger brother and I both work as head of security for two different schools."

"Do you have someone who can vouch for you?"

"Yes. I work for Washington High. Mrs. Weaton is here."

Bobby said, "And Commissioner I work for Central High. Patterson."

I nodded my head at Tom and he left us and reentered the room.

Bobby spoke, "Commissioner, I want to apologize for the actions of my brother and myself. I followed your action from the first day you took office. I have a scrapbook of everything you've done."

"Seeing this town has had a lot of Commissioners you must have a large collection of scrapbooks."

"No Sir. You're the only person I've followed. When I heard you put the reporters in their place I knew you'd do something to change our town and you have."

"I hope the two of you like what we're doing."

"Commissioner, we're your two biggest fans."

"Then why did you almost let me arrest you?"

"That's my fault Commissioner. I told my little brother to let me handle everything if we got caught. I wanted to see how you'd handle things."

"What do you think?'

"No excessive force, no brutality, simply good police work. I'm impressed. I just don't know how you've done everything you've done."

"We've had a lot of help from the Gods."

At that point the door opened and Tom brought the two people out.

Before they could speak I asked them, "Do these boys work for you folks?"

"I'll claim Bobby," said Mr. Patterson.

"And Joe is the head of my team," added Mrs. Weaton.

"Thank you folks, if you'll return to your seats we'll get started in a few minutes."

They left and I looked at the young men for a few seconds. They looked to be in their early thirties. "Now what am I going to do with you boys?"

Bobby said, "You could let us sit in on the meeting Commissioner. We promise to be good."

I smiled and said, "For some reason the Gods wanted you here. So I'll let you stay."

They both had smiles from ear to ear.

"You need to be the last ones to leave. I want to talk to both of you when we have a little more time."

Joe said, "We'll stick around Commissioner."

I wasn't sure why I wanted them to stick around but something inside said it was the right thing to do.

After they got inside I said, "Tom, Jim, the door. Yoto, Lynda, in front of the group with me. Let's move it people. We're behind schedule."

As we sat down the Mayor got up. He walked to the podium that had a mike on it. He slid the mike out of its cradle and spoke to the group. I never heard the Mayor so sharp and to the point. He did about a minute and a half and turned the floor over to Pete. Pete used about 45 seconds, and the last thing he did was introduce me.

"Now people, before we get started we need to get the air cleared in the room. I noticed a half a dozen newspapers under the arms of people. If you have comments; good or bad; let's hear them now. Raise your hand and someone will get a portable mike to you. I know you're all principals of schools, so before you ask a question give me your name. You may call me Commissioner. Now, who's first?"

Eight hands went into the air.

"The lady in the back wearing the light blue dress."

"Commissioner, I'm Mrs. Stahlsworth. Was it necessary to kill all eight of the boys last night?"

"Before I answer your question allow me to clear up some of your English terminology. Now I really feel funny, me, Larry Towers, correcting a school principal's English."

Everyone started to laugh including the woman asking the question.

When things quieted down Mrs. Stahlsworth replied, "I won't take it personally Commissioner."

"Thank you Mrs. Stahlsworth, that makes me feel better. The term I have a problem with is 'boys'. Young animals, the imperfection of nature, or Gods misfits, any of these terms would fit the animals that were here last night."

"Aren't you a bit overbearing in your thinking?"

"No ma'am. I don't think so. The eight animals you refer to were the nucleus of the Southside Hornets. Without them there is one less mob to worry about."

"Is that how you're going to get rid of the 'mobs', as you call them?"

"That's up to them, not me. Everybody last night had a gun and an opportunity not to use it. They chose otherwise and ended up dead."

"Somehow Commissioner, killing kids doesn't seem to be the answer."

"Mrs. Stahlsworth, if these were kids I'd agree with you 100 percent. But we're not dealing with kids. We're dealing with young animals who feel they can do what they want without anyone doing anything to them."

"I can't believe they were that bad."

"Chief, would you step up here for a second?"

He moved up next to me and asked, "How may I assist you Commissioner?"

"Would you tell Mrs. Stahlsworth how may murders that your people know these animals had a hand in but they couldn't get enough evidence to convict them?"

"Mrs. Stahlsworth, we know for sure that they committed 12 murders and we have them connected to a total of 20 murders."

"Then why don't you put them in prison?"

"Because our witnesses were all scared off."

"I don't believe they could do that."

A hand went up in the second row.

I pointed to the man, "Can you help us out with a pro or a con?"

"I can give you a pro Commissioner."

Tom handed him a mike.

"You have the floor. Please introduce yourself to the group."

"I'm Mr. Tucker. I have a real close friend who I need to tell you about. She's a teacher and a very beautiful woman. Most of the mob members in question attend my school. One evening when this teacher was working late, trying to help one of these animals, he had four of his gang members join him and they took turns raping her. When she was going to press charges they beat her son, who is 12 years old enough to put him in the hospital. Then she was informed that if she pressed charges they would kill her son. Now that was three months ago. Last week they broke into her house and made her son watch as all eight of them raped her. They told her they'd be back soon because she was good. The next day she did the only thing she could. She put her house up for sale. All I can say, Commissioner, I talked to her this morning before I left to come here. She told me that every one of the boys in the paper were the ones who attacked her. She didn't know I was coming here when she said, "I'd love to thank the Commissioner for giving me back my feeling of security." Neither she nor her son has been out of their house since the last attack. I've done what I could for her. The minute she called me I dropped everything and got to her side. I lent her my pistol. If nothing else it makes her feel more secure. Commissioner, they called her about six o'clock last night and said they'd be over later after they took care of some important business."

"Why didn't you go to her?"

"She didn't tell me about it until this morning. She also said that she and her son prayed all night that something bad would happen to this scum. She asked God for someone to strike this scum down. Now she thinks you are her savior."

"I'm glad we helped her."

"I'm not done yet Commissioner."

"Please finish."

"Mrs. Stahlsworth, to you and anyone else in this room who tries to defend this scum, in my opinion, you are no better than they are! You defending them just helps to put them out on the street to do more crime."

"Now are you finished?"

"Yes Sir!"

He handed the mike back to Tom as her sat down. Mrs. Stahlsworth was still standing.

"Do you have another question Mrs. Stahlsworth?"

"No Commissioner, just a statement."

"Which is?"

"Until it hits home you don't really know what you're talking about. And after hearing it from one of our own, I'm sorry I questioned what you did."

"I'm not Mrs. Stahlsworth. We're not a police state. I don't mind being questioned about my tactics. I'm only human. I can make mistakes. But if we all work together the mistakes will be small ones. If all I wanted to do was to run around shooting mob members we wouldn't be here this morning. Are there any other questions before I get started?"

No one said a word so I started in. "The way I understand it you have exams at your different schools over the next three weeks. Then everyone has a week off. Am I correct?"

I could see heads in the audience bobbing up and down. "I see I'm correct. Now let me explain what I have in mind doing with your help. Before I start, let me get a few ground rules out of the way. When I ask you a direct question I'd like you to respond by raising your hand if your answer is 'Yes'. Do nothing if the answer is 'No'. Let's try it. Did everyone, to the best of your knowledge keep this meeting a secret?"

Every hand in the room went up.

"Good. Everyone's with me. It's important to keep our meeting today a secret until we put it into effect. Does everyone agree?"

All their hands went up.

"Then I'd like everyone to rise and swear this oath. "I, your name, swear to make my school the best it can be. I will do what is right and true to accomplish this. I will tell no one what has and will transpire before we go public with our plan. So help me God." Please take your seats. Seeing you are some of the smartest people in town I know I can trust you. Just remember, your word is your bond. If you say the wrong thing at the wrong time it could jeopardize you as well as a lot of other people. Now, to our meeting. We're only going to be discussing one subject today. That's the 125 mobs we have in our city. I have noticed that when I say 'mobs' some of you give me a strange look. The people of our town used to call them gangs. Being educated the way you people are, you know that's the wrong terminology. The dictionary defines a gang as a group of person working or associated together; which means a school band could be called a gang. Would you like to make these young animals your equal by calling them a gang? That's why we call them what they are; a mob; which is a large, disorderly crowd. That's all they are. Now, rather than calling them a gang, does everyone agree that we should call them what they are; 'a mob'?"

They all raised their hands.

"That's good. I'll continue. You may take notes but you'll leave them here when you leave. I noticed a couple of mini-tape recorders. If you use them you'll leave the tapes here. It's so easy for the information to fall into the wrong hands."

A hand went up and I pointed to her, "Yes ma'am!"

Tom hurried to her with the mike.

She put the mike up to her mouth and said, "Marjory Castal, Commissioner. I have only one question."

"Ask it."

"Why is everything so secretive?"

"That question will answer itself by the time I finish. But let me hit a high spot for you."

"Please do. I'm starting to feel like I'm in the army."

"You are Mrs. Castal. All of you are now in my army! Teachers are trained to teach, administrators are trained to administrate, the police are trained to protect. That's the way it should be and by the time we are finished in our town that's the way it will be again!"

"You really didn't answer my question Commissioner."

"Answer one for me first."

"Be glad to."

"If I took your hard core trouble makers out of your school would you be able to handle the daily troubles that occur?"

"Yes."

"If these people knew what was ahead for them don't you think they'd do their best to keep it from happening?"

"They'd probably threaten, hurt, or kill someone to keep their hold on the school."

"I knew you people were brilliant. Mrs. Castal, you just answered your own question. Thank you."

"I guess I did. You're welcome."

She handed Tom the mike and took her seat.

"I think everyone has gotten a memo about people out of your district who want to come to your school. They now need to apply and then be invited by you to attend. By the time we're ready to move you'll have a complete list of undesirable people. If I hear of anyone using this situation to discriminate against another individual you will never work in any field again. And the answer is 'Yes' I can do that. Now during finals I need you to make a list of everyone you feel you have no control of. I mean the kind of student who drops a piece of paper in the hall, and when you ask him to pick it up he spits in your face and says, 'If you want it picked up do it yourself.' Those are the kids we want; the ones who have no respect for authority."

A hand went up and I pointed to and said, "Yes?"

Jim had the closest mike. He took it to the man.

"Benny Waldus, Commissioner. What if the student is border line?"

"If you feel by taking away his scummy friends you can make a good citizen out of him; do it. If not, send him to me."

"Thank you Sir."

"You're welcome. I'm glad to see you're starting to understand the program. I'm tired of less than 1 percent of the students destroying the ability of 99 percent of the students to get a good education. I see other people in the room who were educated in the late fifties and early sixties. What I can't understand is how did we ever get an education without drugs, guns, and gang violence in our schools?"

Everyone had a little chuckle.

"I know that everyone was aware that I was being a little facetious. But think about it, we used to call our teachers Sir and Ma'am or by their last name. We were taught at home to respect our elders and people in a position of authority. Our school teachers reinforced what we were taught at home. Would you like things that way again?"

All hands went up.

"If you back me 100 percent, that day isn't far off. Now after you finish your lists, you'll make a copy for yourself and send a copy to the Chief. Please keep yours in a safe place. If you need help in making your list, get it. Just use a different approach. After having trouble for so long you all must have some kind of a list at the beginning of each year. Ask your same people to help you update your list. I know you're all smart enough to do this as a regular humdrum thing. That way no one will ask any question you don't want to answer. Are you all still with me?"

All of their hands went up again.

"Do you like what you've heard so far?"

All of their hands went up again.

"Good. After finals are over I want you to personally send out the report cards and a letter to the mob members parents stating the following: 'Due to 'Johnny's' grades and long list of deportment violations we will no longer allow him to attend classes at our school.' I want it done as formal and nicely as you can. I want you to send it to the parents by certified mail with a return receipt requested. Does everyone understand me?"

All their hands went up again.

"No other school will accept them either. I hope everyone understands that."

All of their hands went up again.

"Now comes the fun part. They have only one place they can go. That happens to be one of our new schools. You heard me right…new schools. I hope you don't run to your union and tell them we're running a school with scab labor."

Everyone laughed.

"I didn't think you would. What we plan to do is use some volunteer help, plus military personnel."

A couple of hands went up.

"You want to know where the schools are, right?"

They took their hands down.

"We've been working with volunteers for the last few months converting the two closed military bases into running private schools. One's on the east side of town and one's on the west. The armed forces have given us uniforms, shoes, food, and sleeping materials for the barracks. The school is all high tech and so is the security. These people will come and go when we say they can. They'll be in bed by ten and up by six. And the last thing they'll want to do is get lippy with someone. Now your responsibility is this; the government is supplying us with surplus items, plus other things they have we need. The one thing they can't give us is money. Don't look at me like that…I'm not going to pass the hat."

Everyone laughed.

"What I do need from you is the following: Someone to test each student. I feel the majority of them will test out between the third and fifth grade level. That's where they'll start classes. I need you to supply books, paper, pencils, pens, and everything else they need to learn. I hope you're getting the picture. If we give them an education 90 to 95 percent of them will get turned around. That people is a job well done. Don't anyone tell me they can't afford to do this. The money you'll save on extra security alone will more than cover this. If you can afford to send something extra, do so. Everything will be utilized. You folks need to talk to one another and coordinate who will send what. I also need volunteer testers for the students. Again you need to work together on this. You need to make up tests or use what you have. I don't care how you do it I just want you to get it done. You'll start your classes back on a Monday. We'll give you a whole week to take flack from parents. I don't think you'll get a lot of problems. You'll supply the parents with an application to our school as the only school that will accept their child. But they have your permission to fill out an application for any school in the city. When the application comes into your office you will pick it up immediately and call the parents and tell them that their student cannot enroll in your school. That will mean for a week you will have to check applications three times per day. Because not only will you have the undesirable students trying to get into your school you may also have some desirable students applying. You must stay on top of it. I want all my students starting their new life on the Monday a week from your school reopening. Does everyone understand me?"

All their hands went up.

"Let me give you an idea why your selection has to be done accurately. The boys and girls you send to us will get from us what they've been dishing out for a long time. They will do a bit of crying and learning. Someday soon they will do a bit more learning than crying."

"Commissioner!" He had his hand in the air as he spoke.

"Yes Mr. Tucker?"

Without the mike he stood up and spoke out in a loud voice, "Am I understanding you correctly? You're going to sort of lock these kids up?" After speaking he sat down.

"Yes Mr. Tucker. That's what we have in mind doing. They're not in jail. They're in a very strict private school. In order for them to get out on leave they'll have to earn it through grades and merit. Keep in mind people this is their last hope. If we expel them the next place they go is to jail or the cemetery. Or they can leave town but that's not very likely. I'd like every one of you to try to be home the Sunday evening before school reopens. After six P.M. a squad car will deliver a packet with all the information and forms in it. You'll need to show them a picture I.D. to receive it. Now, before opening the floor to questions I'd like to say something to all of you. I'm not just proud of you, I'm extremely proud of you. You were asked to be here. You were given very little information yet every one of you showed up. That shows me you care about your school, your students, and your community. For that I thank you very much. Now for the sake of time if the answer to a question is in the packet you'll receive I'll tell you that and we'll move on. First question."

Tom and Jim were once again floating around with the portable mikes. About a dozen hands were in the air.

"Let me start in the front with my new friend Mr. Tucker."

He took the mike from Jim, "Just a comment Commissioner. I want to thank you for giving us an opportunity to make a difference in our student's lives."

"You're welcome Mr. Tucker. You folks are the ones who can make a difference and we're glad to have you aboard. Next, the lady about three seats behind Mr. Tucker."

She stood and took the mike, "Mrs. Yancy, Commissioner. I'd like to know what you're going to do with the dopers."

"I'll answer that question in two ways. If they're selling they'll be out of business. If they're users we've already set up a pretty impressive rehab unit. Next is the gentleman next to her."

"Mr. Alders, Commissioner. How do we get in touch with you?"

"My private number will be in your packet. Next, same row, the gentleman on the other end."

"Mr. Simons, Commissioner. How long before they can have visitors?"

"Mr. Simons, I'll expand the answer for you. In thirty days they can have Sunday afternoon visitors. In 60 days they can earn phone privileges. In 90 days they can apply for leave; a half to a whole day, nothing overnight. Next, is the person behind Mr.Simons."

"Mr. Waters, Commissioner. What if a student goes 'over the wall' or whatever you call it?"

"In the military we call it AWOL, which means 'absent without leave'. If they're dumb enough to do that they can just keep on going. We don't want them back. The first day in orientation we'll tell them that this is their last chance at education. If at any time they wish to leave all they need to do is tell their supervisor and then go pack. The officer of the day will speak to them and then he will get them a ride home. End of story. Folks this isn't a prison. It's a means of putting all of the rotten apples in two barrels. Next question and it looks like the last one."

"I'm Mrs. Downer, Commissioner. How are the kids going to get to school on the first day?"

"We'll have an area where they will meet a bus. All the kids on the east side will be bused to the west side and vice versa. They get a new school and a new area to live in. This will be explained in detail in your packet. I haven't seen anyone taking notes, but if I missed you please deposit them in the wastebasket when you leave. I suggest you folks mill around after we leave and meet one another, maybe put together some kind of structure so when this happens you have people in charge. The last person to leave please close the double doors, they will lock automatically. The elevators will only take you down. So again I want to thank you and you may stay in this room as long as you wish."

Everyone of my team stood up. As we started to leave we received a standing ovation.

I pulled Yoto close to me and said in his ear, "Bring our new friends out into the hall."

Yoto and the two brothers, Joe and Bobby Fisher, caught up to us at the elevators. I faced them as they approached. "What did you boys think of the meeting?"

Joe said, "It was great Commissioner. You're going to make our job a whole lot simpler. I want to thank you again for allowing us to stay."

"You're welcome. Bobby, what did you think?"

"After reading, listening to, and studying you every chance I had, the meeting was a little better than I had imagined."

Lynda said, "You sure are a fan."

"Ma'am, could you tell me anyone better to emulate?"

"No Bobby, I couldn't. The Commissioner is a great person who is here to clean up our town with everyone's help."

I said, "Thank you to everyone. Now can we get to work?"

Lynda replied, "Yes Sir!"

"You boys were sent here by the Gods for a reason. And by the time I finished the meeting I figured out what it was. Two things; if you can't handle the jobs tell me. The first thing is the week you go back to school after the break I want you to overlap and over spend on your security. One of you if not both of you will have big trouble."

"You're talking 24 hours a day Sir?"

"Yes I am Bobby."

Joe said, "We can handle that."

"Keep in mind you're not just looking for our young animals. Trouble may be coming from another direction. So stay alert and stay alive. There's been a lot of school shootings and bombings around the country. I don't want us to make the 5 o'clock news. Understood?"

They both said, "Yes Sir!"

"The next job is a little tougher. I need the two of you to head up a security system. Like the principals are in there setting up as we speak. Can you do that?"

Bobby said, "Between Joe and me, we know just about all the people working in the city. We're also competitive, Commissioner, so we bowl and do other family things together."

"For now you only need to set up communications with the security heads of the different schools."

"What do we tell them?"

"Nothing, you and your brother are trying to set up something that may be helpful in the future."

Joe said, "We got it and we'll handle it Sir."

"Good. Anything you need from us, call the Chief. He'll get back to you ASAP."

Pete said, "Yes I will Commissioner. Also during that first week back I'll assign each of you four cops, two in uniform and two in plain clothes. You'll be in charge of them. If I was in charge of them I'd allow the two plain clothes men to float around the school. New eyes see out of place things better than old eyes."

"I agree Chief and we'll do it. Won't we Bobby?"

"Yeah Joe, sounds like a plan to me."

I said, "That's not all boys. I'm also going to double the street patrol around your areas for that week. If your people are wandering around outside the buildings they better have picture I.D.s with them. Do you understand?"

They both said, "Yes Commissioner."

I said, "Unless you have a question, we have work to do."

Joe said, "I can't wait until things get half way normal. I know we can't make things perfect. But we should be able to get to some kind of normal standard."

"We will Joe. Do you have a last thought Bobby?"

"Yes Commissioner. How many hours a day do you work?"

"Don't quote me."

"I won't."

"Usually 16 to 18 hours a day. When we started we all figured out that our town would not clean itself up at 8 hours a day. So we do what is necessary. And 'no' we're not paid extra for it."

"Thank you Commissioner. That's what I wanted to know. I think if we had to name what you're doing it would be called 'dedication'. Am I right?"

"That and 'commitment'. We all have both. Now you're a part of our team, so do what you feel is enough to cure your problems."

Joe said, "We will Commissioner."

At that time our elevator was ready to go. We stepped in and wished the boys 'good luck' as the doors closed. As we rode down to the second floor I thought, 'those boys will work out just fine'. When the doors opened I instructed Yoto to stay on the elevator and go to the parking garage and bring the limo around.

"Anyone wishing to go with him may do so. I need to get everything we have on Tammy to show Doc."

Yoto kept pressure on the button on the inside panel that kept the doors open.

"Larry, I need to run down to my office for a minute."

"All right Mayor."

Pete said, "I'll join him Larry."

"Then we'll see the two of you at the limo, anyone else?"

Tom answered, "After last night, Jim and I are with you."

We left the elevator and headed down the hallway to my office. Lynda and I got the file and papers out of the safe. We stacked them neatly on my desk. I went into my lounge area. Inside the walk-in closet on a shelf I pulled down a box that said 'briefcase'. I opened the end of the box and pulled out a beautiful natural leather briefcase. It was soft sided, a satchel type. I took it into my office and we filled it with papers and the file. Tom zipped it closed and picked it up.

"Are we ready to go?"

"I think so Tom. Let's go have lunch."

It was close to 1:30 P.M. when we arrived at the hospital. Yoto parked the limo by the emergency doors. As we got close to the doors they automatically opened. We walked back to the admittance area. Doc was standing there with a clip board in hand. He was giving out assignments to people. We stood back from the crowd and waited a few minutes until he was finished. He saw us and gave the clipboard to the woman standing beside him. He said something to her and then headed toward us. As he got close enough I stuck out my right hand and he did the same. As we shook hands I asked,

"How are you doing?"

He replied as he shook everyone else's hands, "I'm doing great, or can't you tell?"

"Looking around I think you're doing better than great."

"Have you got a little time? I have so much I want to show you."

"We have plenty of time for a full tour of your operation."

"Then follow me please. You notice we have the emergency doors working? The admitting area we're leaving is about 90 percent finished."

He took us up and down and all around. We kept complimenting him on how great a job he had done. This was easy to do because it was a great job. We ended up in the lunch area on the first floor.

"This area will give us some room Larry. But if you wish we could go to my office, which is one of the smaller offices in the building."

"This area will do just fine. We have Tom, Jim, and Yoto to see that we won't be disturbed. The first thing I want to do is show you the medical reports of a young woman. I need you to see if you can spot something they missed. While you're doing that, is that ice chest over there full of cold drinks?"

"Yes it is. The refrigerator over there is full of bottled water."

"Thanks, you read, and we'll fetch."

We all walked over to the refrigerator and got a cold bottle of water. We stood there quietly talking for about five minutes.

Seeing the room was empty Doc said, "Larry, would you all come over here?"

"Did you find something?"

"Do you have any recent pictures of the lady?"

"I have ones from when she got married almost two years ago up to last week."

"I'd like to see one of each. I'd prefer a good shot of her face."

I produced what he wanted in 8 by 10 forms.

He laid them side by side on the table in front of him. "Larry, correct me if I'm wrong."

Tom said, "Look out, Doc's bucking for Larry's job."

We all laughed.

"I'm not! I'd just like to show you guys that I know what I'm talking about when it comes to medicine."

"Doc, do whatever you wish. I'm on your side."

"Thank you Larry, I will."
"You're welcome. Go ahead."
"First off, if this is what I think it is, it's one of the worst cases I've ever seen. The girl lives somewhere in the inner city and is mentally deficient."
We all busted out laughing.
Tom said, "Your job is definitely safe Larry."
Jim said, "I agree Tom. You have nothing to worry about Larry."
Doc said, "I guess I blew it."
I said, "Did you notice the caliber of specialists this lady has seen?"
"I know some of them personally and others by reputation. They're all from very wealthy families. I didn't have their fortune or misfortune, depending on how you look at it. But once in a while they will do a diagnosis for nothing."
"This isn't the case. Her mother is one of the wealthiest women in our town. She's also a member of our personal team."
"Is this the same person I talked to Robert about?"
"Yes."
"Then maybe I'm wrong. She has to ingest what I'm thinking of. She probably lives in a new expensive house."
"That's right."
"Here I thought it was easy."
"Would you mind enlightening us with your thoughts?"
"As I said a minute ago no one gave me anything. I had to work my way through medical school. I never forgot my roots. I spent all my free time at a small downtown clinic helping out any way I could. That's where I saw what I thought she had. I had seen it in so many youngsters."
"What did you see?"
"Asbestos poisoning. In the older buildings where the roofs would leak through and penetrate the old asbestos ceilings, the water would distribute the asbestos around the house. It would then, at times be ingested by the babies by accident. Or after it dried out it would be moved around by the people in the place becoming airborne. Then the little ones would breathe it in. It would play havoc on their lungs. If they'd breathe in enough it could cause death."
"Doc, I'm glad you were born poor. I don't care how good a

Doctor is, if he's never seen a problem he sure as heck wouldn't be able to recognize it. Three cheers for Doc!"

"Hip Hip"

"Hooray!"

"Hip Hip"

"Hooray!"

"Hip Hip"

"Hooray!"

"Do you think that's what's wrong with her Larry?"

"Oh, do I ever Doc!"

"But how is she being exposed?"

"We haven't figured that out yet. Look at the rest of the photos and see if you can figure out what we couldn't."

We spread out all the pictures for him. He walked around the table looking and talking. "How long after they got married did she become bedridden?"

"About six months."

"Why wasn't he exposed?"

I picked up the Christmas picture. "Look at this picture and see if you can tell us."

"Look at his morning hair. I'd be willing to bet you a month's pay that he wore an air filtration mask all night."

"How'd you pick up on it so quickly Doc?"

"When I was in med school there were times when we had to wear them. My hair was always a big mess and the straps didn't make things any better."

"Well Doc, before we came we knew What, Who, Why, Where, and now we need to know when and how he's doing it."

"Would you agree he's doing whatever it is he's doing at night?"

"I agree Doc. That's the only time she's left alone with him. Now if I understand you correctly, for her to ingest the asbestos, it would have to be airborne."

"That's right Larry."

I thumbed through the pictures and found a good shot of her room to show Doc. "Check this one out and see if it brings anything to mind."

"The humidifier would do the trick."

"Mayor, tell Doc about it!"

"When they analyzed everything in Tammy's room they tore that machine apart. Except for the normal contaminates in tap water and some Vapo Rub there was nothing else there."

"There's nothing else in any of these pictures that would deliver the airborne asbestos."

"Doc, you've been a big help. Would you like to go for a short ride with us?"

"Where are we going?"

"To look at all the properties we now own and the four we don't own."

"Sounds like fun. I need to tell everyone where I'm going. I'll meet you at the car."

We drove around a six block area.

"Do you people own all this Larry?"

"Mayor, I pass to you."

"Well Doc, we own everything except two empty lots and the grey building we just passed and the tin building in the next block."

"Are you sure we own the warehouse we just passed?"

"Yes Larry. We own everything to the end of the block."

"Yoto, did you notice anything in the warehouse we just passed?'

"I saw movement by one of the windows. What did you see Sir?"

"What looked like a sentry on the roof. Pull around the next corner, the four story corner building will give us plenty of cover."

I reached down and moved Lynda's feet over to her left. I then opened the compartment that went under our seat. When I pressed the button three times the door flipped open and landed on the floor.

"Yoto, how are you armed?"

"Two guns and my boot knife."

"Do you want anything else?"

"Am I going in alone?"

"No I'll be with you."

"Then I'm fine."

The boys started to mumble. "Before you guys say anything, can any of you Walk Silent and Walk Deadly?"

Pete said, "You know we can't Larry. But in less than 10 minutes I can have a dozen cars here plus our SWAT Team."

"Pete, I appreciate that but this is a recon mission. It's possible that a large group of homeless people have taken over the building. I don't want to scare them or hurt them. We'll move them out of the building later."

"What if it's something else?"

"Pete, if you haven't heard from us in 20 minutes come in and get us."

"You want us to wait 20 minutes?"

"Yes, from the time we leave, Pete."

"All right, how will you signal us?'

"Lynda, could I have our cell phone?"

She reached in her purse and got it out and handed it to me.

"Thank you. I'll keep it off until I'm going to use it."

Yoto opened his door and slipped out of the driver's seat. He walked around the front of the car. I kissed Lynda and told everyone to "Hang tough. We'll be back soon." I got out of the limo and joined Yoto. I looked at Pete and pointed to my watch. He understood and looked at his. Yoto and I walked in the direction the limo was pointing. When we got to the alley we took a right and jogged up the alley. We stopped two buildings shy of our target building. Our target building was only two stories high. We figured we'd take out the guard on the roof and then take a look around. I pointed up to the roof. Yoto scaled the blind side of the building. I watched as Yoto put the roof guard in a sleeper hold and secured him. Then he checked out things from the top side, and headed down off the top of the building to me. I started to move forward as Yoto returned. As I went around the corner Yoto grabbed my coat and pulled me back behind the building. He pointed to his eyes and then around the corner of the building. I put my head far enough around the corner of the building to see what Yoto had seen from the roof. A guard at the back door, Yoto and I took a few steps backward.

"You know Yoto, I'm glad that building isn't built out to the alley."

"I agree Larry. I also agree with your next statement."

"We've been together for a long time Yoto. Just like the old days you know what I'm thinking before I say it."

"That's right Larry. These boys aren't homeless people."

"Correct. And with this many guards there's a big operation of something going on inside our building. You know what hurts me

the most?"
"They're not paying rent?"
"That's right."
We chuckled.
"Let me call the limo. Then we're going in and evict our unwanted tenants."
I dialed and Lynda answered the phone in the back seat.
"Yes?"
"We don't know what's inside yet but whatever it is its big and bad. Get Pete on the horn!"
"Hold on he's in the front seat."
Pete picked up the front seat phone, "What is it Larry?"
"Get our people rolling, you have ten minutes. Put the word out that Yoto and I will be inside."
"Do you want us to wait for your signal?"
"No! I want you to drive through the gates and then the front door with whatever help you have in exactly ten minutes. Don't forget to cover the back. Code Two! Got it?"
"It shall be done."
I disconnected my phone, turned it off and put it in my pocket.
"We have ten minutes to secure the perimeter."
"Give me ninety seconds and I'll be behind the guard."
"Go! I'll distract him for you."
While I was waiting for Yoto to get into position I gathered up a bunch of loose papers from the alley and rolled them so they looked like building plans from a distance. I looked at my watch. Five seconds to go. I put the pretend plans under my arm and walked around the corner of the building I was hiding behind. I kept looking up at it with great interest. The man guarding the rear door left his post and started to stroll my way. He got about two steps when Yoto hit him on the back of the head with his pistol butt. I dropped the papers and went to where Yoto was standing close to the building. I walked by him pointing up to a steel bar protruding from the back of the building. It was about ten feet in the air. I interlocked my fingers and squatted a little. Yoto knew what to do. He took a short run and stepped into my hand and I propelled him up to the steel bar. From there it was a snap to get to the roof. He pulled himself up onto the bar and started to climb to the roof. While he was doing that I cuffed

and gagged the fallen guard.

As I moved to enter the door I could no longer see Yoto. I opened the door and moved quickly and quietly inside. There were a lot of boxes and junk by the door which told me that somebody doesn't want me to see what's happening in here. As I moved further into the building I could see a lot of people, around twenty. I spent enough time in the military to know what they were unloading from the four half tracks in front of me. As I took a better look around I noticed four soldiers with their hands out. There was a civilian paying one of the soldiers, who in turn paid his men. The soldier boys put their loot in their pockets and headed for their truck. By my watch Pete still had over four minutes. There was no way I was going to let these soldier boys drive out of here. So I did the only thing I could. I walked out into the open.

"Gentlemen! Gentlemen! Could someone tell me where I wait for the streetcar?"

Everything went quiet.

The man who had paid the soldiers walked my way, "Who the hell are you?"

"Do you really need that information to point out the streetcar to me?"

He pulled out a gun and pointed it at me.

"You don't need a gun! I'm unarmed!" I grabbed my lapels and pulled my jacket open.

He put his gun down on a tall box next to himself. "Let me ask you one more time, who are you and what do you want?"

"I can answer that for you. I'm the Commissioner of Police for the town of Pertsville, and what I want is for everyone to put their hands in the air. You're all under arrest!"

Everyone laughed.

"Just like that, you want us to surrender to an unarmed man?"

"If you do, you'll walk out of here alive. Otherwise you'll be carried out of here in a body bag."

I was now standing about 10 feet from him.

"We're not surrendering are we boys?"

They all started laughing again.

At that moment I heard Pete heading to the front doors. My host turned toward the doors as our SWAT Truck came barreling through them He turned back and reached for his gun. Before his hand could make contact with the steel my knife hit its mark deep in his chest. I moved to his position and picked up his gun. Shots were being fired everywhere. I dropped two guys close to me. A third guy had the drop on me, but Yoto got him before he could shoot.

Soon I was standing with Yoto at my side. Our boys had half the bad guys in cuffs. The other half were either dead or wounded. From what I could see one of the soldiers was dead and one wounded.

Pete joined us. "Chief, you have one on the roof. Don't forget him. Also, he's wearing Officer Yoto's cuffs and the one in the back is wearing mine."

Pete assigned a few boys to get our cuffs. While he was doing that I pulled my knife out of my host's chest. I wiped it off on a rag that was on a stack of boxes. "Chief, Get everyone out of the SWAT Truck. I want to use it for interrogation." I motioned to Yoto. He came close to me."Get the three soldiers. Just like the spy we turned in Nam."

He nodded his head in a positive motion.

As he walked the men over to the truck he explained that what they had done is considered treason. "One of you will get life, maybe with parole. Two of you will hang by the neck until dead. Commissioner Towers is also Colonel Towers. He has the power to do as I just explained. It's real simple, the one who tells the truth lives. Or all three of you die. It makes no difference to him."

Everyone had gotten out of the limo. So on my way to the SWAT Truck I took a detour and asked Lynda, Tom, and Jim to join me. As we walked to the SWAT Truck I gave Tom and Jim their instructions, "After my interrogation I'll open the rear door and hand you the prisoner. You'll not say a word. You'll take him to a squad car and stuff him inside and post a guard outside. I want them in separate cars. Understood?"

"Yes Sir!"

I opened the back door and Lynda and I got inside the truck. Yoto had the soldiers waiting outside.

I quietly said, "Lynda, not a word. If I ask something or say something you're only reply is a nodding of your head. Understood?"

She nodded her head.

"Cute, real cute."

We both chuckled.

I handed her a clipboard the boys had in the truck.

"Take good notes and make sure you get names and ranks."

"I'll do my best Larry."

"That'll be good enough.

I hit the sidewall of the truck closest to Yoto. He sent in the Sergeant. I knew he wouldn't say a word so I spent almost ten minutes with him talking about nothing. When I finished with him I opened the rear door and turned him over to my boys.

As they led him away I spoke loud enough for the other two prisoners to hear. "Thank you for your cooperation Sergeant."

I hit the wall again and Yoto sent in the next soldier. He was as helpful as the first one. After I felt we had been together long enough I turned him over to my boys. Now came the young man I had been waiting for. I had a feeling he was 'Mr. Big' or very close to 'Mr. Big'. What tipped me off to this was that earlier when I watched the payoff he took the money and paid everyone else.

He walked over to where I was seated and sat on the side seat across from me.

"Corporal Rogers, I know you're wounded so I won't keep you. We have enough information from your two friends to pretty well crack this case wide open. So you can leave by the backdoor."

"Wait a minute Colonel! You are a Colonel?"

"Yes I am."

"Well Colonel I'm not leaving until you hear me out."

"But I just explained that we have enough information."

"You don't know everything."

"This is a waste of time." I started to slowly get up.

"Sit down Colonel! I'm a martial arts expert. Even with being wounded and having my hands handcuffed I can still kill you before you can stand up."

"If you're that determined my secretary will start a clean sheet of paper."

"That's better. It all started about….."

He was the boss. He told me things I wouldn't even have asked him. After we finished our young man was pretty wiped out from his blood loss. My boys helped him to a squad car. They secured him and reported back to me. Pete joined us.

"Chief, call the base and talk to the commanding officer if you can. It's Saturday so he may be on the golf course. If you can't get him, talk to the officer of the day. Tell him we'll guard their trucks and weapons until they send a platoon to relieve our men."

"I'll take care of it right away Commissioner."

"We'll see you in the limo when you're finished."

Pete went to make his call. He also wanted to secure the area before leaving.

I walked over to the limo and opened the back door. As I sat down I must have let out a sigh of relief. Doc, Lynda, and the Mayor had followed me into the limo.

"It sounds like you're glad it's over."

"I am Doc. The part that makes me feel the best is the fact that none of our people got hurt. We won't always be this lucky."

Pete got in with Yoto. Yoto was behind the wheel and Pete was sitting behind him and they were both laughing.

The Mayor asked, "Can anyone get in on this?"

Pete replied, "It's too funny."

Tom said, "Now you've got my curiosity up. Tell us!"

"Yoto, tell them."

"Larry did it again. The soldier boys were getting ready to leave and Pete hadn't arrived yet so Larry walked up on the 20 bad guys and said, 'Put your hands in the air! You're all under arrest!'."

Everyone started to laugh.

"I told them I didn't want to kill them."

Yoto said, "The only way they would have died is if they laughed themselves to death."

Everyone kept laughing.

Pete said, "I bet you really had them scared!"

Yoto said, "He had the leader of the gang so scared that when Larry showed them he was unarmed the guy put his gun down on a box."

The laughter continued.

"Thanks Yoto. Did you miss anything?"

"Just that it took an awful lot of guts, and I wish in the future you'd refrain from such activities. You and I are good but 20 to 2 out in the open is suicide."

"I agree old friend and I'll try not to let it happen again."
Lynda said, "You better not."
The Mayor added, "That goes for me too."
And Doc piped in, "I'm a good surgeon, but I couldn't even plug up that many holes."
"All right guys, I got the idea. Now back to business. Pete, do you have our boys checking for drugs?"
"Yes Larry. They have a dog on the way."
"Oh! I forgot to ask. I must be a terrible host. Doc, are you having a good time?"
"Surprisingly Larry, I'm having a blast. But I do have a question."
"Two's your limit. Go ahead."
"Did you get the information you wanted from the soldiers?"
"Oh yes! Did I ever. These boys are out of business for good. Plus I have a good lead for the F.B.I. What's your second question?"
"Why didn't you allow me to look at the soldier's wound?"
"That's real simple. This is his fourth shipment of stolen weapons. His guns have supplied every gang in our town and some across the border. Plus the military prefer to take care of their own. Lastly, Yoto looked at the wound. What did it look like Yoto?"
"A simple flesh wound. I told him it was a lot worse than it really was. That helped lower his resistance during our interrogation. He wanted to be patched up, as well as not getting hung for his crime."
Doc asked, "Do they still hang you for treason?"
"That's your third question Doc, but I'll answer it anyway. No."
As we were driving back I said, "Doc, about half these buildings are going to be leveled. They'll make great parking lots. Do you have any ideas what we can do with the rest of them?"
"Here's something I've been working on with our two major universities. It's an elaborate intern program. I could use one of your buildings for a sort of men's dorm."
"Great thinking Doc, what exactly does that do for us?"
"Counting myself and my recruits, we'll have six full time Doctors. Two to start with, and as we finish the rest of the floors, we'll take on more staff. Naturally our case load will be the main thing that dictates our staffing. Our hospital will be too large for our people to fill. I haven't forgotten that you want this to be a police force only hospital. I can run it, taking overflow from other hospitals

and just about keep us in the black. Our people always have first priority. What do you think?"

"Let me try your memory Doc. I gave you an order when you took on this job. Do you remember what it was?"

"Yes, 'this is your baby, run with it'."

"Nothing has changed. You know our directive. As long as it's our hospital that's all that counts. Staffing is a very hard problem. Without patients it's even harder. So far I like what I'm hearing."

"Good. Then I have one more for you."

"Shoot!"

"Can I have a second building?"

"If you can use it, sure, what's your idea?"

"I know someone who wants to expand their nursing school. He gets a low rent building and we get all the interns we need."

"Knowing how hard it is to get nurses, I like the idea. Can your people wait a few months? We need to get the last four properties before we do anything."

"The colleges will work into our schedule when we're ready for them. The owner of the nursing school is a friend of mine. He told me if I assured him the space he could wait a year if necessary."

"Assure him, and we'll get together with him as soon as possible."

"Thank you Larry. I'll take care of it."

"Pete, you and the Mayor need to take care of the last four properties, they look like they'd make good parking lots."

The Mayor spoke, "That's all we can do with three of them. The other one has good steel structure but we'll need to replace a lot of concrete. If the owner wants to do it he can keep it otherwise we'll condemn it. I'll try to let you know what we can do by the end of next week."

"Don't call me, call Doc. He's the one who needs the information. Doc, you'll have your architect and builder look at the buildings."

"When I get the addresses from the Mayor we'll look at them and get back to you with our ideas."

I said, "Sounds good Doc."

As we finished talking Yoto pulled the limo up to the hospital. We said our 'goodbyes' and headed back to my office.

Chapter 20

I knew Doc was right. All we had to do now was prove it. How could Charles possibly do this night after night to Tammy without being caught? I didn't know, but I knew we'd find out.

As we left the hospital I had Lynda on the phone calling everyone to a five o'clock meeting.

It was 4:30 P.M. when we walked into my office. The boys had carried up the papers I had shown Doc.

Jim asked, "Do you want the papers on the conference table Larry?"

"Yes. Please. Spread them out and start examining them. I have to go to the bathroom."

When I came out of the bathroom I was fresh and ready to go to work. I walked up to the table and noticed Robert had joined us.

"How'd you get here so fast Robert?"

"I was doing a little work next door. So I had my home phone on call forwarding. I didn't want to miss anything Larry."

"The boys probably told you that all we're doing is going over the photos looking for something we missed."

"I've gone over my set so many times that I've almost worn them out."

"This case has really gotten to you hasn't it Robert?"

"You never lie to the group Larry, so I won't either. I think I've fallen in love with her. I know it sounds stupid because I haven't even met her. There's this feeling I get every time I see her picture. Do you think I could be in love with her Larry?"

"I can't see any reason to doubt you or your feelings. If that's the way you feel go with it. She looks like a wonderful lady and from what her mother says she's also a great person."

"Larry, I'm not foolish enough to think there could ever be anything between us. I'm just a cop and she's a millionaire."

"Don't sell yourself short. Robert. You're a great person and a great friend."

"Thank you Larry. I'll just love her from afar."

I moved around the photos on the table until I came up with the best single shot of Tammy. I picked it up and handed it to Robert. "Before everyone gets here take this to your office and put it with your photos."

"Thank you Larry."

He got up and left. When my office door closed I spoke, "I want to thank everyone for not making any wise cracks."

Lynda said, "When a man is pouring out his feelings to his friends only an idiot would say something."

By the time she finished speaking Robert came back in the door and the rest of the boys followed him.

I looked at my watch. It was five to five. "I see everyone is here. Let's take our seats and get started. Unless it's an emergency I only want to hear about Tammy."

Sam said, "Then Wade and I had better get started."

"Must be a heavy report if it takes two of you."

"I'll guarantee one thing Larry. You're going to love it."

"By all means, get started."

"The glass that Mrs. Baker gave us was fantastic! We got three clear fingers and a thumb print of the right hand. I sent them out last night. I had to call in two favors, but I had the results by noon. I'll do this slowly. I know none of us are dummies, but I had to go through this information twice with Wade before it was clear to us."

"It goes like this: Thomas Randell of New York was dishonorably discharged from the Army for almost killing an officer with his bare hands. He spent one year in the 'loony bin' and then was released cured. At that point Thomas Randell fell off the face of the earth. Forgive us if we have his age off a little. Wade and I tried to figure it as best we could."

"Around the age of twenty five, Les Baxter came up with those fingerprints. He was 28 when he was printed in Ohio after his wife of three years died of mysterious natural causes listed as pneumonia. The Captain I got a hold of told me he was a lieutenant at the time he was in charge of the case. He said, 'I knew it was murder but there was no way to prove it. Mr. Baxter collected a $100,000.00 life insurance policy plus the older widow he married had left him everything, about another $250,000.00. We checked everything we could about him; other women, none; drugs, none; high life; none. All he did do was a little gambling. I hope you can get him, I never closed the case'."

"Once again he stepped off the face of the earth. The next time the prints showed up were in Aurora, Illinois. He was about 32 when he was printed under the name of Jay Watson. His wife had died accidently by drowning. She had been sick for almost a year and a half. Once again the police suspected foul play but they couldn't find any. He had his wife insured for $250,000.00 Accidental death gave him double indemnity. He collected half a million plus her estate of about the same amount."

"Don't tell me! Jay Watson fell off the face of the earth!"

"Yes Larry, he did. Until this morning when the results came back on the fingerprints we sent out. Our Mr. Charles T. Winder is really Mr. Thomas Randell."

"You were right about one thing Sam that was a mouthful."

As Sam had explained everything to us, Wade was passing around police photos of the way Charles looked as he portrayed different identities.

"The man was good at what he was doing."

"Yes Larry he was. I also have something else that we figured out that you will not like."

"The sooner you tell me the faster we can solve the problem."

"It's the date of his attempted murder in the service and the deaths of his two wives. They're all on the same date. That date is three days from now. If we figured it right Tammy is supposed to die on Tuesday evening before midnight."

"After looking at what Wade passed around I'd have to agree with you."

Lynda spoke, "It's a good thing Mrs. Baker came to us when she did."

The Mayor said, "If we don't figure out how he's doing it, it won't make any difference."

"Don't worry Mayor, we'll figure it out. Anyone have anything else?"

Robert said, "Could you use some more bad news?"

"Let's hear it."

"Right after they got married they each took out a million dollar life insurance policy. His elapsed after the second payment but her policy is still in force."

Jim said, "We know Robert, double indemnity on accidental death."

Robert said, "Yes. He's looking forward to a two million dollar payday plus, Larry."

"I know boys. Mayor, go to my desk and call Mrs. Baker. Make sure he's going out of town Monday. If possible have her take him to the airport and make sure the plane takes off with him on it."

"I got it. I'll be right back."

"Robert, it's a little warm in here, will you check the thermostat?"

As he got up and headed to the thermostat I continued on. "Gentlemen, it's there in the pictures. Let's go over and over them until we come up with……"

As Robert sat down I could feel the cool air on the back of my neck.

"That feels good."

"I put the fan on to re-circulate the air in here."

"Robert, I could kiss you!"

Lynda said, "You better not, you're spoken for."

As everyone was chuckling Pete said, "You figured out how he's doing it, didn't you Larry."

Everyone got quiet.

"Yes I did with the help of the Gods and Robert." I took my hanky out of my pocket. I took my half full glass of water and said, "Pretend this is a solution of water and asbestos." I pretended to put my hanky in the glass. I pretended to ring out my hanky. I got out of my chair and walked over to the air conditioning duct work near the ceiling. I hung the hanky in front of it. "As it dries through the night the asbestos will be pushed out and become airborne. He is probably using a cheese cloth material or something even more porous." I put my hanky in my pocket and returned to my seat.

"What's everybody looking at?"

Tom said, "I for one agree with you. But the parts that are throwing me are the Gods and Robert."

"By the look on everyone's faces I'd say you all have the same question, even you Robert."

"I'm sorry Larry, I'd like to understand but I don't."

"Some of you weren't here earlier when Robert told us he's in love with Tammy. You see Robert, not only did you tell us, you also told the Gods. Like it says in the bible, God is everywhere. It only stands to reason one of anything can't be everywhere so the Gods heard your true feelings and decided to help you protect your loved one. Question… Since we've been in this office how many times have we changed the thermostat?"

They all looked at one another.

"Let me make it easier. I've never touched it. Has anyone else?"

I still got no response.

"I take it that no one has touched it. Next question, Robert, why did you put the recirculation fan on when I asked you to put the air on?"

"I don't know Larry. It just felt right to do it."

"You also felt right coming back to the table and telling me you disobeyed my order."

"I apologize for that, but I did."

"Does anyone have any questions?"

They all still had dumb looks on their faces.

"Guys, they've been helping us all along, so stop looking so surprised. We need to map out what we're going to do. I'm sorry Mayor I didn't give you a chance to report."

"I talked to Mrs. Baker. She already had arranged to pick him up and have breakfast with him at the airport. He seemed to like the idea."

Jim said, "His next target."

"I think you're right Jim, but it'll never happen."

Robert asked, "What do we do now Larry?"

"Robert and everyone else, there isn't a lot we can do until we can get into the house. So I want everyone to take this evening off, as well as tomorrow. We'll meet here Monday morning at nine for our regular meeting. Before noon we'll be in Tammy's house. Pete, call Doc and tell him someone will pick him up Monday. Have him bring as much gear as he can to examine Tammy."

"I'll take care of it."

"Mayor, is Mrs. Baker calling us when Charles is gone?"

"She'll call us from the airport. She'll then meet us at the house."

"Gentlemen, we roll when she calls. Mayor, what time is his flight?"

"Ten o'clock."

"Sam and Wade, if you have other pressing things you may do them."

Sam said, "What do you think Wade?"

"It's just like Larry, we do all the work, get him all the information, and now he wants to grab all the glory."

Through the laughter I said, "Cute Wade. Real cute."

"I'm sorry Larry. You left yourself wide open."

"I know Wade. And you guys know you're welcome."

"Good. Then we'll go with you."

Pete said, "Larry, at the F.B.I. Monday is paperwork day."

Sam said, "Pete caught us Larry."

"That's all right. You guys can still come. Now Pete, I need you to contact your Hollywood people. We need a stunt lady that looks a little like Tammy. We need her to be able to fall out a window or down a flight of steps, things like that."

"For Tuesday evening?"

"Yes. We need her here around two."

"Got it."

"Can anyone think of anything I'm missing?"

"Larry?"

"Yes Robert?"

"Who takes care of Tammy when her mother and her husband are gone?"

"They have a nursing service. It will be gone by the time we get to the house. Right Mayor?"

"I'll call and make sure."

"Good."

"Larry?"

"Yes Mayor?"

"What can I tell Mrs. Baker?"

"Not a whole lot Mayor. Just tell her that everything is going fine and we'll tell her more Monday. I want her to stay worried so she doesn't tip our hand."

"I understand and I'll handle it accordingly."

"Anything else?"

Robert asked, "What about the staff?"

"They'll also be gone, right Mayor?"

He nodded his head so I knew he understood.

"Once again, anything else?"

No one said anything so I did, "Seeing there's nothing else let's call it a night. I need a driver and someone who'd like to have dinner with us."

Yoto said, "I'm still the driver of the day."

"All right."

Robert said, "I'd like to come."

"We'd love having you."

We all said our good nights. As everyone was leaving I was heading to the lounge area to wash up.

We left and went to a nice steak house. After dinner we were enjoying our brandy when the band started to play. I took Lynda out on the dance floor and we had a great time. I consider myself a great dancer. The nice part is Lynda is a good follower. When we sat back down Robert started in, "You two looked like Fred Astaire and Ginger Rogers out there. You were great!"

I asked, "Robert, I'm curious. Which one did I look like?"

We all laughed.

"I was serious Larry. You two looked great out there."

"Lynda I think Robert is hinting for a dance with you."

"Is that right Robert?"

"That would be a great honor for me, but I don't know how to dance."

By the look on his face we could tell he was serious.

Lynda responded to him very sweetly, "If you're going to have any chance at all with Tammy you better know how to dance." She took him by the hand and led him to the dance floor.

Yoto asked, "Larry have you noticed the three guys over my left shoulder?"

"Yes. They seem to have more than a casual interest in us."

"I think a better pronoun would be 'you'."

"Well there's only one way to find out what they want. I think you have to go to the bathroom. Before you leave screen me so I can get Lynda's pistol out of her purse."

Yoto did as I asked as he got up and excused himself from the table. I held Lynda's gun in my left hand. I had it cocked and ready to fire. No sooner had Yoto left one of the three men got out of his seat and walked to my table and stopped in front of me.

In broken English I had a little trouble understanding he spoke to me. "Excuse me Sir, I know you. You are Police Commissioner. Am

I right?"

"Yes you are. I'm Commissioner Larry Towers."

I extended my right hand and he reached over and shook it. "I'm glad to meet you Commissioner. I'm Hestro Gonzales. May I sit down for a minute, please?"

"Be my guest."

I was watching him as well as his two friends. I knew Yoto would have the two of them dead before they could do anything. And mine wouldn't be a problem.

He said, "Thank you Sir." as he sat down.

"How can I help you Mr. Gonzales?"

"My friends, they tell me not to bother you. You are a busy man. But I read about you in the newspaper. I feel you are a good man. I tell my friends you will help. They say you are white and I'm Mexican so you won't help."

"Mr. Gonzales, are you an American citizen?"

"Yes. I study hard and I pass test. I'm made citizen of this country a long time ago."

"If we went to war tomorrow and you were needed to fight to protect our country would you do that?"

"Yes Sir. My son is in the Army."

"Then Mr. Gonzales, all I have to say is your skin is a little darker than mine which means nothing to me because we are both Americans. Americans don't have a color. They're not black, white, brown, red, yellow, or any other color. They're Americans. The sooner the people of our country understand that the sooner we'll have a greater country. Now that we have that out of the way, what can I do for you?"

"It's my son. He's 24 years old and been in the Army for six years. He made Sergeant."

"That's very good."

"Yes. His sister and me are so proud. He is home on a 30 day leave. His little sister, she's 17, is running with a neighborhood gang. My son wants to quit the Army so he can be here to help protect his family."

"Your daughter may be wild but it looks like you've raised a good son."

"Yes. He makes me so proud."

"How long has your son been home?"

"Three days."

"Could you bring him downtown to my office at 10:30 in the morning on Wednesday of next week?"

"Then you will help us?"

"If the two of you are there I will try my best."

He stood up and shook my hand, "Thank you so much Commissioner. We'll see you Wednesday."

He headed back toward his table and his two friends got up and met him. They all turned and headed toward the front door exit. While they were leaving I un-cocked Lynda's gun and put it back in her purse. Yoto rejoined me at the table.

"Everything all right?"

"Yes Yoto. The man needs our help and he's going to get it Wednesday morning at 10:30."

"Sounds good to me."

As we listened we noticed the band had taken a break. Soon Lynda and Robert returned to the table.

As they sat down Lynda said, "He's got the slow dancing down pat. If no one has any objections we're going to work on the fast dancing a little more when the band returns."

"Sounds like a great plan to me, how about you Yoto?"

"If I can get some more iced tea I'll be fine."

It was 12:30 A.M. when we finally got home.

"I want to thank you for taking care of Robert tonight. By the end of the night he was doing pretty good."

"I enjoyed helping him. He may be big and mean looking but inside he's as gentle as a lamb."

"Mrs. Baker didn't seem overly thrilled when I told her that I thought Robert had a crush on her daughter."

"No she didn't. But we have to remember that she's under a lot of stress, worry and constant disappointments."

"That's true. I think we'll just let the Gods do their thing. If it's meant to be it'll happen."

"I agree."

We had finished undressing while we were talking. I put some background music on. Lynda said, "There was one thing I missed tonight Larry."

"And what was that?"
"Dancing with you, having you hold me in your strong arms."
"I hear the music. Come here."
"I've never danced naked before."
By the time we finished making love it was two in the morning. We slept in Sunday morning. The rest of the day was very relaxing. The nicest part of it was the fact that no one bothered us all day long.

Before we knew it we were in my office for our Monday morning meeting. Everyone showed up by nine so we got started on time.
"Sam."
"I know I'm first Larry but there isn't much happening right now. So I pass to Wade."
"I pass to the Mayor."
"I pass to Pete."
"I have a few things. We're starting to evaluate our disabled men to see where and how we can use them."
"How do they feel about this opportunity?"
"The anticipation factor has been fantastic. What you've done for this police force is simply amazing. You think of your men first. All of your men. We give our lives for our town and then they forget. Not anymore. With our new Commissioner we're always a part of the force. Those are a few of the things I've been hearing."
"Pete I need you to get it across to the men that these people are not being hired back as charity. They may not do the most glorified job that we have but they will be doing a job that frees another cop up for outside duty. The 40 cops we're putting back on the force puts 40 more cops in the field. With the partial disability they are being paid we're getting them at a bargain price. Lastly if I hear of any officer degrading the work these people are doing that officer will take over that assignment. If these people weren't needed we wouldn't be hiring them back. One of the big things I want them to tackle is all the records in boxes that we have on unsolved cases. I want those cases set up on the computer in some kind of order. If we can I'd like to get the cases to a point where we can easily access them. If we get them in some kind of order I'll be willing to bet we'll find a lot of the crimes were done by the same person. By linking them together like this we may find more clues to close

some of these cases. Do you understand what I'm saying Pete?"

"Yes I do Larry. I'll take care of it."

"Thanks Pete. Continue."

"I got a lot of positive feedback from the school principals. No negative feedback at all. They can't believe they may soon be back to teaching instead of running a war zone."

"I'm glad we can give them this opportunity. What else?"

"We're still harassing the mobs with good results. They're still having problems recruiting new members."

"Good. What else?"

"Our real estate boys are working closely with the Mayor on the last four properties. My people know I'm here for the day. Lastly our Hollywood person will be here tomorrow. That's about it."

"Before you pass, let me ask you the following: Are the military people ready to run the school?"

"Yes Sir, Larry."

"And how's our ranch down by the Mexican border doing?"

"It's still in the planning stage. You wanted to use it for a lot of different things. It takes time to coordinate things together. You never mentioned us being on a time table."

"No time table Pete. I was just curious."

"If that's all, I'll pass to Tom."

Tom looked at me and then he said, "Everything is status quo. I pass to Jim."

"I pass to Lynda."

"Hold on a minute. Does anyone have anything to talk about?"

No one said a word.

"Then I have a few things to say. Our main objective today is Tammy. I've called Coop and Josh. They'll meet us at Tammy's house at 10:45 A.M. They'll park in the street and wait in their car until we get there. Yoto, Coop, and Josh are going to help me check out Charles' room. No one else will enter that room. For no reason! Does everyone understand?"

They all nodded their heads in the affirmative.

"Next, at...." Before I could say another word my intercom went off. I knew it had to be something special or Mrs. Thompkin wouldn't interrupt my meeting. Lynda started to get up. "Stay seated Lynda. I'll get it. It's for me."

As I was walking toward my desk she asked, "If it's for you who is it?"

"The commanding officer of the military base we sent the thieves back to on Saturday."

"Oh."

I pushed the intercom button, "Yes?"

"Sorry to bother you Sir but I have a Colonel Cox on the line."

"Put him through Mrs. Thompkin."

"Yes Commissioner."

My phone rang and I picked it up.

"Good morning Colonel. This is Commissioner Larry Towers speaking."

"Hello Commissioner Towers or should I say Colonel Towers?"

"Commissioner is just fine. But at least it tells me you checked me out."

"I hope I didn't offend you."

"No Colonel. I like people who are thorough. You got a good report I hope?"

"In checking you out the computer said 'Top Secret' for further information contact General Hatchaway."

"He's not easy to get a hold of."

"When I told his assistant who I was calling about the General called me back within five minutes. He was on the golf course. What he said impressed me. The fact he called me back immediately from his golf cart impressed me more. So Commissioner I don't know who you really are, but I'm glad to meet you."

"Thank you Colonel. I take it you're calling to thank me for the three presents I sent you Saturday."

"Yes. A matter of fact you did two things for me Saturday. One; you broke a theft ring we've been trying to catch for the last six months; Two, you filled my stockade."

"I'm glad I could help out. As long as we're talking I want to thank you for all the help you're giving us with our school projects."

"It's my pleasure. If there's anything you need don't hesitate calling me."

"I won't Colonel. You do the same if I can help you."

I hung up the phone and headed back to the table, "Sorry for the interruption but Colonel Cox wanted to thank us for Saturday afternoon."

Sam said, "Did we miss something?"

The Mayor responded, "Did you ever!"

"Pete or the Mayor can explain it to everyone who wasn't there after the meeting. Now I'll finish what I started to say before the phone interrupted me. We have a meeting Wednesday morning at 10:30 for anyone who would like to be here."

Lynda asked, "How did I miss that?"

"I met the man at the restaurant Saturday evening. You and Robert were dancing. Yoto and I had the situation well in hand."

Robert said, "Sorry Larry."

"Don't be. If I had felt uneasy about the situation I would have chewed both of you out. Next, for the people who weren't there, the hospital is coming along just fine. Pete, how's our tip line doing?"

"A little slow but it's still working."

"Good. That's about all I have. If no one else has anything the meeting is adjourned. We probably have over an hour to wait. Feel free to hang around here or do whatever. I'm going to have some more orange juice and go over the photos."

Robert piped up, "I'll get the photos for you."

Jim said, "I'll help him lay them out on the table."

"And I'll get your juice."

"Thank you Lynda and everyone else." I looked over at the Mayor, "If I'm not careful I could grow to like this job."

He laughed and said, "Lord help us if you get any more enthused."

With that we all started to laugh.

We spent the next hour and a half talking and discussing everything. At 10:40 A.M. my intercom buzzed.

"Mayor, why don't you see if it's Mrs. Baker? If so you take the call."

He walked over and took the call.

"Boys it's almost time to rock and roll. Jim, go get the Polaroid and four rolls of film. Do you have that many?"

"Yes Larry. I just got a new case the other day."

"Good. Meet us in the reception area."

As he was walking out the Mayor returned.

The Mayor said, "By the time we get there the house will be clear."

"She called from the house?"
"Yes Larry. I didn't ask her why she didn't call from the airport."
"That's all right, in her condition we should be happy that she called at all. Everybody…let's saddle up and move on out of here."
I sent Jim in his own car to get Doc.
We arrived at Tammy's house at ten after eleven. The Mayor rang the bell and Mrs. Baker answered the door. By the time we said our hellos and I introduced Coop and Josh, Jim was pulling up. He and Doc got out of the car. Doc was carrying a black bag. He reminded me of the old time Doctors when they made house calls. As he approached Mrs. Baker I introduced him to her. "Mrs. Baker, May I introduce Doctor Samuel Kaplin?"
She shook his hand, "Doctor Kaplin, thank you for coming."
"Mrs. Baker I wish we were meeting under better circumstances."
"So do I Doctor Kaplin."
"Larry explained to me that you are one of our team so would you please call me Doc?"
"I'll be happy to."
"Now I'd like to see my patient."
I said, "Mrs. Baker why don't you show Doc Tammy? Lynda, go with them and give Doc a hand. If you don't mind Mrs. Baker the rest of us are going to carefully search the house."
"Be my guest Larry, Doc and Lynda please follow me."
After they left I split my force into teams. As we entered the house it felt strange. I'd studied the pictures so much it felt like I'd been here before. As we entered one of the 10 foot hand carved double doors and stepped on the white marble floor we were looking at a beautifully carpeted stairway about 15 feet in front of us. The house had all six bedrooms upstairs. The only bedroom downstairs was the maid's quarters in the rear of the house. Looking at the furniture and the antiques I could easily see another million dollars for Charles. God, that man is a piece of dirt. For what he's done he doesn't deserve to live. But that's not my decision. That's up to the courts and the Gods to decide. But between here and the other states that will want him, he'll never see daylight again. I don't care how nuts he claims to be.
As I looked at the living room to my left and the stairway to the right I thought that we could hide in the living room if we had to. I

took my team of Yoto, Coop, and Josh with me upstairs. I walked by the first bedroom which belonged to Charles and went to the end of the hall to Tammy's room.

"Yoto, take the boys back to Charles' room. Pretend you are dealing with a sophisticated spy. Remember boys, people who are nuts will do different things. We don't want him to know we were here. We don't want him to change his plans."

They left and I entered Tammy's room. It was large and a beautiful master bedroom. As I approached the bed Doc was standing talking to Mrs. Baker and Lynda was seated on the edge of the bed buttoning the last button on Tammy's pajama top.

"I hope I'm not interrupting Doc."

"No Larry, I'm glad you came in."

"Were you able to find out anything?"

"I was just telling Mrs. Baker how my earlier diagnosis was correct."

She spoke, "Why didn't you tell me Commissioner? I could have gotten Tammy out of here."

"And Charles would find another way to kill her. Plus we didn't know for sure without Doc looking at her."

"I'm sorry Larry. You're right. Doc, can I ask how you were able to pick up on her illness by just seeing her picture? I had some of the best Doctors around looking at her and testing her to no avail."

Doc said, "The Doctors you used were born with silver spoons in their mouths."

"How does being rich fit into this?"

"The only time you see asbestos poisoning anymore is in poor small children. So if you don't deal with the poor you would never recognize the disease."

"I see."

I added, "Mrs. Baker Doc is one of the best, if not the best surgeon in our town. He worked his way through school with his ability, not with who his parents are. And we're proud to have him on our team."

"I'm also glad he's a part of our team."

Doc asked, "Mrs. Baker, how good of an actress is Tammy?"

"What do you mean?"

"Do you hear her labored breathing?"

"Yes I do."

"If I make that go away do you think she can duplicate it for Charles?"

"For a short time if she's coherent."

"Will that work for you Larry? I can have her very coherent by morning if you don't mind me spending the night."

Mrs. Baker said, "You're more than welcome."

I said, "I have an idea. Does Tammy have a small tape recorder?"

Lynda said, "Good idea."

Mrs. Baker said, "I'll get you one Larry." She left the room.

"Now what Doc?"

"I have some equipment in the car. But I'll need a hand carrying it up."

"Do me a favor. I have Robert checking the outside. Get him to help you. He's dying to see Tammy."

"Lynda will you join me?"

"Yes Doc."

As they left Mrs. Baker returned with a mini tape recorder. It was about 2 inches by 4 inches. "It has new batteries and a fresh tape."

"Put it close to her mouth and start taping the minute I close her door. I'll wait out in the hall for Doc. He went for some equipment."

"Larry, I don't know how......"

I cut her off, "We need the tape NOW. We'll have plenty of time to talk later." By the time I finished my statement I was closing the door. She did as I asked.

I walked up the hallway to Charles' bedroom. I stuck my head in and asked, "How's it going boys?"

Coop answered, "This nut must have seen every James Bond movie made. Hopefully we've seen all the ways of detecting if someone has been in his room."

"Did you find anything?"

"Yes, a six foot piece of clear plastic rope hidden under his bed."

"He had it lying on the floor?"

"No. We sent Yoto under the bed and he found it. Charles had put some small nails along the inside of the bed side board and laid the rope on top of them."

"That's good. It fits into my thinking. I now know how she's going to accidently die."

"With the rope?"

"Yes Yoto, with the rope and a large stairway. If she's in love and feels her husband is in trouble her motherly instincts will set in. She will pull herself out of her sickbed and go to help him. She will stagger to the stairway and go down one or two steps before she trips on the rope she can't see and falls all the way down to the bottom. End of life, end of story."

Coop said, "That sounds good to me."

When I had looked into the room I noticed a dresser that was made to sit at an angle in the corner of the room. "Josh?"

"Yes Larry?"

"Why would someone have a dresser like that made when he has more room than he has furniture?"

"I don't know Larry, but I'll check it out."

Coop and Yoto joined him in his investigation of the dresser.

I heard Josh say, "Hold on I think I got the release."

I watched as Josh's right hand, which was behind the right side of the dresser, pulled something and the whole dresser pivoted out from the wall.

Josh said, "I don't believe it!"

Coop replied, "Me either!"

Yoto asked, "Larry, can you see this?"

"I sure can. I also can see the little red light that says its recording."

Coop said, "What you can't see is the sensor that started the camera."

"How does he have it set up?"

Coop answered, "It covers the front door. If it's opened, it goes off."

"All right. One of you get Pete up here."

Josh walked by me. He also passed Doc.

I said, "You guys wait here. I'll be back to get you."

I walked back to Tammy's room. I then Walked Silent and Walked Deadly. I came up on Mrs. Baker and put my hand over her mouth. I wanted nothing on the tape but Tammy's breathing. Mrs. Baker was startled for a moment. Then she relaxed when she realized it was me. I reached down to the tape player on Tammy's pillow and turned it off.

"I didn't hear you enter the room."

"I didn't want any sound on that tape except her breathing. Why don't you take the tape recorder over to the dresser and make sure it's okay?"

"All right."

I walked over to the double doors and swung them open and motioned down the hallway for Doc, Lynda, and Robert to join me. And they did just that.

"It's going to take a few minutes to build this unit. I borrowed it from the clinic I volunteer at."

"Can you and Robert handle it?"

"Can Lynda also stay?"

"Sure. Can I help with anything?"

"Well you could help move the bed out from the wall but it's already out far enough."

"Oh, what an idiot I am!"

"What do you mean Larry?"

"Simple Lynda. Robert get me the chair by the make-up counter."

He brought the chair and put it right in front of where I had moved to. I stepped up on the chair. I was in front of the soffit that was about 2 feet from the wall and it went the whole way around the room. The soffit contained the air conditioning ducts. I was looking at the vent that was directly over Tammy's bed, as well as her head. I reached in my pocket and took out my Swiss Army knife and opened the flat screwdriver blade. There were only two screws holding the air vent in place. I turned one screw and it went around but it seemed like it was just sitting there. The second one acted the same. So I put my knife away and put a hand on each side of the vent and pulled it out. I held it upright so the screws wouldn't fall out. I handed it to Robert. And there it was! Hanging in the air conditioning duct, a large bag of a powdery substance, it looked like a large teabag. I took it down remembering exactly how it was up there, so I could return it the same way. But if I had everything in my mind correctly Charles wouldn't be touching this bag again until after the murder.

"Doc, can you relax until I'm done here?"

"Actually Larry there are things I can do while I'm waiting for you."

"Great! I'll only be a few minutes. Robert, keep the vent cover level to the ground. I'll be back in a couple of minutes."

"Okay Larry."

Robert was standing looking directly at Tammy. I walked real close to Robert and whispered in his right ear, "How does she look in the flesh?"

He whispered back, "Beautiful."

I patted him on his upper arm as I walked away.

"Mrs. Baker could you find me some light, clear, unscented hair spray?"

"Sure. Tammy should have some in her master bathroom." We walked through the doorway into the master bath. "Here it is."

"Spray it toward me. I have to make sure you can't smell it."

She did and it was perfect. I couldn't smell it.

I laid the bag on the counter and opened it. I pulled out my sleeve knife and Mrs. Baker did a double take. "I use it to clean my finger nails."

She laughed, "Sure you do."

"It sounded good to me."

"Larry, you're just full of surprises."

"I hope they don't bother you."

"No, they don't Larry. They just show me more and more why I'm glad we hired you."

"Thank you."

"You're welcome."

I used my knife to gently move around the asbestos. As I did, with my other hand I sprayed lightly over the powder, just enough to keep it from becoming airborne. I then put the can down and wiped off my knife with a tissue. I put my knife away and flushed the tissue down the toilet. I watched it to make sure it went down. I resealed the bag and took it back into the bedroom. I climbed up onto the chair and replaced the bag and then the vent cover. I got down and Robert took the chair and returned it to where he found it. I bent down and fluffed the carpet back up so you couldn't see where the chair had been. I looked over and Robert was doing the same to the cushion of the chair.

"It's all yours Doc. I'm going to check on the other boys."

He was giving Tammy a shot when I left. He seemed to have his part of the situation well in hand.

I went back to Charles' room to see what the boys were up to. Pete was inside with the boys so I walked in and joined them.

"Can you fix it Pete?"

"I think so Larry. I called in my two experts on the subject. They'll be here in about 15 minutes."

"Good, anything else?"

"Yes Larry. We found two tapes back here. I wonder what's on them?"

"I'm sure there's a VCR in the family room. Why don't we check them out while we're waiting?"

As we walked out of the room Mrs. Baker was standing there.

"Are they finished?"

"No Mrs. Baker. They just needed a break. They're going downstairs to check something out." Everyone filed past us and headed downstairs. "I'd like to take one myself, but I'm going to give the boys a hand."

"Well, I better go back inside and see if I can help."

She turned and headed back to the master bedroom and I headed downstairs. When I got to the family room everyone was waiting. The T.V. and VCR were on and Pete was sitting with the VCR remote in his hand.

"If you're waiting for me, I'm here so let's get started."

Pete pushed play. A light came on showing a young, good looking, well built woman. Behind her was Charles. They closed the door and started to embrace. Hot and heavy, then they started to grope one another. Next came the undressing and the statements of undying love for one another. When they were both naked Charles picked her up and laid her on his bed. He crawled beside her and kissed her a couple of times. Then he rolled over on top of her.

We then heard Mrs. Baker, "I can't believe it! He's doing this in the bedroom right down the hall from my baby's room! Commissioner!"

Pete turned off the VCR.

"You leave me a gun and I'll be happy to kill this skunk myself! Next I'll take care of his girlfriend. She works for me as a lady's ready to wear buyer."

I put my arm around Mrs. Baker. I nodded my head and everyone left the room in haste.

"Let it out Mrs. Baker. It's been a long time building."

She turned her head to me and buried her face in my chest and started to cry uncontrollably.

"That's a girl. Let it all out."

I knew this was the best medicine for her.

"Tell me everything's going to be all right."

"It is. No question about it."

"And your Doctor knows what he's doing?"

"If Doc said Tammy could play golf tomorrow at noon, I'd get a tee time."

"He's that good?"

"So far he's saved three members of our team; my ex-driver Jack, the Mayor, and little old me. To say he's good is an understatement. Your daughter will be fine. So don't worry about her. She's not going to die as long as we're alive. She'll probably have some permanent lung damage, but that's something we'll know more about when we get her to a proper hospital."

She hugged me again. "Larry, I'm so glad you're here."

"So am I Mrs. Baker. So am I."

"I better let you go and join your men."

"Only if you tell me you're okay, and you can finish the job we've started."

"Don't worry Larry. I'll hold up my end."

"Good. You said Charles will be landing at eight tomorrow evening, right?"

"That's right. I told him I'd be watching Tammy so he should take a cab home."

"He liked the idea, didn't he?"

"Yes he did. Who knows, it may give him a chance to call his bimbo before coming home."

"Mrs. Baker!"

"All right Commissioner. I'll be good."

"Look at it this way, with what we have on him he's going away for a long, long time."

"I guess that's good enough."

"No, I think the good part is he'll have plenty of new lovers in prison. He's so pretty every guy in the joint will want him."

"Now I feel better Commissioner."
"I'm glad. Keep that in mind when you talk to him."
"I will. Now we better get back to work."
She went upstairs and I went outside with the boys. Our boys had showed up to work on the camera.
"Officer Yoto, why don't you show the boys our problem and see if they can fix it?"
"Yes Sir."
After they left, John, who was working outside with Robert asked, "Larry, where's Robert?"
"He's in seventh heaven."
"He's upstairs with Tammy?"
"You're quick John, real quick."
"Since he's looked at her picture she's all he talks about. We all try to be nice but at times it's hard. He thinks she's a raving beauty, but she isn't. Her mother doesn't even think so."
"For me guys, try to remember a couple of things. Beauty is in the eye of the beholder. In this world there is someone for everyone. And the last thing to remember is, if you really upset him he'll probably rip off your arms and beat you to death with the bloody ends."
Everyone broke out laughing.
John said, "I wouldn't laugh too hard. I think Larry's right."
We kept laughing.
Jim walked up and said, "I'm sorry I missed it. Someone can fill me in later. I'm glad I caught you out here Larry. Would everyone like to take a walk to the workshop in the garage area?"
I said, "Let's go guys."
The workshop was large enough for all of us to enter. Tom was looking at a toolbox he had put on the workbench.
"What you got Tom?"
"I'd bet a weeks' pay it's 'death in a bottle'." He had removed the top tray from the toolbox. He reached inside the toolbox and brought out a bottle about the size of a small peanut butter jar. He held it up so we could see it. "There are five more of them, each in its own little compartment in the bottom of the toolbox."
"And the powder inside?"
"I think its asbestos."

"Does everyone agree?"

Everyone nodded their heads and made little comments.

The Mayor said, "He is one sick individual."

"That he is Mayor. That he is."

Jim said, "Larry we also found some real sheer cloth."

"Could I see it?"

He went over to where it was on the shelf. "It isn't hidden, but it just looked like something that could do the job as you described it."

I took one look at it, "Jim you hit the nail on the head. That's the same stuff that was upstairs. Put everything back the way you found it boys. We have everything we need. All we need to do now is work up a good plan. Pete, do we have a good stunt girl coming tomorrow?"

"Yes Larry. She'll be at your office tomorrow at one."

"Cost?"

"She and her makeup person cost $2500.00. My friend says she's one of the best. I sent him a complete description of Tammy. This girl is as close as he could get."

"Sounds good, all I need now is a good plan."

Coop said, "I bet it has something to do with that 6 feet of rope Larry."

"I bet you're right Coop. Jim, see that ball of twine on your left to the rear of the next shelf up?"

"Yes Larry."

"Use that yardstick in the corner and cut off a six foot piece. One of you guys give him a hand."

When Jim had finished he handed me the twine.

"Let's go inside. I can only think of one place this will work."

As we got inside the house I stood on the marble floor at the base of the stairway.

"How many of you think this rope will fit across the stairway and have enough left over to tie it securely?"

Everyone raised their hands.

"Coop, you and Josh found the rope, why don't you do the honors?"

"If he does it the way we used to, we should use the second step from the top."

"Sounds professional to me. Do it."

We watched as they worked.

"Larry, it fits like a glove."

"If the glove fits we must convict."

"Cute Larry."

Everyone was laughing.

"Untie it and get rid of the twine. Coop, what's left to do in Charles' room?"

"Just replace the tapes we have downstairs, the dresser, and fix the camera."

"Pete, go upstairs and get a progress report."

As he climbed the steps I said, "Sam and Wade." I handed them a hundred dollar bill. "Enough pizza and coke for everyone. We'll eat out front. Let us know when you're back."

Coop stood up, "Sam, take my car. It's not as conspicuous as the limo." He tossed his keys down to Sam.

"Thanks Coop."

As they were leaving I told everyone else, "Recheck all your areas downstairs to make sure you haven't left something amiss. I'm going upstairs to check on Tammy."

As I walked up the steps Coop and Josh were standing on the landing. "See if you can help out in Charles' room."

Josh said, "Okay Larry."

"I'll be down the hall checking on Tammy."

As I entered Tammy's room Mrs. Baker was the first person to reach me. She stopped in front of me. You know how you feel when a person wants to hug or kiss you? I could tell she wanted to give me a hug so I opened my arms.

As Mrs. Baker hugged me she said, "She's responding to what Doc is doing."

I hugged her back and then let her go, "I'm very happy and relieved for you. Doc, what exactly are you doing?"

"In simple terms, I've given her drugs to open up all her breathing passages as well as her lungs. I'm using a special oxygen tent to regulate the flow of oxygen she gets. I could do a faster job in the hospital. But even after everything she's been through, she's still a strong willed lady. I can see why he wants to murder her. It would take another year to kill her at the rate he's going. It would be pure hell for her to be bedridden and speechless for another year."

"How do you know she's doing better?"

"You had to be here the whole time, but you can tell by the sound of her breathing."

"I'd like to go see her."

As we approached the bed the phone rang. I put my index finger to my lips and said, "Shhh."

Mrs. Baker answered the phone, "Hello? Yes. Yes. Yes. Thank you, Joyce. I'll see you Wednesday morning. Goodbye."

When she hung up the phone I asked, "Is everything okay?"

"Yes Commissioner. Everything is fine. I sent Charles to the New York store. And guess where our little girl in the movie happens to be right now?"

"New York?"

"That's right. I hope and pray to God that he gets his."

"Remember what I told you. One way or another he'll get his. Now let's see how Tammy's doing."

As I looked I commented, "You're right Doc. Her breathing is less labored. I can also see a little more color under her fingernails."

Doc came closer and said, "You're right Larry."

"Mrs. Baker, she's going to be all right. Robert, I want you to stay with Doc tonight and help him monitor Tammy."

"Yes Sir. I'll take good care of her."

Doc was checking gauges.

"Robert, stay close to Doc and learn what he's doing. Doc, do you still need Lynda?"

"No Larry, we've got it handled."

"Good. I've ordered pizza and cokes. I'll send some up for you when it gets here."

"Thanks Larry. Now that you mention it I could use some food."

"I figured you could Doc."

Lynda and I went downstairs. The boys were in the family room doing what boys do when they're left alone.

"I know you boys are studying the evidence."

Lynda said, "My God! That's Charles and a real good looking young lady!"

"I don't know if making love to a married man in a bed down the hall from his dying wife is someone I'd call a lady."

"You're right Mayor. I wouldn't call her a lady either."

"You know what I meant Larry."

"Yes I do Lynda. We were just having fun with you. Boys, we've done everything we can here. After lunch we're going back to work."

John said, "By the time we get back to work it'll be time to go home."

"Yes it will, John. Come on Lynda let's go outside and wait for Sam and Wade and leave these perverts to their movie."

Everyone was laughing as we left.

A few minutes later Pete came outside and joined us. "What's the verdict Pete?"

"Our boys are taking the movie back to the station. There they can erase the film. They'll bring it back in the morning. The camera has a sixty second timer. This allows Charles to set it and then leave the room. Anyone coming in after that trips the electric eye and they become movie stars as long as the motion detector senses someone in the area."

"Then in the morning we'll seal Charles' room?"

"Yes we will."

A few minutes later our food arrived. We ate and then we left and headed back to my office. It was 4:30 P.M. when we arrived.

As I walked by my receptionist I asked, "Any messages Mrs. Thompkin?"

"None Commissioner. It's been kind of a dull day."

"In that case close up and get out of here!"

"Yes Sir. See you in the morning."

As we walked into my office I was mentally putting the last touches on tomorrow night's plan. Everybody had gone their respective ways. Lynda and I were alone. I was sitting behind my desk and Lynda was sitting on the edge of it. When the phone rang Lynda picked it up. My phone rings you right through if you have my private number, otherwise you get the switchboard and then my receptionist, Mrs. Thompkin.

"Hello, Commissioner Tower's office. May I help you?"

"May I speak to the Commissioner? This is Bobby Fisher, head of security for Central High."

"One moment please." She covered the mouthpiece with her hand, "It's a Bobby Fisher."

"I'll take it." I took the phone out of her hand and said, "Hello Mr. Fisher, how may I help you?"

"You told me to call if I heard anything out of the ordinary. I've already heard almost the same story three times. Next week, in the middle of exams, we're going to have a 'Black Tuesday'. I don't know what that means but it doesn't sound good."

"It's not. That term usually refers to the crash on Wall Street which took place on Tuesday, thus the name 'Black Tuesday'. 'Black Tuesday' killed a lot of people which means someone has something bad in mind."

"Then it wasn't wrong for me to bother you?"

"I was sincere when I told you and your brother to call if there was a problem you couldn't handle. I'm glad you called. Keep me posted. Have you told your brother?"

"Not yet. I'll see him later tonight and I'll tell him then."

"Sounds good. I'll talk to you again when you have more information."

"All right Commissioner. Good bye."

"Good bye Mr. Fisher." I hung up the phone.

"What's up?"

"There may be some trouble at Central High School next week."

"That's it?"

"You'll know more when I know more."

"That works for me. Shall we call it a day?"

"Good idea Lynda. Let's get out of here."

The next day nothing exciting happened until just before one when our stunt lady showed up with her makeup artist. I had to admit she did resemble Tammy. The stunt lady introduced herself as Darlene and her makeup artist was Clair.

"It's amazing Darlene, your hair color is almost the same as Tammy's. That's what I call good casting."

"Not really Commissioner. I dyed my hair to look like the photo we had. I knew we'd be short on time so I've already done the tough part."

"Good thinking. Thank you for thinking ahead."

"You're welcome."

"Is anyone hungry?"

"We ate a full meal before we got here Commissioner. But a drink would be in order."

"Would tea be all right?"

"Yes it would Sir."

While Lynda got a pitcher of tea I went over what I had in mind with the girls.

"What do you think?"

"Of course I need to see the area, but from what you say I should be able to handle it. I would say a lot of blood is in order."

"Where do we get that?"

"It's in the extra case I was forced to bring with me."

"That's good."

"The best part is, between Clair and me, we'll make Tammy look like death warmed over."

Clair said, "I can put a split in her skull that will scare you to death."

"Sounds great, just what I was thinking of. How long will you need Clair?"

"With the two of us working together three to four hours."

"Then we better get out of here and over there."

It was 2:30 P.M. when we arrived. The girls liked the whole setup.

"Commissioner, I can make this fall very noisy and brutal sounding. He'll be surprised when she's still alive."

"You have no idea how nice that sounds."

"Where's our victim Commissioner?"

"Let's go upstairs. She's in the master bedroom."

We made a right at the top of the steps and went straight into Tammy's room. We entered the room and went over to the bed area. There I introduced the girls to Mrs. Baker, Doc, and Robert.

"Now Mrs. Baker, you're going to have to introduce us to this lovely young lady sitting up in her bed," she was still under the oxygen tent. As her mother introduced everyone Tammy had her eyes wide open as she nodded her head.

"Doc will she be ready by eight o'clock?"

Tammy was nodding her head up and down.

"Larry, she's ready right now. She's built of the same stock as her mother. I would like to keep her under the tent as long as possible."

Clair spoke, "If I could just get a clip of her hair to make sure we're close enough in color."

Mrs. Baker said, "I'll take care of that." She walked to the dressing table and came back with scissors in her hand. She put her hand on the zipper of the tent, "Is it okay Doc?"

"Yes go ahead."

Tammy had long hair and she brought a handful of her hair to the area her mother was in. Mrs. Baker took a clipping of her hair and zipped the tent back up. She then handed Clair the hair.

"Will that do?"

"Yes Ma'am. Thank you. Can we use Tammy's bathroom area?"

Mrs. Baker said, "You don't have to ask. Use whatever you need to make this work."

Darlene said, "Thank you, we will."

The girls walked off toward the bathroom and walk-in closet area. A few minutes later Darlene came out with two long nightgown and robe combinations. They were very similar.

"Tammy will wear one and I'll wear the other."

I said, "It looks good to me. You'll change her later, right?"

"Yes, and we're going to rip it and cover it with blood. Now, I have a lot to do if I'm going to become Tammy." She walked back to the bath area.

At this time I figured a little small talk would be in order. "How are things with Mrs. Baker today?"

"Oh Larry, I don't know how to answer that. I don't want to be happy, I might spoil something."

"You won't. And before midnight tonight you'll be happier."

"How do I thank all of you?"

"You are family. You'd do the same for us."

"You're right Larry. I would."

We heard a tap on the oxygen tent. We looked at it and Tammy pointed to herself and put up two fingers.

Mrs. Baker said, "From what I'm seeing I have to correct my statement. 'We' would be happy to help."

"I know you would. You're good people. Now I need to ask you about the two zombies you have working here."

"Robert and Doc do look tired don't they?"

"How are you boys holding up?"

Robert said, "We'll be all right Larry."

"Are you sure? Doc?"

"Robert gave you the answer Larry. We each got a little sleep last night and we're going to get a lot tonight."

"You boys are over 3 times 7 so I'll take your word for it. Everyone needs to eat. Are you boys hungry?"

They both nodded 'yes'.

"Good. I'll order in chicken and fixin's. We'll eat outside. I'll let you know when it gets here."

I walked downstairs with Lynda. Coop and Josh had arrived while we were upstairs. Yoto was keeping them company. We said our 'hi's' and then I asked if everything had gone according to plan in Charles' room.

"Larry, he could use a magnifying glass and still not know that we were there."

"I believe you Coop. I know you just got here but I'd like you to run an errand for me."

Josh said, "I hope it's a food run."

"Don't tell me! Coop didn't feed you?"

"He said, 'Don't worry, Larry will feed us'."

"There he goes reading my mind again." I gave them some money and sent them on their way.

We were standing in the foyer next to the living room, "Let's take a look at what the living room has to offer. The last place Charles will be tonight will be the living room."

Mrs. Baker was descending the staircase as I spoke, "What's your idea Larry?"

"Mrs. Baker, I think we'll do the 'Old Switcheroo'. As Darlene screams and hits the floor we'll help pull her out of the way and slide Tammy in her place. It'll be done before Charles can see it happen."

"You don't think Charles will be watching?"

"No Ma'am. He's too smart for that."

"What do you mean Larry?"

"It's actually very simple. After the death, if anyone feels there was foul play, they'll ask everyone in the house to take a lie detector test. If he didn't see it he doesn't have to lie."

"I see your point. And from what you said, you'll be hiding in the living room."

"Along with Coop, Josh, Clair, Doc, and Tammy. Until we're

needed we'll be hiding behind that large oriental black and gold lacquer screen. It covers almost half the room so we can easily sit behind it to await what's going to happen. There's one thing you must remember tonight Mrs. Baker, neither you nor Tammy will drink anything Charles offers you. I figure he'll give you a sedative and Tammy a stimulant."

"Do you really think he'll do that?"

"Yes I do. So be careful tonight. Take whatever he gives you and thank him. After he leaves get rid of whatever he gave you. Pour it in a plant, or under the bed, or the dresser, or a pillow. In Tammy's case, under her bed, then you want to make sure you head off to bed and give Charles the empty glasses. If you're already in your nightgown you can say you are tired and head for your room. Before he goes to work on Tammy he'll come by your room and call for you. Be sure you don't answer. Then he's going to lure Tammy out of her room and down the stairs. You can come out once he's downstairs. For your added safety Robert's going to be in your closet area."

"What about Darlene?"

"Yoto will be with her."

"Have you missed anything?"

"I hope not Mrs. Baker. A lot depends on us."

We ate and awaited the return of Charles. At 8:30 P.M. my cell phone rang. It was dispatch. The network Pete had set up was watching Charles. "Commissioner, he just left the parking lot with a young lady in her car, heading your way."

"Keep me posted. Lynda, that's your cue. Go park the limo somewhere close by and I'll call you when it's all clear. Josh, you moved your car after dinner didn't you?"

"Yes Larry, it's a block away."

I walked Lynda to the door and kissed her good bye. "Be careful. I'll call you before midnight."

"You be careful too Larry. And I love you."

"I love you too, now get out of here."

While Clair was doing the makeup on Tammy, Doc and Robert took the equipment apart and put it in the closet of one of the other spare bedrooms. By the time I got dispatch's last call everyone was in their places.

We listened as Charles got out of a car and shut the door. Next we heard his key in the front door. He came in and closed the door and walked straight up the stairs. I heard his bag hit the floor outside his room. Then I heard Tammy's door open.

As I was told later this is how it went down:

"I'm home Mom. I had a good trip. How's Tammy doing?"

"She's resting." She got up from where she was sitting and walked to Charles before he could get a good look at Darlene. She grabbed him by the arm and led him out into the hallway. "I think we should let her rest."

"Good idea. Would you like to hear about my trip?"

"I'd like to wash up and put my night gown on. I'm awfully tired."

"Would you like me to get you a warm glass of milk?"

"Oh, that would be so sweet of you."

By the time she changed he had returned with the milk.

He walked right into her room without knocking, "I brought you your milk."

She took the glass from him and set it on the nightstand by her bed. "Thank you Charles. I would have fallen to pieces around her if it hadn't been for you and your strength."

He took her in his arms and gave her a gentle hug. "I'll always be here for you."

Mrs. Baker thought, "That's what you think." Then she said, "I should have had you bring one for Tammy."

"I did, it's on the stair post. I was going to give it to her."

"Why don't you unpack and I'll take care of Tammy? Tomorrow we'll get together for dinner and we'll discuss your trip, just the two of us."

"I'd like that."

I'm glad Larry told me that he had me lined up as his next victim. Also if I played up to him a little it would help keep him off guard and it seemed to be doing just that. We walked down the hallway. He stopped and picked up his bag and walked into his room. I went to Tammy's room and poured the milk down the sink. I gave Yoto the okay sign and took the glass and stayed by Darlene for a few minutes. I then got up and headed back to my room. I quickly got rid of my milk and winked at Robert. I slowly walked out into the hallway. "Charles."

He walked out of his room. He was still dressed in his slacks and white shirt. He had taken off his jacket and tie and unbuttoned his collar. "Yes Ma'am?"

I had an empty glass in each hand. "I was going to talk a little but all of a sudden I really feel tired. Would you mind taking these glasses downstairs for me?"

"No. You go get some rest. Tomorrow will be a new day."

"Good night Charles."

As we waited in the living room I heard Charles coming down the stairs. He went to his left and down the hall to the kitchen. I looked at my watch and we waited. Before we knew it we heard footsteps coming toward us and then heading up the stairs towards Tammy's room. We heard a door open and about 30 seconds later we heard it close.

Coop whispered, "He's got the rope."

I nodded.

Everything was quiet for a few minutes.

Then we heard, "Mom. Mrs. Baker." There of course was no answer.

Then we heard how 'Mr. Slick' was going to kill Tammy. He opened her door and called her. "Tammy! Tammy!! I'm in the family room and I need your help!! Tammy! Don't let me die! Tammy! Help me!!"

Darlene slowly got out of bed and pretended to be very weak. She slipped her silk robe on as she walked. She let it hang open.

"Tammy! Hurry!!" Charles moved down the staircase still yelling. "Hurry! Tammy!! I can't breathe!"

I whispered to Clair, "Showtime!"

She had a spray bottle of blood. She started to spray Tammy as Charles' voice got further away. We all moved right next to the living room entrance and waited for Darlene to fall. It wasn't long in coming. We could hear her panting and it sounded like the tape recording of Tammy. Then it happened. The loud scream! The noise on the stairway as she tumbled down and when she hit bottom it was scary. I grabbed her and pulled her into the living room as Josh laid Tammy down. Clair gave her one last spray.

The next thing we heard was Charles whistling a happy tune. He approached Tammy. "Are you dead my dear, dumb wife? What I had to put up with the last two years was unbelievable. But now that you're dead......"

Tammy moaned, "Ooohh."

"Well it looks like you're still alive, but you won't be for long. I have to go up and remove the rope I tied across the stairs. Then I'll go back to the den and fall asleep watching T.V. while you bleed to death."

He stepped around her careful not to get any blood on himself. He also watched as he walked up the stairs. He started to reach for the rope when Mrs. Baker showed up at the top of the staircase.

"If she dies, you'll get the gas chamber!"

"Not if all the witnesses are dead!" He leaped to the top of the steps and grabbed her throat. His mind must have snapped because he said, "I'll hide your body in the old well behind the house with my other mother."

He barely got a good squeeze when over Mrs. Baker's right shoulder came a huge right hand. It hit Charles square in the face. It had to break something because I heard a 'Crack' downstairs. It had to be a nose or cheek bone. Charles grabbed his face with both hands like a little boy who lost his first fight with a bloody nose. He turned and started to run down the stairs. He got as far as the second step when he tripped on his own rope.

The first words to break the silence were Robert's, "Larry, get Tammy out of the way!!!!"

I took one large step into the foyer and grabbed Tammy's arm and slid her into the living room. She slid across the polished marble floor like a hot knife through butter. By the time I had her half out of the way Coop was pulling me backwards. We no sooner cleared the foyer when Charles' body hit the floor head first. Without being too gruesome...his head split open like a ripe melon.

"Doc, check Tammy."

I had fallen backwards with Tammy in my lap and I was in Coop's lap. We untangled with Coop and I laughing.

Doc said, "Tammy, are you okay?"

In a small whispery voice she spoke, "Yes."

We all cheered as her mother, Robert, and Yoto walked in.

"Do you always cheer when someone dies?"

"That wasn't why we were cheering Mrs. Baker." I still had

Tammy in my lap. "Would you come over here?" She moved very close to me. "Could you lean down here? I want to say something only to you." I nudged Tammy.

When her mother got close to Tammy's face Tammy said in a whisper, "I love you mommy."

Mrs. Baker knelt down and grabbed her daughter and hugged her and started to cry.

Coop slid back and got up and I did the same.

"Doc, make sure Charles is dead."

He was that…very dead. I called Pete to come over with the coroner.

"What happened?"

"Charles accidently killed himself. He fell down a flight of stairs."

"Then it's true what they say."

"What's that?"

"Most fatal accidents happen around the house."

"Putting it that way…..it's true."

I called Lynda to come and get us. I left Robert and Doc to rebuild the oxygen tent and spend the night.

Yoto took Lynda and me home. Then he took our guests to a hotel.

"Lynda we need to get some rest. We have a meeting in the morning with Mr. Gonzales."

Chapter 21

At this point in my thinking Lynda nudged me, "Larry, are you asleep again?"

I opened my eyes, "Nope! Just in deep thought. Are we at the auditorium yet?"

John answered, "Not yet. We're in a traffic jam. Go back to relaxing. They won't start the ceremonies without you."

"I may just do that."

The End
(Or should I say the end for now…..)

Watch for Book Four of this Mystery Series
"CHANGING OUR TOWN"
Coming Soon!